the SILVER WIND

NINA ALLAN

TITAN BOOKS

To Peter

The Silver Wind
Print edition ISBN: 9781789091694
E-book edition ISBN: 9781789091700

Published by Titan Books
A division of Titan Publishing Group Ltd
144 Southwark Street, London SE1 0UP

First edition: September 2019
1 3 5 7 9 10 8 6 4 2

A CIP catalogue record for this title is available from the British Library.

Printed and bound in the United States.

Did you enjoy this book? We love to hear from our readers.
Please email us at: readerfeedback@titanemail.com

To receive advance information, news, competitions, and exclusive offers online,
please sign up for the Titan newsletter on our website:
titanbooks.com

the
SILVER WIND

AUTHOR'S FOREWORD

It is now more than ten years since I first found myself writing about a character named Martin Newland. Martin originally turned up in 'Darkroom', which was commissioned for an anthology of slipstream stories entitled *Subtle Edens*. He wasn't even real at the time – he was a figment of another character's imagination – though rereading that story now I can still see why Martin kept pestering me, insisting that there was more to his walk-on role than I'd given him credit for.

There are a lot of things I would change about 'Darkroom', were I to imagine it again from the beginning, but Martin Newland would not be one of them. Though it hardly seems fair on the other characters to say so, the most interesting thing about 'Darkroom' is the way it relates to the stories that came after it. My own shorthand for these is 'the Martin stories', which together make up the book you are holding, *The Silver Wind*.

The original incarnation of this book took me four years to write. Longer than might reasonably have been expected, given the volume's relatively small number of pages, though as must be the case with most fiction, the book that eventually appeared represented only a fraction of the material that had been written, the work that had been going on behind the scenes. What I was battling with through those years was not so much how the story should go as what narrative should be. Then, as now, I found the concept of straightforward linear storytelling difficult to justify. The novel is a uniquely flexible, perennially interesting art form, both as a means of self-expression and as a forum in which broader questions of reality and experience can and should be asked. As such, it seems normal and desirable to me that the form the novel takes should itself be interesting and flexible.

As both reader and writer, I want a novel to do more than simply 'tell a story'. The practical application of such an ambition still forms most of the ongoing drama of my working practice. As the writer I was then, in 2008, it felt like trying to stuff an inflated balloon through a letterbox without it bursting. Although I instinctively knew what I wanted, the technicalities involved in achieving it were more long-winded.

In short, I wrote a lot of stuff about Martin, and not all of it worked in the context I was providing. There was a long-running story strand devoted to his battle with the rat-catcher in 'Darkroom', for example – I still have an abnormal number of books on rats and the Black Death to prove it. But while there is still mileage in those ideas – Harry Phelps was a great character, and rats are fascinating creatures – I had in the end to accept that this wasn't their story. The book

I eventually settled on contained the essence of the ideas I had been playing with – about the unreliability of time when applied to memory, about sibling relationships and our own relationship with the past and future, about my personal love for H. G. Wells's novel *The Time Machine*, about the ordinary miracles of mechanical engineering, and of course about narrative's natural tendency towards the non-linear – but even at the time of publication I felt painfully aware that the text as it existed was not complete.

There were stories that did belong, but were not present, simply because of my technical difficulty – then – in making them come out the way I wanted. At the heart of that dissatisfaction lay the story of Owen Andrews's apprenticeship in Southwark, a segment of narrative that formed much of the logistical and emotional underpinning of what came later but that I could never seem to resolve in a manner that felt in keeping with the story as a whole. When I was asked if I might write a new Martin story to celebrate the publication of this new edition, it was Owen Andrews's missing pages that leapt immediately to mind, and I am delighted to present them – completely reworked – for the first time here.

Also present is the story 'Ten Days', a straight-up Silver Wind story I wrote for the NewCon Press anniversary anthology *Now We Are Ten* in 2016. Originally inspired by the image of Johann Conrad Wolf's extraordinary watch in the form of a skull, made in Germany in 1660, combined with a reading of Leonora Klein's 2006 study of Albert Pierrepoint, *A Very English Hangman*, this story too had been with me from the beginning. It was not until I realised that the narrator should not be Martin but his sister Dora that I was finally able to make it work as I knew it should.

The result is particularly pleasing to me. Over the somewhat protracted interval of writing these stories, I have come to understand that the real hero of *The Silver Wind* is not Martin at all, but Owen Andrews, followed closely by Martin's brilliant sister, Dora Newland. To find Dora's voice fully revealed has been perhaps the greatest reward among many in revisiting these stories.

If *The Silver Wind* is a book about time, it is almost equally a book about place. All these stories – with the exception of the last one, which transports me back a decade, just as Dora is transported backwards to a pre-war Camden – were written while I was living in London, getting to know the city as a subject even as I was exploring it obsessively as a geographical entity. And so 'Darkroom' is my Ladbroke Grove and Kensal Rise, 'Time's Chariot' my Greenwich and Blackheath, 'The Hurricane' my hymn to beloved Southwark. 'The Silver Wind' is a story as much about my own bus rides out to Shooter's Hill and Oxleas Woods as Martin's search for answers about Owen Andrews.

The locations of these stories are ordinary, but I love them to my bones. Even in the half-dozen years between the imagining of 'Darkroom' and the publication of the first edition of *The Silver Wind*, London was changing rapidly. In the months immediately before I left the city, the Shard had just gone up, the area around London Bridge Station altered irrevocably from what it had been like when I drafted 'The Hurricane'. Nicholas Morton's house on Trinity Street is still there though, and lovely Merrick Square. As Dora says in 'Ten Days', even when houses, when whole streets have been torn down and built over, the old shadows remain. These are stories of a time in my life as a writer, a collation of memory. Time is strange, and so are memories. If these stories are about anything, they are about that.

Nina Allan, Rothesay,
Isle of Bute, August 2018

part one

THE HURRICANE

He was enchanted with his room.

Morton had shown him into it with an air of apology but for Owen the space was the realisation of all he had hoped for, or all he would have hoped for, had he dared to imagine it. At home, in the cottage, he had moved out of the bedroom he used to share with his younger brother Anthony, and made a place for himself in the disused privy, which led off the back of the kitchen. The privy had one window, high up but giving light enough to read by through the summer months. He had whitewashed the interior walls, and there was just enough room for his bed frame and the old school desk he used as a work table. His brothers and father jokingly referred to it as his study.

The room at Morton's was in the attic, a long, low space, the bare floorboards sealed with an opaque black varnish. A high wooden bedstead, a stained deal table beneath the single skylight. At the far end of the room a narrow doorway led to a small, windowless chamber that contained a heavy claw-footed bathtub and a tottering armoire.

"The toilet's out the back," Morton said. "It's three flights down." He glanced at Owen's cane and cleared his throat, plainly embarrassed. "Can you manage the stairs?"

"It's a fine house, sir," Owen said. It had become his habit since he was a boy to sidestep or ignore any questions or name-calling he experienced on account of his club foot. He felt bad doing this with Morton, whose concern was genuine, but the response was automatic. Owen himself had been shocked in turn by how frail the old man seemed in person. Morton's letters had radiated garrulous good humour and a fierce independence. He had known of the old man's problems with arthritis – this was at least part of the reason for his coming to London to serve as Morton's apprentice – but his mentor's mental alacrity and professional expertise had made it easy for Owen to forget that Nicholas Morton was not far off his eightieth birthday. On arrival at Trinity Street, he had been confronted by a skinny, bent figure with wispy white hair and a voice so cracked and so quiet Owen had had to strain, at least at first, to understand him. The old man's clothes hung in loose folds, as if he had lost a lot of weight recently. He seemed unsteady on his feet, and it had been Morton, not Owen, who had been forced to stop and rest for a moment on every landing before continuing upwards.

Most shocking of all was the state of his hands, the knuckles swollen and reddened, the thumb joints grossly enlarged. Owen could hardly bear to look at them. How Morton had been able to carry on working up until now, he could not imagine.

Only his eyes were as Owen had pictured them, the dense metallic blue of tempered steel. They blazed with intellect and commitment, with everything that had become familiar from his letters.

"The stairs are no trouble," Owen added. He smiled. "The room is perfect."

"It can get cold in winter. I've arranged to have them reopen the fire."

A lumpy section of green-grey wallpaper to the left of the door showed where the chimney had been boarded up. A picture had been hung there to disguise the damage, a medium-sized oil painting depicting a castle surrounded by a moat overhung by trees. An amateur work, most likely, but still fine, still interesting in a way that made you want to keep looking. Owen found himself wondering if Morton would permit him to keep the picture in the room once the work on the fireplace had been completed.

"That's Herstmonceux Castle," Morton said. "Before the bombing, of course. My niece painted it."

"I can pay for having the fire done," Owen said. "Or you can take the money out of my wages."

"Wouldn't dream of it," Morton said. "Come down when you're ready and I'll get some supper going. You must be famished."

He left the room. Owen listened to him going downstairs one step at a time and felt a powerful urge to go after the old man, to make sure he was all right, but resisted it. He knew Morton would no more enjoy being reminded of his limitations than he would himself. They were alike, Owen supposed, more even than he had realised. It seemed a good omen.

He began to unpack his things. He had brought with

him only the bare minimum, enough to fill the Gladstone bag that had been a gift from his mother's brother, his Uncle Henry, who had also given him the money he needed to make a start in London. The bag had been purchased second-hand. The paisley lining was faded and the leather was scuffed in places but Owen prized it all the more for that – it showed the bag had been out in the world a year or two. There was an inner compartment that could be locked with a small brass key, where Owen kept his money, the reference that had been written for him by his school headmaster, the watchmaker's loupe he had saved up to purchase from a clockmaker on Fore Street, Exeter. Aside from that, his possessions were few: the clothes he stood up in, plus two spare shirts, a best pair of trousers in fine tweed, a corduroy jacket. He had packed also writing materials and two books – Cutmore's *The Pocket Watch Handbook* and *The Time Machine*, by H. G. Wells, a Christmas present from his brother, Anthony.

His winter coat he had been forced to carry, a burden that would have proved all but insurmountable had it not been for the extra money his uncle had given him so he could take a taxi from Paddington Station instead of using the tube. A ridiculous extravagance, perhaps, but on that evening of his arrival a necessary one. He hung the coat in the armoire with his jacket and shirts. In the depths of the wardrobe the clothes looked different, the clothes of a stranger. He placed his two books in the bedside cabinet and the writing things in the drawer of the desk. In the box with the notepaper and safely out of sight he kept the photograph of Dora Newland he had once persuaded his eldest brother, Charles, to purloin from the top of the sideboard in the Newlands' drawing room – Charles was good friends with Martin Newland, and at their house often. It had been a mistake to let Charles know of his feelings for Dora, one he often regretted, but at least he had the photograph.

Outside it was growing dusk. The tall houses opposite presented their closed facades, shadowy and impenetrable as fortresses, as the castle in the painting over the chimney breast. People passed along the pavement, leaving the shops and businesses of Borough High Street as they headed towards their homes in East Southwark and Bermondsey. He wished he had someone to write to, someone for whom he could describe this room, the all-night coffee stand at Paddington, the black cabs lined up like beetles outside the station entrance. *Dearest Dora*, he imagined writing, and then banished the thought. Later, after supper, he would write to Uncle Henry. If it wasn't for his uncle, he probably wouldn't be here in London at all.

Owen slept late. He washed quickly and then dressed. In Morton's kitchen on the floor below, the table was laid for breakfast: bread and butter and cheese and a pot of coffee simmering on the stove. Owen ate standing up, ashamed to discover that Morton was up and about before him. He rinsed his plate and cup under the tap and then started downstairs.

To the rear of the house was a small paved courtyard, hemmed in on all sides by high red walls. Weeds sprouted from between the flagstones, groundsel and chicory and the miniature yellow sunbursts of a dozen dandelions. The privy was dark and cramped, its mildewed walls permeated by the odours of damp and spent urine. Owen used the toilet quickly and went to find Morton.

The ground floor was Morton's showroom, where he saw his clients. The front and back rooms had been knocked into one, creating a large, bright space looking directly on to the street. There was a seating area with armchairs, an oriental rug atop the polished parquet, a sideboard with a crystal decanter and glasses. Further towards the back, a cabinet with brass locks stood in an alcove. The room was spotless, bathed in early morning sunlight, but there was no sign of Morton. Owen knew already from his letters that the old man worked in the basement. He had had the cellar converted exactly to his requirements some decades before.

The cellar ran the full width of the house, partitioned roughly in two by a wide brick archway. Natural daylight penetrated through the two half-height windows at the front, with Morton's main work area immediately to the right of the archway. Owen noted two lathes and a circular saw, a set of the new balance-sprung weighing scales, a rack of loupes gradated in order of power. Aside from this newer machinery there was all the usual paraphernalia you would expect to find littering a watchmaker's studio: soldering iron, anvil, fire tongs, carefully miniaturised replicas of equipment he had seen in use a thousand times in the yard of Pat Gilmour, the blacksmith.

To the left of the archway, a workspace had been prepared for Owen. A bench and a lathe, an electric lamp on an articulated metal stand. There was also a partitioned wooden box filled with various tools – pliers and bradawls, tweezers and a set of the fiendishly expensive new steel shears specifically designed for cutting sheet metal. The box smelled sweetly of linseed oil. Every piece of equipment looked brand new.

Owen felt himself flush with emotion. There could be no adequate way of thanking Morton, whose efforts to make him feel welcome – to feel needed – had gone far beyond anything he might have expected. Morton, perhaps sensing his new apprentice's discomfort, coughed and sniffed. He held up a thin strip of shining metal, offering it to Owen as if it were some important artefact, only recently discovered.

"Titanium steel," he said. "One of the most durable alloys known to man."

The metal was cool to the touch, with a peculiar greyish sheen. Owen knew that many modern horologists had adopted steel as their material of choice for watch casings – in terms of stability and durability it was preferable to both gold and silver – but he was surprised to find that Morton was familiar with it.

"What would you like me to do?" Owen said. "Would you like me to cut this for you?"

"I would like you to show me your watch," said the old man. "Let's see what you're made of, young man."

The watch had a silver case and a plain white dial. Owen had constructed it using a barrel and fusée rather than the more modern lever escapement, simply so as to master the finer points of the earlier, more complicated mechanism. The watch kept perfect time, losing less than one second a month. Owen had completed it earlier that spring. It had taken him nine months to make and was the first piece of work that satisfied the standards he had set for himself. His prentice piece. He was inordinately proud of the watch, but this did not mean he was not terrified of showing it to Morton. If Morton were to reject it as not good enough, Owen would feel that it was he, Owen Andrews, who had been rejected. He felt new colour rising in his cheeks as he unbuckled the strap from his wrist and handed it over.

The old man settled the watch beneath his bench lamp and unfastened the back. It was one of the new-style cases, fitted with a concealed spring. Morton worked it without difficulty, his hands so confident and steady Owen found it hard to reconcile this Morton, so comfortable in his element, with the frail and arthritic figure of the evening before.

"Nice and clean," Morton said. "Why did you use a fusée?"

"To see if I could," said Owen. Morton laughed, but in a way that suggested pleasure rather than mockery, and Owen felt swept by relief. Perhaps Morton meant to praise him, after all.

"What do you hope to learn from me?" Morton said. "You already possess more skill than any apprentice I have worked with. You would probably benefit more by going abroad."

Owen was startled by the old man's honesty. He remembered one of his father's best carpenters, a craftsman of such technical skill and inventive power he could make the meanest piece of pine look like seasoned maple wood. Owen had once seen him use leftover strips of walnut to construct a card case so beautifully jointed it slid open and closed as if upon oiled runners. The man had made it during his lunch hours. Owen had asked if he could purchase it from him but the man had refused. He was a difficult character. He did not like it when his father hired other joiners, even to work beneath him, and much preferred working alone. It was as if he feared other people stealing his ideas.

Morton seemed the very opposite, so little concerned with his own talent as to eliminate it from the equation. What interested him was the craft itself, the pure and abstract art of the measurement of time.

"You are mistaken, sir," Owen said. He tried to choose his words carefully, full of gratitude for Morton's candour. "I still have much to learn, and you inspire me simply by being here, by existing. I want to know how to build a tourbillon. I know you have done it. I know you can teach me how."

Morton raised his eyebrows. The gesture, full of irony and humour, made him look twenty years younger. "The tourbillon is redundant, don't you know? An indulgence, a foible, as anachronistic as the bicycle in the age of the aeroplane." He paused, as if waiting for his words to take effect. "I read it the other day in *Scientific American*."

"But that is a nonsense, and you know it," Owen shot back at him. "Like saying that books should be done away with, now we have film."

"Well," said Morton, laughing. "Shouldn't they?"

Owen frowned, then laughed also, delighted that the

easy familiarity that had built up between them during the years of their correspondence seemed so easily restored. They spent the remainder of the morning in the workshop, Morton explaining the workings of the new machines. Though Owen was familiar with them from books and periodicals, this was the first time he had seen many of them in action. At one o'clock they walked up to Long Lane and had their luncheon at The Almoners, a public house that Morton referred to as his local.

"The family who run the place came here from Poland," Morton told him. "Their food is the finest in Southwark."

They ate bowls of spiced goulash, served with a dark rye bread baked at a continental bakery just three streets away. Owen felt elated by the sound of foreign voices, the fresh tastes. He found it hard to believe he had been in the city less than twenty-four hours. When the young woman serving behind the bar smiled at him, he found himself smiling back. Owen noticed that Morton was grinning and blushed furiously. Nonetheless, he felt blessed, illustrious. Could it be possible that here in the city he was simply a man among other men, busy in his chosen profession, his disability as unremarkable and unremarked upon as the nose on his face? It scarcely seemed possible, yet here he was, living a life he had believed existed only in dreams.

He could not help wondering what Dora might think of him, were she to see him now, the apprentice of a renowned watchmaker, relaxed in the company of other workingmen as he took his lunch in the saloon of a busy London pub, whether it would make a difference.

Dream on, little brother. The voice of his brother Charles. *A cripple is still a cripple, wherever he drinks. Women like us to think they don't care about such things, but they do. Dora Newland would no more look at you than at the man who cleans and oils her father's motor car.*

Charles and Stephen had been against Owen coming to London at all. They did not see the point of it, not when there was a post ready and waiting for him as business accountant to their father's building firm. His two older brothers, who both worked as site overseers, had tried to pressurise their father into making him stay, though Ted Andrews had seemed indifferent to his leaving, some might say relieved. Owen always had the feeling he made his father uncomfortable, not so much because he was crippled as because he reminded Ted too much of Owen's mother Evelyn.

His younger brother Anthony was now in line for the accountant's job. Well, he must make his own decisions. Of all his brothers, Anthony was the only one who had seemed sorry to see him go. There had been tears in his eyes, even though Anthony was a hard nut, obstinate as their father and wild-spirited as their mother. Whatever he chose to do, he would fare well enough without the scant protection Owen could afford him.

The subject of brothers would not leave him alone that day, it seemed. Back at the workshop on Trinity Street, Morton set Owen to work cutting and hammering back plates for a pair of wristwatches he had been commissioned to make for two regular clients, identical twins.

"They're a strange pair," Morton explained. "They work

as a cabaret act, the Gemini Twins. I've made pieces for them before and they have been most appreciative. The only thing you should be aware of is that these watches must be identical in every detail. I don't just mean that they should look the same from the outside. They must be exactly alike, even down to the smallest component of the mechanism. Any discrepancy is liable to make them physically ill."

Owen watched his face carefully, wanting to be sure he was not joking, but his features remained impassive and Owen was bound to take him at his word. The subtext, that Morton would never have trusted such intricate work to Owen unless he felt him capable, was both daunting and thrilling. Owen worked steadily for several hours, measuring and cutting the silver, then stretching the plates. The method for this was called bouging, and involved striking the metal with his hammer in a series of repeated spiral motions that both thinned it evenly and stretched it into shape. The work was routine, some might say mind-numbing, though Owen had always found it almost hypnotically satisfying. It did not demand the pitch-point accuracy required to build a mechanism but the constant rhythm of the hammer, the minute movements of his fingers as he steadied and turned the silver calmed and reassured him in a way the company of people never had.

His thoughts were free to wander, and he found himself remembering his last Guy Fawkes Night in Ottery St Mary, when he had tried to explain the wonder of the tourbillon to Anthony. They had just come down off the Hurricane, the huge spinning wheel that had been brought all the way from the goose fair in Tavistock and had proved so popular there were queues around the fairground most of the night.

Anthony was laughing, his head flung back, his arms outstretched as he struggled to regain his balance on the too-solid ground.

"You felt weightless up there, didn't you?" Owen said. "Well, for all the time you were in the capsule you *were* weightless, or as good as. That's what the tourbillon does to the watch mechanism. It suspends it from gravity. There's effectively no friction, nothing to stop the watch from keeping perfect time."

"You're not telling me your tourbillon is better than a quartz watch," his brother said, snapping back to reality. "My friend Giles Wellesley from school has a quartz watch his father brought back from America. He says that in ten years' time everyone will have them, that you'll never have to wind a watch again. Wellesley reckons quartz watches will be so cheap to make there'll be no point in having them repaired, that if your watch stops working you'll throw it away, and get a new one instead."

Anthony folded his arms, seeming to challenge him, and all Owen could think was that he had not explained the thing well enough. The tourbillon was a technical marvel, but for Owen it was more than that: a miraculous alignment of art and science that compelled attention and awe, as perfect and inviolable as the arrangement of the planets around the sun.

He had never yet seen a quartz watch, but he knew already that such a thing had no majesty, that it was a dead thing, a reanimation at best, a Frankenstein's monster of a watch that worked by trepanning a crystal shard with a microscopic lightning bolt. A quartz watch did not tick, and for Owen there was something monstrous in that, in and of itself.

The inventor of the tourbillon, Louis Breguet, had been eighty-nine when he died, a Methuselah of his time and still in the midst of his researches. In his final years he had come to believe that the tourbillon could be improved still further, that the gravitational stasis it induced could be extended to control the fabric of time itself. There were many who insisted he was confused at the end, unable to distinguish fantasy from reality. His youngest son Georges-Louis swore his mind was clear as a bell, as impervious to time's passing as the miraculous watches he had set in motion. Some years after his death, Georges-Louis published his father's diaries in the hope that some future genius might one day make sense of them.

So far, none had.

The days soon fell into a rhythm. Owen would rise at eight o'clock, have breakfast and work until one, when he would go along to The Almoners for something to eat. Morton would sometimes accompany him, though more often than not he preferred to take lunch in his rooms. He would return to the workshop at two, working on through the afternoon until Morton ordered him to down tools, always insisting that Owen break off before he became too tired.

"Rest is a part of the work, don't forget that," he said. "Push yourself too hard and you'll make mistakes."

After supper, Owen would sometimes return to The Almoners to down a pint or two, or play a hand of rummy with Sergius and Andrzej, two medical students from the nearby Guy's Hospital who were friendly with the proprietor's son. When he tired of the pub, he would take the tube up to Charing Cross and spend the evening in one of the drinking clubs in Soho. He never consumed much alcohol – Morton never made enquiries as to where he spent his evenings but Owen knew that if his work began to be affected he would think less of him – but he liked to sit and listen, the gruff voices of merchant seamen mixing with the raucous laughter of doctors, lawyers, artisans, bank clerks off the leash. He had been horribly nervous the first time he had dared to enter one of these places, the smoky upstairs rooms with their red plush and chandeliers, their mirrored alcoves and mahogany bars, though he soon discovered that so long as he could pay his way he was welcome anywhere, no questions asked. No one cared who he was or what he did. No one passed comment on his uneven gait, or poked fun at his cane, and indeed the drinking clubs were full of misfits, dwarfs, transvestites, homosexuals, gamblers. Criminals too, Owen suspected, and their associates. A year ago, he would have been shocked at the idea that he would feel fellowship with such people. Now, he frequently found himself nodding to one or other of them as they passed each other on the stairs.

The light of London's night life entranced him, the unearthly mixture of sunset and street lighting as it glanced off the proud facades, translucent washes of saffron and rose, and then the deeper dark, the night light that was so different from moonlight, so different from the dark of the country, mostly because it never became truly dark in London at all. Often he would not return to Trinity Street until well after midnight. Morton usually retired to bed at around ten o'clock, but whenever Owen rose in the night to use the privy he would invariably see light seeping in a soft yellow band from beneath Morton's door. The old man must suffer from insomnia, no doubt exacerbated by the pain of his arthritis.

Owen wondered how the old man got through these lonely night hours, whether he liked to read or simply sat in his armchair and stared out of the window. The streets of Southwark fell strangely silent after the pubs closed. Owen had never been afraid of the dark but he found the hours between one and four curiously unsettling. Time seemed to pass more slowly then, bent out of shape and beyond its natural limits, stretched to brittleness and fatigue like a badly worked piece of silver. He sometimes had the sense that if he were to go downstairs and open the front door he would find himself stepping over the threshold into some other universe, a world that looked the same but wasn't, a world in which you might look into the eyes of your brother and find a stranger staring back.

He would lie awake in the slippery half-light of four o'clock, the silence so deep he could hear the milk carts beginning their rounds in Stepney and Whitechapel, and wonder if Morton was also lying awake in the room below. He wondered if Morton was afraid of death or simply resigned to it. Owen could not imagine how anyone might think of death – how they might fully open their mind to its hideous possibilities – and still face it with equanimity.

Often in these grey hours he would take solace in thoughts of Dora, tormenting himself with her image until the darkness receded and urgency overtook him. The relief was a double blessing, a rejoining of himself with the world as well as a simple slaking of his lust. In spite of the inevitable guilt, he usually found he could sleep afterwards, right through until the morning and with no dreams.

Owen spent his first four months at Trinity Street working on the watches for the Gemini Twins, whose real name was Bentall. What the brothers wanted, Morton told him, was not so much novelty as elegance, pieces whose quality was obvious yet would still be unobtrusive when worn on stage. A gentleman's dress watch, in other words, with few complications. For Owen the work was satisfying but straightforward, and he quickly realised that Morton had given him the commission mostly as an opportunity to observe how he worked.

Morton's sole contribution was to engrave his own name on the twin dials. He apologised to Owen for claiming the work as his own, explaining that it was easier that way, and less likely to upset the Bentall brothers.

"It's my name they're expecting to see," he said. "And they're used to getting everything they expect."

Owen tried not to feel disheartened. He knew it was common practice for an apprentice to have his work signed by his master, that he owed the old man a great debt. He reminded himself that these might be among the last projects Morton would see to fruition. His own callousness surprised him, but he accepted it as part of his new self, his London self, as he had accepted the humiliation of having his first society commission effectively stolen from beneath his nose.

He felt a thrill of righteous satisfaction when Morton informed the Gemini Twins that their watches had mostly been the work of his apprentice.

"Owen Andrews is one of the most gifted horologists I have ever encountered," he said. "You'll be hearing his name again."

"Magnificent," the twins said, simultaneously. The brothers were an unusual spectacle. Before meeting Arthur and Simeon Bentall, Owen had known only one set of identical twins, the Sisley brothers, who had gone to substantial lengths to assert their individuality by adopting different hairstyles, different professions and manners of dress. The Bentall brothers, by contrast, seemed not only content with their sameness but fixated upon it. They did not speak much, and when they did speak they held a kind of silent conference beforehand, with one brother delivering the verdict at a nod from the other. They were scrupulously polite, but restrained in their manner to an almost unnatural degree, refraining from any overt displays of emotion as if they believed that to expose themselves in such a way would be as unseemly as removing their clothes.

They gazed at the watches on their velvet cushions, tipping their heads from side to side, exchanging nods and smiles and covert glances, their pale eyes shielded by their long eyelashes. When they expressed themselves satisfied, Morton served China tea, which they appeared to relish. At the end of exactly half an hour they rose to leave. As they headed for the door, one of the brothers reached into his jacket pocket and produced a cardboard wallet.

"For you," said the other. He nodded then offered the wallet to Owen. "We trust that you and your young lady will enjoy the show."

The wallet contained two tickets to the Gemini Twins' stage show at the London Palladium. Owen bowed his head, stammered his thanks. He glanced briefly at Morton, wanting to gauge his reaction, but the old man was shaking hands with the other twin and refused to meet his eye. It was only once the brothers had departed that Morton congratulated him on his decorum.

"They're not the easiest of clients," he said. "But you did well, they liked you."

He said nothing about the tickets. Nor did he express any curiosity about the 'young lady'. Morton cleared away the tea things and then they returned to work.

Once the Bentall commission was complete, Morton put Owen on repairs, routine work that nonetheless required a high degree of accuracy and offered Owen the opportunity to familiarise himself with the work of some of the greatest watchmakers in the world. Morton's regular client list included two headmasters, half a dozen consultants from Guy's, a number of prominent local businessmen, a high court judge and several members of parliament, each of them owning at least one timepiece of above average quality. Owen's workload soon encompassed watches he had thus far only seen in periodicals or museums.

Christmas came and went. Owen had planned on returning to Devon for the holiday, but the weather had turned suddenly colder and on December 18th a prolonged and heavy snowfall closed the railway line west of Reading. By Christmas Eve, workmen had succeeded in making one of the tracks passable but there were few trains and major delays to those that did run. Owen worried about further snowfalls, his return to London postponed by days or even weeks. In the end, he decided it would be better to remain in town. He telegraphed his father, promising to come at New Year if the weather improved. He spent Christmas with Morton, the two of them enjoying a turkey dinner at The Almoners. The dark-haired girl who served behind the bar had just become engaged to the pub's chef and many toasts were drunk. Owen enjoyed himself more than at any Christmas he could remember since his mother died. He barely thought of Dora Newland, and felt pleased with the way things had turned out.

On December 27th the thaw set in. He travelled down to Exeter on the 29th. Anthony collected him from the station in Eric Butts's motor car. On the drive back to the village, his brother regaled him with news and items of gossip from the past six months. Benny Dixon had been brought before the magistrate, charged with affray, Old Dan Blakeley had died of a heart attack during harvest festival, Julie Wetherall who ran the post office was married again, to a sailor she met on the dockside in Plymouth.

"Dora Newland got engaged," he added, seemingly as an afterthought.

Owen, who had just seconds before been laughing merrily over the widow Wetherall's apparently inexhaustible appetite for men in uniform, felt his heart skip a beat, the tips of his fingers suddenly stiff with cold.

"Who to?" he said. He tried to make the question seem casual, as offhand as Anthony's original remark. He had no idea whether he succeeded, what, if anything, Anthony might notice about the change in his demeanour. Owen doubted his brother even remembered Dora was special to him – he could not recall Anthony ever having taken even the most cursory interest in a woman, and when Charles and Stephen fell into boasting about their conquests he usually made a point of leaving the room.

He prefers his machines, and chess games, Owen thought. And maybe Billy Deuce, who had been at school with Anthony until he won a paid scholarship to the Cathedral School, in Exeter. Yes, it was obvious, though were it not for his Soho nights, the revelation would probably not have come upon him.

Should he speak to his brother, try and reassure him, or no? His musing upon the subject almost cut through the pain of what he was hearing. Almost but not quite.

"Tommy Stowells, of course. The big hero."

Tommy Stowells was the son of a stonemason, a skilled bricklayer who had been one of his father's regular crew until he went and joined the army. The whole village had cheered him off, him and the others who went, and now as Anthony said, Stowells was a hero; Victoria Cross, Veterans' Pension and not a mark on his handsome face to show he'd ever left the county.

The lads who had joined up with him had not been so lucky.

It all made sense. Owen sighed. At least it was over. He kept his eyes on the road. As they turned off the main thoroughfare and on to the narrow, winding lane that led to the village, Anthony pointed out their father's latest construction site, where work had just begun on a house for a retired opera singer.

"He's from Milan," Anthony said, excitedly. The subject of Tommy Stowells seemed to be closed.

Owen spent a week in Devon altogether, mainly working on the site with his father and brothers. His father was short-handed because of the holiday, and Owen found himself mixing mortar and cutting bricks, relishing the cleansing sting of the December air. He found himself enjoying the work, as familiar to him as an old suit of clothes and a welcome distraction from thoughts of Dora, though he dreaded to think what Morton would say if he knew how his gifted apprentice was risking his hands.

He caught sight of Dora Newland only once, at a distance, riding out across the frosted fields on her father's hunter Brewster. She was wearing trews, a luxurious ermine-trimmed cloak about her shoulders, and the combination of the plain workingmen's garment with the almost fantastical elegance of the cloak stabbed Owen to the heart with rapture and hopeless longing. The look, the daring, unconventional beauty of it, was so very Dora. At least she was alone, and not with Tommy Stowells. Owen didn't think he could bear the sight of Tommy right now, although Tommy had always been kind to him when he was a boy, never mocking his crippled leg the way many of the men on the sites had done, at least when Owen's father was nowhere near.

Yes, it was over. For a long time afterwards, Owen would look back at that moment – that gorgeous image of Dora on horseback, her face turned away, one elbow jutting as she adjusted her hood – as the final severance from his old life, the true beginning of the new.

On January 4th, Owen went back to London.

The snows returned at the end of January. With much of the transport network suspended or only partially operational, the city seemed static, eerily gridlocked. Certain foods were in short supply, and there were whispers of a serious outbreak of influenza in the slums of Canning Town. Then as suddenly as it had descended, the freeze lifted. Crocuses bloomed in the squares, the street markets reopened, burgeoning with newly imported goods. Spring arrived early. They received the commission from Lionel Norman in the last week of March.

Owen came down to breakfast to find Morton reading

a letter, hand-written in blue ink, a tightly elongated script that sprawled haphazardly across the page. The sender, who Morton insisted was not a regular client, described himself as a businessman who collected watches as a pastime. He wanted Morton to create a timepiece for him, specifying that it should incorporate a tourbillon regulator. He invited Morton to lunch at his home in Worthing, West Sussex.

"Do you fancy a trip to the coast, then?" Morton said. There was a mischievous light in his eyes. He had not looked so lively since Christmas.

They travelled from London Bridge to East Croydon, where they changed on to the Littlehampton train, which ran down to Worthing via Haywards Heath and Portslade. The war zone, some people still called it. Owen had been nine years old when the war broke out. He remembered vividly Tommy Stowells coming home on his first leave, resplendent in uniform. He remembered the foreign coin Tommy had given him – he thought he might still have it somewhere – Tommy claiming he had taken it from the body of a German soldier. Owen had cherished the coin for years as a lucky charm, even when he found out it was a Belgian franc and not a German coin at all.

He would never forget the day the telegram came, announcing that Tommy's comrade Warren Baxter was missing in action. Becky Baxter running down the High Street still in her dressing gown, clutching the piece of paper and screaming no, not her son, it couldn't be true, falling to her knees outside the Fox and Hounds, Martha Wellesley opening the doors and taking her inside. Owen's mother Evelyn, scrubbing away her tears with the edge of a tea towel before sitting down at her desk in the corner of the living room and dashing off another letter of protest to *The Times*.

"What a ridiculous waste of life," she had stormed, when she saw the newspaper photographs of the ruins of the armaments research station at Herstmonceux. More than two hundred civilians had been killed in the bombing, and worse was to come. Evelyn Andrews had not lived to see the long, drawn-out, deadly endgame that laid waste to the Romney Marshes and the ports of Dover and Newhaven. Owen had never been in Sussex. He had no clue what he might see, how widespread the destruction. He had an idea the bombing had not extended as far west as Worthing and Angmering but wasn't sure. He did not want to ask Morton, for fear of seeming ignorant.

There had been talk at the time that the terms of the Armistice had been too harsh, that there was a danger of revolution in Germany, possibly a new war. So far it hadn't happened, and Owen had not paid the talk much heed. The whole idea of war sickened him, and he had other things to think about, now more than ever.

The land immediately to the south of London formed a series of waste lots, a mixture of scrub and cleared underbrush, scrapyards and gravel pits and closed-down factories, the ordinary detritus of urban expansion. South of Horley seemed somewhat less squalid, and by the time they reached Haywards Heath they were passing through large tracts of open countryside, less extreme in terms of colour and contour than the county of Devonshire but with a delicacy and subtlety of ambience that lent it a beauty of its own. From time to time, Owen noticed odd sections of railway track branching off from the main line but clearly going nowhere, the rails and sleepers sunk in thickets of nettle and brambles.

"What are they?" Owen asked Morton, unable to help himself.

"The lines that used to serve the garrisons," Morton replied. "There's no use for them now."

The journey took almost two hours. They alighted at West Worthing. Lionel Norman was there to meet them at the station, his car, a gleaming green Austin, parked outside. Norman shook first Morton and then Owen jovially by the hand.

"So glad you could make it," he said. "It's quite a hike from London."

A stoop-shouldered, sinewy man, he was not in the least as Owen had expected. His face, with its high cheekbones and clear grey eyes, was good-looking but in a tired, dissolute sort of way. With his thinning hair and gold tiepin he reminded Owen of the upper-class drug dealers that congregated around certain pubs in Soho. As he opened the back door of the car for him to get in, Owen noticed he was wearing a Rihm, a watch of almost grotesque ostentation, the horological equivalent of one of the more outlandish castles of mad King Ludwig of Bavaria. Personally, Owen found Rihm watches to be ridiculous, yet one could not doubt their pedigree, equal to Breitling and Lange in terms of quality and rarer than the both of them put together.

None of Morton's clients owned a Rihm, so far as he knew, and Owen had never seen one outside of the magazines. If Norman had dressed to impress, he had surely succeeded.

Norman's house, on the western outskirts of the town and close to the sea, was a detached modern villa with a glazed veranda running along the front and a gated service entrance to the side. A nice-looking house, built from flint and brick and to a pleasingly simple design. Owen was surprised. He had been expecting something grandiose and elaborate, like Norman's wristwatch. The interior was similarly understated, almost modest – mellow pine, with just a scattering of more valuable-looking antique pieces – and Owen found it difficult to believe that Norman had chosen the furnishings himself. Norman's wife, Owen supposed, although the house bore no immediately discernible signs of a spouse or children.

Lionel Norman showed them where to put their coats and then offered them drinks. Owen asked for a Scotch. He had developed a taste for malt whisky since coming to London. Morton opted for the Amontillado he always preferred. With a drink in his hand, Morton immediately became more animated, almost garrulous. Owen had seen him like this before, and it saddened him a little. Morton claimed to enjoy alcohol for its blood-thinning qualities, though Owen suspected he drank mostly in order to gain a respite from his arthritis.

"You should be talking to my apprentice, not to me," Morton said, once all the necessary pleasantries had been exchanged. "When it comes to the tourbillon regulator, Owen is something of an expert."

Lionel Norman turned to look at him. His eyes had a peculiar cold radiance, like chips of mica in granite. When Morton mentioned the tourbillon they had seemed to flare with a sudden light, like flames doused with paraffin.

"You seem very young," Norman said, disdainfully. "Have you actually constructed a tourbillon before?"

Owen flushed. "I've been conducting experiments," he said. "I have been reading about a new kind of tourbillon, a mechanism that will change the way we think about time. It is complicated work, very intense. Mr Morton has been generous enough to act as my sponsor."

Owen was amazed by his own capacity for invention. He stole a glance at Morton, but the old man seemed entirely unperturbed, and Owen realised the truth of the matter: that Morton had planned it this way, that from the moment he received Norman's commission he had always intended that it would be Owen who would complete it. Another test, like the one he had pulled with the Bentall brothers, only infinitely greater. Owen felt excitement, gratitude and terror in equal parts. For the moment at least it did not matter that the closest he had come to making a tourbillon was a series of tentative drawings at the back of his work log. He had read everything about the apparatus he could lay his hands on. In a discussion with a layman like Norman he had the advantage.

"I'm lucky to have him," Morton added. "It's like being given a new pair of hands." He seemed about to say something else, then found himself interrupted by the sound of a door slamming.

"At last," Norman said. "Her Highness returns. I thought we were going to have to start our lunch without her."

He ducked out into the hall and began talking to someone, a woman. Owen wondered if this was Norman's wife at last. He felt excited suddenly, as if something important was about to happen. He heard footsteps going upstairs, then Lionel Norman came back into the room.

"My daughter," he said. "She'll be down in a minute. She's been up in the woods all morning." He went over to the sideboard and refreshed his drink from the decanter. Like Owen, he was drinking whisky. The tumblers were exquisite, a greenish crystal, the bases embedded with tiny metallic spheres. "You know what it's like with children," he said. "You don't always see eye to eye, but then I have to make allowances with Angela. It hasn't been easy for her, losing her mother." He told them his daughter had just been awarded a place at Cambridge University, to read mathematics, and was due to take up her scholarship in the autumn of the following year. Once again Owen found himself swept with a peculiar sense of anticipation. This girl – Angela – had lost her mother, just as he had. She enjoyed exploring the outdoors. She was a gifted mathematician.

Might it be possible that they would become friends, he and this Angela? Even on such short acquaintance, Owen was beginning to realise he disliked Lionel Norman intensely, even as he relished the idea of Norman's commission, Norman's approval, Norman's money. The thought of having an ally against him – a spy in the midst – was disconcertingly attractive.

"Shall we take our drinks through?" Norman said. "Angela won't be long."

They passed through an archway into a dining room. The table was already laid. A heated hostess trolley stood off to one side, laden with serving dishes and condiments. The idea of Norman preparing food was somehow ridiculous. He must have a cook, Owen supposed, or else he had hired an outside caterer for the occasion. He took his place at the table where Norman indicated. As he settled himself in his seat, Angela Norman entered the room.

She had a careful way of moving, Owen noticed, as if she were afraid of bumping into something and upsetting it. She was wearing a loose, shapeless dress in a biscuit-coloured jersey fabric, heavy horn-rimmed spectacles and a preoccupied expression. Her dark, frizzy hair was gathered on top of her head in a velvet band. Owen smiled at her nervously.

"Hello," he said. He extended his hand. "Owen Andrews."

"I'm Angela." She smiled, and when she took his hand in hers, Owen noticed that two of her knuckles were grazed. "Don't worry about that," she said, seeing him looking. "I scraped it on a rock, that's all. I was looking for snails."

"She's always poking about, seeking out vermin," Norman said. "You'll have to humour her, I'm afraid."

Angela raised her eyebrows, a gesture so slight and so swift that if Owen had not been looking right at her he would have missed it. They were grinning at each other, he realised, as if they had known one another a great deal longer than the approximately thirty seconds that had so far elapsed.

"Let's eat," said Lionel Norman. He uncovered a large Delft tureen, releasing the warm and spicy fragrance of mulligatawny soup. Owen's stomach growled. The soup tasted as delicious as it smelled and Owen found he had emptied his dish in less than five minutes. How uncouth I must seem to her, he mused. He glanced across at Angela but she seemed lost in thought, her spoon suspended midway between her mouth and her half-empty plate.

Morton had abandoned his sherry in favour of red wine. Owen filled his own glass with water from a carafe on the sideboard. He did not want to risk becoming even slightly drunk in front of Angela. Morton's good mood continued. He seemed unaware both of Owen's growing dislike of their client and of Norman's general odiousness, and Owen thought that anyone observing the scene from outside could be forgiven for thinking that this was Morton's home, Morton's wine, Morton's lunch party. Norman himself seemed unchastened by being so volubly upstaged. He was already on his third or fourth glass of wine. Beads of sweat gleamed on his forehead and temples. A section of his slicked-back hair had fallen forward, making him resemble a card sharp in a Roman casino.

"Do tell us about your collection," Morton was saying. "What gave you the bug?"

"You want me to talk about watches? Don't get me started."

Empty rhetoric, as it turned out, as Norman seemed happy to hold forth on the subject with no further persuasion whatsoever. He told them how he had been given his first watch by his father, a Longines Solar Eclipse with a silvered dial and thirteen complications.

"Dad gave me it as a reward for passing my eleven-plus. I was never what you'd call academic, but I knew how to work hard. Dad was a self-made man. The headmaster of my school looked down on him, but I swear Dad taught me more about life than that old bastard ever did." He leaned back in his seat, brandishing his wine glass. "Of course Dad would never have guessed that most of the money I earned would end up going on expensive watches."

He laughed loudly, and pushed back his hair. The gesture disarmed him, and Owen was dismayed to discern something of himself in Norman's story, only in his case it had been his Uncle Henry's pocket watch that had hooked him. Henry worked as a bookkeeper for a local grain merchant, though his true passion was for history, and his narrow cottage was crammed with books and periodicals and interesting curios. Henry's pocket watch was gold, with a skull and candle etched into the back of the case.

"It's called a vanitas," Henry had told him. "The vanitas shows us that the clock is always ticking, even when the candle burns most brightly."

The watch had once belonged to a doctor, Henry said. Owen was enthralled by it, by its rotund, golden smoothness, its mellow, patient ticking, most of all by its self-containment, which to Owen seemed more reminiscent of eternity than mortality. He began to save the pennies and shillings he earned doing jobs for his father on site and bought an instruction manual on the care and repair of pocket watches. By studying the manual he learned to draw and name the parts of a watch mechanism, and to understand their function. Gradually it dawned on him that watches were not simply objects to be purchased and admired, they were machines that had first to be manufactured by an expert craftsman. That he himself might design such a machine, much as his own father might design and build a new school washroom, or a stable block.

Owen felt a brief burst of pride in himself that his own instincts had been creative rather than acquisitive, but the emotion felt sordid, unworthy, and Owen recognised it as nothing more than an outburst of his personal animosity towards Norman himself. He asked himself why it was, exactly, that he disliked Norman so much on such cursory acquaintance. It was not as if Norman had done anything to harm him – rather the opposite – and it had never previously been his habit to take against people. He sensed that Norman was a bully, yet he had no evidence. His treatment of Angela was patronising but then Owen supposed he was like that with everyone.

Norman told them he had decided to commission Morton because he had been recommended by a client, and because Norman felt it was important to support English watchmaking. He used phrases like 'an investment in creativity' and 'giving something back to society', the kind of highfalutin talk rich men were apt to spout when they had a bit of extra money to splash around.

Once again, Owen felt mean-spirited and guilty, but there seemed nothing he could do to banish his misgivings.

What it came down to was he simply did not trust the man. As he tried casting around for something more solid to back up his suspicions, all he could come up with was that much as Lionel Norman seemed to enjoy informing them of how he spent his money, he had not said a word about how he earned it.

They came to the end of the meal. Norman and Morton had polished off three bottles of claret between them while Owen worked his way through the selection of meat dishes and seasoned vegetables in the seemingly endless array of covered platters contained within the hostess trolley. He felt drowsy, piggish, his stomach heavy from overindulgence, discomfited at being so ready to take advantage of Lionel Norman's hospitality whilst harbouring such rancour against him. He kept glancing towards Angela, desperate to know what she might be thinking. Suddenly she turned to look at him, her eyes behind the heavy glasses golden and clear.

"Would you care to see the garden?" she said.

Her approach was so direct he was taken aback, yet he felt certain he sensed at the root of it the shared desire to get away from her father, at least for a time.

"That would be excellent," Owen said. "I could do with some fresh air."

"Don't let her lead you astray," Norman drawled, his voice sluggish from the wine. "Her and her ridiculous animals."

Owen gave a short laugh, not trusting himself to speak. As he and Angela both made for the door, he felt his fingers brush accidentally against the back of her hand. He opened his mouth to apologise but she was already halfway down the hall. He could feel his fury at Norman receding and he put that down to Angela, the calmness of her presence, the otherworldliness that felt simultaneously strange and utterly familiar. He ached to touch her hand again, this time for longer.

The outside air invigorated his senses like a draught of cool water. Owen smelled the sharp tang of seaweed and brine, at once rank and medicinal, antiseptic and corrosive. He recalled stranded flotsam and kelp on the beach at Dawlish, the rotting, barnacle-encrusted breakwater at low tide, and for a second he found he could almost hear the high, outraged shriek of his brother Anthony as the paper kite he had made at scout camp ditched itself like a shot-down pheasant into the waves. The garden immediately behind the house had been arranged formally, a wide lawn bordered by shrubs. At the bottom of the garden was a low wall. On the other side of the wall were the wilds, not woods exactly but a tract of scrubland, thick with bushy outcrops of tamarisk and dune grass, scattered here and there with stunted trees.

"Trees don't grow well here," Angela said. "They don't like the salt." She led him through a gap in the wall, presumably where a gate had been. A stony path wound its way through the undergrowth.

"Is all this land yours?" Owen asked.

"It's my father's. He bought it because he wanted to put more houses on it, but the council won't let him. Not so far, anyway. He's been at war with them for years." She turned to face him. "I've told him that if he ever builds on this land I'll never speak to him again. Most of this stretch of coast has been developed now, but the land between Goring and Ferring is still unspoiled. My father wants to use it for executive homes." She paused. "When I was small I called it the Mermaids' Garden. I used to play out here for hours. Now I'm making a study of the plants and invertebrates here. This land is home to a rare variety of land snail. Not that my father gives a damn about that."

She stood looking out over the tangled underbrush, loose strands of her hair blown back by the breeze, and Owen sensed a passion in her, a current of feeling so highly charged it seemed to galvanise her. Angela Norman had remained mostly silent through their long luncheon. Here in the open and away from her father she seemed a different person.

"Are you looking forward to Cambridge?" Owen said.

"I'm afraid he'll find a way to stop me from going," she said. "I know that sounds stupid, but I can't help worrying."

She meant her father, of course, and Owen felt his fury at the man rising in his gut again.

"He can't. Not once you're eighteen."

"You don't know my father. Not yet." She smiled and then shrugged, a slow, contemplative gesture, drawing her shoulders up to meet her hair in a manner that reminded him of the ravens he often saw in Merrick Square, just across from the workshop, sheltering from the rain. "I don't want to talk about him. Can I write to you in London?"

Once again, her question was so direct and so unexpected it was almost shocking, and he wondered what it was she found to like in him, a cripple who had done nothing but slouch at the table and stuff his face with food, all the while dancing attendance on her hated father.

The idea of receiving a letter from her sent a shiver along his nerves. He knew instinctively that Lionel Norman would be vehemently against the idea of a correspondence, would try to prevent it if he could, and the knowledge filled him with glee. But behind the more frivolous emotion was something else, a feeling that had nothing to do with Lionel Norman and everything to do with Angela. When he woke up that morning he had not known she existed, yet already the thought of losing her was unbearable.

"I would like that very much," Owen said. "I don't think I'm much good at letters, though."

"I bet you are," Angela said. She smiled again, and for a second he glimpsed the child who had played in the Mermaids' Garden. "Write to me about your work. We'd better go in now or Daddy will begin to wonder where we've got to."

They turned back towards the house, and as Owen moved aside to let her pass through the gap in the wall their shoulders collided. Owen put out his hand to steady her, and in the same moment she flung up her own hand, their fingers intertwining as they came to rest. Her face was so close to his he could feel her breath upon his cheek.

"I'm sorry," he said. He felt an ache deep inside him that was like homesickness.

"It's all right." Angela laughed softly. "Come on."

They hurried towards the house. Owen sensed the urgency they both felt, to get inside before Lionel Norman began to suspect something and came looking for them. The idea of seeing him appear at the head of the garden was somehow unthinkable. They needn't have worried. Morton and Norman had moved back into the lounge. The whisky decanter stood on a low table in front of them and they were deep in conversation about the state of the international silver market.

"I hope she's not been boring you with those snails of hers," Norman muttered. He raised his glass to his lips, the Rihm clamped against his wrist like a large golden spider.

"Your gardens are very special," Owen said. "It was kind of Angela to show them to me."

Lionel Norman gazed back at him steadily with his topaz eyes. He knows, Owen thought, though what precisely he believed Norman knew he could not have said. He glanced down at Morton, slumped in his armchair, and felt annoyed with himself for leaving the old man alone for so long. He was not used to drinking alcohol in such quantity and would be bound to suffer for it later. "It's getting late," he added. "We should really be going. We've trespassed on your hospitality for too long already." He thought afterwards that this was when the balance of power in the room shifted, away from Morton and in his favour. It was him and Lionel Norman now, the battle lines were drawn. Morton was an old man. It was Owen's responsibility to protect him.

Norman too seemed to sense the change. He curled his lip. "I'll call you a cab," he said. "It's been a real pleasure." He seized Owen's hand, then Morton's, crushing his swollen knuckles. Owen saw the old man wince and felt enraged. He turned to Angela to say goodbye and found she had already left the room. He felt his heart clench in panic, then realised it was better this way. He and Angela had said everything to each other they needed to say, for the moment at least. Soon she would write to him. The idea of exchanging pleasantries with her in front of her father made him feel sick.

Morton fell asleep almost as soon as they settled themselves in the railway carriage. It was getting on for six o'clock. Beyond the windows the darkening countryside slipped by, folding itself into the shadows. By the time they pulled away from Three Bridges it was completely dark. The light in the compartment was a dingy yellow, making Owen think of the paraffin stove his father's men used for brewing tea when they were working on site. He watched the old man sleeping, glad of his presence yet grateful that he could sit in silence and not be thought rude.

He closed his eyes, thinking of Angela, and knew with absolute certainty that she was thinking of him. The train ran over the tracks, beating out a steady, ratcheting rhythm that put him in mind of a great loom, weaving a cloth of the world, iridescent with miraculous patterns. He jerked awake suddenly just before East Croydon, heart racing, wondering where he was and where he was going.

He shook Morton gently by the shoulder to wake him.

"Time to change trains," he said. "We're almost home."

* * *

For a week following their visit to Lionel Norman, Owen did not go near the workshop. Instead he walked, pacing the streets of Southwark and on across London Bridge into the City. He walked the length of the Embankment from Chelsea to Rotherhithe. He observed the great clocks in their towers, All Saints and St Martin's and Bow. Constantly and everywhere he thought about time. He felt himself suspended within it, the city swerving and changing about him, mutable as the sea, as the coloured chips of glass inside a kaleidoscope, while he himself remained ageless and immortal.

Morton did not appear to question the changes in his behaviour, offering neither advice nor consolation. He seemed to accept Owen's withdrawal for what it was: a preparation for the ordeal that lay ahead. And it was true that Owen was terrified at what lay before him, the work by which he must prove himself, or fail.

He thought a great deal about Angela Norman. He had expected her to write to him soon, and when several days had passed without a letter from her he began drafting one of his own, which he destroyed. He went into a cartographer's store on the Strand, where he bought a large-scale Ordnance Survey map of West Sussex. He traced the route of the railway line, down through the suburbs of London, on through Purley and Horley and Wivelsfield, eventually arriving at the ragged silhouette of the coastline, the Mermaids' Garden. He noted that the garrison railways, the spurs of track that no longer led anywhere, did not appear on the map at all.

Ten days after the journey to Sussex, Owen made an

appointment to examine the Breguet watches he knew were held at the Guildhall, as part of the collection belonging to the Guild of London's Worshipful Company of Clockmakers. One of their members, Horatio Lowndes, agreed to show him round. Lowndes was courteous, tall and quiet, and seemed rather shy. Only the watch he wore, a stunning tonneau Paysage with an openwork dial, hinted at his elevated status within the Guild. He seemed to know without being told the watch Owen most wanted to see, the Breguet Chrysóthome, bequeathed to the museum by a Russian exile, who some had believed to be the cousin of the murdered Tsar Nicholas.

"Breguet's son Georges-Louis helped him to complete it, as he did all his later pieces," said Lowndes. "But it is Breguet's vision you see, a sure example, and one of the finest tourbillons ever made."

They were in a small, white-papered side-room leading off Lowndes's office. Lowndes stood beside him to begin with, but after a while he seemed satisfied that Owen could be trusted and went back to his desk. Owen was vaguely aware of papers being shuffled, drawers being opened, occasionally a phone ringing, but these distractions seemed insignificant, unreal. He studied the tourbillon through his four-loupe for more than two hours, until its pattern of rotation became as familiar to him as the cycling of the blood in his own veins. He grew dizzy with the motion, the breadth of his world shrunk to a space of less than three inches. He thought of the Hurricane, its green and gold lanterns reflected in the waters of the River Otter,

Anthony's cries of delight as the thrust of its momentum rendered him dizzy and finally weightless.

When he arrived back at Trinity Street, he found a letter waiting for him from Angela Norman.

Dearest Owen, she began. *I have thought of you every day.*

The work took him over completely. Time seemed to shrink and compress. Owen had known this would happen – indeed it seemed to him now that the fortnight of walking and planning had been a respite, a breathing space. He cut templates and formulated diagrams, calibrating the wheel train. Morton kept out of sight, and there were days when Owen glimpsed him only at breakfast, or occasionally in the saloon bar of The Almoners much later in the evening. He asked no questions about the work, or how it was going, and Owen was glad. He was too tired to talk, even if he had wanted to. The long hours with the loupe, the lathe, the hand saw and the callipers, the reduction of his world to four square feet of bench space meant that by the end of the day his hands were shaking and his eyes, red and raw from close focus, seemed incapable of taking in the wider world. Leaving the workshop, he suffered bouts of vertigo and nausea as the real world teetered around him, brash and unwieldy, its brutal colours and textures too vast and crude to bear.

The only peace to be found came in the hour or two before he turned down the light, when he would either write to Angela or reread her letters. To her alone he charted his progress, his letters a daily record of travails and triumphs. In her own letters, Angela would report the latest adventures of the rare snails in the Mermaids' Garden, or the peculiarities of a problem of calculus set by her teacher. Sometimes, if she was having difficulties, she would copy out the problem in full and ask Owen if he had any ideas.

Every time she did this it made him laugh aloud. He had tried to explain to her that his own mathematical ability was of the kindergarten in comparison with hers, the rude practice of a mechanic, that her theoretical flights of fancy were beyond him. Nonetheless, he liked to gaze at her blue sheets of paper with their deftly etched symbols. They seemed to tell a story, even if it was in code. He even loved the way she formed her numbers, their blunt, squared-off corners, the pluses and minuses and square roots as smoothly and mysteriously executed as musical notation.

In the moments before he slept, he liked to imagine her in her room, in the lamplight, her hair pushed back from her face as she commanded her hordes of numbers as a general might command his armies. When towards the end of the summer Angela wrote that she intended to travel to London and meet with him – that it was a matter of urgency – Owen's first reaction was to feel disconcerted. He had grown used to things the way they were, the soothing symmetry of their days, the close companionship that had grown up between them without any of the constraints or embarrassment that would inevitably have been a part of any fuller liaison. Angela's physical absence was a part of their closeness. Owen was nervous, he supposed – nervous in case they were unable to translate the intimacy of their letters into real life. He had disclosed so much of himself to her that it was difficult to believe they had met only once, that they had spent less than half an hour alone together. What if he had moulded his idea of her to suit his needs, creating an ideal in his mind that she could not possibly live up to in reality?

Angela planned to travel on one of the many days when Lionel Norman was away on business. It would be easy, she wrote, so long as she was careful. She could get up to town and back without Norman ever knowing she had left the house. Owen wondered, all the same, what could be so urgent that she would risk a journey to London without her father's permission? There was also the question of his work, which was at a delicate stage. He did not relish the prospect of being interrupted, even for a day.

He stifled his worries and wrote that she should come, of course she should come if she could, they would spend the day together and it would be wonderful. This was Angela, after all, he could refuse her nothing, and if she really was in trouble then he needed to know. As the hour of their meeting came closer, his doubts receded, his stomach alternately heavy and light at the prospect of seeing her, speaking with her, holding her hand.

Her train came in on time. Owen saw her approaching from the other side of the barrier. She was wearing a red summer dress, belted at the waist, and carrying a leather satchel. She had brushed her unruly dark hair into smooth-flowing waves.

"Hello, Owen," she said. She smiled, her cheeks flushed

from the heat. Other passengers were streaming past them on to the concourse. Owen found himself holding her hands, realising he had made no plans at all for the day, that he had thought no further than the moment of her arrival. He wondered about taking her for lunch at The Almoners, but rejected the idea almost immediately. Morton might be there, the students from Guy's. He had no wish to answer their questions, then or later.

"What would you like to do?" he asked, lamely. All he wanted was to find somewhere private where they could sit close together with no one watching and keep holding hands.

"Is there a coffee house near here?" she said at once. "We really do need to talk, Owen. There are things I must tell you."

They left the station by the Tooley Street entrance. There was an eating place Owen knew close by, The Bridge Lounge, popular with commuters and businessmen, busy enough for them not to be noticed and to speak in private. It was still relatively early, so not too crowded, and they managed to find a table by the window.

"Have you been up to London often?" Owen asked.

"Only with my father. He has a lot of friends here, people he knows through his business." She fell silent, and a warmth emanated from her, a scent of the sea that reminded Owen immediately of the Mermaids' Garden. A memory came to him of his mother reading him a story from the book of Hans Andersen's fairy tales that, she said, had been a present from her grandmother when she was a girl. The book was illustrated with ten colour plates, each protected by a sheet of semi-transparent paper to stop their brightness from fading. In the story of the Little Mermaid, Andersen had described how each of the seven mermaid sisters kept her own garden at the bottom of the sea, how each of the gardens was decorated with the treasures the mermaids had gathered from sunken ships: sea chests, anchor chains, the bones of drowned sailors.

The youngest sister had one thing only in her garden, the statue of a young boy carved from white marble. In time she fell in love with the statue, believing it represented the face of her beloved. Owen forgot how the story ended. It was a distant memory, distant and gentle as the memory of his mother herself. He listened to the thump and grind of the coffee machine, the shrieks and laughter of children at another table.

"Is it too noisy here?" he asked Angela, concerned that the sudden onslaught of the city might be too much for her.

"I like it," Angela said. She reached across the table, caught hold of his hand. "I like being here with you."

That was when he knew his worries had been ridiculous, that their letters had been real because their feelings were real, that whatever happened next they were in it together. He smiled back at her, momentarily speechless, stupefied with happiness. He realised there had been a part of him that had always believed he would spend his life alone. Not just on account of his club foot, but something deeper, a strangeness that was in his nature and could not be altered. He had believed himself resigned to it – had welcomed it, even.

Now, with Angela before him, the idea of aloneness seemed as distant and as alien as the ocean floor.

They ordered coffee and, suddenly ravenous, two double rounds of sandwiches. As they waited for their food, Angela reached into her satchel and drew out an envelope.

"I need you to look at this," she said, sounding serious. "I think it might be important."

Inside the envelope was a black-and-white photograph. It showed a pocket watch, a chronograph with a split-dial setting and elegant Roman numerals. The dial was silver, or possibly platinum, intricately engraved with a pattern of roses.

Owen held the photograph up to the light. It had been taken at close range, making the image slightly blurred. In spite of this he could see at once that the timepiece was of extraordinary quality, not just in the harmoniousness of its design but in its exemplary finish.

"What a marvellous watch," he said. "Do you happen to know who it's by?" The dial, Owen saw, was unsigned. The maker had probably signed the back plate instead.

Angela gave him an odd look. "You don't recognise it?"

"I've never seen a piece quite like it."

"I found this photograph in my father's office," she said. "If I tell you what I think it is, will you believe me?"

"Of course. Why wouldn't I?"

She stared down at her hands, tapping her fingers against the varnished surface of the table. Then she appeared to come to a decision. "I believe this is a photograph of the watch you are working on now, the watch you are making for my father."

"You mean this is a design he would like me to copy?"

She shook her head. "No," she said. "I mean, this is the

actual watch, the watch my father is going to buy from you once it is finished."

Owen frowned. "I don't understand."

At that moment the waitress brought their coffee. Owen took a sip, scorching his lips. The burnt sienna aroma was harsh and delicious. "You have to tell me what you mean," he said at last. He felt confused, afraid, excited, the same feeling he had experienced in Lionel Norman's drawing room in the moments before Angela had first entered the room and entered his life. As if he was standing on the cusp of something marvellous and new.

What Angela seemed to be suggesting was impossible, and yet he knew it was real. He wondered later how things might have turned out if he had torn the photograph in two and refused to discuss it. He saw himself taking Angela by the hand, leaving the inn and walking with her over London Bridge, into the late August sunshine and another life.

"You don't like my father, do you?" Angela said.

Owen started, broken out of his reverie, confused by her seeming change of tack. "I wouldn't say that," he said. "I'm not entirely sure that I can trust him, I suppose."

"It's all right for you to admit it. I'm glad you don't like him. It shows you have fine instincts. But liking him or not liking him isn't the point. The point is, my father is dangerous. I don't mean just to us, although of course if he knew what we were doing he would try to stop us. I mean he's ruthless and greedy and he'll risk anything to get what he wants. It's why my mother left him. I think she was even afraid of him in the end."

Owen felt a thrill of vindication. He had been right then,

to take against Lionel Norman. His aversion was natural, the same fear and disgust experienced by the hare at the sight of the fox.

"Your mother," he said. "I thought – your father said—"

"Mama isn't dead, if that's what you mean. My father likes to pretend she is, because he still can't stand the fact that she walked out on him. She's living in France now, in a town called Sommières, near Montpellier. She writes to me care of the post office in Goring, because she doesn't want my father to find out where she is."

"She left you alone with him?"

"She knows how badly I want to go to Cambridge. She won't let anything get in the way of that." She looked down again at her hands. "17, rue de Durel," she said suddenly. "That's where I'll be. If anything were to go wrong, I mean. Don't tell anyone."

She gazed at him earnestly from behind her glasses, her eyes the same greenish gold he remembered from their brief half hour in the Mermaids' Garden.

"I wouldn't," Owen said. "I won't." His heart seemed to twist inside his chest. "Please, tell me about the watch."

For a moment she said nothing. She toyed with the breadcrumbs on her plate. They had eaten their sandwiches almost without realising it. "My father came from a poor family," Angela said finally. "He left home at sixteen. His parents were Jehovah's Witnesses. They wanted my father to go into the Faith, but he ran away to London instead. He got a job selling dress and curtain fabric off a market stall in Whitechapel. He turned out to be good at it – not just at persuading people to buy things, but finding the things that people wanted to buy. He was never out of work after that, not even after the Crash. He made most of his money during the war."

"Are you trying to tell me your father was smuggling arms?"

The possibility had not occurred to him before, yet Owen found now that it had, it made perfect sense.

Angela smiled, a wan, resigned smile that suggested she had rehearsed the facts so many times in her head she could no longer doubt them. "To be an arms trader you need money and you need influence. When the war broke out, my father had neither – not enough, anyway. What he did have was an eye for opportunity and a talent for doing business. He broke the trade embargo with Germany, both during the war and immediately afterwards. That makes him guilty of treason. My father knew that if he was caught he could face the death penalty, but that was the kind of risk he was willing to take."

"You mean he was a German spy?"

Angela laughed. "Daddy was never a spy. He doesn't care about politics, he's a natural mercenary. He shipped German goods to anyone who wanted to buy them, which turned out to be a lot of people. The Germans had scientific resources – radar technology, navigational equipment, new kinds of weapons – that were more advanced than any developed in Britain. If you were to argue with him about it, he would say it was his way of helping the war effort, by evening things up. It's a sound argument, in one sense, but my mother never forgave him and what he wants to do now is even more dangerous."

"What does he want to do?"

"He wants to import technology from the future. He believes your watch – your tourbillon – will give him a way to do it."

Owen stared at her in consternation. Then he laughed. "What you're suggesting is impossible," he said. "I make watches, not time machines." Hearing his own words spoken aloud made him want to laugh still harder, a wild, shrill laughter tinged with the sound of madness. *For what is a watch but a time machine?* he thought. *If this is madness I am half in love with it already.*

"You do know about Breguet's diaries?" Angela said.

"Of course." He felt momentarily surprised that Angela should speak so casually of the great Swiss watchmaker, that she would have heard of him even, the man who had invented the tourbillon, who had created some of the greatest timepieces in the world, almost losing his head to the guillotine in the process. But then, why should she not have done? Angela's hero was the mathematician Sophie Germain. Mathematics was her lifeblood, and Abram-Louis Breguet was one of the greatest engineers who ever lived. "They're a nonsense though, an old man's fantasy. There's no such thing as the Time Stasis. There never could be."

"There was no such thing as the motor car or the aeroplane until someone invented them."

"Not me," Owen said. "I still count on my fingers, especially when I'm tired. I'm a mechanic, not a physicist."

"You don't know what you are," she said. "Not yet."

He felt suddenly dizzy, seized by claustrophobia.

His surroundings grew indistinct, an unfocussed, noisy jumble of colour and sound. "Let's go outside," he said. "It's difficult to think straight in here."

He fumbled in his pocket for coins, and as he walked up to the bar to pay the bill he found his hands were shaking. He glanced back at Angela, suddenly anxious that she would be gone, the past hour a kind of fugue state, a fantasy. He wondered if this was how people began to lose their minds – not in a catastrophic meltdown, but in a slow and insidious seeping away of what was real.

Angela was still there, looking out of the window at the people passing by, her arms folded on the table in front of her. If anything, she seemed more real than those around her, the drinkers and diners at the other tables, whose appearance and costume and manner of speech meant as little to him as if they were stage dressing, a company of extras paid by the hour who would disperse amidst merry chatter once this scene was over.

Could there be even an iota of reason in what Angela was suggesting? Time travel? Smuggling weapons that could avert or more likely cause a new world war? The kind of ideas that would appeal to Mr Wells, perhaps – Owen had read *The Time Machine* and enjoyed it well enough but for all its gorgeous invention it was still just a story.

Why then did he feel so afraid? For it was fear he felt, he realised, the kind that seizes the heart when you sense a lurking presence in a darkened hallway yet refuse to make a light.

They crossed the road and went down the steps into Potters Fields. The park was busy with lunchtime strollers, office clerks and shop girls, children playing tricks on their au pairs. They walked companionably side by side, sunshine dappling the pathway in front of them, and Owen thought how happy he would be to make light of what Angela had told him, or better still, to forget it entirely. What he wanted was simply to be with her, to feel again the nervous excitement that had overcome him when he first saw her at the station, as if everything around him were gifted with a peculiar brightness.

He tried pointing things out to her – a trio of nuns, a Dalmatian dog, two schoolboys trying to get a kite down from a tree. The kite was red, like a sail, like that kite of Anthony's that had dived into the sea that day at Dawlish. Owen hoped these sights would capture Angela's attention, help to draw her out of herself, yet still there was a tension between them, that odd sense of hiatus that always descends in the wake of an unfinished conversation. Angela smiled distractedly, hugging her satchel to her chest. Her desire to return to the subject they had been discussing was obvious, insinuating itself between them like a third person. In the end he had no choice but to give in to it.

"Where did your father come by the photograph?" he said at last. "The photograph of the watch, I mean."

"That's the strange part." She spoke without missing a beat, as if their twenty minutes of awkward, inconsequential small talk had never happened. "He's been travelling a lot recently – Amsterdam, Brussels, Berlin. Sometimes he comes back filled with energy, at other times he's so exhausted he sleeps for days. I don't know which scares me more. I stole the photograph out of his desk last week, while he was in Manchester. There were several copies, half a dozen at least, so I'm hoping he won't notice that one has gone missing. The photographs were in an envelope – a stamped, addressed envelope sent to our house in Worthing. I know you're going to find this difficult to believe, which is why I needed to tell you in person. The date on the postmark was – well, it was twenty years from now, or almost. June 1943."

"You're telling me someone sent these photographs to your father from the future?" A burst of laughter escaped him, finally, and for a split second he felt furious with her at the preposterousness of it all. Why was he wasting time here when he could be working? Only children believed in time travel, as only children believed in ghosts and goblins, and however brilliant she might be, Angela Norman was still a child, barely eighteen years old. He should never have let himself become seduced by her.

"Not just someone," Angela said. "You sent them, Owen. The writing on the envelope was yours. I recognised it the instant I saw it."

Her face was flushed, and there were tears in her eyes. "I thought we trusted each other," she added. Her hands were curled tightly into fists, and Owen saw she was not so much upset as angry. He had failed her, he realised. Their first serious test of courage, and he had not been equal to it. He grabbed both her hands, tried to uncurl her fingers.

"I'm sorry," he said. "I'm trying to understand, that's all." He touched her hair, which was softer than he had imagined, with the grainy, rippling texture of raw silk.

"I've been trying to understand for days," she said, relenting. "I haven't worked it out – yet. All I have is the envelope. And you are working on the tourbillon, aren't you? You are using Breguet's calculations?"

"Yes – but that still doesn't mean I can build a time machine. You might call the tourbillon a miraculous device, a miraculous invention, but it cannot perform miracles. What Breguet believed at the end – it was just a theory, a flight of fancy, the same as anyone might have, watching a skein of geese crossing the sky and imagining what it might be like to be flying with them. I don't believe Breguet was senile but I do think he let his imagination run away with him."

"In order for a thing to be invented, it must first be imagined," Angela said. "Breguet imagined it, but he was already old, he died. You may not believe in the Time Stasis, but you have imagined it, you imagine it constantly. You are already further along the pathway than you know."

"I'm an apprentice still – I couldn't possibly achieve the things you say I can."

"Not now, maybe, but soon. And my father is waiting. He knows all this already, don't you see?"

"Are you telling me – I don't know, that I should refuse his commission?"

The idea that he should stop, that he should abandon work on the watch, slammed against his insides like a death knell. He wouldn't do it – whatever he promised Angela, he felt bound to press onwards. *That's what he's depending on*, Owen thought. *Lionel Norman – that's why he hired you. Because really you are brothers under the skin. Because he knew you would sacrifice anything rather than fail.* The dismay must have shown in his face because Angela grabbed his hands and shook her head.

"That's not what I mean at all. You have to keep going. I thought at first I would have to beg you to stop, but now I understand that this work is your destiny. It's what you were born for. I can see you're laughing at me again, but you know it's true. We have to keep my father from getting his hands on it, that's all. At least we know what he's up to. Some of it, anyway. That should make things easier."

We know nothing, Owen thought, but did not say. He imagined a world in which the things Angela said were possible and might really happen – a world in which the motherless son of a builder grew up to become a genius, a genius who made watches that could alter time. A marvellous world, in which diseases were cured, the hungry fed, the impassable gulf between the past and the future reduced to the status of an ancient legend. Or would it be a world of horrors, in which those men who least deserved power seized it for themselves, laying waste to their enemies with terrible weapons, with those who dared resist them expunged from history?

A flight of fancy, Owen thought. *I'm getting as bad as Anthony, with his Martian war machines.* He nodded slowly. "All right," he said, and he found that it was. What he wanted was to carry on working on the tourbillon and writing to Angela. The rest he could simply ignore, at least for now. The idea that he might somehow cheat Lionel Norman of what he desired was also appealing, a way of showing the man that money could not buy everything, whatever he thought.

He drew Angela closer, kissed her forehead. The gesture felt natural, as if he had done it a hundred times before. *And what if you have, or will do? How would you know?*

He felt like laughing again. The sun emerged from behind a cloud, spilled dazzling light across his face and into his eyes. He put up a hand to shade them. "Will you come back with me, to the house?" he asked her. "Morton would love to see you again. I could show you the workshop, you could stay for supper."

She shook her head. "That would be wonderful, but I can't. My father will telephone later – he always does when he's away. If I'm not there when he calls he'll want to know why. I'll never hear the end of it. The last thing we want to do now is to make him suspicious."

They walked back to London Bridge Station. The rush hour was just beginning, the streets filling up with commuters hurrying to catch the trains that would take them out of the city, returning them to their homes in the dormitory towns of Surrey and Sussex and Kent.

"When will I see you again?" Owen said, as Angela's train was announced. Until they were actually on the platform, the idea that he would soon be parting from her had seemed distant and unreal.

"I don't know. I'll come up again at half-term if I can but that depends on where my father is. It's not safe for you to be in Sussex."

The idea of having to sneak around like a naughty schoolboy riled him, but he supposed Angela was right, it was better that they kept their relationship secret, at least for now. Owen imagined that even under normal circumstances, Lionel Norman would be the type to oppose any friendship of his daughter's that he had not personally sanctioned. Confronting Norman directly would only make things worse for Angela. Everything would be different once she was at Cambridge.

They embraced briefly, and then Angela got onto the train. Owen stood on the platform, gazing through the window into the compartment: the brass trim, the blue seat covers, the red flash of Angela's dress as she sat down. There were others in the compartment with her, an elderly vicar reading a newspaper and a young black woman with a baby in her arms. Angela pressed her fingers to the glass. Her lips were moving but Owen could not make out what she was trying to say. He found he had to resist the urge to leap aboard, to hold her hands one more time before they parted. When the train pulled out of the station he was almost glad.

Owen crossed the taxi rank, dodging between the bus lanes and emerging on to Borough High Street. Cars and lorries thundered past him over London Bridge. At the junction of Long Lane and Great Dover Street he crossed over on to Marshalsea Road, losing himself in the tangle of side streets and alleyways tucked into the right angle between Bridge Road and Great Suffolk Street. He had no reason to be there but it was a part of town he liked, crammed with corner newsagents and Turkish restaurants, dingy junk shops stuffed with pre-war bric-a-brac and mildewed books.

Most of these shops had already closed for the day. Their dusty window displays glowed blue or rose under neon lighting. Owen paused in front of one of them, a nameless, peeling premises that advertised itself as a specialist in modern electrical goods, though many of the objects on show in the window looked as if they would have been out of date even before the war.

Most of the window space was taken up by a large aquarium in which silvery, triangular fish glided up and down as if suspended on invisible strings. Owen gazed at them, momentarily mesmerised, wondering if they were for sale or just for show. He remembered his old Latin teacher, Stanley Simpson, who had kept tropical fish as a hobby. Mr Simpson had insisted his fish were not insentient as most people imagined them to be, but could recognise the person who fed them and could even be trained to rise to the surface of the water and take food from your hand.

As a boy, Owen had been spooked by the idea. He wondered if it was true. It was beginning to grow dusk he realised; time for him to return to Trinity Street. Shadows massed in the alleys and doorways, seeming to block his path. Owen felt confused, realising he could not remember the exact direction he had approached from, or how he should find his way back to the main road. He walked to the end of the street, casting about in both directions for a familiar landmark, but the lanes that led off into the shadows seemed completely alien. He doubled back, passing the shop again and then emerging into a narrow courtyard he thought he recognised. There was a burst of coarse laughter, the sound of running feet, and then suddenly he was in Marshalsea Road again, with the brighter lights of Borough High Street clearly before him.

He made for home as quickly as he could, cutting across the High Street then into Great Dover and Trinity. A figure loomed up at him out of the twilight, a middle-aged man carrying a briefcase. Owen's heart began to race, convinced for a second that this was Lionel Norman, though when he looked again he saw he was nothing like him.

The basement of Trinity Street was dark, the windows shuttered. Owen stood on the pavement outside, wondering where the time had gone. In some small yet infinitely distressing way, the house seemed different, and Owen realised he was afraid to enter. He thought about calling out, just to see if Morton would come to the window, inwardly chastising himself for his own foolishness.

You'd scare him half out of his wits. You're as mad as Louis Breguet, after all.

He thought of retracing his steps to the station, taking a room at the Tooley Hotel, but it had grown so late he doubted they would let him in. Aside from that, his foot was aching badly. He would not be able to walk much further, even if he wanted to.

Finally he was left no choice but to go inside.

The hallway was dark as he expected it to be, but faint traces of light were visible on the upper landing, a sure sign that Morton was still awake, reading in his armchair or listening to the radio. Owen hurried upstairs, eager to reach the safety of his attic. He fumbled his way into the room then lit the lamp, turning everything a grainy yellow. The bed was neatly made, the books and papers on his desk untouched.

All at once, his fears seemed groundless, the kind of half-awake, nameless anxieties experienced in the small hours, in the wake of a nightmare. As he crossed to the window to draw the curtains, he noticed something lying on the bed. When he stooped to pick it up, he saw it was the photograph of the watch that Angela had given him.

How it had arrived in the room before him he had no idea. Was it even the same photograph? He wondered if it might not be Morton's – an image the old man had found, and wanted him to see. The question seemed suddenly wearying, less important than the watch itself, which was a gem. Owen gazed for a long time at the elegant lines of the hands, the silvered dial with its pattern of roses. As he slipped out of his clothes and into bed it occurred to him that he could indeed copy it, that he could make the design his own.

He fell asleep quickly, and slept a full eight hours. He awoke thinking about Lionel Norman, about how satisfying it would feel to fool him into believing the watch he, Owen, had made him was the watch in the photograph.

He was now working twelve hours a day. Often he was so immersed in what he was doing that he was aware of Morton only as a hazy, beneficent figure on the periphery of his existence. Occasionally he would go to Morton with questions – minor technical problems that needed solving, queries regarding the melting points of various alloys. Morton seemed happy to share his experience, and never offered advice unless Owen specifically asked for it.

His inattention to Morton sometimes made Owen feel guilty, though never guilty enough for him to change his behaviour. He felt the old man's presence as a steadying influence. There were times, late at night, when Owen felt tempted to go to Morton and tell him about Angela, just for the relief of finally having a reason to speak her name aloud. He wondered what the old man would say if he were to tell him what Angela had said about her father, if he were to ask him if he could identify the maker of the watch in the photograph Angela had stolen from Norman's desk. He burned to confide in his master, yet something held him back. He told himself it was because he didn't want to worry the old man, though he knew there was more to it, that his hesitation had more to do with his own anxiety over what might happen than concern for Morton.

He was worried that Morton might tell him to stop, that he might forbid him from entering the workshop until they were able to establish for certain what was going on. The prospect of that was unbearable, and so he said nothing.

He asked him about Breguet instead.

"Was he mad at the end, do you think?"

"The man was a genius," Morton said. "There's a fine line between the two."

One morning Morton came down to breakfast holding a tattered copy of Georges-Louis's edition of Breguet's diaries.

"Keep it," he said to Owen. "I think my days of fretting over insoluble puzzles are almost done."

Owen had laid eyes on Breguet's diaries only once before, in a heavily abridged edition he had managed to obtain via the inter-library loan scheme in Exeter. He had made little sense of them at the time, though then as now he had been enthralled by Breguet's drawings. Owen himself had never been a good draughtsman. Even his most careful efforts showed little discernible improvement from the lopsided, inarticulate doodles that had once littered the pages of his school exercise books. Breguet drew with the accuracy of an architect, the impassioned fluency of the fine artist. The drawings he made detailing the design and mechanism of his watches had a finesse and a flair, above all an energy that reminded Owen of the sketchbooks of Leonardo da Vinci.

Breguet's earlier diaries consisted mainly of such drawings, accompanied by sparse notes about materials he needed to buy, clients he was appointed to see, monies he had received from commissions fulfilled. Latterly they became more confusing, a disorderly hotchpotch of horological history, scientific methodology and what appeared to be some sort of fictitious narrative, complete with named characters and snatches of fully articulated dialogue.

In the midst of all this there were conventional diary entries: sarcastic comments about the weather or diatribes on contemporary politics.

Owen hardly knew what to make of it. He purchased a stack of sketching paper from a stationer's on Borough High Street and spent a part of each day attempting to make copies of Breguet's more elaborate drawings, striving for accuracy insofar as his limited ability would allow him. When enlarged in scale, the components of Breguet's watches appeared to take on a life of their own, an individualistic, almost organic quality, like some of the nameless objects he had observed in Cubist paintings by Miró and Gris.

He sent some of his drawings to Angela, who pronounced them beautiful. Their letters continued as before, and as before he would spend the final hour before sleep in recounting anecdotes from The Almoners, or other incidents from his day he thought would interest or amuse her. The weeks passed, and then the months, and as his second Christmas in London approached, Owen found himself wondering if this would be his life from now on, a never-ending pursuit of the impossible, indifferent to the weather, undifferentiated by high days or holidays. He thought of his New Year's sojourn in Devon with detached nostalgia, his pain over Dora Newland a dusty jewel in a hoard of useless mementoes he had forgotten existed. The snows came again, and Owen thought about how the past itself seemed to have become smaller, a self-contained and isolated region that had no bearing on the present. He could visit it through memories and photographs if he really wanted to, but what would be the point?

He remembered a snow dome that used to stand on his mother's dressing table, a miniature city behind curved glass that had entranced him so much he had begged and pleaded to be allowed to keep it in his room.

"You'll only break it," his mother said. "Then there'll be tears."

After she died it disappeared. Owen had no idea where it went.

As work on the watch gathered pace, Owen began a series of new experiments, making enlarged templates of the mechanism's most complicated components from the same steel and brass alloy Breguet would have used before finally recreating them in Invar, a newly invented alloy of iron and nickel. Less susceptible to corrosion or heat expansion, although it was more expensive than brass and steel, most of the top horologists considered Invar to be superior in every way.

Owen planned to construct the tourbillon cage itself from Nivarox, an alloy containing beryllium that was more durable even than Invar. The plates and case of the final article would be constructed from gold. For the prototype he contented himself with silver and stainless steel. He assembled the enlarged components into a travelling clock, with a glass panel inserted into the back plate, making it possible to view the mechanism in action. He engraved the dial with roses, copying the pattern in the photograph Angela had stolen from her father's desk. Seeing the design brought fully to life gave him a strange sensation of déjà vu, a feeling he brushed aside as predictable and irrelevant. Of course the pattern seemed familiar, because it was – if he had examined the photograph once, he had examined it a hundred times. There was nothing uncanny in this. He had seen the pattern and liked it. That was all.

When Owen showed the clock to Morton, he immediately removed the back plate and began examining the mechanism through his loupe.

"These are Breguet's measurements," he said at once. "You've been working from the drawings he made before he died?"

"The drawings are incomplete," Owen said. "I've had to

improvise a little. But yes, the design of the mechanism is taken from Breguet."

The old man's expression became suddenly inscrutable, almost stern. "What makes you think you can succeed where Breguet failed? Breguet was a genius. You, young man, are barely out of school."

Owen flushed. He had secretly thought his machine so fine he had expected Morton to gush unqualified praise, all but bowing down before him in his admiration. He had become so wrapped up in the work he had forgotten himself. "Breguet did not fail," he said. "He ran out of time. If he had not been so old and so ill he would have completed his work, for sure."

He felt his flush deepen. He feared that Morton, who was old and ill himself, almost certainly dying, might interpret his remark as a criticism, a young Turk's sarcastic revenge on his duller master. He was amazed to see that Morton was smiling.

"You're a brave lad, Owen Andrews." The old man touched him briefly on the shoulder. "Would you mind if I kept the clock?"

"I would be honoured," Owen said. "It's yours."

Almost exactly a year from the day Morton had first accepted the commission from Lionel Norman, a second letter arrived, this time addressed to Owen personally. In it, Norman enquired after Owen's health, delivered a humorous account of an auction he had recently attended in Geneva, expressed excitement over the watch, which, he trusted, must be nearing completion. The tone of the letter was outwardly friendly, but beneath the surface Owen felt sure he could detect an accusatory tone, a warning, even. He reread the letter several times in an attempt to quantify his suspicions more precisely, but came up with nothing.

As before and as always, there was his simple dislike of the man, that instinctive mistrust, and he was reminded of a story he had chanced to read once in one of the pulp magazines Anthony was so keen on, in which the devil, in the guise of a travelling salesman, terrorises the residents of a cheap boarding house. He replied to Norman's letter with a careful courtesy, stating that although the presentation of the final article was still some way off, the prototype was indeed complete, that Norman was welcome to call at the workshop when he was next in London.

He did not discuss the matter with Angela, or even tell her that her father had been in contact. He felt determined that Norman should intrude on their lives as little as possible. He assumed Angela must feel the same. The only time she referred to her father directly was when she wrote advising Owen they should not try to see one another again until she started at Cambridge.

I think my father has begun to suspect something, she wrote. *If he discovers the truth he will make our lives hell, maybe even find a way to destroy us. It is better this way, if you can bear it. There are less than six months to go now, after all.*

He resented Norman for interfering, and most of all for the power he still exerted over Angela. But still, he could not deny it would be inconvenient, perhaps even dangerous, to confront Norman directly, especially now. Once the watch was finished, Owen would be paid, and handsomely. With money like that, he and Angela could go anywhere, do anything. Lionel Norman would be unimportant, out of their lives.

He found he thought less and less about what Angela had told him of her father's ambitions to travel in time. As the weeks passed, the idea became less real, like a conversation they might have had once in a dream. Angela's letters were the reality, and in the absence of Angela herself, Owen came to rely on them more and more. When towards the end of June a whole week went by without even a single postcard from her, Owen started to worry. He began to listen out for the postman, hurrying upstairs from the workshop the moment he heard the heavy clack and thump of Morton's letterbox. When another week passed and there was still no word from her, his worry turned to fear. His first thought was that Norman must have found out about them somehow, intercepted their letters. Then he began to wonder if the explanation might be more prosaic – a young Cambridge don perhaps, an unknown rival approved by her father, who had been steadfastly courting Angela's affections all along.

Owen knew such suppositions were ludicrous, but the thoughts kept swarming through his mind nonetheless, nagging away at his sanity and preventing him from working. What could have happened? Although he had promised Angela he would never telephone the house he found he could no longer help himself. He called on a

Wednesday, in the afternoon, when he thought it most likely Lionel Norman would be out. There was no reply, and as he replaced the receiver Owen could not help feeling he had somehow made things worse.

Finally, his endurance was at an end. Owen decided he would travel to Sussex, that he would call at Norman's house under the pretext of showing Norman the samples of gold he had procured for making the watch case. At least then he would know if Angela was still at the house, and if he was able to be alone with her even for a moment he would try and persuade her to return to London with him immediately.

He caught an eight o'clock train. Although it was early, the air was already humid, the station concourse muggy with the heat of the day before. A bus had broken down in the station entrance, and a mechanic in a fluorescent safety jacket was attempting to restart it, his hands black with grease. A small girl, perhaps seven or eight, darted around him, hopping on and off the kerb in her dusty plimsolls. She had a dirty mark on one cheek and a crooked smile. As Owen watched, she grabbed a wrench from the mechanic's tool bag and handed it over.

"Not to worry, mate, she's mine," said the mechanic. "Got to keep them out of mischief somehow, haven't you? She's been crazy about the buses since she could walk."

Owen smiled his understanding, and passed on to the station concourse. He remembered himself at the same age, perhaps a little older, mucking about on the site after school and begging one of his father's contractors to let him work the cement mixer. It was one of the old ones, still cranked by hand, and it needed the whole weight of Owen's small body to get it moving. He had returned home triumphant, the solidifying cement dust caked in his clothes and hair. It was the only time he could remember his mother being angry with him.

"Do you know how much that blazer cost?" she yelled. "Do you think new school uniforms grow on trees?"

She had taught Music and History at the Priory School, and yet she had fallen in love with Ted Andrews, the builder. Crazy about him was what they said in the village, was what Owen heard time and again in the weeks and months after she died. For the first time in many years, Owen had a clear memory of her face, the quick light in her eyes, the loose strands of hair at her temples, the hectic flush in her cheeks when she raised her voice. She had come to him later and asked him gently how it had felt, to work the machine. Then she had offered him a sheet of paper and asked him to draw it for her. While he did, she mended his blazer, sewing shut the rip in the pocket using tiny, overarm stitches in pale grey thread.

The train heaved itself out of London. To the south of Croydon, Owen saw again the waste tracts and abandoned factories, the scrapyards piled high with rusting machinery, the gathered detritus that was the aftermath of war. For the first time, he perceived how vulnerable a city could be to enemy attack, and wondered what might have happened to London if the bombing had continued.

The government had forced a peace because they had proved equal strength, but what if their threat to use nuclear weapons had not been heeded? The newspapers had always insisted it was common soldiers like Tommy Stowells who had won the war with their perseverance and courage. Owen saw now that this was a lie, that it had been traders like Lionel Norman, with their illegal arms deals and industrial espionage, criminals who had acquired the blueprints for jet engines and radar, the contraband, illicit knowledge of atomic power. Thieves who cared for nothing so long as they were paid.

The military research station at Herstmonceux had been smashed to its foundations, but that had proved only a temporary setback. Buildings and machines could be destroyed, but not the knowledge they contained. And men like Lionel Norman were left alone to conduct their business, even while they were guilty of treason. Even if, in spite of the Armistice, the world they were creating was viler and more dangerous.

As the train drew nearer to its destination, Owen found himself taken over by a growing resolve. Lionel Norman would not have his work, whatever he proposed to do with it. There were other ways of making money. The only thing that mattered was getting Angela away from him.

There were no taxis at the station entrance and so he was forced to walk. Norman's house was some distance from the station, perhaps two miles, and his foot always ached worse in hot weather. He leaned heavily on his cane, his weak leg dragging a little as he made his way slowly uphill. He felt uncomfortably exposed, vulnerable to scrutiny in a way he never did in London. The houses on Elizabeth Avenue were large and expensive. Some were modern, like Lionel Norman's. Others seemed much older, their pale facades gleaming behind granite gateposts. Many of their lawns were cracked and dry, and he remembered Angela telling him there had been a hosepipe ban. He kept looking around for Norman, but the street seemed empty.

Finally the house was in sight. The green Austin was not in the drive, Owen noticed. It seemed reasonable to suppose that Norman was out, though he knew it would be dangerous to take that for granted. He approached the front door, trying to appear confident and relaxed, though the pain in his leg would have made that difficult whatever the circumstances. He could feel the sweat gleaming on his brow. More than anything he longed to sit down, to take the weight off his feet. He rang the doorbell and waited. For a moment he thought he saw someone moving behind the frosted glass panels of the entrance porch, but nobody came to open the door and the house remained silent. He tried the doorbell again, stepping shakily back off the step and gazing up at the windows. He realised there were no curtains, and when a moment later he pressed his face to the glass of the drawing room window he saw that the space beyond was completely empty. The leather armchairs, the sideboard, the whisky decanter – everything was gone.

His breath came hot and fast. The parched garden flickered before his eyes, and Owen realised he was about to faint. He leaned forward, gasping, using his cane for support. As he stared at the ground, trying to bring it into focus, he noticed a folded-up newspaper on the path to the right of the step. He bent slowly to pick it up. It was dated 18th July, three days before.

All that time he had been sitting waiting in London, and Angela was – where? He had been fiendishly outplayed, Owen realised. It was almost as if Lionel Norman had known all along what he was planning, and like a chess player making a knight's move, stepped in to obstruct him.

Short of breaking into the house, there was nothing more he could do here. It occurred to him that Lionel Norman wanted Owen to break in – getting himself into trouble with the police would provide a timely distraction, an opportunity for Norman to more thoroughly cover his tracks. In this respect at least Owen had no intention of giving Norman satisfaction. He walked, almost staggered towards the gate, wondering how he would ever make it back to the station. He might wait, he supposed, in the hope of hailing a passing taxi cab. But in a quiet residential area like this, he might wait for hours, attracting unwelcome attention all the while.

Somehow, he would have to walk. He leaned against the gatepost, steeling himself. The pain in his foot was excruciating, a lump of steaming lead at the end of his leg.

"Can I help you?" said a voice. "You don't look at all well." It was a woman, and for a single breathless second he allowed himself to believe that it was Angela, that she had escaped from Lionel Norman and come back to find him. But of course it was not, could never be. Angela was gone, and this woman was indisputably present: older than Angela by twenty years at least, her fair hair in an immaculate permanent wave, her slim wrists adorned with golden bracelets. She was looking at Owen with an expression caught midway between admonishment and concern.

My guardian angel, disguised as someone's aunt. Owen's thoughts tumbled haphazardly through his mind like leaves of dropped paper. *There are stranger things in life.*

"I don't suppose you could call me a taxi?" he said, trying to straighten his back. "I came here to keep an appointment, but the person I was meant to be meeting seems to be out."

"If you think I'm leaving you out here in this state, you've got another think coming," she said. "Can you manage?"

She offered him her arm, and Owen found himself taking it, leaning his full weight on her as she steered him away from the entrance to the Normans' place and up the driveway of the house next door. Her own, Owen assumed, a mirror image of its neighbour, only without the scrubby expanse of the Mermaids' Garden to the rear. The woman was glad not to have to be bothered with it, probably, for how could anyone hope to keep such an unruly domain in order? She brought him inside, and Owen all but collapsed on to the wide, cream-coloured sofa in the spotless living room. His sweat-stained, dust-defiled presence seemed an affront, though the instant relief of most of his pain was like a miracle. He exhaled audibly, tears in his eyes.

"Hold on a moment and I'll bring you a drink," said the woman. She left the room, and Owen was glad simply to be there, unobserved. He closed his eyes and leaned back against the sofa cushions, relishing the sensation of weightlessness. *Higher than the Hurricane,* he thought, and he must have dropped off for a second because when he next opened his eyes the woman was back, a tray with two glasses of what looked like lemonade and a plate of frosted buns on the low table in front of him.

He reached for the lemonade, surprised to discover that he was, after all, ravenous and parched. The drink, tart and delicious, brought him back to himself.

"I apologise," he said. "It must be the heat."

"That, and the fact that you were clearly in agony," the woman said. "My older brother has a club foot. They've tried innumerable operations but if anything they've made things worse. The problem with doctors is that they only know what they're doing half of the time. The other half, you might as well pray to God, and I'm sure you're well aware of how useless he is. What on earth are you doing here?"

"I came to see Angela," Owen said. "Angela Norman, from next door." He could not see the point in lying. It seemed ungrateful, somehow. And there was always the chance that this woman might know where Angela was.

"They're gone," the woman said softly. "The house is packed up. The removal men came a month ago."

"That can't be true." The words burst from him, unbidden. He had received Angela's most recent letter just three weeks before. She had spoken of the house, the street, the Mermaids' Garden, the lack of rain. There had been no mention of moving – she would be moving soon enough, to Cambridge. And yet the house was empty.

"She seems like a nice girl. I never did take to him, though. The father, I mean. Too fond of splashing his money about. No wonder his wife left him."

"I thought she was dead," Owen said, distracted.

The woman snorted. "Dead, my foot. Caroline left him. She's in France now, I think."

France, Owen thought – remembered – and a wave of relief overcame him, hit him so hard he found himself imagining it as real, an ocean wave striking his chest and throwing him backwards, laughing, overbalancing him in the sun-spangled water. Himself and Anthony, on Dawlish beach, chasing a kite.

If anything happens, that's where I'll be, Angela had said. *17, rue de Durel, Sommières*. Angela had prepared him for exactly this eventuality. How could he have forgotten?

"Thank you," Owen said. He feared he was beaming.

"No need. Now, I'll call that taxi if you're feeling better."

"Much better."

"You'll take these buns for the journey? They'll only go stale otherwise."

It was only later, at the station, that the strangeness of the encounter came home to him. The woman had taken him into her home, she had seemed unsurprised to discover why he was there. It was almost as if – yet the idea was preposterous – Angela had told her to expect him.

He saw from the timetable that he had just missed a train, that there was half an hour to wait before the next one. He went to the station cloakroom to use the toilet. His face in the mirror was filthy, streaked with sweat and dust. His shirt stank, and there was a dirty, map-shaped mark on the breast pocket of his blazer. He scrubbed at it ineffectually with a dampened paper towel, splashed water on his face, smoothed back his hair. The pain in his foot had lessened to a dull throb. Now that he knew for certain that Angela was no longer in Sussex, he was desperate to be on his way back to London.

In order to pass the time before the train came, he searched idly through the books on a stall that had been put out beside the refreshments kiosk, spy stories and romances, ancient-looking recipe books and manuals for birdwatchers. Most were in poor condition and some were without dust jackets. None held much interest, and Owen was about to turn away when one caught his eye, a novel entitled *An Unknown Country*, by an author he had never heard of called Sylvester John. The cover showed a dark-haired, lean-faced man reading a letter, while in the background a creature that looked like a giant octopus seemed to be in the process of devouring a factory.

Peter Strickland never wanted to be a spy, read the text on the inside flap, *but when his brother Harry is kidnapped his life begins to spiral out of control. As a maniacal dictator seizes power in Germany, a team of rogue scientists open the gateway to a new kind of terror. As millions flee the alien armies and the hell of the labour camps, for Peter Strickland the nightmare is only just beginning...*

Owen smiled. *An Unknown Country* was exactly the kind of book Anthony would enjoy. Anthony had no memory of their mother, but of all the Andrews brothers it was Anthony who was most like her, a dreamy, mercurial child who had suffered from nightmares throughout his childhood and was afraid of the dark.

"It's all this rubbish you're reading," their father had once insisted, after a particularly bad episode. He had threatened to confiscate Anthony's books, a jumbled assortment of no fixed hierarchy, in which Mary Shelley's *Frankenstein* sat side by side with Einstein's *Theory of Relativity*, and Wells's scientific romances rubbed shoulders with Darwin and Freud. Anthony had refused to hand the books over, curling his body around them protectively, as if they were living things.

"Oh, leave him be, Pa," Stephen had said. "He'll soon grow out of it."

Anthony had grown out of the nightmares, but he had never grown out of the books, and Owen was seized with the desire to buy the John novel and send it on to him. He now knew it might be some time – maybe years – before he saw Anthony again, and it seemed important to let his brother know that he was thinking of him. He looked around for an attendant, someone he could pass the money to, but there were none about and after a moment he spotted a metal cash box bolted to one end of the stand. A slip of paper taped to the side invited customers to leave a donation.

Owen dropped a shilling through the slot and tucked the book under his arm. Five minutes later the train came. Owen settled back in his seat and began to read the John book, simply for something to do, but his eyes kept falling shut and he was asleep before the train reached Portslade. He awakened briefly at Haywards Heath, where they were held at the station to let another train pass, one of the new high-speed locomotives that ran on electricity, its sleek, bullet-shaped carriages a gunmetal grey. Owen pressed his face to the glass, trying to get a better look at it, but the train rushed by so swiftly it was hard to see and later he wondered if the whole thing had been a dream. He went back to sleep, jerking awake what seemed like seconds later to the bawling of station announcements at London Bridge.

He stumbled from the train. When he looked to see what the time was, he found his watch had stopped and realised he must have let it wind down. He wasn't able to find a clock on the station concourse either. He made for the Borough exit, which should have brought him out on the High Street opposite the Marshalsea Road, but when he came back up to street level he found himself at the crossroads between Sanctuary Street and Disney Place, close to where he had become lost after seeing Angela back on to the train the day she came to London.

There must be another underpass, he thought, *an exit I've not used before*. He made off down Sanctuary Street. He knew that if he cut through the houses on the right side of the road he would eventually come out at the lower end of the High Street, opposite Long Lane, but the route was more complicated than he remembered and in just a few minutes he was lost again. He told himself it did not matter, that he should simply keep walking until he came to a place he recognised, which in London you always did, sooner or later. He made his way unsteadily through a number of closes and narrow courtyards, some of them stinking of refuse, others piled high with nameless junk. He was beginning to panic.

His foot was hurting badly again, and more than that, he had the feeling of being *elsewhere*, not in his London at all but in Peter Strickland's, from the John novel, where there were spies on every corner and government officials who could send you to the labour camps just for speaking out of turn.

He began retracing his steps towards Sanctuary Street and the Marshalsea Road, thinking he would make his way home from there instead, take a cab from the station taxi rank if necessary. He passed several small shops, two boarded up, the other a drab-looking premises he thought he recognised. He looked more closely, and realised he had indeed passed by it once before, that it was the store selling used electrical goods with the fish tank on display. He leaned against the wall, resisting the urge to sit down on the pavement and rest his leg. Some of the junk in the window seemed familiar – a Bakelite telephone, a hand-operated Singer sewing machine – but there were other things too, things that made no sense. A black box, its metallic surface shiny as lacquer, a panel of what appeared to be glass covering most of its front. The glass was greyish, and opaque, slightly convex, giving no clue as to its function. Owen stared at it, stupefied. The fish tank was still there, he noticed, but watching the fish sliding up and down on their invisible wires, he saw they were not in fact fish at all, but silvery, many-tentacled crayfish, or maybe small squid. They moved with a darting liquid grace, weightless in the greenish water. In the uncertain light from the window they appeared more shadow than substance.

They're like the things in the book, thought Owen wildly. *The book I bought for Anthony at the station*. He patted his blazer pockets, fruitlessly searching, before realising he must have left the Sylvester John novel behind on the train. He backed away from the window, hobbling to the opposite pavement and then taking the first street he came to, uncertain of where he was going but desperate to put some distance between himself and the things in the aquarium. By some fluke, he emerged almost immediately on to Borough High Street, the large intersection by Newington Causeway and Harper Road. A diesel coach thundered by in the direction of the Elephant and Castle. Ignoring the pain in his leg, Owen walked back up the road to the traffic lights just to the left of the turning into Trinity Street. He crossed the road, trying to appear nonchalant, though he could by now barely stand.

Finally, he was at the house. The first floor lights were on, a sure sign that Morton had finished work for the day and was having supper. Owen felt in his pocket for the key, then discovered he didn't need it; the front door was unlocked and standing ajar. His sense of foreboding returned. Morton would not have left the door open, it was as simple as that. He stood in the doorway, listening. At first he could hear nothing but the aggravated susurrus of blood in his own ears, but gradually he was able to make out the murmur of voices, coming from upstairs. He crept forward to the foot of the steps, only to draw back in surprise as the voices were suddenly replaced by a burst of music.

He realised it was the old man's radio. Morton was definitely in, then. This should have set him at ease, but still it did not. He closed the front door behind him and switched on the hall light. There was a note on the telephone pad, a date underlined and what looked like a telephone number. On the chair beside the hall stand was a copy of the *Evening Standard*. He reached for it automatically. The headline was about a bank robbery in Clapham.

The paper was dated 30th July, more than a week in the future. He was reading about a crime that hadn't happened yet.

Owen's mind rejected the idea, not so much because it made no sense but because it seemed to have no bearing on the matter in hand. He dropped the paper back on the chair and began to make his way upstairs.

"Morton," he called. "Are you there? Please answer me." He gripped the banister, breathing hard. He knew that calling would do no good – if the old man had the radio on and the door closed he would not hear him. He would have to go up there and see what had happened. The thought filled him with a deep unease. His stomach heaved, and Owen knew that if there had been more in it he would have been sick. Step by painful step he climbed the staircase, straining his ears for the least sign of movement. He could hear the radio more clearly now, a musical quiz show Morton was fond of.

I'm going to play you the opening bars of a symphony, the announcer was saying. *I want to hear the name of the composer. Fingers on your buzzers and here we go.*

There was a bright upward flourish, the sound of massed strings. Owen knew nothing about music. It always amazed him how quickly Morton came out with the answers. He had sometimes joked that the old man should apply to be on the show himself, but Morton only laughed.

There was no light on in Morton's rooms. The sound of the music in the twilight was eerie and somehow mocking. Owen felt desperate to be rid of it. Quickly he made a light, his hand shaking. The first thing he saw was that the long wooden stool Morton used to rest his supper tray on had been overturned. Spilled tea and broken crockery had made a mess of the carpet. Morton's body was by the window. The old man lay on his side, a rust-red trail of congealed blood issuing from his right nostril. His eyes were closed, one of them swollen shut, the eyelid rudely disfigured by a heavy bruise.

His body was cold. Owen had never seen anyone dead before. He had begged to see his mother, to say goodbye, but his father said no.

"You're too young for that," he said. "It's best you try and remember her the way she was."

He had remembered her as she was, clasping the memory close like a priceless possession, yet he had never stopped wishing he had been able to see her after the doctor left, to clasp her hand one more time. He had always felt this gap in his knowledge of her as an abandonment, a turning away of his face when she was most in need.

He leaned over the old man's body, stroked back the wispy hair from the stony brow. He felt no pain, no horror, just an enormous puzzlement, a lack of comprehension that, he realised only hours later, was his first numbed presentiment of grief.

He could not yet grasp that Morton was absent. He kept wanting to ask the old man what had happened. Apart from the broken tea cup and Morton's body, the room looked as it always did. The Meissen figurines on the mantel shelf had not been disturbed, and the corner bureau, where Morton kept his bank book and a supply of cash, seemed to be in order. Owen moved slowly around the room, touching things like a blind man, searching for clues. Eventually, he realised the only object missing was the clock he had made and given to Morton, the prototype of the tourbillon watch he had decided to christen the Hurricane.

It was then that he knew for certain who Morton's murderer was – Lionel Norman, or if not Norman himself then someone who had come here on Norman's behalf. He remembered the letter Norman had sent – the avuncular tone, the trite little anecdotes – and felt a dull rage. The idea came to him again that Norman had planned this, that somehow he had known when Owen would be out of London, and made his move accordingly.

And Morton – frail and slow and utterly defenceless – would have been an easy target. Owen sat down on the floor by the old man's body and took hold of his hand. The radio was still playing. The music quiz finished and the news came on. After that there was a documentary on the common toad. Owen listened, the tears flowing down his face, thinking how much Morton would have enjoyed the programme. Morton was like his Uncle Henry in that way – he loved collecting facts.

When the programme finished, Owen covered Morton with the chequered blanket from the back of the sofa, tucking it gently about his shoulders as if he were sleeping. He found he could not bear to cover his face. Then he went down to the hall and dialled the number the old man had scribbled on the telephone pad.

The phone was answered almost immediately, as if the person at the other end had been expecting his call.

".Who's there?" Owen said. "Angela, is that you?"

The line was terrible, heavy with static, but he thought he could just make out someone saying his name. He pressed the receiver against his ear, straining to hear, and then it slipped from his hand. He bent to snatch it up, almost pulling the phone off the table.

"Are you still there?" he said. "Can you hear me?"

There was a series of clicks, and then the line went dead. Owen dialled the number again but this time he got the engaged tone. He tried once more with the same result. He began to doubt he had heard anything in the first place.

He bolted the front door and went back upstairs. In his room, he pulled off his filthy shirt and washed himself in the bathtub. The act of cleansing made him feel immediately stronger. He put on fresh clothes and then began to pack.

He left the house at first light, taking Morton's money stash with him. He knew the old man would not mind, that he would want him to have it. On the way to the station he bought a copy of *The Times*. The date beneath the masthead was 22nd July, the day after his journey to Worthing and still just over a week before Morton's murder. He had eight clear days before anyone came looking for him. He hoped it would be enough to make his escape. He was entirely innocent of the old man's death, but still there were certain questions he would rather not be asked.

He took the Northern Line to St Pancras, and while he waited for his train he bought a postcard of the recently renovated terminal, the vast engine shed designed by WH Barlow in the 1860s. He addressed the card to Angela Norman, c/o 17 rue de Durel, Sommières, France.

I am on my way, he wrote. *My thoughts are with you always.*

At a little after ten o'clock, Owen found himself on the Eurostar, bound for Paris.

part two

TIME'S CHARIOT

My first time machine was a Longines. It was given to me for my eighteenth birthday by my mother's brother, Henry Pullinger. I suppose we should have called him uncle but we never did. With my sister Dora it was because she disliked ranks or titles of any kind. With me it was just that I never thought of him that way. The word *uncle* always conjured up images of sinister good humour shading to idiocy. Henry Pullinger was a kind but serious man who was always trying to make up for Dora and me not having a father. He was central to both our lives, although not for the reasons he seemed to think he ought to be. His nervous attempts at discipline, the pep talks relating to school or sex or what we ought to aim for in the future – these things made us laugh behind his back when we were children and feel embarrassed as we grew older. What we loved about Henry were precisely those things he tried to hide from us: his shyness in the company of strangers, his taste for foreign food and expensive clothes, most of all his outlaw status, his indifference to social norms.

He looked very like my mother, the same dark colouring and frowning expression. People often mistook them for twins. Dora was the spit of Henry. I was the odd one out. With my fair hair and pale skin I was given to understand from an early age that I took after my father.

Henry lived alone in a flat in West Kensington. He hated clutter and dust, and kept the place scrupulously clean. For some years during my early teens he shared the flat with a young architect called Thomas Byrne, who designed metro systems and sewer complexes, anything involving tunnels. I loathed Thom because I didn't like having to compete for Henry's attention. Dora claimed to be in love with him. There was a game we played in which Dora would concoct all kinds of lurid fantasies about Thom and I would pretend to get angry. Thom went away in the end. He got involved with some minor film director but it turned out to be his wife he was interested in, a lanky Yemeni girl with slim hips and bitten nails. Henry seemed to take it philosophically, as he seemed to take everything. He had his books and his students after all. At the time of Thom's departure he had just started work on what he jokingly called his magnum opus, a biography of Rimbaud that took him ten years to write. It was a strange book, mixing conventional biography with passages of fabricated reportage and Henry's own personal diary during those years. It left the critics divided.

Henry dedicated the book to my mother. Her name was Violet. When my father left she went back to her maiden name and became Violet Pullinger once more. I always liked the name. It suited her long pale hands and bony wrists, her frizz of dark hair. Dorothy and I were left stranded with our father's name, which was Newland. It seemed right for us, Dora and I. We were a new land after all, a country of two.

I never set much store by birthdays. I disliked the fuss and bother on account of something you had no say in. I paid my eighteenth birthday even less attention than usual because I was in the thick of A level exams. On the day itself I had a difficult history paper and wanted nothing more than to get the day over with. In the evening Dora and I had been planning to sneak up to town and see the new Brian de Palma movie but Henry had other ideas. When I arrived back at the house after finishing the exam I found my mother looking put upon and Henry looking portentous. He had dug out some crystal glasses from the box under the stairs where my mother kept the tableware and china that had been given to her as wedding presents. There was a silver toast rack, I remember, some horn napkin rings, a sherry decanter. Henry was filling the glasses with champagne.

"Happy birthday, Martin!" he said as soon as he saw me. "Did the paper go well?"

I took a glass of champagne and in the business of clinking glasses with Henry managed to avoid answering the question about the history exam. As far as Henry was concerned this was an important day for me and he wanted to celebrate it accordingly. I glanced at Dora. She was wearing a green velvet dress that was too tight for her. She shrugged and said nothing. Our plans were ruined but neither of us could bear to disappoint Henry. He was all set on going up to town but I suggested we try somewhere local instead.

"It's beautiful out," I said. "Let's walk across the park."

I didn't want us to end up at one of Henry's usual haunts because I knew my mother didn't like them. She never much enjoyed eating out because she felt uncomfortable being on show. In the smart Soho restaurants Henry favoured she would eat even less than usual.

"Do you know anywhere suitable?" asked Henry doubtfully. He was always mystified by South London, which he thought of as a repository of knife crime, grubby takeaways and discount supermarkets. I told him there was a good Chinese restaurant in Blackheath. Dora and I loved Chinese food and so did Henry. I took Dora's hand. The sky had the colour and translucency of amethyst.

Henry ordered the food. He loved to take charge in these situations and we were happy to leave him to it. Dora and Henry and I made short work of the meal, while my mother picked at a small bowl of chicken satay. When Henry ordered another bottle of champagne she perked up a little.

"I'd like to propose a toast," said Henry. He tapped the end of his knife on the rim of his glass. "To Martin, who today makes the transition from boy to man."

My mother giggled. With her fuzzy hair slightly awry and her open-necked white silk shirt she looked like a recalcitrant schoolgirl. I thanked Henry for the meal. I was relieved it would soon be over, even though I had enjoyed the food.

"I wanted to give you this," said Henry. "Just a little something to mark the occasion." He took a small oblong package wrapped in a dull gold paper from his jacket pocket and pushed it towards me across the tablecloth. I hated to think what was in it, some fancy pair of cufflinks or one of the expensive fountain pens he was so fond of. Henry was always giving me pens. He liked to think of me as a scholar in the making. He, far more than my mother, had been distraught when I failed half my mock O levels. He offered to pay for a private tutor to help get me through the exams but my mother had turned him down flat.

"There's no point in you wasting your money," she said. "Martin's just lazy, that's all."

She was right of course. I'm sure the only reason I finally managed to scrape into university was because I didn't want to see the look on Henry's face if I failed my A levels.

Dora was different. She passed everything, although much of what she was taught held little of real interest for her.

I tore off the paper, revealing a flat leather box. I liked the box at once. It had the patina of age, and a wonderful workmanlike quality that reminded me of the plain but elegant decor of Henry's flat. I opened it quickly, preparing for disappointment at the sight of cufflinks or a tiepin and wanting to put the moment behind me. When I saw the watch the first thing I felt was surprise at being wrong.

It was the simplest and loveliest of objects: steel case, black strap, white face. The hands had been set to the correct time, and the long, needle-like second hand was sweeping around the dial with a graceful gliding motion that tugged at my heart. I realised I wanted it. I smiled, in amazement at myself.

"It's a Longines," said Henry. He leaned over and pointed at the dial, where the unfamiliar name was printed in black. "Longines were one of the finest Swiss firms in their heyday.

Lindberg wore a Longines to fly the Atlantic. This one is a military model. It was made just after the war."

"I'm sure it was too expensive," said my mother. "He'll only go and lose it, you know."

That was unfair of her. We both knew I didn't lose things. I think she felt uncomfortable sometimes, being dependent on Henry for so much.

"Henry," I said. "Thank you."

I passed the box to Dora. She held it between her hands and looked down at the watch inside. With her long green dress and dark hair pulled back from her face she looked like a mediaeval astronomer consulting an astrolabe. Henry beamed, the kind of pure, untroubled smile that was rare with him. He could tell how pleased I was and no further words were necessary. We understood each other perfectly. It was a special moment between us.

Henry paid the bill. We walked with him to the station, where he insisted on calling a taxi to take us home. My mother sat in the front seat beside the driver, Dora and I sat close together in the back. It was still not quite dark. I could see my mother's face in the rear view mirror. Her hands were folded in her lap and her eyes were closed. She seemed to be asleep but I knew that she was not, that she was pretending because she didn't want the taxi man to talk to her. She had a dislike of casual conversation. My mother and I were alike in this, as I suppose we were alike in so much.

Dora stared straight ahead, her face bathed in the orange light from the oncoming traffic. She smelled of nettles, or pine needles, some new shampoo she was using. I wanted to kiss her mouth hard, so our teeth would grind together and perhaps draw blood.

When we got home we went straight upstairs. We went to my room, where the bed was still unmade from the morning. I pulled the cover up over the duvet and we lay down. I held her for some minutes in silence, relishing her closeness and warmth. She was seventeen then, just eleven months younger than me. That morning she had given me her own present, a recent biography of Brunel and a silver bookmark shaped like a rose.

Dora's presents were often bizarre but I always enjoyed them. They led me into territory I might never have explored otherwise. And while I was no scholar in the way Henry would have liked me to be, I had an appetite for books of any kind.

"You like it a lot, don't you?" said Dora. "The watch Henry gave you, I mean." Her voice was muffled against my shoulder but I had no trouble understanding her. I stroked her head, feeling the bumpy fragile contours of her skull.

"I think it's beautiful," I said. "It's such a perfect thing."

"Clocks make me nervous sometimes," she said. "They remind me of how little time we have left."

It was a strange thing for her to say. I had never known Dora to be morbid. She had a steady pragmatic mind and was too absorbed in the life she was living to worry unduly about the future. I put it down to the champagne and forgot all about it. In later years when I remembered her words I always had to push them away.

"Does it bother you then?" I said. "My having it?"

"I love you having it. It reminds me of your mind, all

ordered and silver and neat." She giggled and I rolled her on her back. She always saw me as orderly and painstaking, even though I saw myself as obdurate and chaotic. It was strange, how right she was. It was as if she instinctively recognised that in the luminous dial and the intricate mechanism behind it I had found everything I was looking for, an ideal of perfection and constructive order I had been striving towards without even realising it.

She squirmed away from me and got up from the bed. "I'm tired," she said. "Goodnight." She kissed me on the forehead and left the room. A moment later I heard her in the bathroom, the toilet flushing and then the sound of running water. Dora's baths were so hot they drained the immersion tank. It drove our mother crazy.

It had been some years since Dora and I had shared a bed. We had often spent nights together before that, crammed side by side into either my bed or hers, but the older we grew the more difficult and dangerous this became. It was Dora who put a stop to it, although I had the sense that this physical separation was a temporary thing, a measure she had introduced while she, in her pragmatic way, considered the implications of doing otherwise.

I could stand it, be resigned to it even, so long as there was nobody else.

I lay back on the bed. It had grown dark while we were talking, but I didn't turn on the light. I took the leather box from my jacket pocket and laid the watch gently on my pillow. It came to me that time itself had no material presence, that it did not truly exist until it had been taken up by the watch and passed through its mechanism like thread through the eye of a needle. In becoming the owner of the Longines my relationship to time had changed. I felt I had acquired rights over it. The idea had a strange power. With extreme care I raised the crown of the watch and moved the hands backwards by a quarter of an hour. I wished Dora were still with me in the room, as she had been fifteen minutes ago. I waited but she did not come. The watch's ticking was measured and patient, like the beating of a tiny mechanical heart. I had never considered what made a watch tick before, any more than I really understood how the human heart pumped blood around the body that contained it. On that evening it was enough simply to listen. The sound was infinitely consoling. I moved the watch closer to my ear and felt my breathing become more even, my eyes begin to close.

A college friend once told me how large parts of his childhood had been shaped by his father's phobia of clocks. It wasn't clocks so much, he said, as the sound they made. He could never wear a mechanical watch next to his skin because he could feel its vibrations. If there was a clock in the room he would almost instantly become aware of it to the exclusion of all other things, even much louder sounds such as voices or music.

"Chiming clocks were the worst," he said. "We once went on holiday to a small village in the Spanish Pyrenees. It was one of those places you read about, where the cafés stay open past midnight and the old men play boules in the street. We rented a villa near the village centre. It had slate floors and a massive step-down bath made of marble. My mother and sister thought they'd died and gone to heaven. But we were only able to stay there one night.

"There was a town clock in the square that chimed the hours, and not just the hours but the quarters and the half hours, too. I remember my father's face when he heard it, when he first realised it was there. He went rigid all over, as if he had been injected with some paralysing drug. He didn't sleep a wink all night. The next day we returned the keys of the villa to the agency and drove to the nearest big town. We found a good hotel and had a good holiday. But there was always this tension, this wondering if my dad would be all right. You hear about some people having the same thing with aeroplanes, or spiders. My father was never afraid of spiders, though. In fact he quite liked them."

When I asked him what his father had been afraid of exactly, the man just shrugged. "Time getting away from him, I think," he said. "He once told me that lying there in the dark listening to the bells chiming off the hours was like hearing the four horsemen of the apocalypse thundering towards him across the desert."

In theory I could understand it but never in fact. I found the ticking of my watch to be the most soothing, the most companionable of sounds. I finally got undressed and into bed. I slipped the watch under my pillow. I went to sleep then quickly, and slept well.

I have no memories of my father. He left us when I was less than a year old and before Dora had even been born. For many years I didn't even know what he looked like. Later I found a whole cache of photographs. They were in a shoebox in the airing cupboard, wedged in behind an old duvet and the spare blankets. The pictures showed a young man with dark blond, combed-back hair and thin cheeks. Some showed him with my mother, his arm around her shoulders, his hand on her knee. He was good-looking in his way. I knew I was supposed to resemble him but I just couldn't see it. I don't know if this was because I didn't want to see it or if my mother had been mistaken. In any case it seemed not to matter. I had been curious to see the photographs but I wanted nothing to do with my father and was never tempted to seek him out. He, after all, had wanted nothing to do with me.

His name was Peter Newland. He had been a sales rep for one of the first computer software companies. My mother never talked about him and apart from those bare essentials she made it clear she didn't want to answer any questions. I once asked Henry why Peter Newland had walked out on her.

"He claimed he never wanted children," he said. "When he found out Violet was pregnant with Dora that was it."

I thought it was a cowardly action but I didn't want to dwell on it. I knew nothing of my father, of what factors might have influenced his decisions, and had no wish to know. I did not want to be defined by someone else's actions, least of all by the actions of someone I had never known. I put the photographs back in the shoebox and stuffed them to the back of my wardrobe. I knew that I would keep them, but I didn't think I would look at them very often.

My mother went to school locally in Greenwich, but that was not where she met my father. It was Peter Newland though who put down the deposit on the house in Calvert Road, and perhaps it said something about him that when he left he relinquished all claim to the house and the equity that was in it. I think Henry helped with the mortgage payments at first. Later on, when Dora and I had started going to school, my mother worked part-time as a medical receptionist.

My first memories are of the house: the long downstairs hallway with its black and white tiles, the sour and brackish odour of the small galley kitchen, the fake William Morris wallpaper on the upstairs landing. There was a concrete yard out the back and a scrappy lawn where my mother had the rotary clothes dryer. On one side lived an old man who wore a tweed cap and bred budgerigars. On the other there was a smartly dressed young woman of a similar age to my mother, although as far as I knew the two never exchanged a word. On the wall of my bedroom was a large coloured map of the world, an early and beloved present from Henry. I learned most of it by heart and would often send myself to sleep by mentally reciting the names of all the countries in Africa or the capital cities of South America. For some reason none of this ever did me much good in my geography classes. It was a private thing, and had no connection with schoolwork.

I remember my mother's hands, long and slightly rough, the opal ring on the middle finger of her right. I remember how she talked on the telephone, sometimes for hours, after I had gone to bed at night.

I have no memories of Dorothy from before the age of four but from that moment on my memories are continuous, conscious, what you might call adult.

It is true to say I loved her at first sight, though I had no understanding of her as a sister. From the first days of my awareness of her I was thrilled by her otherness, her identity as a separate person. Until then I had lived a child's solipsistic view of the world. If I thought about other people at all it was mostly to calculate how their actions might impact upon me. With Dora I was struck almost mute by the idea that she could be herself and yet love me, that she could ally her will with mine and yet remain intact, inviolable, gloriously private.

Perhaps it was because we were so close in age. Perhaps it was because our mother was distant, lost in her world of troubles, and we fell back on one another. I believe none of these things. They explain closeness and sympathy but they do not explain Dora and me.

She was a sturdy, unsmiling child who would sometimes think for a long time before speaking. Some might have said she was prone to moods. She had my mother's coarse dark hair, Henry's bottle-green eyes. When she was very young she would come into my arms whenever I came near her, laying her face against my chest and locking her small square hands behind my back. As she grew older she became physically less demonstrative but even so we were never apart for long.

I never experienced a moment's guilt over what we felt for one another and so long as there had been no question of children we might easily have flouted the law. Our mother saw what went on and ignored it. Her experience with Peter Newland had left her with little time for social conventions and she preferred to keep herself to herself.

As a family we were peculiar. As three people sharing a house we got along surprisingly well.

I loved Dora so completely that the feeling was inseparable from being alive, but I was envious of her too. What I envied was her sense of herself, her pragmatism, her ability to concentrate her mind on something and succeed at it. She was interested in so many things and was good at all of them. She could have taken her life in any one of a dozen directions.

Compared with her I felt like a fraud, a dilettante, someone kicking around on the sidelines while the game went on.

I think Henry might have realised how I felt and he did everything he could to encourage me in my interests, but the fault wasn't in my family or teachers, it was in me. My mind was a closed room from which I looked out at the world with a sense of incredulity that was almost entirely passive. I watched, but I took no action. Nothing affected me strongly enough to make me want to grab it and not let go.

Henry had an old-fashioned slide-viewer, an oblong plastic box with a slit in the top. When you put in a slide a light came on, projecting the transparency against a white background. The photographs showed groups of people: at the seaside or on board an aeroplane, seated around a table in paper hats. They seemed frozen in time. I had no idea who any of them were but that didn't matter to me. Their world seemed magical, softly lit and private, poised somehow between our own world and the past.

I used to imagine that in a world like that anything would become possible. I would lie on my back in the middle of Henry's living room floor, one eye pressed to the viewfinder of the slide projector and wondering how I could arrange to be transported inside it. I wanted to be like those strangers, moving through the half-light at one remove.

When I told Dora this she was angry. "That's horrible," she said. "What if you got in and then couldn't get out?"

She was seven years old then. I imagined her snatching up the plastic box and staring through the viewfinder, searching the unknown faces in the old photographs, desperately looking for the one she recognised.

When Henry gave me the Longines everything changed. It was like a light going on inside me. Everything in the world seemed to gather focus, to become a function of this new passion, and finally I began to make sense of my life. I discovered in the Longines's mechanics all the perfection and idiosyncrasy of a world in miniature. In apprehending that world I also became a part of it. I had discovered what I wanted to do: I wanted to become a connoisseur of time.

Dorothy and my mother didn't get on. My mother thought Dora was cold. Dora thought my mother had let her life drown in indecision. They never fought or argued but they were uneasy in each other's company. They sometimes went several days without speaking, though this was never the result of any particular grievance.

When Dora became ill my mother had no idea how to cope with it. The practical things she left to Henry, and when it was all over she made her escape as quickly as she could. She had a friend, Leonie Sutton, someone she had known since school. Leonie Sutton had married an Australian, a medical student, and had gone to join him in Melbourne as soon as she graduated from college. She and my mother had kept in touch though. Their friendship was remarkable in that Leonie remained my mother's only real friend and the only person apart from Henry that had known her before she married my father. When Dora and I were children we always saw the arrival of Leonie's Christmas card as the signal for the start of the holiday. The cards themselves were always of the same type: small and highly-coloured on a stiff, slightly waxy white paper. Sometimes they contained a photograph of Leonie, by herself or with her husband and three children. There was always a letter, too, but those we were forbidden to look at.

I have no idea what my mother wrote in her letters to Leonie Sutton, but the fact that they existed were proof to me of something mysterious: that my mother had a private inner life that had nothing to do with me and Dora and perhaps was even kept secret from Henry.

Dora had been dead less than three months when my mother told me she was going to visit Leonie Sutton in Australia. She said she would be gone for six weeks.

"You don't mind, do you?" she said. "Leonie has always wanted me to go."

I couldn't remember the last time she had asked me how I felt about something. Since Dora's death we had lived side by side in the Greenwich house as usual but more than ever we had communicated through Henry. There was no hatred, no blame, no dislike, even – just nothing, and nowhere to go. I looked at her, this strange, scrawny woman with the fuzz of dark hair so like Dora's, and thought suddenly how pitiless her life had been. I still knew almost nothing about her.

"Of course I don't mind," I said. I gazed at her hands, the still beautiful tapering fingers, the opal ring. "Opals come from Australia, don't they?"

She smiled, and her eyes were bright. "Yes," she said. "Yes, they do."

It was Henry, of course, that helped her with the form-filling, but she showed me the visa when it came, the crested document in its plastic folder with her photograph, and VIOLET JANE PULLINGER blocked out in inky black capitals. There was something different about her, a nervous excitement. There were points of colour in her cheeks and I realised with a shock that she was happy.

Henry and I went with her to Heathrow. I kissed her on the cheek and watched her walk towards the barrier. Henry caught her by the wrist, whispered briefly into her ear then let her go. The next time he saw her, she was an Australian citizen.

She turned back once and waved to us. She had her hand luggage with her, a new flight bag in red leather with gold zips and a turtle motif. She had never owned anything like it, and I felt startled each time I saw it, thinking she had picked up someone else's luggage by mistake.

She looked dauntingly young, as if the whole of the last twenty years had been wiped out. My heart turned over. Dora's absence struck me like a physical blow.

Dora had set her heart on going to Cambridge. She was going to read physics and maths. She had exchanged a couple of letters with one of the fellows of Clare College, a Dr Rosine Gerstheimer who had done work with Schelling and Auel. She seemed nervous about the interview. I told her she would walk it. The idea that they might turn her down was laughable.

I didn't really want her to go. We had never been separated for more than a couple of hours and I knew that if she went to Cambridge everything would change. I dreaded change. I equated it with destruction.

She showed me a photograph of Rosine Gerstheimer in the Clare College yearbook, a surprisingly young-looking, tall woman with her hair gathered softly at the nape of her neck.

"She worked in engineering for ten years before she went into teaching," said Dora. "I really want to meet her. She won a prize for her book on Sophie Germain."

The name rang a bell, but I couldn't place it. I leafed through the rest of the yearbook, looking at photographs of the chapel and the Backs and the frontage of Heffers Bookshop and the Fitzwilliam Museum. I knew the museum had a small but interesting collection of clocks and watches, including a key-wound London pocket watch that had supposedly belonged to Beethoven.

I went to Liverpool Street and picked up a railway

timetable. I kept telling myself that Cambridge was less than two hours away by train.

The weather over Christmas was mild but January was icy and three girls in Dora's class went down with glandular fever. Dora looked tired and pale. Sometimes when I went to her room after supper I would find her already in bed.

With her eyes closed she looked barely alive. My mother wrote a note to her form tutor, saying that Dorothy was unwell and would not be attending classes for the rest of the week. It was so unlike my mother to interfere in anything Dora or I did that when I saw the letter in its long white envelope I felt a stab of anxiety. The fact that Dora made no objection worried me even more.

"How do you feel?" I said. It was a question I had rarely had to ask.

"Like stone," she said. "Like I'm wading through treacle."

I sat on the bed and read aloud to her from the crime thriller we had both been reading, Arkady Solovey's *Muczinski Boulevard*. It was set in a future Warsaw, a convoluted epic about a stolen necklace and the series of murders that resulted from the theft. It was over a thousand pages long and we had been racing each other to the finish, but now I had to ration it out at one or two chapters each night. Sometimes she would fall asleep without me noticing, and I would have to do a recap the next day.

She returned to school the following week and seemed a little better for a while. In the evenings she worked on her maths problems, copying down equations from a thin red pamphlet Dr Gerstheimer had sent her from Cambridge.

She seemed closed in on herself, almost frightened. She liked to have me sit beside her but often hours would go by without either one of us speaking. Before this had seemed natural, a kind of telepathy, but now it was as if each of us were hiding something.

At the end of a month Henry and my mother took her to the doctor. I stayed at home in my room, feeling terror for the first time in my life. There was a sour taste in my mouth. The air felt sharp at the edges, too painful to breathe. I didn't know why I hadn't gone with them. I didn't know what to do.

It was a rare form of leukaemia. They tried giving her a blood transfusion but it didn't work. The doctors said afterwards that there was no point in trying again, because the new cells were being killed off almost from the moment they entered her bloodstream.

"Virulent," they called it. I couldn't get the word out of my head. When I offered my own blood the surgeon shook his head, a quick, embarrassed gesture, a dismissal of a suggestion that had already been considered and found to be useless.

"You have a different blood group from Dorothy," he said. "Didn't you know that?"

I hadn't known. I had never thought about it. He might as well have told me my blood was soiled.

There was a noise in my head, white noise, as if somebody had clipped me hard around the ear. I walked home, cutting through the self-generating miasma of wharf-side developments, industrial estates and sports centres that rimes the south bank of the Thames. Amidst the welter of glass and concrete the inns and terraces of Bermondsey and Rotherhithe hung on regardless, like a time stream in a different universe. An old man walked his dog, a grey and grizzled Jack Russell terrier. Three children, two boys and a girl, chased a leather football across the street. The girl had long red plaits and a t-shirt that said *cannon fodder* in white letters on a black background. I had always felt at home in this corner of London. There was an unbending spirit in the place, a filthy-cheeked defiance that I found both subversive and consoling. But that morning it seemed as if the city itself had abandoned me, had turned its back in embarrassment at such naked emotion. The walk back took me more than three hours. By the time I got home there were huge blisters on both my heels and another on the sole of my foot, a tapering isthmus of red-tinged transparency that visibly distorted the curve of my right instep. I went to the bathroom and burst the blisters with the edge of my fingernail, rinsing off the pus under the tap. The outermost layer of skin came away, leaving ragged patches of red too tender to touch. I felt giddy with vertigo. It came to me that I had been out of the house for hours; hours in a sequence of days and weeks that now by some hideous accident appeared to be finite.

I went to her in her room. I slammed the door hard. The reverberations ran down through the walls and into the floor, spreading beneath my feet like ripples on water. She was wearing a loose grey shirt dress with a cardigan over. Her hair had been brushed down smooth. I clung to her, digging my fingers into the flesh of her shoulders. I felt that so long as I held her fast she could not leave.

This is how you stop it from happening, I thought. *You have to stay awake, stay on guard.* I pulled her down onto the bed and tugged the cover over our heads. I touched her face in the dark. The rim of her cheek was damp with perspiration or tears.

I kissed her breasts and belly, stroked the curves of her buttocks and thighs. I had never touched her like this before but I had imagined it so many times that her body felt familiar under my hands.

"It's all right," said Dora. "I want us to do it. I want you to try and make it last for hours."

I pressed my palm against her pelvis and slid my hand between her legs. Then I kissed her, biting her lips, grinding my mouth against hers and tasting blood. She was breathing heavily through her mouth, as if she had a cold. Her odour was stronger than usual, acrid as seaweed. I began to tug at her clothing, hitching up her dress around her waist. I pulled down her knickers and slipped two fingers inside her. She was slippery with mucous. When I finally entered her it was over in seconds. I shouted and pulled at her hair.

"Don't worry," she said. "It's all right." She tightened her arms around my waist and pulled me up hard against her where we were joined. Her body gave a brief, tight hitch, as if she were stifling a sneeze. Then she lay still. I had a sudden, painful sense that I had injured her in some way. Then I remembered she was dying.

I got up and went to the bathroom. I splashed water on my face and wet back my hair. The face in the glass seemed not to belong to me. I put out my fingers to touch it, half expecting it to ripple and dissolve.

In the final two months of her life she became fragile,

brittle-boned, with a translucent pallor that made her beautiful in a way she had not been when she was well. She was always tired, even from the moment she woke up. She seemed not to know the difference between night and day. Sometimes she was asleep and sometimes she was awake and that was all. It was high summer by then. The morning light was painful, bright as a spear.

"I feel so angry," she said. "I feel like setting fire to things."

I remembered her on the beach in Brighton, a sturdy girl in a blue sailor dress with sun-reddened dimpled knees. Henry had friends in Brighton, a female couple, both teachers, who lived in one of the post-war prefabricated bungalows not far from the seafront. Their names were Judith and Myra. We had jokingly called them the Aunts. Judith had given Dora a red plastic bucket and spade to make sandcastles with. I remembered how Dora had applied herself to the task, diligent and careful as a stonemason. When the tide came in and drowned the castles she had looked away.

"Do you remember the Aunts?" I said.

"Judith and Myra," she said. "Myra had golden eyes, like a cat. I remember the Circus Man."

The Circus Man had been Dora's name for the middle-aged beach bum who went up and down the promenade dressed always in the same shabby pinstripe suit and straw boater. He walked with a stiff, shuffling gait, leaning heavily upon a cane. The cane was black, with a silver handle in the shape of a horse's head. The Circus Man would sometimes flap the cane about and swear at the tourists, but apart from these occasional outbursts he seemed harmless enough.

The sight of him had always unnerved me a little but to Dora he was an object of endless fascination.

"I don't believe he's real," she said. Once she went right up to him, gazing in wonder as if he were an exhibit in a museum. Then she put out her hand and touched his knee. At first he seemed not to notice, then he leaned down very slowly and stared into her face, as if he were marking her out. For some hours afterwards I felt cold inside, somehow tainted. My sense of him had faded with the years, but I remembered him now.

In the end Dora stopped eating completely. I told her I had sent a letter to Rosine Gerstheimer, explaining that she had been unwell.

"I told her you would write to her again once you were feeling stronger," I said. I tried to get her to drink, but she would only let the water moisten her lips.

"I don't want us to tell each other lies," she said. "We're stronger than that."

"It's not a lie," I said. "We can beat this." I put my face close to hers. A fine down had begun to grow on her upper lip. The hairs were silky and almost colourless, shading to a silvery grey at the very tip.

"Don't leave me," she said. "I know I won't be frightened if you're here."

Her final days were spent in hospital. She was semi-conscious most of the time, her lovely mind made dull and heavy with morphine. I don't know how much she was aware of. The drugs made her unable to speak. When she died I was in the hospital cafeteria getting myself a coffee. My mother was on the phone. Only Henry was actually with her. He tried to speak to me afterwards but I refused to look at him.

We came back to Calvert Road. I still felt no real pain. She was still too close, too present. I dreaded what I knew was to come. I held on to the dusk, exhausted but afraid to sleep because I knew that when I woke the separation from her would have become permanent.

The sheets still smelled of her. I lay down on the bed, watching as the sky turned from Prussian blue to the faded, sequined black that passes for night in the city. The extruded beams of car headlights criss-crossed the ceiling. I heard a door slam further along the street. I took off my watch and held it by its strap in front of my eyes. Its slender luminous hands stood at eleven o'clock. It was such a graceful thing, so lovely. I held it next to my ear, trying to soothe my heart with its familiar tick.

I lay there for what seemed like a long time, but the hands of my watch scarcely moved. My thoughts ran unchecked through channels and intersections that remained obscure to me. Sleep seemed impossible. I wondered if my watch had developed a fault, some kind of irregularity, a heart murmur. *Tachycardia*, that was called. From the Greek, meaning swift, or fast.

I remembered a physics class I had been in where the class brain Lindsay Ballantine had asked Mr Gibbon about tachyon particles. Lindsay Ballantine was so good at science that a lot of the teachers were scared of him. Gibbon had gibbered something about tachyons being particles that travelled faster than light but even I could see that he didn't really know what he was talking about.

"Is it true that tachyons are time particles?" asked

Lindsay Ballantine. "That they're too unstable to exist in the known universe?"

"We haven't got time for this," said Mr Gibbon. "It isn't part of the syllabus."

I wondered what such particles might look like, whether they drifted about in a shapeless mass like a temporal fog, or whether they were fiery and glistening, streaking across the sky fast enough to smash a hole in the side of one universe and right through the wall of another.

I remembered a painting I had seen in the National Gallery, 'The Fall of Phaeton', by Johann Liss. It was a large painting and rich in colour. It told the simple story of a boy who borrowed his father's car and wound up dead.

What would happen if the sun fell out of the sky? I thought. *What would happen if I forgot how to sleep?*

Time was a treacherous thing. It moved on when you least expected it. But it came to me that in the strange hinterland between one day and another it was possible to bend the rules. I raised the crown of my watch and turned the hands backward eight hours. It was late in the afternoon and Dora had still been alive. Tomorrow she would be a memory. I closed my eyes and listened. At the far end of the street I heard the crash and rattle of a metal dustbin lid falling onto concrete. There was a burst of stifled laughter, the rapid sound of running feet.

"*That's it now. We're in deep excrement.*"

"*You dorkus.*" There was more laughter. The voices were hushed to stage whispers but I could hear them quite clearly, as if the exchange had taken place in the hallway outside my room. The footsteps disappeared along the street. For some moments afterwards there was silence, and then I heard the sound of someone calling my name.

I understood at once that it was her. She spoke in an undertone, as if she were afraid of waking the neighbours. I went to the window and looked out. I could see her quite plainly. She was wearing her old parka. It was zipped right up to the neck, and I thought how she didn't really need it, that it was warm outside. Then I remembered how ill she had been and decided it must be that.

"I've lost my key," she said. "Can you come down and let me in?" Her face was upturned towards the window. The light from the streetlamp opposite smoothed her features, making her look like a ghost girl, an alien spirit with Dora's familiar face.

She folded her arms across her chest and jigged around a little on the spot. "Hurry up," she said. "I'm getting cold."

Dorothy means gift of God. In that moment of seeing her again I loved her more fiercely and tenderly than in all the years leading up to it. I understood completely what love meant.

I ran downstairs and opened the door. The night air brushed against my face, warm and soft and redolent with the perfumes of dried nettles and frying onions. There was a car at the kerb, a blue Citroen. The street was empty.

I went back upstairs and closed the curtains. Then I undressed and got into bed. I put the Longines under my pillow and closed my eyes. In the silence of the morning I could hear the watch ticking. Its sweet voice soothed and caressed me, taking me down.

MY BROTHER'S KEEPER

My brother died before I was born, but that didn't stop him looking out for me. He was my earliest companion, my closest friend. His name was Stephen. My mother missed him terribly but he never appeared to her.

"What good would it do?" he said. "It isn't going to bring me back."

Stephen's best friend was Rye Levin, who was the same age as Stephen and five years older than me. If Stephen had still been alive they would have been in the same class at school. Rye's full Christian name was Rainer, with the 'ai' pronounced like 'eye.' People couldn't cope with that though, they insisted on calling him Rayner, so in the end he stuck to Levin or simply Rye. I admired Rye for his independence but I was afraid to approach him in case he gave me the brush-off. Rye didn't care to make friends. The only person he would tolerate was Stephen.

"Rye's OK," Stephen said. "He takes after his granddad, that's all." I knew nothing of Levin's grandfather and for some reason Stephen refused to tell me about him. Levin's father had been born and raised in London. He was an antiques dealer in Spitalfields. I had only seen him the once, when he had been called into school in the aftermath of the gun incident. Rye Levin had smuggled a gun into school in his duffel bag. The gun wasn't loaded, and looked about as threatening as a cap gun. It was one of his father's antiques, with an engraved barrel and a mother-of-pearl handle, what was known in collectors' circles as a Ladies' Weapon. The headmaster made Rye stand up in school assembly. He hated what he saw as Rye's insolence and wanted to make an example of him. He asked Levin what he thought he'd been playing at and Levin said the gun had been a present from his father.

"You'll come to a bad end if you're not careful," said the headmaster. "Young men like you always do." He made a violent dismissive gesture and I could see his hands were shaking. Levin was kept in detention for a week. For two hours each day after school he sat alone in the gym filling an exercise book with obscene drawings and chemical equations. I never found out what became of the gun.

Rye Levin was tall and lanky with dirty brown-blond hair that was always flopping forward into his eyes. Stephen was dark, like me. Levin dropped out of school halfway through the sixth form but I still saw him in the street sometimes. He was always alone. Occasionally he would speak to me. I once ran into him in the local newsagent's. He was buying cigarettes, Silk Cuts. His clothes were crumpled and smelled stale. The stubble showed on his chin, as if he hadn't shaved for several days.

"I've not seen your brother around much lately," he said. "Tell him I said hello."

I nodded and mumbled assent. I was thirteen then. I did

still see Stephen, but usually it was at a distance, ahead of me in the cinema queue or coming down the opposite escalator at London Bridge Station. Perhaps he thought I no longer needed him, that I was old enough to look after myself. On the rare occasions we were together I tried to ask him about it but he would never answer. Every time I saw him I was afraid it might be the last.

My first time machine was a Smith, one of the post-war models with a stainless steel Dennison case and a silvered dial. It was given to me for my thirteenth birthday by my aunts, Judith Greening and Myra Dillon. They weren't my real aunts, just friends of my Uncle Henry, but I had known them all my life and they were like family. Uncle Henry was my mother's brother, and lived north of the river in West Kensington. The Aunts lived in Brighton, close to the sea. We often went to Brighton to visit them, but I quickly came to realise that my mother didn't enjoy these trips as much as I did. At first I thought she was uncomfortable with the fact that they were lesbians, but later on I came to believe it was because they had known my father. My mother never talked about my father. She was reluctant to tell me even his name.

Judith and Myra's bungalow was one of the asbestos prefabs that had been put up after the war in an effort to cure the housing shortage. Most of them were later demolished and replaced with traditional brick-built houses. There were even grants to help with the cost of doing this but the Aunts refused to apply for one. They saw their home as a part of history and they preferred to keep it exactly the way it was. The outside was painted yellow and trimmed with narrow black beams in a casual approximation of mock Tudor. The bungalow had been built to a strange design, with the kitchen and bedrooms and dining room arranged around the living room like the cells in a honeycomb. The living room itself had no exterior windows. My mother used to say it was the ugliest place she had ever seen but I adored it. I found its very ugliness enticing. I loved also the small glazed veranda that the Aunts called the loggia. In winter when the rains came it felt like the observation turret of a submarine. In summer it smelled of creosote and peeling paint.

Judith and Myra were both history teachers. Myra was tall and thin with spindly wire-framed glasses. She wore her hair in a long grey plait that fell straight as a bell rope between her jutting shoulder blades. My mother used to call her the Spider. Judith's hair was curly and still dark. Her eyes were different colours, one a translucent green, the other a light hazel. In certain lights the hazel eye looked almost golden, like a cat's eye. When we arrived for my birthday visit it was Judith who opened the door.

"Happy birthday, Martin!" She flung her arms around me, hugging me fiercely against her flat chest. I could smell her usual aroma, a dense, dry scent like almonds or marzipan. Of the two Aunts it was Myra who usually talked the most but Judith was the more affectionate. When I was younger she often took me for walks on the beach and I had always enjoyed these times alone with her. She was older than my mother, but had a playful innocence that kept her seeming young. She loved animals. Once when we were down on the sand we came across a fish that had been left stranded when the tide went out. It was trapped in a shallow pool between two low hillocks of sand. It was a flatfish, a bottom feeder, a ray of some kind. Its speckled colouring made it all but invisible.

"Oh no, the poor thing!" cried Judith. "Wait here."

She ran off up the beach, leaving me standing beside the pool. I watched her tiny figure receding, the thin cotton skirt flapping against her shins. She was gone for almost half an hour and I had started to worry about what was going to happen to the fish. It was a hot day. The water in the pool had begun to go down.

Finally Judith returned, haring towards me across the sand, carrying the red plastic bucket and spade that I had used for building sandcastles when I was small. She went down on her knees in the sand, filled the bucket with water from the pool and used the back of the spade to chase the fish inside.

"Got him," she said. "Just in time." We went to the edge of the sea, to where the rock pools were deep and secure and shaded from the sun. Judith lowered the bucket into the water and sighed as the fish swam free.

"They're so beautiful, aren't they?" she said. She kissed the top of my head and shortly after that we went back to the house.

My birthday seemed to have got her very excited. "I can't believe you're a teenager already," she whispered. "How does it feel?"

Myra kissed my mother on the cheek. "Violet, how lovely to see you," she said. "Is Martin allowed to try a glass of champagne?"

"I don't see why not, but I doubt he'll drink it," said my mother. "He never likes trying new things."

That was not true, and both of us knew it. I knew also it was not me she was trying to get at, but Myra. I sensed again my mother's resistance, not hostility exactly but a cool dislike. The Aunts were Henry's friends after all, not hers. Thomas Byrne, the man Henry had lived with for more than a decade, had been at school with Myra's brother Edwin. Henry and Myra had known one another for years.

The table was already laid, the white lace tablecloth, the glasses like crystal trumpets on twisted stems. There was something beside my plate, a small oblong package wrapped in a dull gold paper.

The champagne tasted bitter and yellow. It filled the back of my throat with a strange dry heat.

Bloody hell, said Stephen. *It's the real McCoy. No cheapskate Tesco's Cava for the Spider*. It was the first time I had seen him for several weeks.

"Should we eat first, do you think?" said Myra. "Or would Martin like to open his present?"

"Oh, the present first, of course," said Judith. "It isn't fair to make him wait."

It was unusual for her to express a preference ahead of Myra. My mother looked up at her sharply. Their eyes met briefly then each of them looked away. I had been feeling curious about the gold package but now I was nervous. It seemed there was a lot riding on it.

Get a move on then, said Stephen. *Best get it over with.*

I knew Stephen hated birthdays. He thought they were a lot of fuss about nothing. For my last birthday the Aunts had given me a pair of cloisonné cufflinks. He had teased me about them for weeks.

I tore off the paper, revealing a hinged box covered in brown leather. I liked the box at once. It had a workmanlike feel about it, and a smell of wax polish, and for some reason made me think of the gun Rye Levin had brought into school, the swatch of yellow silk he had used to wrap it in. I opened the box quickly, steeling myself for disappointment at what might be inside. When I saw the watch I was left speechless. It came as such a total surprise.

"Henry helped us choose it," said Judith. "He has such immaculate taste."

Henry had given me a gift already that morning, *Cusk's Illustrated Guide to Clocks and Watches*, an expensive-looking brick-shaped book full of colour plates. I had thought it was another of Henry's attempts to educate me. Now that I had the watch it all made sense.

"It's beautiful," I murmured. I could not take my eyes off it.

"It's a Smith watch," said Henry. "Smith made all the watches for the army and the air force during the war. They were a good firm, one of the last of the great English watchmakers."

The Smith's design was elegant but simple, like a child's drawing. I loved it on sight. You might say I lost my heart to it. I recognised its beauty instinctively, but that wasn't the point. I loved the fact not just that it was, but that it did something, that it was mechanics in miniature, a perfectly constructed machine. When I held the watch to my ear I heard its robust, reassuring tick as the dynamic throbbing of a mighty engine.

I thrilled at the idea of it, so secret and so alive in the palm of my hand. In that instant of recognition I was lost.

Slowly I came back to the present. To the lunch table with its lace tablecloth and champagne glasses and Viennese dinner rolls. Henry and the Aunts were smiling broad smiles. My mother was staring down at her empty plate. Her expression was grim and closed, reminding me of a spy drama I had seen on television in which a captured female agent was interrogated many times but never confessed.

"Thanks," I said. "I love it."

"Aren't you going to wear it?" said Judith. "Aren't we going to see you try it on?"

The idea made me nervous. I would have preferred to keep the watch in its box, but I didn't want to spoil the moment by making a fuss. I unhooked the Smith from its elastic fastening and strapped it on. The leather wristband was soft and pliable, and I could tell from the way the strap holes were stretched that the watch had already been worn a great many times. I felt a strange sense of kinship with the previous owner. I wondered who he was, what had happened to him. I knew he must be dead. It did not seem possible to me that he would have given the Smith away or sold it of his own accord. I made him a silent promise: that I would cherish and look after the watch just as he had.

I had owned other watches before of course, a black Casio with a digital display that Henry had given me, a cheap plastic Swatch with a cartoon cat on the dial that I had won in a Christmas cracker. Neither watch had meant anything to me; they were just a convenient means of telling the time.

The Smith made me feel different, powerful. It made me feel as if I *owned* time, as if my relationship to time had somehow been changed.

"Look how well it suits you," said Judith. "I want to get a photograph."

She darted off to the bedroom to fetch the camera, an ancient Kodak in a box case that the Aunts had had ever since I'd known them. A moment later I was made to smile and hold out my wrist. Stephen made a face and stuck out his tongue at the camera. That was all right for him, he wouldn't show up in the picture. The flashgun went several times.

"Let's get one of you all together," said Henry. "I'll take it."

Judith put her arm around my shoulders and squeezed me tightly against her.

"Say cheese," she said. I saw my mother try to smile and fail.

What's wrong with her? I thought.

She can't stand being around Judith, said Stephen. *She can't wait to get home.*

I turned in my seat to face him.

What do you mean? I said. *Why?*

"Oh, Martin," said Henry. "You moved. I'll have to take the picture again."

Stephen's father was called Peter Newland. He was a sales rep for one of the first computer software companies and much of his work involved travelling. He died soon after Stephen was born.

"He had a heart attack," Henry had told me. "He was in a hotel somewhere on the outskirts of Manchester. Apparently it ran in the family. His father and his brother both died from heart attacks. There was nothing that could have been done."

Stephen had the same condition but even worse. He was five years old when he died. The doctors said he was something of a miracle. Most children with his kind of defect died soon after birth.

My mother didn't keep any photographs of Peter Newland around the house and until I was sixteen I had no idea what he looked like. It was Myra who showed me his picture, a faded snapshot that showed him wearing shorts and sitting astride a bicycle. Seeing it made me realise how much Stephen resembled my mother. Peter Newland had fair hair and well-muscled legs and a clean-shaven boyish face. He was handsome but in an ordinary way. He could have been anyone.

"Peter was a nice boy," said Myra. "But Violet could never forgive him for dying. She saw it as a betrayal."

Myra took the photograph out of my hand and put it away in a drawer. She was a senior lecturer by then, and held an important position in the History Department of Sussex University. My own father had been a friend of hers, another history lecturer who was visiting from Düsseldorf. So far as I knew he had no idea I existed.

My mother had been beautiful once. There was a photograph in Henry's flat that showed her in her last year of school, the same year she met Peter Newland. Her hair was fuzzy and dark, and stood out in a soft corona around her head. Her bare shoulders were narrow and pale, like the wings of a dove. Henry told me she had been keen on studying medicine at one point but had never followed it up.

"Everything happened so quickly," he said. "She and Peter met and married in less than three months."

He told me that she had been very depressed after Stephen's death and that had made her stop caring about her appearance. She wore shapeless, frowsy clothes that made her look pallid and spinsterish, years older than she was. Her one remaining vanity was her shoes. On the day of my thirteenth birthday she was wearing a pair of sleek brown sandals with four-inch stiletto heels. The narrow straps crisscrossed her ankles like the bridle on a Lipizzaner horse.

"Have some more bread, Violet," said Myra. "It's awfully good." She held out the basket of rolls. My mother took one and immediately laid it aside on the edge of her plate.

"He's wonderful, our baker," said Judith. "Everything's organic, and made by hand." She selected a roll and appeared to study it, turning it in her hands as if it were some small but highly significant work of art. "His son Lindsay obviously takes after him. He loves making things. He does these amazing model aircraft, all to scale."

"He's about Martin's age actually," said Myra. "Perhaps we should introduce them one of these days."

"He goes to school just round the corner," said Judith. "It's a wonderful place, one of the new technology colleges. The headmaster there is marvellous. He gets the most outstanding results. His Ofsted report this year was one of the best in the country."

"It would do Martin the world of good to go to a place like that," said Myra. "The emphasis is very much on individual attention for every child."

"Martin's fine where he is, thank you," said my mother. "And he has plenty of friends of his own."

She darted me a frightened glance and then looked down again at her plate. I had the oddest feeling, as if I had stumbled on the edge of something, a piece of rusted metal half-buried in sand.

I knew it, said Stephen. *Time to boogie.*

What's going on? I said. *What are they talking about?*

"You shouldn't dismiss it out of hand, you know, Violet," said Henry. "That school he's at is hardly a centre of excellence."

"I don't believe this," said my mother. "You're on their side."

"I'm not on anyone's side. I just think you could do with a break."

"A break?" said my mother. "From my own son?"

There was a sudden crushing silence around the table. I stared at my mother's hands, her slim, still graceful fingers laced rigidly together in her lap. There was an opal ring on the middle finger of her right hand, a beautiful thing, a large oval stone in a gold claw setting that she had worn for as long as I could remember. When I was a small child she had occasionally let me play with it. I loved the way its colours seemed to run together beneath the surface, making the whole stone pulse with a rainbow light.

"The best opals come from Australia," she told me. "The Aborigines believe they hold magical powers."

She had a friend in Australia called Leonie Sutton, someone she had known since her schooldays. Leonie Sutton had married an Australian medical student and gone to live with him in Melbourne. She was always asking my mother to visit but she never had. She said she couldn't afford it, even though Henry would have been glad to pay her airfare. She collected books on Australia and knew a lot about its history. Whenever she heard the place mentioned a fierce opalescent light came into her eyes.

"You should go and have a look at the beach, Martin," said Henry. "It's a shame to be cooped up inside on a day like this."

Sounds ideal, said Stephen. *Let's get out of here.*

I knew it was pointless to stay. Whatever was going on I could tell from their stony faces that they had no intention of talking about it while I was there. I set off towards the promenade, smelling the familiar odours of seaweed and brine. Stephen ambled beside me, kicking a stone.

"Where shall we go?" he said.

For the moment I made no reply. I knew that Stephen was keeping something back from me and I resented him for it, for coming the older brother. But gradually my anger subsided. Stephen was dead, after all. He was bound to have the inside track.

"Let's go along by the beach huts," I said. "I want to have a look at the pier."

We set off across the shingle. The tide was a long way out. Close to the edge of the sea two men were digging for lugworms, and a boy in shorts and a T-shirt was throwing a yellow Frisbee. He had a dog with him, a Dalmatian. Each time the boy threw the Frisbee the dog would sprint after it, its ears flapping. The boy looked about my own age, and made me think of the boy the Aunts had been talking about, the baker's son who made model aircraft and went to the local technology college. I had no real friends apart from Stephen. I shivered in the stiffening breeze.

"Look over there," said Stephen suddenly. "Look who it is." He picked up a piece of shingle and threw it towards the sea. I thought at first that he was talking about the boy and his dog, that he had noticed me watching the game of Frisbee. I felt a surge of guilt, wondering if my unconscious desire for a companion meant I had betrayed my own brother.

"That's a Dalmatian he's got there," I said. "Did you know their spots are perfectly round?"

"Not the dog, silly," said Stephen. "Further along."

He pointed to a spot to the left of the boy, further towards the West Pier, and suddenly I saw the Circus Man. It was impossible not to recognise him, even at a distance. The straw boater and striped blazer made him unmistakable. He was performing some kind of dance, a repeated pattern of steps that brought him up the beach and then down again, an identical distance each time.

"Let's go back," I said. "He gives me the creeps."

"Just keep walking," said Stephen. "He's not going to do anything."

"He's a weirdo."

Stephen shrugged. "He's harmless. I bet he'd run a mile if you tried to speak to him."

"Speak to him?" I said. "You must be joking."

The first time I saw the Circus Man he had been running in and out of the sea. He was doing the same mad dance, and gesticulating at the waves with the black cane he always carried. The cane had a silver head in the shape of a dog's paw. His trousers were soaked to the knee. I was five years old. Judith had been taking me for a walk along the promenade. It was a grey and windy day, not the weather for sea-bathing.

"Oh look," said Judith, pointing. "There goes the sandman." She seemed unafraid, as if the sight of this monster was something she was used to. I was dismayed by her lack of concern. I found it all too easy to imagine the strange darting figure breaking off from its games and dashing up the beach towards us. I don't know what I thought he was going to do to me but all the same I was terrified of him. I didn't see him every time I came to Brighton but the thought that I might spoiled my anticipation of the visits even more than the tension between my mother and the Aunts. In all the years I had been seeing him he did not appear to have changed. He always wore the same clothes, or versions of them, always walked with the same dancing gait. He behaved as if he was putting on a performance, and it was this that had first led me to call him the Circus Man. His face and hands were very pale, as if he were wearing some kind of stage makeup. Whenever I saw him it seemed like a bad omen.

I said nothing of this to Stephen. He thought my fear of the Circus Man was childish and irrational. I suspected that he had drawn my attention to the Circus Man for precisely this reason, as a way of curing me of a groundless superstition, of exerting his authority. We walked side by side, saying nothing, our faces turned into the wind. I was determined not to show my weakness and in the end it was Stephen who broke the silence.

"I'm worried about Mum," he said. "I don't like the way they gang up on her."

At first I thought that this was just Stephen's way of trying to change the subject without conceding defeat but when I turned to look at him I saw at once that he had forgotten all about the Circus Man, that his thoughts were now clearly elsewhere. Stephen never called my mother 'Mum.' Sometimes he called her Violet, but mostly it was just 'she' or 'her.' Again I found myself feeling uneasy, wondering what it was that he thought he knew.

"I don't know what you're on about," I said. My voice came out sounding churlish and petulant. "They're always scoring points off each other. Today is no different from the rest."

"It is, though. It's your birthday."

"So what?"

"It makes Judith jealous of Mum. Because she has you with her all the time." He began to walk more quickly, his shoulders slightly hunched beneath his jacket. He looked cold, but I knew that was impossible. Stephen never noticed the weather.

"Wait up," I said. "What's the rush?"

"Judith had a child once, you know." He shot me a glance, as if trying to appraise my reaction.

"But what about Myra?" I felt embarrassed and out of my depth. When it came to sex I was still mostly in the dark. I didn't want to discuss it, not even with Stephen, but Stephen wouldn't let the matter drop.

"Judith had boyfriends before she met Myra," he said.

"Myra knows all about it. She doesn't mind. It's all in the past."

I carried on walking in silence, not knowing what I was supposed to say. I didn't see why Stephen was telling me this, or what it had to do with my mother. I wondered what had happened to Judith's child.

"Judith's baby didn't die, if that's what you're thinking," said Stephen. "She had him adopted at birth."

"Him?"

"Yes, it was a boy. He weighed seven pounds and three ounces."

"Did this happen before she met Myra?"

"No, they'd already been together a couple of years. Judith got drunk at a party and slept with a lecturer who was visiting from Germany. It was just one of those things and they soon got over it. But she had never planned on having children and neither had Myra. And in any case there were other reasons."

"What other reasons?"

"They had a friend who had just lost a child. This woman had been very ill, she even tried to kill herself. They thought it might help her get better, you know, if she had another little boy to think about."

He gave me a long, meaningful look, and suddenly I felt faint, giddy, as if all the blood had rushed to my head.

"How old would he be now?" I said. "Judith's little boy, I mean."

"Thirteen," Stephen said. "Exactly the same age as you."

There was a roaring sound in my ears, wide as the sea.

"That's rubbish," I said. "You're making it up."

The things he appeared to be telling me – that I was

really Judith's child and not my mother's, that my mother had attempted suicide – were so fantastical they didn't seem real. The only thing that really registered was that Stephen wasn't really my brother. I felt tears starting in my eyes, a dry and prickling heat at the back of my throat.

"I'm sorry," Stephen said. He held up his hands for a moment as if in surrender and then let them fall to his sides. "I just thought you should know. I can't stand them arguing over you, talking about you when you're not there. Henry thinks they should tell you everything but Mum's terrified you'll turn against her. She's convinced you've always preferred Judith to her. She thinks it's some kind of gut instinct, the way a lamb recognises its mother even if they get separated at birth."

"Why would you care?" I said. "Seeing as we're not even related?"

I flung the words like an accusation. I wanted to strike him, to pound him with my fists. I felt his ghostliness as just one more betrayal.

"You're still my brother, Marty," Stephen said. "You always will be. I don't give a damn about all this other stuff. What does it matter whose kid you are? I just wish they'd all get lost."

He picked up a stone and lobbed it towards the sea.

"What should I do?" I said.

"Do what's best for you," he said. "Don't let anyone bully you."

I dropped to the ground, landing heavily and jarring my spine. I dug my fingers into the shingle. The stones underneath were smaller and slightly damp. I put my fingers to my mouth and tasted salt.

"Is it true about the lamb recognising its mother?" I said.

"It's what people say. It's all rubbish if you ask me."

I rested my face against my knees. I knew I could not leave my mother. I loved her with the irrational, unconditional love that comes from years of close proximity, even if that togetherness is habitual rather than voluntary. In spite of her moods and silences I knew she needed me. I didn't know how I felt about Judith. We looked so alike it was laughable really. It seemed impossible I hadn't noticed this before.

"Did you mean that?" I said to Stephen. "About always being my brother?"

He didn't answer. I looked up to find him gone.

I scrambled to my feet. "Steve," I said. "Don't do this, come back." I scanned the horizon in all directions but there was no sign of him. I felt an upsurge of fury that quickly collapsed into despair. He had walked away from me when I needed him most. Quite suddenly I knew things would always be like this, that I had no way of preventing it and no way of confronting him until or unless he chose to show himself. The only sanction I had was a negative one: to reject him, to refuse to let him into my life.

Yet how could I reject my own brother? I choked back my tears. I knew I would forgive him everything if only I could see him again.

I carried on down the beach, walking once again in the direction of the West Pier. Eventually the shingle gave out and I was walking on bare sand. I began to run, loving the feel of it, the wind tugging at my hair, my trainers hitting the ground with a muffled thump. I let my mind go, gradually losing awareness of everything but the wind and the sea and the sound of my footfalls on the sand. My breath sawed in my lungs and there was a stitch in my side but I forced myself to keep going. The West Pier loomed up ahead of me, its wasted hulk rising out of the sea like the desiccated carcass of a beached sea monster. I had stood with Judith many times at evening on the edge of the sand, watching the starlings circle above the pier in the violet air. There were so many they darkened the sky. Judith told me they came every evening, that the flocks of starlings over the West Pier had become something of a tourist attraction. The flocks were called murmurations.

"Nobody knows why they do it," she said. "Some people think they're the spirits of the dead."

I imagined Stephen flying with them, the clamour of wings in abandoned places, the desolate splendour of the ruined ballroom, the faint sweet chiming of phantom music.

On evenings like that, when the twilight was a soft mauve and a pale moon rose gracefully out of the sea, I could almost let myself believe he was better off dead.

My fall was sudden and terrifying. I was catapulted forward, one of my trainers torn free. I put out a hand to save myself but instead of sand there was something hard, something that hurt. The force of the impact made my wrist turn back on itself. I felt the delicate bundle of bones slide and compact together, trying to control the movement. The pain was sickening.

I had tripped over a piece of rusted iron, a section of scaffolding, some tag-end of broken machinery. The metal was half-buried in the sand close to what turned out to be the remains of a concrete ramp once used by local yachtsmen to launch their boats into the sea. Later on that afternoon I would discover that the rusted stanchion had torn a hole in my jeans and cut deeply into my thigh. My knee was so badly bruised it was painful to walk on for several weeks afterwards. But in the moments after the fall I noticed none of this. My first thoughts were for my watch. I was sure I had bashed it on the concrete as I went down. The idea of seeing it damaged or broken made my stomach turn, although later when I came to examine my injured leg I felt quite calm.

The watch glass was cracked across the dial. Seen from above the crack was scarcely visible but when you tilted the watch towards the light it became disastrously apparent, a transparent greenish ribbon, like a fissure in a block of ice. Logic told me that the glass could easily be replaced, that such accidents were commonplace. But this knowing made no difference to how I felt. It seemed to me that the new glass would not be the same as the old glass, that its beauty was ruined and smashed beyond repair.

And there could be no doubt that the watch itself was broken. The second hand had stopped moving. Time stood still at twenty-six minutes past three.

I had never felt so desperately ashamed. It was not just the thought of having to face Myra and Judith and Henry with what I had done. The idea was horrible to contemplate, but it did not matter. What mattered was that the Smith had trusted me and through my own carelessness I had destroyed it. I felt as if my world had come to an end.

I locked my arms around my knees and started to cry. These were not the choked-back tears I had cried earlier over Stephen, the stunted, voiceless crying that comes from repressing an emotion rather than expressing it. This was an all-out wailing, a sobbing so boundless and intense it seemed to break me apart.

I don't know how long I would have gone on crying if he had not come to me. When I felt his hand on my shoulder I thought at first that it was Stephen, that he had taken pity on me for what had happened and come back. I gave a violent start, mortified that anyone should see me in this state, even if it was my own brother. But when I looked up it was not Stephen I saw but the Circus Man.

I was surprised at how young he was. He had a delicate girlish beauty, like the angels in the Renaissance paintings Henry was so fond of. I had always imagined that his natural expression would be obscured by some awful kind of madness. What I saw instead were light blue eyes of an almost preternatural clarity. Beneath the straw boater his head was closely shaven, showing a dark stubble. His skin was white as porcelain, with the same bluish undertint.

"What is it?" he said. "What's wrong?"

He spoke with gentleness and warmth. I realised with a shock that I was no longer afraid of him.

"It's my watch," I said. "It's broken."

He put out his hand. His fingers were long and graceful, white as his face, the fingers of a concert artist or travelling musician. I handed him the watch. I found I trusted him completely. It was as if it was impossible not to trust him, as if I had been put under some kind of spell.

"Oh, what a beauty!" he said. "I love these London watches." He held it up to the light. The sun flashed in the broken glass.

"It was an accident," I said. "I fell over and banged my wrist." I thought of trying to explain further but was afraid that if I did I might start crying again. "It was a present from my aunts," I said instead. "Today is my birthday."

"Oh dear," he said. "I should think you'll be in for the high jump when you get home."

It was the kind of thing Henry used to say when I was about six. The Circus Man smiled, a sweet smile with just a hint of mockery. I managed to smile faintly in return.

"It's not that," I said. "It's the watch. I love it, and now it's ruined." The last word caught in my throat, starting a fresh rush of tears.

"Oh, I don't know," said the Circus Man. "These things aren't always as bad as they look." He glanced at the Smith again and then made it disappear. He worked the sleight as deftly as a conjuror palming a coin. He sat down beside me on the concrete ramp, brushing away the sand with the flat of his hand. His clothes smelled strongly of the sea, the same rank odour that came up off the beaches after a storm. His shoes were a spotless black, tap dancing shoes, with shiny half-moons of steel on the heel and toe.

"Tell me about the watch," he said. "Tell me what you love about it."

I was silent for a moment, listening to the sound of the

waves. The sound was louder and more insistent and I knew this meant the tide had started to turn. I wanted to tell him how powerful the watch made me feel, the rush of dark excitement that had coursed through me when I first realised it was mine. I found these feelings impossible to describe. They seemed to touch on everything: my mother's tired beauty, the joy I had felt in running, even the sound of the sea.

"Time is alive and real," I said at last. "It's something you can measure, like water or gold. The watch is so beautiful. When I hold it in my hand I feel as if I'm at the control centre of the universe." I gave an embarrassed laugh. "I know I'm not making sense."

"Yes, you are," he said. "I understand perfectly. Now tell me about your brother."

The question knocked me sideways, and once more I felt a little afraid.

"Did you see us on the beach earlier?" I said. "We were having a bit of an argument."

He didn't answer the question, but I assumed it was a safe assumption. It wasn't as if Stephen was invisible. Rye Levin had been seeing him for years.

"He told me things I didn't know," I said. "Things about my mother and my aunt."

"Did you believe him?"

"I don't know," I shook my head. "I don't care."

"I had a friend once," said the Circus Man. "He always used to say that it isn't where you come from that matters, but where you are going."

"Stephen said he would still be my brother," I said. "That's all that matters to me."

"Time is even stranger than you think," he said. "Most people think of time as a straight line, a road that leads in only one direction. But I've always found that time is more like a garden, or a labyrinth, a place where you might wander in circles and never come out." He reached into the pocket of his blazer and produced the Smith. "A beautiful watch is not just a measuring device. A special watch like this can open doors."

He took my hand in his, then placed the watch in the centre of my palm and closed my fingers securely around it.

"What's your name?" he said. When I told him he smiled and seemed pleased.

"Martin," he said. "That means 'dedicated to Mars.' Did you know that Mars is the god of war? You must be a fighter." He laughed out loud. "You've certainly been in the wars today." He pointed at my jeans. I saw that they were torn and stained with red.

"You'd better get going," he said. "You ought to get that seen to." He stood up, springing to his feet in a single bound. Before I could say anything he had set off across the sand, walking, almost dancing, in the direction of the West Pier. I started to go after him, but was brought up short by the pain in my injured leg.

"Wait," I called. He was moving rapidly out of earshot, and I cupped my hands around my mouth to amplify the sound. "I don't even know your name."

"Ferenc," he called back to me. "It means 'free man.'"

He smiled, but it was not the smile I had seen on him earlier. It was a wide and mischievous grin, almost a leer. He waved, and spun his cane in the air, and suddenly he seemed as dangerous and unpredictable as I had always imagined him to be. I took a step backwards, bumping my heel against the edge of the concrete ramp. I glanced down to check my footing, and when I looked up he was gone.

I felt a deep and unaccountable relief. I began inching my way up the beach. My injured leg made even slow walking painful, especially on the rough shingle, and by the time I reached the promenade I had started to sweat. Normally I could walk for hours and not feel tired, but now I found I had to concentrate all my efforts just to keep going. I was almost all the way back to the bungalow before I realised I was still holding the watch, still clutching it in my palm just as Ferenc had presented it to me. I also realised something else: I could feel the watch ticking, the miniscule rapid vibrations of its secret heart.

I stopped walking at once. The sudden cessation of movement sent a spasm of pain through my bruised knee but I barely registered it. I was listening with my whole body, straining every nerve outwards. I could hear waves falling and sighing on the beach, the distant grumbling of traffic on the coast road. It was impossible that I could hear the watch, so small a sound against that background of noise, but I heard it anyway, the steady, immutable beat that had become the living centre of my life.

Slowly I unfolded my fingers. The second hand was sweeping the dial. I held the watch so I could examine it better, half afraid that what I was seeing was a trick of the light. Sunlight flashed off the unbroken glass. The elegant blued-steel hands showed me four o'clock.

I knew this was impossible, that it had to be later than that. The watch had stopped at twenty past three, and I had spent a half an hour at least talking to Ferenc. Added to that there was the time it had taken to get from the beach to the bungalow. Thirty minutes of my life had disappeared.

I started to tell myself that the Smith had simply stopped for half an hour and then started working again. I could even persuade myself that there was some kind of crazy logic in what Ferenc had done, that it had been the beat of his heart that had set the watch going, as garage mechanics might use jump leads to start a flat car battery.

But none of that felt right to me. The day now seemed different, older. I had the same feeling I had after an afternoon nap: bleary-eyed and slightly confused, with the sense that something important had happened while I had been asleep, that the world had a secret it was determined to keep from me.

What I needed was evidence. I thought suddenly of the old Westclox alarm clock that the Aunts always kept in the kitchen pantry. It was made of tin and its tick was so loud that you could hear it even when the pantry door was closed. I had always thought it rather ugly but Myra seemed inordinately fond of it.

"I had that clock when I was up at Oxford," she had told me on several occasions. "It has always kept excellent time."

If the Westclox read five o'clock or later then it would prove that the Smith had simply stopped for half an hour and then started running again. In a sense how that might have happened was immaterial. But if the Smith and the Westclox agreed then that would seem to suggest something else entirely. It occurred to me that Ferenc could have moved the hands himself, that he could have reset the watch to the correct time before giving it back to me, but I had not seen him do it. Besides that I could have sworn he had not been wearing a watch of his own. He would have had to guess the time, and any attempt to reset the hands would have been an estimate at best.

I could think of nothing that would explain the mended glass.

I approached the bungalow from the road. There was another way in, a shortcut, a narrow gravelled path that ran straight from the promenade into a service lane behind the garden, but I didn't want to use it that day. I knew that everyone would be in the loggia and if I came in through the garden they would see me at once. That was the last thing I wanted. I needed a couple of minutes to myself.

The front door opened directly into the kitchen. I went straight to the pantry, to the Westclox alarm clock, sandwiched in its usual place between the toast rack and the egg timer.

It read twelve minutes past four, the same as the Smith. There was less than a second's difference between the two.

I put the Westclox back on the shelf and closed the door. I leaned upon it, letting it take my weight. It was hot in the kitchen, hot and buzzing as a beehive. All at once I felt very tired. My bruised knee began to throb.

I stood like that for a couple of minutes, trying to recover myself. The dazed feeling started to recede and I supposed it had been brought on by the heat. I took a glass from the shelf under the window and filled it with water from the tap. The water was tepid, with the sour, slightly sulphurous taste that was always a feature of the water at the Aunts'. The door to the rest of the bungalow was open, and I could hear Henry and Myra in one of their interminable political discussions, this one about the American oil tycoon who had recently announced his intention to stand for president.

"It's a blatant case of vested interests," said Myra. "If his motives weren't so transparent I might be less furious."

"Everyone has vested interests if you look closely enough," said Henry. "It's what politics is all about."

Judith appeared in the doorway, carrying a tray. The tray was loaded with empty glasses and a china dish containing the remains of a trifle.

"My God, Martin," she cried. "What on earth happened to you?"

She dumped the tray on the counter and rushed to my side. She caught me by the shoulders, almost knocking the glass of water out of my hand.

"Did someone do this to you?" she said.

"No," I said. I tried to back away from her a little. "I fell over, that's all. It was an accident."

"You'll have to get out of those things. Go and run a bath. I'll see what I can do with those jeans."

I did as she said, mostly to escape all the fuss. I lay back in the bath, listening to the slow dripping of water from the hot tap. When I put my big toe to the mouth of the tap the dripping stopped. The cut on my leg was puckered at the edges and a deep red at the centre. It looked like a small jagged mouth. Bruises were already forming, a blue-green skein of silk that gradually ate up most of my upper thigh. After I got out of the bath Judith doused my leg with TCP. The pain was fierce and stinging but I hardly cared. The thing that bothered me was Judith. I was all but naked, wrapped only in a bath towel. Her closeness, her touch, made me almost frantic with embarrassment. For some moments afterwards I wondered how I would ever be able to look at her again.

She appeared not to notice how uncomfortable I was. Finally she handed me my jeans.

"I've cleaned them off a bit," she said. "They'll have to do until you get home." She screwed the cap back on the bottle of surgical spirit and replaced it in the bathroom cabinet. As soon as she was gone I put on my clothes.

I returned to the lounge. Myra was cutting a chocolate cake into large slices. Henry was pouring sherry into glasses, the striped Murano goblets he had found and bought in a junk shop near the Lanes.

"Are you all right?" said my mother. They were the first words I'd heard her speak since I came in. She looked battered and exhausted, like a frightened bird. I wanted somehow to reassure her, but I had no idea what to say.

"I'm fine," I said. "It was just a stupid accident." I briefly touched the back of her hand. She jumped as if I had burned her then turned away.

We left just after seven o'clock. We usually walked to the station but because of my leg we took a taxi instead. Henry sat in the front and chatted to the driver. I sat next to my mother in the back. She was very quiet, and I didn't try to speak to her. It was dusk by then; the sky was full of an ambient, amethyst light.

Henry found us seats on the train and then announced that he was going to the buffet car. My mother sat in silence, her shoulder pressed tight up against the window. Eventually I asked if she was feeling unwell. Her eyes seemed to sparkle with an unnatural brightness and I realised with a shock that she was crying.

"They want you to live with them and go to that school," she said. "Is that what you want to do?" Her words came out in a rush, as if she had been holding them back against their will.

"No, Mum, it's not," I said. "I'm absolutely fine where I am."

She peered at me balefully, as if trying to catch me out in a lie. I thought as I had often thought how beautiful her eyes were, navy blue, just like Stephen's. I felt as if there were other things I should say but words failed me. It had been a tiring day.

In the end she seemed satisfied. She rummaged in her handbag and took out a book, a new paperback about doctors in Africa. She leaned back in her seat and started to read. I put my face close to the window and watched the fields roll by. I longed to be home. I wanted to go upstairs to my room and shut the door. Once there I would turn on the bedside lamp and read the introduction to the book on watches that Henry had given me. Then I would slowly begin to go through the pictures.

I felt in my pocket for the Smith. It was there, safe in its neat leather box.

You're like the mad dwarf in that awful opera, said Stephen. *Gloating over his treasure.*

Henry had once tried to make us listen to the whole of Wagner's *Ring Cycle* but he had never got further than *Das Rheingold* because Stephen had done something to his record player. I smiled to myself at the memory, but when I turned to look at Stephen he was gone.

It never occurred to me to try and dismiss what had taken place that day. I knew already that miracles could happen, that the important thing was not that they happened but the significance you attached to them. By the time we changed trains at London Bridge I had made a decision: I would become a connoisseur of time, a time-savant. I would collect information and evidence, the way any conventional biographer might build up a file on his subject. I would do my best to tell time's story. I hoped that by doing this I might eventually understand the story I was trying to tell.

Three months later I received a letter from Rye Levin. I was surprised to get it. I hadn't known he knew my address. He told me he had decided to join the army and was about to start basic training. He wished me luck with my GCSEs. Tucked into the envelope with his note was a photograph, an old Polaroid.

I found this when I was sorting my stuff, he wrote. *I thought you might like to have it. I still miss him.*

The photograph was of my brother Stephen. Rye Levin was standing beside him, making a rude gesture with one hand and miming a gun with the other. Stephen was smiling. The colours of the photograph had corrupted slightly, and his blue eyes looked green, like the sea.

They were on Brighton beach, standing beneath the entrance to the West Pier. In a booth just off to one side a man in a boater and blazer was handing out flyers. His skin was very pale, as if he were wearing stage makeup, and I saw at once that it was Ferenc. He was wearing white gloves, like a mime artist. His black cane was tucked under his arm.

THE SILVER WIND

Shooter's Hill had a rough reputation. The reforestation policy had returned the place to its original state, and the tract of woodland between Blackheath and Woolwich was now as dense and extensive as it had once been in the years and centuries before the first industrial revolution. The woods were rife with carjackers and highwaymen, and scarcely a week went by without reports of some new atrocity. The situation had become so serious that there were moves in parliament to reinstate the death penalty for highway robbery as it had already been reinstated for high treason. During the course of certain conversations I noticed that local people had taken to calling Oxleas Wood by its old name, the Hanging Wood, although no hangings had occurred there as yet. At least not officially.

There was still a regular bus service out to Shooter's Hill, although I heard rumours that the drivers rostered on to it had to be paid danger money. I made up my mind to call on

Owen Andrews in the afternoon. The evening curfew was strictly enforced in that part of London.

"How on earth do you manage, living alone out here?" I asked him. "Don't you get nervous?"

He laughed. "I've lived here for most of my life," he said. "Why should I leave?"

Owen Andrews was an achondroplasic dwarf, and as such he was subject to all the usual restrictions. He could not marry, he could not register children, and I wondered if this question was now academic, if he had been sterilised or even castrated in one of the holding camps. Everyone had heard of such cases, and to knowingly pass on defective genes had been a custodial offence ever since Clive Billings's British Nationalists came to power.

There was a photograph on the mantelpiece in Andrews's living room, a picture of Owen Andrews when he was young. The photograph showed him seated at a table playing cards with a young woman. The woman was smiling, her fingers pressed to her parted lips. Andrews's face was grave, his head bent in concentration over his cards. He had a handsome profile, and the camera had been angled in such a way as to conceal the most obvious aspects of his disability. There was something about the picture that disturbed me, that hinted at some private tragedy, and I turned away from it quickly. I asked him again about the Shooter's Hill Road and about the carjackers, but he insisted the whole thing had been exaggerated by the media.

"This place has always had a history to it, and history has a habit of repeating itself. If you don't believe me read

Samuel Pepys. People feared the Hill in his day too. You'll find Mr Pepys particularly eloquent on the subject of what they used to do to the highwaymen." He paused. "Those of them they caught up with, that is."

I first learned about Owen Andrews through one of my clients. Lewis Usher had once been a rich man, but when the Americans abandoned Europe for China he lost everything more or less overnight. His wife was Zoë Clifford, the film actress. She died giving birth to their daughter, or from complications after the birth, I'm not sure which. The child was taken away by relatives of Zoë's and Lewis Usher was left alone in an enormous rambling house at the top end of Crooms Hill, less than half a mile from the centre of Greenwich. The place would have been worth a fortune in the old days, but it was far too big for him, and after the crash he could no longer afford to maintain it. In spite of its poor condition it was the kind of property my agency specialised in and I was able to negotiate a very good price with an independent pharmaceuticals company. They were attracted by the council tax rates, which were still much lower on the south side of the Thames. The firm's representative, a Hugo Greenlove, said they were planning to turn the house into a research facility. He rattled on excitedly, making exaggerated arm gestures to demonstrate how rooms might be divided and walls torn down, and although I thought it was tactless of Greenlove to talk that way in front of the property's current owner, Lewis Usher seemed completely unmoved. Once Greenlove had left, he told me to get rid of the lot, not just the house itself but everything in it. He didn't say as much but I had the impression he was planning to use the proceeds of the sale to get him to America. I imagined he had contacts there already.

"You really want to sell everything?" I said. In spite of my sympathy for Usher I was excited by the prospect. The house was stuffed with things I could move on for a handy profit, paintings and small bronzes and so on, and my files back at the office were stuffed with the names of people who would be happy to buy them.

"There are some things of Zoë's I want, but that's about it," he said. There were framed photographs of his wife everywhere about the place, detailing the course of her career from stage to screen. She had been a tall, angular woman with a crooked mouth and a wide forehead but the pictures hinted at a deep sensuality and a striking screen presence. Usher was still very much in mourning for her, and I think it was the fact that I was also a widower that made him trust me. He said I could have first refusal on anything I wanted from the house, and when I tentatively mentioned a few of the things that caught my fancy he named a price so low I felt filthy with guilt even as I agreed to it. Usher must have seen some of this in my expression because he thumped me hard on the shoulder and began to laugh.

"You'll be doing me a favour," he said. "It's surprising how little you need, when you come right down to it."

He laughed again, the laugh quickly turning into a painful-sounding cough that made me wonder if there was something more than grief that was consuming him. This could certainly account for his indifference to his material possessions. Yet when a couple of moments later I pointed to a small brass travelling clock and asked him how much he wanted for it his whole demeanour changed. An excited light came into his eyes and he looked ten years younger.

"That's an Owen Andrews clock," he said. "Or at least it's supposed to be. I've never had it authenticated. I accepted it in lieu of a debt. I've had it for years."

He looked down at the clock approvingly, his face registering the sort of personal pride that suggested that even if he had not made the clock himself it was people like him, people with money and influence, that made such things possible, and I glimpsed for a moment the man who for twenty years had been on the directorial board of a successful multinational company.

"Who is Owen Andrews?" I said. I knew little about clocks and their makers, just as I knew little of furniture or scrimshaw or glass. I had never counted myself as an antiques expert. I was an estate agent who indulged in a little antiques trading on the side. I counted my successes as luck, and the willingness to let myself be guided by instinct rather than knowledge.

"Owen Andrews makes alchemical clocks," Usher said. "More popularly known as time machines."

It was my turn to laugh, a trifle uneasily. "You're not serious?" I said. "You don't believe in such nonsense, surely?"

I had watched several TV documentaries on the subject of the new physics but I had never taken any of it seriously. It was my wife Miranda who was interested. Miranda had been like that, fascinated by the unknown and always wanting to believe in the impossible. It was this openness to experience that had convinced her she could help her father, even when his doctors had warned her that his illness had made him unpredictable and possibly dangerous. Her faith in the possibility of miracles was one of the things I loved most about her. I wondered if Usher was trying to set me up in some way, trying to make the clock seem more valuable by spinning an elaborate yarn around it. Why he would do this when he seemed willing to more or less give away the other items I had no idea. I glanced at the clock again, its case gleaming with a bronze lustre. It was only a small thing, and quite plain, but the more I gazed at it the more I wanted to buy it. I had already made up my mind not to sell it, to keep it for myself. But if Usher named some ridiculous price then the game was over.

Usher shrugged. "I think they're all deluded," he said. "I happen to believe that time is like water pouring out of a tap, that once it's been spilled there's no calling it back again, not for love nor money nor any of these newfangled gadgets they're dreaming up now. The man who gave me that clock offered it to me because he thought it was valuable but I accepted it because I liked it. I thought it was beautifully made."

"But surely he can't have believed it was a time machine? It looks like an ordinary carriage clock to me."

Usher smiled. "What else is a clock if not a time machine?" He narrowed his eyes, locking them on mine for a moment as if challenging me to a duel, then glanced off to one side, shaking his head. "But in the way you mean, no, it's not a time machine. From what I gather it's one of his 'dry' clocks, designed to tell the time and nothing more. It's accurate of course and rather lovely but the case is brass, not gold, and in today's market that makes it practically worthless. If you like it that much you can have it for nothing. The deal you just did on the house has solved a lot of problems. Call it a little extra bonus on top of your fee."

My heart leapt. I had to concentrate hard to stop myself snatching the clock right off the shelf there and then, just so I could feel its weight in my hand.

"Is the maker still alive, this Owen Andrews?" I said instead.

"I have no idea," said Usher. "I know nothing about him other than what I've told you."

I think it was in that moment that I made my decision, that I would seek out Owen Andrews and discover the truth about him. I told myself that this was because the little brass clock had been the only thing to excite my interest since my wife died. There was more to it than that though. Somewhere deep inside me I was nursing the crazy hope that Owen Andrews was a man who could turn back time.

"I don't think you should get involved with this guy, Martin," Dora said. "I think he's under surveillance." She dragged on her cigarette, leaning to one side to knock the ash into the chipped Meissen saucer she kept permanently at her elbow for this purpose. I had long since given up going on at her about her smoking. Like Samsara perfume and the fake leopard-skin coat she wore, it was simply a part of her. She was wry and canny, with the kind of piercing, analytical intelligence that had sometimes caused me to wonder why she had left her job with the Home Office. The freelance legal work she did now earned her a steady and fairly comfortable income but it was hardly a fortune and only a fraction of what she was really worth. Once in the early days of our friendship, when for a brief while I imagined there might be the possibility of romance between us, I got drunk and asked her about it.

"I can't work for those thugs any more," she said. "I don't believe in doing deals with the devil." She laughed, a brisk 'ha,' then changed the subject. Later that same evening I found out she was married to a chap called Ray Levine, an ex-airline pilot who now grubbed around for work shuttling government ministers to and from their various conferences and crisis summits.

"Ray's a bit of an arsehole, I suppose," Dora said. "But we've known each other since we were kids. We used to smoke rollups together behind the boys' toilets. That's something you can't replace. I don't care what he does on those trips of his, just so long as he doesn't bring it home with him. I learned a long time ago that trust is a lot more important than sexual fidelity."

I first met Dora when I sold her her flat, a three-room conversion in Westcombe Park occupying part of what had once been a private nursing home. It was an attractive property, with high windows, a stained-glass fanlight, and solid oak parquet flooring, but it had serious disadvantages, most crucially the access, which was via a fire escape belonging to the neighbouring property. I knew this could pose legal problems if she ever wanted to sell, and because

I found myself liking her I broke all the usual rules of the business and told her so. The forthrightness of her reaction surprised me but as I came to know her better I realised it was typical of her.

"I can't make a decision to buy something based on whether I might want to get rid of it later," she said. "This is about a home, not a business investment. This is where I want to live."

Then she smiled and told me she was a lawyer. She knew all about flying freehold and compromised access but she was adamant she wanted the flat, as she was adamant about a lot of things. After she moved in I took the liberty of contacting her and asking if she was interested in doing some freelance contract work. Within a year she was working two full days a week for me, clarifying the deadlocks and stalemates that occasionally threatened to upset some of our more lucrative sales. She had a genius for finding a loophole, or for finding anything, really. It was for this reason that I asked her if she could help me track down Owen Andrews. I didn't go into any details and Dora being Dora she didn't ask. A couple of days later she called me at home and asked me if I could come round to her place.

"I have some material to show you," she said. "But it's not the kind of stuff I want to bring into the office."

She opened the door to me dressed in a pair of Ray's old camo pants held up with elastic braces. "Andrews is alive and well and living in Shooter's Hill," she said. "Would you like a drink?" She poured Glenlivet and wafted Samsara, the kind of luxury items that were often difficult to find on open sale but readily available if you had the right contacts. I supposed the whisky and the perfume came via Ray. Levine himself was rarely at the flat. Dora said he spent most of his nights on airbases or in the bed of whichever woman he was currently trying to impress.

"It's like being married to your own younger brother," she said. "But to be honest I think I'd kill him if he was here all the time."

I occasionally wondered what would happen if I tried to spend the night with her. The prospect was tantalising, but in the end I valued our friendship, not to mention our business relationship, too highly to risk ruining it through some misconceived blunder. Also she had liked Miranda.

She handed me my drink then pushed a small stack of papers towards me across the table.

"Here," she said. "Have a look at these."

The documents comprised a mixture of photocopies and computer printouts, with markings and annotations everywhere in Dora's spiky black script. There were copies of a civil service entrance exam and a standard ID card, together with a passport-sized photograph and a printout of an article from a magazine I had never heard of called *Purple Cloud*. The photograph showed a dark-haired, rather handsome man with a high forehead and heavy brows. It was just a head shot, and offered no clue to his stature, but his ID gave his height as 4'10", with the note that between the ages of nine and fourteen he had undergone four major operations to try and correct a curvature of his spine. His address was at Shooter's Hill, just a couple of miles east of where we were sitting, but with its reputation for violence and the strict imposition of the night-time curfew it might as well have been half a world away. In his civil service entrance test Andrews had scored ninety-eight percent.

"This is incredible," I said. "How on earth did you find this?"

"There's more," Dora said. She pulled some papers from the stack and riffled quickly through them until she found what she wanted. "He worked for the MoD on classified projects. That means they could have wiped his whole ID if they'd wanted to, or altered it in some way – anything. What's really strange is that he was dismissed from his post but left alone afterwards. That never happens. Normally they slam you in jail, at least until the work you're involved in is no longer relevant. The fact that Andrews is still out there means he must still be valuable to the MoD in some way. Either that or he's a spy. The very fact that he was working for them at all is suspicious. Owen Andrews is a dwarf – for that read non-person. It's getting harder for people like him even to be granted a work permit." She paused and stubbed out her cigarette. I caught the sweet reek of Marlboro tobacco. "The thing is, his bosses or ex-bosses or whatever are bound to be watching. If you so much as say hello to him they'll be watching you, too. You don't want to get blacklisted."

"I want to ask him about his work, that's all. What harm can it do?"

"On the face of it, none whatsoever. But I've read that article in *Purple Cloud*, all that stuff about time travel. What's this about really?"

"It's not about anything. I have a clock he made and I'm curious about it. Is that so hard to believe?"

"Well, you know what they say about curiosity killing the cat."

We sat side by side at the table, sipping our drinks. I wanted to reassure her in some way, to at least thank her for what she had done for me, but neither of these things seemed possible. I realised we were on new ground, the unstable territory that springs into being whenever the conversation between two people begins to trespass beyond its usual limits. Politics was something that didn't get discussed much, not even in private.

"Can I take all these papers with me?" I said in the end.

"Please do. I don't want them. I had to use my old Home Office passwords to gain access to some of those accounts. I'd be traceable instantly, if anyone had a mind to go looking. It's a ridiculous risk to take. God knows what I was thinking." She ran her hands through her hair, making it stand out about her head like a stiff black halo. "I have to admit it was fun, though. Beats the shit out of verifying leasehold clauses."

She smiled, and I knew we were back on safe ground. I knew also that the subject of Owen Andrews was closed between us, that whatever fleeting thrill she had gained from hacking into classified files, her involvement stopped here. Doubtless she had her reasons. I had no wish to know what these were, just as she had no real wish to know what had prompted my interest in Owen Andrews. I walked home the long way round, skirting the boundary of Greenwich Park, which was kept locked after sundown and was sometimes closed to the public for months at a time. The captive trees made me think of Shooter's Hill, an outpost of an imaginary realm shrouded in a rough twilight. I wondered what Andrews was doing at that precise moment, and the strangeness of it all made my heart turn over. One thing I had noticed and not mentioned to Dora while glancing through his papers was that several of the documents gave contradictory information about his birth date. Neither was it simply a matter of a couple of days – his birth certificate made him a whole fifteen years younger than his ID card, while his medical records showed him as ten years older. I guessed that bureaucratic errors like this must happen constantly, but still, it was peculiar.

When I got home I read the article Dora had copied from *Purple Cloud*. It was an essay about how the previous government had allegedly made use of what the writer called 'time-bridge technology' to try and alter the course of the war in the Middle East. It had the smack of conspiracy theory and sensationalism I associated with the kind of magazine that specialises in UFOs and the so-called paranormal and I found myself not believing a word of it. According to the article Owen Andrews was significant as the pioneer of something called the Silver Wind, a quantum time-stabiliser that certain military scientists had subverted to their own purposes. Apparently Andrews also had connections with the German firm of Lange und Söhne, who had made watches for everyone from Adolf Hitler to Albert Einstein, as well as being pioneers in the field of atomic engineering.

I knew I had to see him, to talk to him. After reading the flimsy bit of theorising in *Purple Cloud* my doubts about the new physics were stronger than ever, but my fascination with Andrews himself remained undiminished. A non-person who was somehow immune to political reality. The three different birthdays. His insistence on living in a place rumoured to be populated by the outlawed and the desperate. I felt as if I had tripped over a loose paving stone, only to discover that it was in fact the secret entrance to an underground city.

It sounds insane to say it, but I had never really questioned the world I grew up in. I remembered the hung parliaments, the power shortages, the forced deportations of millions of blacks and Asians to the so-called 'home-states' of Nigeria, Botswana and the near-uninhabitable wastelands of the exhausted Niger Delta. I remembered the fire on board the *Anubis*, mostly because I happened to know one of the three thousand deportees who died in the blaze. Kwella Cousens taught Business French for a time at the college where I was studying but lost her work permit during the tax revisions and so was forced to take a place on one of the transports. I remembered these things, as generations before me might have remembered the moon landings or the Kennedy assassination, as news flashes and photographic images. They happened when I was in my late teens, busy with college work and desperate to lose my virginity.

The truth was, I remembered them as things that had happened to other people. The new employment laws affected mostly black people and immigrants. If you were white and had a UK ID card you could mostly go on with your life as if nothing had changed. I had seen what happened to people who made a fuss: the small number of students from my college who joined the demonstrations and the dock pickets, the pamphleteers who for a time had littered the streets of the major cities with their samizdat scandal sheets had all spent nights in jail and some of them had had their grants suspended. One young man who chained himself to the railings of Buckingham Palace even had his national insurance number revoked. They bundled him off to Niger with all the other deportees. I remember thinking what a fool he was, to throw away his future over something that didn't concern him.

Up until now the biggest risk I had ever taken was to ask Miranda to marry me. As I went to bed that night I realised I was on the verge of taking actions that could affect my life in ways I could not know about until it was too late. I lay in bed, listening to the steady ticking of Owen Andrews's clock on my bedside table and the distant phut-phutting of the wind-powered generators across the river on the Isle of Dogs, and as I drifted off to sleep it seemed to me that the clock and the generators had combined forces to form one vast machine, a silver wheel, its shafts and spokes catching the moonlight and casting its radiance in a hundred different directions.

The bus was ancient, its wheel arches pitted with rust. The bus was also full of soldiers. Their rambunctious, raucous presence made me nervous, although I realised this was illogical, that there was nothing unusual or sinister in their behaviour, that the presence of forces personnel was entirely to be expected. Shooter's Hill was a restricted zone. Civilians could enter, and the shops and small businesses that had serviced the area prior to its closure were allowed to keep running as usual, at least partly for the benefit of the new influx of military. But after sundown any movement into and out of the village was strictly prohibited. There was a military checkpoint, and it was said that the woods behind the old hospital were alive with snipers, that the turf battles between the military and the carjack gangs that used Oxleas Forest as a hideout had taken on the dimensions of guerrilla warfare.

Officially the place was a shooting range and assault course, like Dartmoor and Romney Marsh, but everyone knew there was more to it than that. There were rumours that the run-down hospital buildings had been turned over to one of the specialist divisions as a testing laboratory for biological weapons. I had always thought the idea was far-fetched, but as the bus pulled further up Maze Hill I began to wonder. Passing into the forest felt strange, almost like crossing the border into another country. The starkly open expanse of Blackheath Common gave way abruptly to massed ranks of oak and ash and beech, the trees growing so closely together that it was as if we had entered a tunnel. The lowest branches scraped the roof of the bus, linking their gnarled green fingers above our heads. Rough tarmac and dirt tracks branched off from the road at regular intervals, and between the trees I could make out the rectangular masses of houses and old apartment blocks. I wondered who would choose to live out here. I knew that much of the housing in the vicinity of the hospital had been demolished by order of the government.

Aside from one burnt-out car at the side of the road I saw no overt signs of violence but in spite of this I found the atmosphere oppressive. The forest seemed unending, and its green stillness unnerved me; I felt as if something was lying in wait, just out of sight.

We passed through a set of traffic lights, then came to a standstill beside the two fluted granite columns that marked the entrance to the hospital. The main building was mostly hidden behind a high stone wall topped with metal spikes and coils of barbed wire. Armed sentries stood on guard beside a swing barrier. The soldiers on the bus all rose to their feet, jostling each other impatiently as they crowded towards the front. Once outside they formed a straggling line, waiting to be admitted. I saw one of them rummaging in his knapsack, presumably for his entrance pass or some other necessary document.

I pressed my face to the window, watching the soldiers go through their ID check. As the bus pulled away I caught a glimpse of narrow windows and blotchy grey walls. Now that the soldiers were gone the bus was almost empty. Towards the rear sat two men in business suits and a stout, middle-aged woman with a wicker basket on her knees. The basket contained three live chickens. On the seat across from me sat a teenage girl. Her pale face and wispy fair hair reminded me a little of Miranda. She glanced past me at the soldiers in the road.

"That's the loony bin," she said to me suddenly. "They

guard it to stop the loonies getting out. Some of them have killed people."

I stared at her in silence for a moment, unsure of what I should say. When I looked back towards the road the hospital and the soldiers were already some distance behind us. I had vague memories of the place from my childhood, when Oxleas Wood had been unrestricted and carjackings less prevalent. The hospital was derelict then, a forgotten eyesore. We used to pretend it was haunted, or believed perhaps that it really was, I was no longer sure. In either case, the gates were always secured against intruders, and the high wall that ringed the perimeter meant that the grounds were impenetrable, even to the most resourceful and daring among our company. Its gloomy edifice had always been a source of vague dread to me. It was not ghosts I feared so much as the building itself. I hated its barred windows, the frowning façade that always made me think of dungeons and prisons. I could never escape the idea that terrible things had happened there.

I was unsurprised to find that the intervening years had done little to moderate my dislike of the place.

"Do you know why the soldiers are here?" I said to the girl. I had taken her for about thirteen, but now that I looked at her closely I saw she was older, eighteen or nineteen perhaps. She did not really resemble Miranda, other than in the colour of her hair. The girl pressed her lips tightly together and shook her head vehemently from side to side. She seemed startled, even frightened that I had spoken to her, even though it was she who had begun the conversation.

It crossed my mind that she might have learning difficulties, though when she finally replied to my question there was no doubt she had understood what I was asking.

"I've been inside," she said. She glanced at me from beneath her colourless lashes, as if checking to see that I was still listening. I felt certain that she was lying. I turned away from her and back towards the window. We were coming into the village. Shooter's Hill had never been much of a place, and the encroachment of the forest made it seem even less significant. I saw a general store and a post office, a church and beside that a recreation hall or perhaps a schoolhouse. One side of the dusty main road was flanked by houses, a mixture of small flint cottages and slightly larger Victorian terraces. On the other side of the street the forest began, stretching in an unbroken swathe as far as the Carshalton Reservoir and beyond that the Sussex Weald.

The bus juddered to a halt beside the Bull Inn. As I rose to my feet the fair-haired girl scampered past me, darting along the pavement and then disappearing down an alleyway between two of the houses. The bus coughed once and then lurched forward, bearing the chicken woman and the suited businessmen on towards the dockyard at Woolwich. The silence closed itself around me, so complete it seemed material, green in colour and with the texture of house dust. I looked back the way I had come. Somewhere to the north of me lay the boulevards and tramlines and bombsites of central London. I hesitated for a moment in front of the pub then headed off down the road. On my left was the water tower, a renovated Victorian structure that I guessed would serve all the houses in the village and probably the hospital too. It soared above the rooftops, its brick-built crenellations weathered to the colour of clay. Owen Andrews's house was on Dover Road, one of a terrace of eight Victorian villas and directly in the shadow of the water tower. The houses were shielded from the road by a thin line of trees. Fifty years ago and as a main route into London the road would have been seething with traffic. The universal tax on private vehicles had changed everything and so had the closure of the woodlands. Dover Road was now a forest byway frequented mainly by logging trucks and army vehicles. Weeds spilled through the cracks in its tarmac. For the first time since setting out that morning I asked myself what I thought I could possibly achieve by coming here.

Andrews's house was approached by a short pathway, a couple of paving slabs laid end to end across a yellowed patch of pockmarked turf. I stepped quickly up to the door and pressed the bell. I heard it ring in the hallway beyond. I stood there waiting for what seemed an age. I had no doubt I was being watched. Whether my visit would have repercussions was something I would only discover later. I bent down and peered in through the letterbox. I caught a glimpse of cream walls and wooden floorboards and then the door was opened so suddenly I almost went flying.

"Can I help you?" said Owen Andrews. "Are you lost?"

"No," I said, staring down at him. "At least I don't think so. It was you that I came to see."

"You'd better come in then," said Andrews. "I don't get many visitors these days." He retreated inside, moving with a slow rolling gait that was almost a waddle. He seemed unsurprised to see me. I followed him into the house. Things were happening so fast they felt unreal.

He took me through to a room at the back. The room was steeped in books, so many of them that the ochre-coloured wallpaper that lined the room showed though only in oddly spaced random patches. Glazed double doors overlooked a narrow strip of garden. A set of library steps on castors stood close to one wall. Andrews heaved himself up on to a battered chaise longue, which from the multitude of books and papers stacked at one end I guessed was his accustomed reading place.

"Sit down," he said, waving at the seat opposite, an upright armchair upholstered in faded green velvet. "Tell me why you're here."

I lowered myself into the chair. "I'm sorry to turn up uninvited like this," I said. "But I bought a clock of yours recently and I wanted to ask you about it. I wanted to talk to you as soon as possible. I hope you don't mind."

"A clock of mine? How fascinating. Which one?"

He leaned forward in his seat, clearly interested. He was very short in stature, with foreshortened limbs and a head that seemed too big for his body, but his torso was powerful and upright and he seemed to take so little account of his disability that it is true to say that within five minutes of meeting him I had stopped thinking of him as different – he was simply Owen Andrews. His force of personality was tangible. I thought he was probably the most extraordinary man I had ever met. I described the clock to him, telling him also how I had come by it.

"I know the one," he said at once. "The case was made from melted-down bell metal."

He grabbed a sheet of paper from the pile at his feet and began to draw on it, sketching in rapid strokes with a blue biro. He gazed at his work appraisingly, tapping the blunt end of the pen against his teeth then handed me the paper. His drawing captured the likeness of my clock in every detail.

"That's it," I said. "That's amazing."

Andrews smiled. "I find them hard to let go of," he said. "It's a weakness of mine. But you didn't come all the way out here to ask me about an old clock. A simple telephone call would have dealt with that. Why don't you tell me what you came for really?"

I could feel myself beginning to blush. The man's forthrightness startled me, and now that I was about to put it into words the thing I had come to ask seemed as ridiculous as the article I had read in *Purple Cloud*. But I had come too far to turn back. And the fact was that I trusted him. I believed that Owen Andrews would tell me the truth, no matter how difficult or unpleasant that truth might be.

"My wife died," I said at last. "Her name was Miranda. She was killed in a car accident. Her father drove his car off a cliff into the sea and drowned them both."

"I'm sorry to hear that," said Andrews. "That's a terrible story." His eyes were clouded with concern, and I was surprised to see that he really was sorry, not just interested as most people were when they first discovered what had happened to Miranda. I didn't blame anyone for being interested. The story was shocking and dramatic, a breakdown in normality that had never become entirely real even to me, even after the wreck was salvaged and the bodies recovered. Who would not be interested? It is all but impossible for one man to climb inside another man's sorrow. But I could see from his face that Owen Andrews was at least trying. I guessed he was more practised than most in enduring heartache.

"I read about you," I said. "About the work you did for the army. I read about the Silver Wind."

His dark eyes flashed, his expression changing so suddenly it was almost as if my words had thrown a switch inside him.

"You're asking me to bring back your wife? That is what you're saying?"

I nodded and looked down at the ground. I felt smaller than an insect.

"Do you have any background in physics?" he said.

"Not in the least."

"Well, if you did you would know that what you are asking is impossible. For one thing, the time sciences are in their infancy. We have about as much control over the time stream as a Neanderthal over a steam train. But mainly it is just not possible. A layman such as yourself tends to think of time as a single thread, an unbroken continuum linking all past events together like the beads on a necklace. We are discovering that time isn't like that. It's an amorphous mass, a ragbag if you like, a ragbag of history. The Time Stasis might grant you access to what you think of as the past, but it wouldn't be the past that you remember. You wouldn't be the same and nor would your wife. There's a good chance you wouldn't even recognise each other, and even if you did it's unlikely that you would have any sense of a shared history together. It would be like that feeling you get when you meet someone at a party and can't remember their name. You know you know them from somewhere, but you can't for the life of you think where. It would be an alternative scenario, not a straight rewind. And Miranda would still probably end up dying in that car crash. We've found that the pivotal events in history still recur, even if the cause and effect are subtly different. It's as if the basic template, the temporal pattern if you like, is to some extent indelible."

He folded his arms across his chest, as if to indicate that this was his last word on the matter. I felt once again the power of his personality, the force of his intellect, and it was as if we were fighting a duel, his knowledge against my despair. I knew the battle was lost, but I could not deny myself one final, miserable onslaught.

"But I would see her again? She would be alive?"

"No. It might be possible to transfer to a version of reality where a version of Miranda did not die in that car accident. But that is all."

"Then that is what I want. I have money."

"No you don't," said Andrews. "And this has nothing to do with money." He fell silent, looking down at his hands, the fingers short and neat, pink as a baby's. I sensed that he was troubled, that such brutal candour was not something he enjoyed dispensing.

"I'm sorry," I said in the end. "I've been very stupid."

"Not at all," said Andrews quickly. "And at least what you

asked for is harmless, beautiful even, the kind of wish one might almost be tempted to grant if it were possible. I've had far worse propositions, believe me. Fortunately they've been equally impossible."

"You're talking about your work with the army? The Billings government?"

Andrews nodded. "I must warn you that this room might be bugged. I've given up bothering about it. They know my views and I have nothing to hide. But I wouldn't want to cause any unpleasantness for my friends." He paused, as if giving me the option to leave, but I stayed where I was and waited for him to continue. I realised two things: firstly that my pilgrimage to Shooter's Hill had always been about Andrews's story rather than mine, and secondly that I felt properly alive for the first time since Miranda had died.

There was also the fact that Owen Andrews had called me his friend. I took this as a mark of trust and a gracious compliment but strangely it also felt *true*. For a brief instant something flickered at the back of my mind, a sense that there were some facts missing, like pieces in a jigsaw puzzle. Then the curtain of logic descended and the feeling was gone. I liked Andrews, and felt a certain kinship with him. That was all.

"What's the matter?" Andrews said. His anger seemed vanished, and an amused smile tweaked the corners of his mouth. I wondered what secrets my face had given away.

"Nothing," I said. "Go on."

He shifted his position on the chaise longue, sitting upright and hugging his knees. He was wearing green velvet slippers and grey schoolboy socks. The combination was both amusing and moving, and I was reminded of images I had seen in books, paintings by Velázquez and Goya of the court dwarfs of Spain. They had been the playthings of the nobility but in some cases they had actually been the secret power behind the throne. "Do you know about the hospital?" he said.

"I've heard the rumours," I replied. "What about it?"

I was surprised to hear him speak of the place, I suppose simply because it was the source of so much ignorant tittle-tattle. I thought of the strange girl I had met on the bus, and my heart sank. If Owen Andrews went spinning off in some similar tale of murderous lunatics it would make me start to doubt everything he had told me.

I was wrong, of course. The girl had not been completely deluded either, although I did not think of her again until much later.

"It's always been a military hospital," Andrews said. "It was designed and built by Florence Nightingale's nephew as a centre for the study and treatment of shell shock. It was the first hospital in the country of its kind."

"I've heard it's being used to test chemical weapons," I said. "Is that true?"

Andrews shook his head, seeming to dismiss the idea out of hand. "You said you read about the Silver Wind," he said. "What did you read, exactly?"

I hesitated, unwilling to reveal that the only hard information I had on Andrews's research had been gleaned from a UFO magazine. "Something about time-bridges," I said in the end. "The article I read said that the army were trying to change the outcome of the Saudi war by stealing technology from the future. It all sounded rather improbable. I wasn't sure what to believe."

Andrews nodded. "Do you know what a tourbillon regulator is?"

"I have no idea."

"It was invented by a watchmaker named Louis Breguet, in the eighteenth century. He became famous for making watches for Napoleon and Marie Antoinette. His grasp of mechanics was extraordinary and at least a century ahead of his time. He discovered a way of making time stand still. Please excuse me, just for one moment. It's better if I show you."

Andrews slid from the chaise longue and shuffled out of the room. A minute later he returned, bringing with him a small wooden box.

"Here's one I made earlier," he said with a smile. He flipped open the lid, and I saw there was a watch inside. Andrews lifted it out, laying the box carefully to one side on the floor. The watch was quite large, a facsimile of a gentleman's pocket watch from the nineteenth or early twentieth century. I was familiar with such articles, having bought and sold them on several occasions. This one had a silver case, and a pattern of roses engraved on the dial. Even to my untutored eye it was a thing of quite exceptional beauty.

"I studied Breguet's diaries for many years," said Andrews. "He died an old man. Many people thought he was losing his faculties in his final years, suffering from Alzheimer's disease or some other form of dementia. It is true that he did lose some clarity of expression at the end, but that may well have been due to the complexity of the ideas he was struggling with. A lot of it was brand new science." He thumbed a catch, opening the back of the watch. I caught a glimpse of wires and levers, a mass of mechanical circuitry that glimmered as it rotated. Andrews cradled the watch in his left hand, using his right to point to first one of the gleaming internal wheels and then another. I quickly lost track of them all. Fortunately his words were somewhat easier to follow.

"The tourbillon is like a cage," he said. "It rotates the whole mechanism about its own axis. Breguet discovered this as a way of preventing gravity from dragging on the mechanism and making the watch run slow. In effect he made the mechanism weightless. The Time Stasis is simply an advancement of this idea. It reduces time to a null state within its area of operation. The stasis creates a kind of temporal anteroom. Think of it as the lobby of a large hotel, with doors and lifts and corridors opening off it. Once you get through the entrance and into the lobby you can go anywhere you like within the building. It's the Time Stasis that reveals the entrance. Do you see?"

"Some of it." I paused. "It's what the article I read referred to as the time-bridge."

"Yes. But I've never liked the term 'time-bridge.' Once again it's too linear. The lobby image is better, and useful, too. You know how easy it is to get lost in one of those big corporate hotels. All the corridors look the same after a while."

I was struggling to make sense of it all. "But what use could this be to the army?" I said. "You've already told me it's not possible to travel in time in the way we imagine it, so where's the point?"

"There isn't any. But the government refuse to believe that. They've set up a stasis field around the hospital and they are conducting experiments there, forcing people through into other realities and trying to control the future before it happens. And I'm not just talking about weapons. My guess is that they have glimpsed something in the future they don't like, somewhere in one of the alternative realities, and are trying to eradicate it as a possibility for this one. Think about what Hitler might have done if he had seen what would happen when he invaded Russia, or if Reagan had changed his mind over North Korea. It's insane, of course, like trying to do brain surgery with a pickaxe. They believe that with the right inducements I might still be persuaded to refine the calculations for them, and that is the only reason they leave me alone."

"But if their experiments can't succeed, what harm can they do?"

"The harm they're doing to individuals, for a start. They snatch people after curfew and then blame it on the carjackers. They snatch carjackers, too. They send them through the Time Stasis, hoping that with enough practice they'll learn to control the direction and duration of travel. They believe that individuals are expendable. Some of the people they send through never come back. Some never seem to leave, but their contact with the stasis seems to alter their substance. They're incomplete somehow, flickering in and out of existence, like ghosts. I have come to think that they *are* ghosts, or rather that the manifestations people think of as ghosts are not the spirits of the dead at all, but the living products of unsuccessful experiments with a Time

Stasis, conducted from a time stream lying parallel to ours. Then there are the mutants, those unfortunate individuals that experience the stasis as an allergy, a chemical reaction that distorts their bodies, leaving them with all manner of deformities. There's nothing that can be done for them. The soldiers simply release them into the forest. They don't mind if someone catches a glimpse of one of these poor creatures once in a while because they're better than any amount of barbed wire and electric fencing for discouraging intruders. I've no doubt that this is how the chemical weapons stories started. And if the mutants start causing trouble then the army simply go out and use them for target practice."

"But that's terrible."

"No more terrible than most of what is happening these days." He looked at me hard, as if holding me personally accountable for the transports and for the Saudi wars, for what had happened to Kwella Cousens aboard the *Anubis*. "No doubt there have been the usual speeches about omelettes and breaking eggs. What none of them seem to realise is the harm they are doing, not just with these local atrocities but on a wider scale. The Time Stasis is a weak point, a lesion in time that could undermine the stability of our own reality. The breach should be closed, at least until we understand its implications. There are people that have an idea of what is happening and are determined to stop it, but they have a tendency to disappear."

"A resistance, you mean?"

"I don't talk about that. I do still have some shreds of a

private life, and I intend to hang on to them. I suppose it is true, that everyone has his price."

A clear image came to me of the young woman in the photograph on the mantelpiece in the other room. Andrews folded the watch in his hand, pressing it shut.

"How long did it take you to make that?" I said.

"A long time," Andrews said. He smiled to himself, as if at some private joke. "Can I offer you something to eat?"

I stayed, and we talked. I told him about Miranda, and he told me about his childhood in Devon, his first encounter with a Breguet watch at the town museum in Exeter, his friendship with the master horologist who had brought him to London as his apprentice. Some details of his stories seemed disconcertingly familiar, and several times I experienced that same feeling I had had earlier, that there was a wider sense to everything, just out of reach.

It was only when Andrews got up to light a lamp that I realised how late it was.

"I should be going," I said. "It will be dark soon."

I had not thought to check what time the last bus departed for Greenwich. In the light of what Andrews had told me about the hospital, the idea of breaking curfew was doubly unthinkable.

"You're welcome to stay," said Andrews. "There's a spare bed upstairs."

"No, thank you," I said. The idea of spending the night marooned in the Hanging Wood was deeply unnerving.

"Then at least say you'll come and visit me again. It's been just like the old days, having you here."

I laughed to show I knew he was joking, but his face remained serious. Suddenly I was anxious to leave.

"I will, I'll come soon," I said.

"See that you do. Mind how you go."

He waved to me from the doorway. I wondered if he ever got lonely. Dover Road stood silent, a ghost place. With the darkness approaching, the scene appeared to me as a mirage, a stage set for some elaborate deception.

The dusk was gathering. The forest loomed before me, its greens leached to lavender by the approaching twilight. In the Bull Inn the lamps were already lit, and further along the road towards the village there were lights showing in the windows of most of the houses. It was not long till curfew, but I reasoned that as long as I could get myself on to a bus within the next half hour there would be nothing to worry about. I set off in the direction of the High Street, walking briskly in what I hoped was a business-like fashion. I had just come in sight of the bus stop when I saw something terrible: a roadblock had been erected outside the post office. There were four soldiers manning it, all of them armed with carbines. I stopped in my tracks, ducking sideways into an alleyway lined with dustbins. My heart was racing. There was no question of approaching the barrier. Even though I had not breached the curfew and it was still my legal right to pass along the street I knew beyond any doubt that in practice this would count for nothing, that the soldiers would find some pretext to arrest me. What might happen after that was something I did not care to think about.

The safest move was to go back the way I had come, to

return to Owen Andrews's house and take him up on his offer of spending the night there. I hesitated, knowing this was the logical course of action but still reluctant to take it. I trusted Andrews completely, the place I did not trust at all. As the dusk came stealthily onwards, seeming to curl out from beneath the trees like tendrils of smoke, I realised that my horror of the place had not diminished, that the thought of spending the night here in Shooter's Hill was almost as impossible for me as the idea of confronting the soldiers at the barricade.

I cowered in the alleyway, staring at the trees opposite and knowing I had to make a decision in the next few minutes or risk breaking the curfew. It was then that it came to me there was a third option: I could bypass the checkpoint by cutting through the forest. The idea seemed simple enough. I was actually within sight of the checkpoint, and less than half a mile from the village boundary. I could walk that in less than fifteen minutes. I would not need to go far into the woods, just enough to keep me out of earshot of the soldiers. I should emerge on the Shooter's Hill Road somewhere between the hospital and Blackheath.

I ran quickly across the road, hoping that one of the soldiers down by the barrier would not choose that moment to turn his gaze in my direction. I slipped in between the trees, my feet crunching through leaf litter. The slope down from the road was steeper than I had imagined. I tripped against an exposed root and almost fell. In what seemed a very few moments I had completely lost sight of the road.

I had imagined there would be a pathway, some kind of track to follow, but there was none, or at least none that

I could find, and in the oncoming darkness it was difficult to see clearly for more than a couple of yards. I kept going, fighting my way through the underbrush in what I hoped was a westerly direction. There were no landmarks to guide me, no sounds other than the scuffling of my feet in the leaves and my own rapid breathing. I stopped moving, straining my ears for the rumble of a logging truck or even for the voices of the soldiers at the barricade, but again, there was nothing. I could not have been more than a mile from the lighted windows of the Bull Inn, yet it was as if I had unwittingly strayed into another universe. I could smell the trees all around me, the pungent odour of tree bark and rising chlorophyll. I remembered something from my schooldays, that it was during the hours of darkness that plants released their pent-up stores of oxygen, and it seemed to me that I could feel their exhalations all around me, the collective green-tinged sigh of a thousand trees. The dark was rising, spreading across the forest floor like marsh gas. From somewhere further off came the echoing melancholy hooting of a night owl.

I walked for what seemed like hours. I could no longer see where I was going, and had no idea of whether I was even vaguely headed in the right direction. I was very afraid, but the state of high nervous tension that had taken me over when I first realized I was lost had worn itself out, blunting my terror to a dull background hum, a mental white noise that drove me incessantly forward whilst slowing the actions and reactions of my brain.

Finally I came to a standstill. The woods seemed to close

in around me, shuffling forward to block my escape like some vast black beast that knows its prey is out of running. I slid to the ground where I stood, the dampness settling at once into my clothes. Until that moment I had not realised how cold it was. I began to shiver. I knew that if I was to spend the night in the open I had to get under cover somehow, but I was too exhausted by my flight through the woods to make any decisions. I closed my eyes, thinking confusedly that this might make the darkness less awful. When I opened them again some minutes later it was to the sight of a yellowish glow, moving slowly towards me from between the trees. I could hear something also, the soft shushing sound of someone or something doing their best to move quietly across a ground that was ankle-deep in twigs and dry leaves.

I moved from a sitting to a lying position, stomach down in the dirt, never taking my eyes from the pale light that though still some distance off appeared to be coming closer with every second. I was torn by indecision. I did not wish to fall into the hands of soldiers or carjackers, but on the other hand I was desperate to be out of the forest. At that moment, any human company seemed better than none. As the light came closer I was able to discern amidst the surrounding darkness of trees the deeper, blacker bulk of a human figure. A woman, I thought, a woman carrying a torch, and coming my way.

In the end the simple need to hear a human voice outweighed my misgivings. I scrambled to my feet, extending my arms towards the figure with the lamp like a blind man trying to feel his way across a crowded room.

"Hello!" I cried. "Hello there. Wait for me!"

I moved forward, my attempt to run reduced by the darkness to an unsteady lurch. I crashed through the treacherous underbrush, stray twigs clawing at my hands and face. The figure stopped dead in its tracks, the torch beam wavering gently up and down. Its light was weak but my eyes had grown used to the darkness and were temporarily blinded. The figure took a step backwards, crackling the leaves underfoot. I sensed she was as much afraid of me as I was of her.

"I'm lost," I said. "Do you know the way out of here?"

I could hear her breathing, slow and heavy, as if she was about to expire. There was a rank odour, a smell like burning fat tinged with underarm sweat. I was by now convinced that the woman was a fugitive, a political detainee or an immigrant without a work permit, someone on the run from the police. None of that mattered to me. All I cared about was getting out of the woods.

"I'm not going to report you," I said. "I just want to find the road." I grabbed at her sleeve, anxious in case she tried to bolt away from me. She was wearing padded mittens, and a padded anorak made from some shiny nylon-coated fabric that was difficult to get a grip on. My fingers tightened involuntarily about her wrist. The woman moaned, a low, inhuman sound that made me go cold all over. I released her abruptly, pushing her backwards. As she flailed her arms to retain balance the torch beam darted upwards, lighting her face. Until that moment she had been shrouded in darkness, her features concealed by the large, loose hood of the nylon anorak. Now I saw she was disfigured, quite literally *de-formed*, squeezed apart and then rammed back together again in a careless and hideous arrangement that bore as little resemblance to an ordinary human face as the face of a corpse in an advanced stage of decomposition. Her skin was thickly corrugated, set into runnels as if burned by acid. Her mouth, a lipless slit, was slanted heavily to one side, dividing the lower portion of her face in two with a raw diagonal slash. One of her eyes was sealed shut, smeared in its socket like a clay eye inadvertently damaged by its sculptor's careless thumb. The other eye shone brightly in the torchlight, gazing at me in what I instinctively knew was sorrow as much as fear. The eye was fringed with long lashes, and quite perfect.

I screamed, I could not help it, though it was more from shock than from fear. I knew that I was seeing one of the mutants Owen Andrews had spoken of, one of the victims of the army's clumsy experiments with the Time Stasis. Andrews had called the mutants unfortunate, but his words had barely scratched the surface of the reality. In my traumatised state I could not grasp how this person could survive, how she did not just *stop*. Her face was an apocalypse in flesh. It was impossible to know what further ravages had been unleashed upon the rest of her body and internal organs.

Her mental torment I could not bear to imagine.

My scream made her flinch, and she stumbled, dropping the torch. She fell to her knees, sweeping her hands back and forth through the leaves in an effort to retrieve it. But either the padded mittens hampered her efforts or she no longer had proper control of her hands because it kept skidding out of her grasp. I saw my chance and made a lunge for it. Suddenly the torch was in my hand. The woman howled, flinging herself at me as if she meant to topple me into the dirt.

I began to run. The woman picked herself up off the ground and began to follow. She was no longer crying, but I could hear her breathing, the raw panting gasp of it, and I felt sick with revulsion. The thought of having to fight her off, of having her ruined face pressed in close to mine as she battled me for the torch did a good deal to keep me moving. I knew the very fact of possessing the torch made me easy to follow, but there was nothing I could do about that. I pointed it ahead of me, panning the ground at my feet and lighting the way in front the best that I could. The beam was weak, a feeble yellow, barely enough to see by. I kept expecting to bash into a tree, or worse still, to catch a foot in some pothole or crevice and twist my ankle.

I have no doubt that one of these two things would have happened eventually but in the event I was saved by the soldiers. I climbed a shallow rise, tearing my hands painfully on brambles in the process, and then I was in the open. I could sense rather than see that there were no more trees around me, and I guessed I had reached the edge of a woodland meadow. I shone the torch frantically about me, trying to work out which was the best direction to follow. Suddenly there were more lights, broad and penetrating beams of white radiance, strafing the ground and dazzling my eyes. They were approaching from the side at a full-on run.

"Halt!" someone screamed. "Get down."

I threw myself to the ground, covering my head instinctively with my arms. A stampede seemed to pass over and around me. Then there was more shouting, a single wild cry that I knew was the woman, and then a burst of gunfire. I covered my ears, cowering against the ground, and the next minute I was being dragged upright, pulled back down the rise and into the trees.

My mind froze and went blank. I felt certain that I would die within the next few seconds. Someone shoved me from behind and I almost fell. The criss-crossing beams of powerful torches showed me half a dozen men with blackened faces and wearing combat fatigues. The woman's body lay face down on the ground, a dark irregular stain spreading across the back of the padded anorak. One of the soldiers kicked her, flipping her on to her side with the toe of his boot. The anorak shifted slightly, revealing a portion of the clothing beneath, a tattered woollen smock over filthy jeans.

With her face turned away from me she was just a dead woman, an unarmed civilian, gunned down in cold blood. Fury coursed through me like an electrical current. I wanted to be sick, but I was terrified to vomit in case these men shot me for it.

"Frigging disgusting," said one of the men. I had the confused impression that he was referring to my weak stomach, then realised he was talking about the woman they had killed. "What do you think would happen if they started breeding?"

"Shut up, Weegie," said another. The tone of authority in his voice left me no doubt that he was in charge. Then he turned to me. "What the fuck are you doing out here?"

My throat gave a dry click, and I felt once more the gagging reflex, but finally I was able to stammer out an answer.

"I came off the road," I said. "I'm lost."

"ID?"

For a second I panicked, wondering what would happen if I had lost my wallet, or left it behind at Andrews's place, but miraculously when I reached into my jacket pocket it was there. I handed it over in silence. The officer flicked through it briefly, letting his eyes rest for a moment upon my photograph and national insurance number, then handed it back.

"Bloody civvies," he said. "Do you *want* to get mistaken for one of these?" He nodded down at the woman's lifeless body. I shook my head, not trusting myself to speak.

"You'll have to come with us. It's for your own protection. I suggest you get moving." He nodded to the man he had called Weegie, who grabbed me by the upper arm and pushed me into line behind the others. I stumbled a couple of times, but with the soldiers' powerful searchlights to see by the going was actually much easier. Now that it seemed they were not going to shoot me, or at least not immediately, my panic had subsided somewhat. I thought back to the night before, when I had lain comfortably in bed contemplating my forthcoming visit to Andrews and the state of my political complacency. It seemed impossible that a mere twenty-four hours could alter my life so completely. I felt inclined to agree with the officer: I had been bloody stupid.

We marched through the forest for about an hour. I was exhausted by then, my mind empty of anything but the desire to stop moving and lie down. At last there were arc lights, shining to meet us through the trees. The forest ended suddenly at a barbed-wire perimeter fence, and I realised we had arrived outside the hospital.

I was too tired to be afraid. I was marched through a set of iron gates then led along a green-tiled corridor that smelled faintly of damp clothes and disinfectant. Unbelievably it reminded me of school. I caught glimpses of a kit store, and a rec room, where soldiers sprawled on bunks were watching a televised boxing match. At the end of the corridor a short flight of concrete steps led down to what was clearly a cell block. The officer in charge nudged open one of the mesh-strengthened doors and gestured me inside.

"I'd get some kip, if I were you. I'd bring you some grub, only the mess will have shut up shop, so you'll have to hang on till morning."

I stepped through the door, which was immediately banged shut behind me. I heard the sound of a key being turned in the lock, the soldier's footsteps trudging back up the stairs. Then there was silence. I stood where I was for a moment, wondering if anything else would happen. The room I was in was small, although curiously it still had the wallpaper and curtains left behind from the time before the soldiers had taken over. The way the wainscoting and ceiling architrave had been divided made it clear that the cell had been partitioned off from a much larger room, possibly the doctors' lounge. There was a bed pushed up against one wall, a metal-framed cot of the kind that is usual in hospitals. In the corner was a bucket and basin, crudely screened from the rest of the room by a section of cotton sheeting strung from a pole. The windows behind their curtains were barred from the outside.

I relieved myself in the bucket then lay down on the bed. It creaked beneath my weight, the springs weary from decades of use. The room was lit by a single bulb, a bald, enervating glare that I feared would be left burning all night, although when I tentatively pressed a switch by the bed the light went out. In contrast with the alien blackness of the forest, the darkness of my cell gave me a feeling of being protected. I lay under the threadbare blanket, listening to the silence and wondering what was going to happen to me. I was a prisoner, but what was I being imprisoned for? If it was a simple matter of breaking the curfew then I could expect a hefty fine and perhaps three months behind bars, as well as the wholly undesirable possibility of finding myself under continued surveillance. This could lead to all sorts of problems at work, not just for me but for my colleagues. Certainly it was no laughing matter, but it was at least a situation with navigable parameters. The thing was, I knew my situation was not that simple. I had witnessed a murder, the execution of a defenceless and vulnerable woman. That I had seen the frightful injuries inflicted upon her by the Time Stasis hardly served to make things less complicated.

There was also the fact of my visit to Owen Andrews, a troublemaker who by his own admission had been repeatedly in conflict with the state.

What if the soldiers decided it was simpler just to get rid of me? Now that Miranda was dead there would be few who cared enough to risk asking questions. Dora might ask, she might even look for me, but in the end she would weigh up the cost of the truth about a dead man and the price of her own safety and Ray's. She would find the balance wanting and I would not blame her.

Probably they would just shoot me, or perhaps they would use me in one of the time travel experiments. I thought of the mutant woman, twisted and bent by the Time Stasis almost beyond the bounds of her humanity. I still found it difficult to contemplate her isolation, the loneliness and horror she must have suffered at the moment of her realisation of what had been done to her. It came to me that there were fates worse than being shot. I even found myself wondering if her death at the hands of the soldiers had been for the best.

All at once the darkness of the room seemed oppressive rather than soothing. I put the light back on and got up from the bed. I paced about my cell, examining the barred window and testing the door handle, wondering if I might discover some means of escape, but for all its ramshackle ambience the room was still a prison. I placed my ear against the door and listened, straining for any sound that might give a clue as to what was happening in the rest of the hospital, but there was nothing, just a deep, eerie silence that suggested I was completely alone. I knew this had to be nonsense: I had seen the rec room, the soldiers on their bunks watching television and playing cards. I supposed the cell had been soundproofed somehow. The thought was not exactly comforting.

In the end I decided the only thing for it was to take advantage of the silence and get some rest. Now that my life was not being directly threatened I found I was ravenously hungry – it was hours since the meal at Andrews's house – but there was nothing I could do about that. I drank some water instead from the tap in the corner. It had a peaty taste and was unpleasantly tepid but it was something to fill my stomach. Then I lay back down on the bed and covered myself with the blanket. I thought I would be awake for hours but I fell asleep in under five minutes.

At some point during the night I was woken by the sound of shouting and running footsteps but no one came to my door and I decided I must have dreamed it. I closed my eyes, hovering on the boundary between sleep and waking, a citizen of both nations but unable to settle permanently in either. I saw sleep as an immense blue forest that I was afraid to enter in case I never found the way out again. Then I woke with a start to bright sunlight, and realised I had been asleep all along.

I was surprised that none of the soldiers had come to wake me. Surely they hadn't forgotten I was here? It occurred to me that I could easily be left in this cell to die and no one would know, that perhaps this had been their plan all along. I leapt from the bed, relieved myself once again in the stinking bucket, then crossed to the door, prepared to rattle at the lock and shout until someone came. I seized the handle, twisting it sharply downwards.

The door opened smoothly and silently in my hand.

I eased it open a crack and peered out into the corridor. I was prepared for a burst of shouting or even of gunfire, but there was nothing, just the silence of my room, magnified in some queer sense by the largeness of the space it now flowed into. There was nothing in the corridor, just a single plastic chair, as if once, many days before, someone had stood guard there but had since been assigned to other duties and ordered away. The doors to the other cells were closed.

I stepped out into the corridor, my footsteps echoing on the bare cement floor. I tried the door to the room next to mine, and like mine it swung open easily. I was afraid of what I might find on the other side, but what I found in fact was nothing at all. The bed had been stripped of all its furnishings, including the mattress. There was a slops bucket but it was empty and perfectly dry. Beside it stood a pile of old newspapers. I glanced down at the one on top. The headline story, about Clive Billings losing his seat in a by-election in Harrogate, did not make sense. The paper was brittled and yellow from sun exposure and dated two years previously. I remembered the by-election to which it referred – who wouldn't? It was the by-election that effectively made Billings prime minister – but it had happened more than two decades ago, just as I was about to enter university. Billings had taken the seat with a huge majority.

Looking at the headline made me feel odd, and the idea of actually touching the paper made me feel queasy, off-kilter in a way I could not properly explain. I felt that by touching the newspaper I would somehow be ratifying the version of reality it was presenting to me, a reality I knew had never happened. It would be as if I were somehow negating my own existence.

I left the room quickly, passing up the short stone staircase and into the hospital proper. The building was empty, not derelict yet but certainly abandoned. The soldiers' rec room was stacked high with dismantled beds and plastic chairs like the one I had seen in the corridor. There were signs everywhere of encroaching damp and roof leakage, peeling wallpaper and buckled linoleum. One more winter without proper attention and the place would sink inexorably into decay.

The main doors had been boarded over but after hunting around for a while I found a side entrance and made my escape. The hospital grounds were a wilderness, the paths choked with weeds and many of the smaller outbuildings partially hidden by rampaging bramble and giant hogweed. Beyond the perimeter wall the trees loomed, whispering together with the passing of the breeze. In spite of the emptiness of the place, and the fact that I was plainly alone there, I felt exposed, watched, as if the trees themselves were spying on me.

The army checkpoint had disappeared and the entrance was unguarded but the high gates were chained shut and it took me some time to find a way out. The perimeter wall was too high to climb without assistance, and I was just starting to think about going in search of a ladder when I discovered a rent in the small section of chain-link fencing that blocked off the access to the service alleyway at the side of the building. The torn wire snagged at my clothes. I smiled to myself, thinking how the breach was most likely the work of schoolchildren for whom the hospital now as then was a realm of dares and bribes, of dangers both imaginary and real. I was glad they had broken through, that some of them at least had been bolder than I.

I came out of the alleyway and wandered down to the main road. I tried to look nonchalant, not wanting to draw attention to my soiled clothes and general unkemptness. There was a bus stop by the hospital gates, just as before, and after only ten minutes of waiting a bus arrived. I got on, swiping my Oyster card. The sensor responded with its usual bleep. The driver did not look at me twice, and I noticed with a start that she was black. I could not remember the last time I had seen a black person in any position of public service in this country. The bus was, once again, full of soldiers, their London accents blending noisily together as they exchanged ribald jokes and squabbled over newspapers and cigarettes. They were white and black and Asian, as racially mixed as the cowed hordes of deportees in the television broadcasts of my adolescence. I stared at them, barely understanding what I was seeing.

"Lost something, mate?" one of them said to me. "Only if you have, then one of these crims has probably already nicked it." He looked Middle Eastern in origin. One of his eyebrows was pierced with a diamond stud. The rest of his company erupted in laughter, but the whole exchange seemed pretty good-natured and they soon fell back to speaking amongst themselves. The bus grunted then lurched off along the road. The woodland seemed to sing with colour and light.

* * *

When I arrived at my house on Frobisher Street the key would not fit in the lock. By then I was not surprised. I had even been expecting something of this kind. I rang the bell, and after a minute or so the door was opened by a young woman. Her hair looked uncombed, her eyes dark from fatigue. A child clung to her knees, a boy of perhaps four or five. In contrast with the woman's scruffy housedress the little boy wore a cleanly pressed playsuit in a cheerful mix of blues and yellows.

"Yes?" she said. "Can I help you?"

I peered over her shoulder into the hall. The black-and-white tiles had been replaced by a dun-coloured carpet. Piles of washing stood heaped at the foot of the stairs.

"How long have you lived here?" I said. The woman took a sudden step backwards, almost tripping over the child. She ran a hand through her hair, and I saw that all her nails were bitten.

"We're registered," she said. "We've been here almost two years. I've got all the forms." Before I could say anything else she had darted away inside the house, disappearing through the door that had once led to my own living room. The toddler stared up at me, his green eyes wide with fascination.

"Are you from the prison?" he said.

"Not at all," I replied. "This used to be my house once, that's all. I wanted to see if it had changed."

He continued to gaze at me as if I were a visitor from another planet. As I stood there wondering whether to stay or go the woman returned. "Here you are," she said. "They're all up to date." She thrust some papers at me. I glanced at them briefly, long enough to see that her name was Violet

Jane Pullinger and she had been born in Manchester, then handed them back.

"It's all right," I said. "I'm not from the council or anything. I used to live round here, that's all. I was just curious. I'm sorry if I scared you. I didn't mean to."

The child looked from me to the woman and slowly back again. "He says he's not from the prison, Mum. Do you think he's my dad?"

"Stephen!" She touched the boy's hair, her face caught somewhere between laughter and embarrassment. When she looked at me again she appeared younger and less frightened. "I don't know where they get their ideas from, do you? Would you like to come in? I could make us a cup of tea?"

"That's very kind," I said. "But I've taken up too much of your time already."

I knew I could not enter the house, that to do so would be a kind of madness. I said a hurried goodbye then turned and walked back to the High Street. I thought about looking to see if my office was still there but my nerve failed me. I went to a cashpoint instead. I inserted my card in the machine and typed in my PIN. I felt certain the card would be swallowed or rejected. If that happened I would not only be homeless, I would be penniless too, aside from the couple of notes that were still in my wallet. I peered at the screen, wondering what I would do if my PIN was rejected, but this was one decision I did not have to make. My debit card, apparently, was still valid. When the machine asked me which service I required I selected 'cash with on-screen balance,' then when prompted

I requested twenty pounds. It seemed a safe enough amount, at least to start with. I waited while the note was disgorged, staring intently at the fluorescent panel where my bank balance was about to be displayed.

When the figure finally appeared I gasped, inhaling so sharply that it set off a fit of coughing. My bank balance was apparently four times what it had been the day before. I was not a rich man by any means, but for a weary time traveller without a roof over his head the money at least provided some temporary security.

I went to the corner newsagent's, where I bought a newspaper and a wrapped falafel. I ate the falafel right there on the street, wolfing it down in three bites then wiping my fingers on the greaseproof paper. Afterwards I headed for the Woolwich Road and a hotel I knew, an enormous Victorian pile mainly frequented by travelling salesmen. It always had something of a dubious reputation, but reputation mattered very little to me at that moment. I only hoped the place still existed in this reality.

The hotel was still there and still a hotel. It looked more down-at-heel than ever. Some of the rooms on the ground floor appeared to have been converted into long-stay bedsitters. There was a pervasive smell of cooking fat and stewed tomatoes.

"I don't do breakfast," said the landlady. "You get that yourself, out the back." She was huge, a vast whale of a woman in a flowered print dress with the most extraordinary violet eyes I had ever seen. I told her that was fine. She looked vaguely familiar, and I wondered what she looked like with her hair down. I shook my head to clear it and headed upstairs. The upper landing was sweltering and my poky little room was even hotter but I didn't care. I sat down on the bed, which creaked alarmingly. It was strange how much the room, with its faded wallpaper and antiquated washstand, resembled the hospital cell where I had spent the previous night.

As well as the bed and the washstand there was a battered mahogany wardrobe and a portable television set with an old-fashioned loop aerial. I opened the window, hoping to let some air into the room, and then switched on the TV. The one o'clock news had just started. There was footage of a refugee encampment like those I had seen previously in Tangier and Sangatte. I was amazed to learn that the camp, a ragged shanty town of tents and standpipes and semi-feral children skinny as rails, was situated on the outskirts of Milton Keynes. A delegation from the camp had delivered a petition to Downing Street, and the prime minister himself appeared on the steps to receive it.

The prime minister was black, a slim, earnest-looking man named Ottmar Chingwe. I had never seen him before in my life.

I watched the broadcast through to the end. Some of the items covered – the famine in Russia, the blockade in the Gulf – were familiar, or at least they seemed to be at first, but other events, reported in the same matter-of-fact tone, were like passages from some elaborate fantasy. The newspaper I had bought was the same. I felt dazed not so much by the scale of the changes as by their subtlety. There were no miracle machines, no robots, no flying saucers; in many ways the world I had entered was the same as the world I had left. What I saw and felt and heard was a change not so much in substance but in emphasis.

Was it this world that the Billings regime had learned of, and sought to eradicate? Certainly Billings's worldview – his 'Fortress Britain,' as he had proudly referred to it – was everywhere conspicuous by its absence. This new England seemed more like a travellers' encampment, a vast airport lounge of peoples, chaotic and noisy and continually on the move.

Yet commerce was clearly active, the homeless were being fed. People of all shades of opinion were expressing their views robustly and at every opportunity.

It was like the London I remembered from when I was a boy.

I watched TV for about an hour then went down to the curry house opposite and ordered a meal. I ate it quickly, still feeling conspicuous, though none of the other diners paid me the slightest attention. Once I had finished eating I returned to the hotel. There was a pay telephone in the hallway. I inserted my card and dialled Dora's number. The phone rang and rang, and was eventually answered by a woman with an Eastern European accent so strong I could barely understand what she was saying. Silently I replaced the receiver.

After a moment's hesitation I lifted it again, this time dialling Owen Andrews's number, reading it off the slip of paper in my wallet. The phone clicked twice and then went dead. I climbed the stairs to my room and watched television into the small hours, trying to gather as many facts as I could about my new world. Eventually I turned out the light and went to sleep.

I had to keep reminding myself that this was not the future. I had jumped forward three months at some point but that was all. The year was the same. The TV channels were more or less the same. Shooter's Hill Road was still rife with carjackings, only now there was no talk of reinstating the death penalty. The increase in my finances I put down to some lucky quirk, an error in accounting between one version of reality and another.

Once my initial nervousness began to wear off my biggest fear was meeting myself, the kind of nightmare you read about in H. G. Wells. I reminded myself that Owen Andrews had not mentioned it as a possibility and as things turned out it did not happen. I began to wonder if each reality was like Schrödinger's theoretical box, its contents uncertain until it was actually opened. I thought that perhaps the very act of me entering this world somehow negated any previous existence I had had within it.

Such thoughts were unnerving yet fascinating, the kind of ideas I would have liked to discuss with Owen Andrews. But so far as I could determine, Owen Andrews did not exist here either.

I returned to what I was good at, which was buying and selling. I was still cautious in those early days, afraid I might reveal myself through some stupid mistake, and so instead of applying for a job with an estate agent I decided to set up by myself selling watches and clocks. I enjoyed reading up on the subject and it wasn't long before I had a lucrative little business. I had learned in my old life that even during the worst times the rich are always with us, all of them eager to spend their money on expensive luxuries. I had never lost sleep over this, preferring to turn the situation to my advantage. I was amused to find that some of my clients were people I knew from my old life, men and women whose houses I had sold for them, or their sons or daughters. None of them recognised me.

The only possession I carried over from before was the photograph of Miranda that I always kept in my wallet, a snapshot of her on Brighton beach soon after we married. Her topaz eyes were lifted towards the camera, her heart-shaped face partially obscured by silvery corkscrewed wisps of her windblown hair. It was like an answered prayer, to have her with me. There were no traces of her death now, no evidence of what had happened. All that remained was my knowledge of my love for her and this final precious image of her face.

One evening in September I left a probate sale I had been attending in Camden and walked towards the tube station at St John's Wood. It was growing dusk, and I stopped for a moment to enjoy the view from the top of Primrose Hill. The sky in the west was a fierce red, what I took to be the afterglow of sunset, but later, at home, when I put on the radio I discovered there had been a fire. The report said that underground fuel stores at the old army hospital at Shooter's Hill had mysteriously ignited, causing them to explode. The resulting conflagration was visible for twenty miles.

The Royal Herbert was a listed building, said the newscaster. *It was originally built for the Woolwich Garrison at the end of the eighteen eighties and was most recently in use as a long-stay care facility for victims of war trauma.*

The police suspected arson, and a forensics team had already been sent in to investigate. I supposed they would find something eventually, a piece of loose circuitry or faulty shielding, but felt certain that unless they were experienced in tracking a crime from one universe to another they would never discover the truth of what had happened.

What I believed was that the resistance fighters Owen Andrews told me about had finally found a way to destroy the hospital and seal the breach. The blast had been so strong it had ripped through the Time Stasis, wiping the building off the map in all versions of reality simultaneously. I had a vision of the great hotel lobby of time Owen Andrews had spoken of, alarm bells clamouring as a line of porters shepherded the guests out of the building and a fire crew worked to extinguish a minor blaze in one of the bedrooms. The fire was soon put out, the loss adjusters called in to assess the damage. By the end of the evening the guests were back in the bar and it was business as usual.

Some old biddy's cigarette, apparently, said one as he sipped at his Scotch.

We're lucky she didn't roast us in our beds, his companion jabbered excitedly. *D'you fancy some peanuts?*

I supposed that my old life was now lost to me for good. Perhaps this should have bothered me but it didn't. The more time passed, the more it was that past life that seemed unreal, a kind of nightmare aberration, a bad photocopy of reality rather than the master version. The world I now inhabited, for all its rough edges, felt more substantial.

I uncorked a bottle of wine – the dreadful Blue Nun that was all you could find in the shops at the time because of the customs embargo – and drank a silent toast to the unknown bombers. I thought of the soldiers in their rec room, their harmless card games and noisy camaraderie, and hoped they had been able to escape before the place went up.

It was not until some years later that I stumbled upon the photograph of Owen Andrews. It was in a book someone had given me about the London watch trade in the nineteenth century. Andrews stood at his work bench. He was wearing a baggy white workman's blouse and had his loupe on a leather cord around his neck.

The caption named him as 'the marvellous Mr Andrews', the 'miracle dwarf' who had successfully perfected a number of new advancements in the science of mechanics. I studied the picture for a long time, wondering what Andrews would make of being called a miracle dwarf. I supposed he would have a good laugh.

The text that went with the picture said that Andrews

had held a position in the Physical Sciences Department of Oxford University but had resigned the post as the result of a disagreement with his superiors. He had come to London soon afterwards, setting up his workshop in Southwark.

Sometimes, on those light summer evenings when I had finished all my appointments and had nothing better to do, I made my way to Paddington and ate a leisurely supper in one of the bars or cafes on the station concourse. I watched the great steam locomotives as they came and went from the platforms, arriving and departing for towns in the north and west. A train came in from Oxford every half hour.

I knew it was futile to wait but I waited anyway. Andrews had said we would meet again and I somehow believed him. I sipped my drink and scanned the faces in the crowd, hoping that one of them one day would be the face of my friend.

REWIND

"Tourbillon is French for whirlwind," said Juliet Caseby. "It is also the name of a mechanical invention, something watchmakers refer to as a complication. Owen Andrews told my grandmother Angela that the tourbillon was the most exacting horological complication ever."

"Was he right, do you think?" Miranda asked.

"I'm sure he was. Even today, with microelectronics and computer circuitry and so on, the basic principles of the tourbillon are still in use. The man who invented it was a genius. His name was Louis Breguet, and he learned and honed his craft at the court of Versailles. Marie Antoinette was one of his clients, and it was partly because of her that he ended up having to flee Paris. It was only with the help of Marat that he escaped the guillotine. Owen Andrews used to say that Breguet was the first human being to defy the laws of gravity."

Marat, Miranda thought. *Wasn't he the one who was murdered in his bath*? She remembered seeing an article about the tourbillon in the *Greenwich Gazette*. The whole of Greenwich seemed obsessed with time. As the home of the

Greenwich Meridian it went with the territory. Miranda had read the article because it included a photograph of a pocket watch with an image of a fox enamelled on the inside of the case and she had always had a fondness for urban foxes. The article described the tourbillon as a *time-cage*, and encouraged its readers to think of it as a tornado in miniature.

Wind itself has no physical substance, the article read. *But it generates enormous power. The tourbillon spins the watch mechanism about its own axis like storm debris caught in a hurricane. Like flicking a switch on gravity and turning it off.*

Miranda thought about the recent television footage of the damage caused by a tornado in the Midwestern United States, the vistas of flattened houses, the cars and lorries and beef cattle flung hundreds of feet into the air then released to smash on the ground like plastic toys.

Later in their hotel room she went online and searched for images of the tourbillon. There were diagrams with pointers and arrows showing how the watch mechanism could be made to fit inside a metal cage that would then spin it around itself, like a sidecar on a fairground ride.

The cage itself reminded her of the gyroscope she had owned as a child, a beautiful and shining thing that her brother Stephen referred to as one of the minor miracles of engineering. He had taught her how to tightrope-walk it across a piece of string stretched between her bedroom windowsill and the door handle. Stephen had a genius for tricks like that.

"But what was it actually used for?" Miranda said. "I can see how it made a watch more complex, but what was the point of it?"

"It helped a watch keep accurate time," said Juliet. "The trouble with the old pocket watches was that they couldn't stand being bumped about. A pocket watch stayed in your pocket and liked it there. Taking it out to look at the time played havoc with the mechanism and even the finest watches in the world could lose as much as twenty minutes in as many hours. A tourbillon freed the mechanism from the pull of external gravity. Breguet's watches were accurate to an eighth of a second."

"Are tourbillon watches expensive?"

Juliet smiled. "You could say that. They take hundreds of hours to make, and cost many thousands of pounds to buy."

Miranda thought of a fairground at night, the big wheel turning majestically against a backcloth of stars. She had once accompanied her mother to a pre-auction viewing at Christie's for a sale of timepieces. The others who had attended were mostly men, though she did see two women, both wearing designer business suits and an air of confidence that made it clear they were used to being looked at. Self-assurance wafted from them like the cool green ground-notes of the expensive scents they wore. Women of this kind used to intimidate Miranda until she came to realise she was invisible to them. Her gaucherie scared them. They shied away from her as if she had a physical deformity.

The men were different. It was as if they saw in the gleaming watch glasses not just a reflection of their own status but the encapsulation of dreams they had once cherished but had since let die. In spite of the Italian shoes and the onyx signet rings she could see her father in each and every one of them.

There was a picture of her father, photographed on the veranda of his childhood home in Cape Town, the house Miranda had never seen but where Stephen now lived. Her father was twelve years old and surrounded by the glinting innards of a war-vintage Bakelite wireless set. There was a second photograph, taken later the same day, that showed the radio restored to working order.

Her father had mended the wireless all by himself.

"Your granddad was a coffee grower," he told Miranda. "He could fix a pick-up truck no problem, but not a radio set."

She could still hear the pride in his voice. Ronnie Coles was never a vain man but he had always experienced a profound joy in making things work.

Stephen was the same, of course. It was a pity he had been unable to mend their father.

Lewis Usher lived alone in one of the fine detached villas at the top end of Crooms Hill. He had let the place go a bit, Martin thought, but for the right price it would be snapped up in no time. Houses on the Hill always were.

Usher said he wanted a quick sale.

"It's time to move on," he said. "That's a moment you only recognise when it comes." Usher coughed and dabbed at his eyes and Martin found himself wondering if the house sale was being forced on him by interfering relatives. It had been the same for him when Dora died. His friend Ray Levin especially kept insisting he should make a fresh start. There were mouse droppings in Usher's larder though, and the rooms on the second floor were festooned with cobwebs. All in all, Martin thought, Usher probably would be better off with something smaller.

He moved from room to room, taking measurements and making notes of the fixtures and fittings. It was work he enjoyed, especially when the house, like this one, was full of curious angles and surprises.

The picture of the two girls brought him up short. It stood on top of a chest of drawers on the upper landing, just one of a collection of objects gathering dust. The girls were both smiling broadly for the camera and standing either side of a dwarf in a panama hat.

The little man was smiling also. He held a dog on a leash, a white chihuahua. There was a seaside pier in the background, posters advertising pleasure boat rides.

The scene was so familiar it made Martin feel faint.

"That's my wife, with her best friend Juliet," Usher said. He touched the top edge of the photo frame and then quickly withdrew his hand. "This was taken long before I met her, of course. They were only sixteen."

Usher's wife had died of cancer at the age of sixty. Martin had the vague idea she had been an actress. Lewis Usher was clearly still in mourning for her.

"It's a lovely picture," he said. "Where was it taken?"

"Hastings, Folkestone, one of those places. That's where she was from."

"Your wife, you mean?"

"Zoë was born in Shoreditch. I'm talking about Juliet. She went to the same school as Zoë and Zoë often used to go down and stay with her during the holidays. I have her address somewhere. Zoë used to write to her every Christmas. I'll go and have a look if you don't mind waiting."

He shuffled off into one of the bedrooms, panting a little with the exertion. He returned after a minute or so, clutching a small leather-bound address book. Its covers bulged with the many additional scraps of paper that had been stuffed between them.

"This was Zoë's," Usher said. "Zoë was the one with all the friends." He leafed clumsily through the pages, grabbing at the loose sheets and markers that kept threatening to fall to the floor. "Here it is," he said finally. He pointed to one of the entries, *Juliet Caseby*, with the surname in brackets, *24 Silcox Square, Hastings*. The postcode began with TN, which Martin knew was for the main sorting office in Tonbridge.

The entry was scrawled in blue biro. Zoë's large, flamboyant handwriting overflowed the lines on the page as if it resented being cooped up in such a confined space.

Most likely the photo was nothing, just a coincidence.

"Do you mind if I take a note of the address?" Martin said. "I'd like to make contact with this lady. My sister and I used to go for holidays in Hastings. I'd be interested in hearing what she remembers about the old days."

"I don't mind at all," Usher said. "I'll leave you to it. Just put the book back on the tallboy when you've finished." For a moment he remained where he was, and Martin sensed he had more to say, but in the end he turned his back and retreated downstairs. After a minute or so Martin heard the radio come on in the kitchen. Martin copied Juliet Caseby's address into the back of his diary and placed the address book carefully down on the chest of drawers.

When he tried to find Lewis Usher to tell him he was leaving, the old man was nowhere in sight.

Leave him be, Dora said to him inside his head. *You must have noticed how upset he was. This house was his life.*

Martin returned to the office, parking his car at the back and entering the building through the side door.

Miranda Coles was in her cubby hole, typing up a batch of new instructions.

"If I download the photos for Crooms Hill would you sort them out for me?" Martin said to her.

Miranda nodded and smiled then returned to her work. She seemed the same as always, calm and pragmatic, but for some reason the sight of her unsettled him.

Their trip to the cinema the week before had been a disaster.

Your fault, Dora said. *You hardly spoke a word to the woman all evening.*

Dora was right of course, but the truth was he had not known how. He had known Miranda for twelve years but had barely exchanged a word with her outside the office. That was something he wanted to change but as to how to go about it he was in the dark.

He put his briefcase down on his desk and switched on his computer. He wondered briefly about asking Miranda to go to lunch with him but decided he wasn't feeling up to it.

He knew from her CV that she was now thirty-eight, though he would have found it difficult to tell her age otherwise. The drab, old-fashioned clothes she wore made her seem middle aged, and yet her skinny arms and pageboy haircut gave her the appearance almost of an adolescent.

She worked hard and was clearly intelligent, though she never made Martin party to her opinions and occasionally he wondered if she even had any. The other women in the office, Jenny Lomax and Janet Carlson, who was head of Land Sales, called her the Mouse. Her meekness seemed to irritate them for some reason, though this never boiled over into open hostility.

Jen Lomax once told him that when Miranda was ten years old she had been abducted.

"She was snatched off the pavement, right in front of her own house," Jen said. "That's probably why she always acts so traumatised. Have you noticed the way she jumps when you say her name?"

Jenny Lomax was loud and confident and her desk resembled the aftermath of a minor apocalypse. She was brash, Martin supposed, but all the clients adored her and she was great at her job. Martin had no idea if she was speaking the truth about Miranda, but listening to her gossip made him uncomfortable. Jen was always teasing him with her coarse remarks and sexual innuendos. He had found this off-putting at first but in time he had grown accustomed to it. Jen lived in New Cross with a sharp suit who worked for Credit Suisse.

Miranda lived in Sidcup with her mother. Just before he went to lunch Martin poked his head round the door of her cubbyhole and asked if he could bring her anything from the coffee shop next door.

"No thank you, Martin," she said. "I brought sandwiches." Her wrists, temporarily suspended above her keyboard, looked fragile as reeds. For the first time he found himself noticing the watch she wore: yellow gold with a patina so rich it was almost buttery.

"I like your watch," he said, and immediately felt stupid.

"Thank you," said Miranda. "It belonged to my grandmother."

Martin coughed, reminding himself idiotically of Lewis Usher. Then suddenly Miranda was slipping the watch from her wrist and passing it across to him. It had an Art Deco chain-link bracelet, a bold design that ought not to have suited her but somehow did. The gold was warm from the contact with her skin.

"My grandmother was German," she said. "She was interned here during the war. She had to report to the police each week or risk being sent to prison. None of those policemen cared that she was Jewish, that the reason she'd come here in the first place was to get away from Hitler. Aren't people strange?"

It was the most Martin had ever heard her speak. Her voice was light, with a sweet timbre, like the voice of her watch. He found himself wanting to take her hand, to slide the gold circle of the watch bracelet over the pearly twin protrusions of her wrist bones. He would feel the blue veins pulsing beneath her skin like tiny, mysterious rivers.

In the end he just handed it back.

"It's lovely," he said. Once again he felt like a fool. That evening when he'd finished supper he took down the photograph album and looked for the picture that Aunt Violet had taken of himself and Dora with the Circus Man, but couldn't find it. Somewhere along the line it must have fallen out of the album and had since been lost.

It was possible that Dora herself had removed it. Dora had always been afraid of the Circus Man.

A mystery then, Dora said. *You never liked mysteries much, did you? You prefer it when things add up.*

He wondered if she was right, if he really was that boring, the kind of man that is called a dry old stick.

I'll write to the Caseby woman, he thought. *Tomorrow.*

He thought about Miranda Coles, the way the pretty gold watch had slipped down over her hand.

He spent an hour in front of the television without paying any attention to what was on then dialled Miranda's home number in Sidcup from his mobile. He had all the staff numbers stored there, hers included. He didn't know if Miranda owned a mobile, only that he had never seen her using one.

A cross-sounding woman answered. When he asked to speak to Miranda the woman said she was out.

Their garden backed on to the railway line. Miranda's mother was fond of saying that they were trapped, that the proximity of the railway made it impossible for them to sell the house even if they wanted to. Miranda had never believed it. There were plenty of people who liked trains, who found the noise they made comforting.

She had always liked the sound of the railway. As a young child and in the difficult years after her father died their measured, regular passage helped her to sleep at night.

She knew the timetable by heart, and could tell the trains apart just from the sounds they made: the jaunty thrust and dash of the new metros, the slower lumbering of the older rolling stock that went on to Gillingham and Gravesend, the fast trains down to the coast that did not stop at all until they reached Orpington.

She had never been afraid of the dark, but it was never completely dark in London anyway. When at five years old she had asked her mother where the trains went at night her mother had told her *Gravesend*. The word and the images it evoked terrified her for years. Later she learned that Gravesend was just the name of a town in Kent.

Most of her afternoon had been spent preparing the brochure for the Crooms Hill property, the house that had been the home of the actress Zoë Clifford. She and Stephen had been to see her in a spy film called *An Unknown Country*, Clifford looking haggard and bewitching in an army greatcoat and mud up to her knees. Stephen had had a thing for her ever since.

Miranda turned away from the tracks and went inside. She hoped her mother would have gone up already but she was fussing about in the kitchen making cocoa, her mug and spoon and cinnamon neatly laid out.

"There was a phone call for you," she said. "He didn't leave his name."

Did you ask for it? Miranda thought to herself but did not say. She knew it would be a mistake to sound too interested. The call had most likely been from Tom Stowells, wanting her to babysit again so he and Melanie could go to some party or other. Or Clive Trewitt, who sometimes called her up for a game of cards. Clive Trewitt was eighty-three but still a dab hand at bezique. Better than she would ever be at any rate.

"Why didn't you call me?" she said. She felt a sudden certainty that the caller had been Martin. She resisted the temptation to ask her mother what the man had sounded like or what he had said.

"I'm not yelling down the garden like a fishwife. And I had nothing on my feet. Anyway, it's too late for people to be ringing." She made a sniffing sound that Miranda recognised as disapproval and added three teaspoons of sugar to the boiling milk.

Nimmie Coles was skinny as a rake, and still young, in spite of the strenuous effort she put into her mean old woman act. She was just sixty-eight, and tenacious as ragwort. Miranda had no idea why she had adopted the role of tragic widow; Nimmie had stopped loving her husband years before he died.

Her mother picked up the mug of cocoa. Her long feet in their worn moccasins poked from the bottom of her dressing gown, her still-fair hair looped untidily behind her ears. "Don't forget to turn out the lights," she said.

"I won't," said Miranda. She watched her mother shuffle towards the stairs. *She's like a crane fly*, she thought. *All angles*. She knew she should leave, just get out of there. Stephen said she could join him in Cape Town at any time, but the idea frightened her. She and Stephen had been close as children, but inevitably they had drifted apart and the truth was that in all but the surface detail they had become strangers.

She stared at the phone on the wall, willing it to ring again, knowing that it would not, that it really was too late now, almost midnight. She wondered what Martin was doing, then wondered if it was rude to wonder, a kind of eavesdropping.

She didn't know why she persisted in thinking about him. Nothing had happened between them, or at least nothing serious.

Something might have, though, she thought. *Only you blew it.*

Miranda had assumed at first that Martin was married but Jenny Lomax had told her that no, he lived with his sister.

"He never talks about her," Jen said. "I think she's sick or something."

She raised one eyebrow as if to imply that Martin was peculiar and that made him a perfect and righteous target for office gossip. Miranda did not take the bait, even though she knew that this could only worsen her relations with Jenny Lomax. She liked Martin. She did not want to gossip about him with Jen or with anyone. But at least now she knew he was not married.

She wondered what the sister was like, whether it was true that she was ill or just another piece of gossip.

But then Martin was off work for three weeks, and Scott Unsworth, the deputy manager, told them he was on compassionate leave following a death in the family.

Martin had not been the same after that, not for a long while. Then suddenly and out of nowhere he asked Miranda to go to the cinema with him. It was a film she had wanted to see, but Martin's unaccustomed proximity made her nervous and when the film was over she realised she couldn't remember a thing about it.

Once they were outside on the street she lost her nerve completely. She told Martin she had to get home because of her mother.

She couldn't decide if he looked disappointed or relieved.

She supposed it was probably better to keep things as they were. Change was something she had grown unused to. She wasn't sure she had the courage to invite it.

Martin had seemed excited though when he came back from the Clifford house. And then there had been that odd conversation about her wristwatch, that moment when she thought he was going to kiss her. It was strange, the way she felt close to him, even though she felt sure that so far as romance went they were doomed. She had seen it in films, read it in books, the couple who were clearly meant to be together but somehow never managed to make things work out.

She brushed her teeth and got ready for bed. Later she dreamed she was in Martin's office. She had gone there thinking she would give Martin her watch, but Martin was nowhere in sight. She opened the door to the stationery cupboard, thinking he might be inside, only to discover that it wasn't the stationery cupboard at all but the downstairs cloakroom at home.

She could hear the watch ticking beneath her pillow. It sounded like a bomb about to go off.

* * *

Dear Ms Caseby, Martin wrote. *I was recently given your address by Lewis Usher. I understand that his late wife Zoë Clifford was a friend of yours. Mr Usher is currently in the process of moving house, and has employed me as estate agent to market his property in Greenwich. In the course of preparing the details I happened to notice a photograph belonging to Mr Usher, a picture of yourself and Zoë Clifford on the seafront in Hastings when you were schoolgirls. This photograph brought back a lot of memories for me as my sister and I spent summers in Hastings at what must have been about the same time, and I was wondering if you were able to tell me anything about your time there. Do you know, for example, the identity of the man in the Panama hat with the little dog? I remember him well, although I never knew his name.*

He finished off the letter with some meaningless pleasantries, taking care to include his email and mobile number as well as his return address. He wondered how soon he might hear from her, if the woman was still alive even. There was also the chance that she might take exception to Usher giving out her address and refuse to communicate. He was surprised to receive an email from her the following day:

I know the gentleman you mean, of course. His name was Owen Andrews, and he earned his living in the town doing clock and watch repairs. He was a very good friend of my grandmother, who kept house for him for a time before she was married. I have some old photos of hers, if you are interested, though I would have to insist on your travelling here to see them. My grandmother's papers are in a fragile condition and I would not feel happy about them leaving the house.

How extraordinary, thought Martin. *She is still alive.*

Why extraordinary? said Dora. *Zoë Clifford was only sixty when she died, wasn't she? This friend of hers can't be much older.*

He knew she was right, but it felt extraordinary anyway to read Juliet Caseby's message, like opening a door into the past. He had never heard anyone refer to the Circus Man as Owen Andrews, although the name caused a stirring inside his head, a trace memory of something he had read perhaps, or seen in a museum. Part of him wanted not to go to Hastings. In a sense things were perfect the way they were, the door ajar with just a chink of light showing. What was he hoping to gain by passing through it?

What lay on the other side could only be commonplace, old furniture under dustsheets in a room that had not been used for many years. But he acknowledged Juliet Caseby's email, thanking her for her reply and adding that he would definitely be interested in seeing her grandmother's photographs. *I will be in touch with you soon to confirm a date*, he wrote. *Thank you again.*

When he arrived at work Miranda informed him that three lots of people had made appointments to view the Crooms Hill house.

"One of them was the guy who runs the Picturehouse,"

she said. "He went on and on about Zoë Clifford, the actress. She used to live in that house, did you know that?"

"I did, actually," said Martin. "The gentleman who's selling is her husband." He guessed the Picturehouse man had no intention of putting in an offer, he was just curious to have a poke around. You couldn't let on that you knew that, though. Being polite to timewasters was part of the job.

It seemed that Zoë Clifford was everywhere all of a sudden. Almost before he realised he meant to, he found himself telling Miranda about the email from Juliet Caseby.

"She was Zoë Clifford's best friend," he said. "She lives in Hastings. My sister and I used to go there on holiday when we were children." He paused. "I saw a photograph of her with Zoë when I was doing the valuation and I asked if I could have her address. There was someone else in the photograph, someone I recognised. I want to find out what this Caseby woman knows about him."

The next moment, he was asking Miranda if she would like to go to Hastings with him.

"It would be nice to have some company," he said. "If you think you could put up with me, that is."

Miranda blushed, her cheeks filling up with the powderpuff, pigeon-breast pink of fine Capodimonte porcelain.

"My dad took us to Hastings once, to visit the castle," she said. "It would be lovely to see it again."

Martin gazed at her in surprise. He noticed that her hands were trembling slightly, that her jaw was set in a rigid line, as if she had bitten down on something sour or very cold.

"Are you sure?" he said, still not certain she had actually

said yes. "It would be better if we stayed overnight, really. We wouldn't have much time there otherwise."

She smiled then, and Martin thought he saw tears in her eyes. He remembered the feeling that had come over him when Dora called him into her room and told him she was going to die.

Don't look like that, she had said. *We've had a good run for our money.* She had cried later on that night, though never again in his presence. Dora used to love travelling, but for those final eighteen months she had barely left the house.

Miranda Coles had spent the whole of the past decade shuffling back and forth between her mother's house in Sidcup and the office in Greenwich, the whole time they had known one another. Most people would see that as a kind of living death, but perhaps it wasn't and perhaps they were wrong.

It was daunting, how little he knew her. He wondered how they would get on alone together, whether things would have changed between them by the time they returned to London. The rest of the day passed in a blur. At around three o'clock he told Miranda he was popping out for a sandwich and spent most of the next hour wandering around the back streets of Greenwich. The sun blazed down, the back gardens and building lots hummed with the sound of crickets. The layout of streets was stamped upon his brain, an interlocking grid of neat black lines. It was the job that had done that, although his decision to become an estate agent had been a complete accident, a way of avoiding stacking shelves at the local supermarket.

What are you going to do, Martin? You can't just do nothing.

His mother's voice, grown steadily more accusing with each passing day.

You in a suit, Dora said. *I can't believe it.*

Dora spent the last days of her life in hospital but for the whole of the time leading up to that Martin had looked after her at home. On the evening of her death Martin returned to the house and removed every visible trace of her illness: the medicines and syringes, the rolls of lint and kitchen towels, the glass tumbler, still smeary with the dregs of the glucose drink that was the only nourishment she would take in her final weeks.

He loathed the smell of these things, their sinister combination of sweetness and acridity. He thought of it as the smell of death itself.

For God's sake don't think about it, Dora said. *It's over.*

It will never be over, Martin thought. *Not while my brain still works and there are thoughts in my head.* He turned back in the direction of the office, then called Jenny Lomax on his mobile and told her he wouldn't be back for the rest of the day. He began to call Miranda and then didn't.

He phoned Ray Levin instead and told him he was going away for the weekend with a woman.

"Hey, Marty," Ray said. "Way to go."

"Nothing's going to happen, she's just a colleague from work."

"For God's sake don't put the mufflers on before you get started. Just see how it goes."

He had known Ray since school. He was the only one who knew about him and Dora.

"You should forget all that now," Ray had once said to him. "You two were just kids. What's done is done."

"I slept with my sister, Ray," Martin replied. "I ruined her life."

"Are you telling me you forced her?"

"It wasn't like that."

"Well there you are then. Time to move on."

If it had happened just the once that might have been possible but the truth was they had become addicted to one another. The first time had been in the aftermath of her broken engagement to Michael Klein. The last had been five weeks before her death.

Martin sometimes imagined the only way he could be at peace with himself would be to serve time in prison for what he had done. Sometimes, ridiculously, he felt he was responsible for Dora's illness and therefore her death.

He could not see any way of telling Miranda the things he had admitted to Ray Levin. Surely that meant they were finished before they'd even begun?

I am miserable, he thought. *I've been wasting my life.*

I can't stand you when you're like this, Dora said. *You're so indecisive.*

Indecisive, Martin thought. *I can't decide.*

A memory caught him off guard like a camera flash, himself in Aunty Violet's garden in Hastings, digging the sandy soil with a red plastic spade. There was a girl with him, a child he had met on the beach with a birthmark on one shoulder and dirty knees.

She had tried to touch him through his shorts and he

had been embarrassed but also excited. Dora had seen them and threatened to tell Violet.

He was surprised at how much the memory of it still aroused him.

Martin had booked them into one of the larger hotels along the seafront, a tall white stuccoed building with sun balconies and potted palm trees flanking the entrance. Miranda had assumed they would have separate rooms, but there had clearly been some kind of mix-up. The room they were shown to had twin beds, pushed together to form a double. Twin bedside cabinets with lamps on stood to either side.

"I'm so sorry," Martin said. "This isn't what I asked for. I couldn't find anywhere with two singles. I thought we were getting a twin. We can move them apart if you like."

"Don't worry," said Miranda. "It's no problem."

She could see how embarrassed he was. She wanted above all to reassure him that the confusion over the booking was not his fault, but in truth she was unsettled by the idea of spending the night in such close proximity to another human being, even if all they did in the room was sleep.

She and Stephen had shared a room once, but they had been children. She tried to imagine what it would be like, undressing in the little bathroom with Martin just a few feet away on the other side of a flimsy pasteboard wall, but the thoughts did not come easily.

She had no experience with men. She was what used to be called an old maid, or at least that was how Jen Lomax and Janet Carlson saw her. They couldn't know of course about her three-week engagement to Edmund Wiley because Edmund Wiley had left the firm long before either of them started working there. She supposed someone might have told them, Scott Unsworth for instance, though she couldn't see that it mattered much. She had never slept with Edmund. She split up with him largely because she knew she could never do so. When she thought about sleeping with Martin her mind went blank.

"Are you sure you're all right with this?" Martin said.

"Of course," she said. "It's a lovely room." She placed her overnight bag on the end of the bed that was closest to her. The bag was burgundy in colour and made of soft leather. She had bought it for the weekend in Oxford Edmund had been planning just before she broke up with him. The bag had never been used.

They were not due at Juliet Caseby's until half past three. Miranda assumed they would have lunch somewhere first, explore the town a bit. She had told Martin she would enjoy revisiting the place but in truth her memories of Hastings were not pleasant.

They had come down for the August Bank Holiday, she remembered that. The roads were heavy with traffic and the heat inside the car close to unbearable. Stephen had not wanted to go. Once Stephen was into his teens he argued with their father more or less continuously and the two of them had started up again almost as soon as they left the house. Ronnie Coles was insisting that Stephen give up his idea of a gap year and concentrate instead on his Oxbridge entrance.

If you let things slide now you'll never catch up. We're talking about an investment in your future.

I don't want to invest in my future. I want to live my life the way I choose.

Stephen bought a second-hand Honda motorbike and rode it all the way from Cherbourg to Cape Town. He wanted to see the land where his grandfather had had his coffee plantation and where their own father had spent most of his childhood. He loved the place so much he never returned.

Their father's depression got worse after Stephen left, though Miranda suspected this would have happened anyway. People were what they were, it was no use blaming others for what happened to them.

She remembered Hastings as a crumbling pile of bricks at the far end of nowhere.

"Is there anything in particular you fancy doing?" said Martin.

"Not especially," Miranda said. "Shall we go and have a look at the sea?"

She wished there was a way around this somehow, the awkward small talk and over-politeness that seemed to be an inevitable part of getting to know someone. Things had been all right on the train but during the taxi ride to the hotel a careful silence had developed and now it seemed they were back at the beginning.

They locked up the room and left the hotel by a side entrance, crossing the main road to the esplanade. There was a stiff breeze blowing. A group of French kids trundled past them on roller blades.

"Is it how you remember?" she asked. She wondered what would happen if she took his arm. She had a sudden image of Jenny Lomax in her halter-neck sundress, the way she had of squeezing her breasts together when she laughed.

"I don't really know," said Martin. He shook his head. "It's all mixed up in my mind, what was real and the games we made out of it. There were times when I was terribly bored. It would rain for what seemed like days on end. Dora didn't mind that, she was just as happy to stay inside and read. She was able to find things to do wherever she was."

"But you couldn't do that?"

"I liked to be outside. I liked going for walks."

He turned to face her, his thinning hair blowing back in the wind. Suddenly he reached out and took her hand.

"Thank you for coming with me, Miranda. I don't think I could have done this alone."

She felt too surprised and overwhelmed to reply. His hand felt dry and warm, his grip firmer than she would have imagined. They walked east along the esplanade, away from the pier and towards the shingle beach known as the Stade and the network of interlinked streets that made up the Old Town. Juliet Caseby lived in the Old Town, Martin had told her. The promenade between the pier and the Stade ran parallel with the main coast road. There was an underground car park, a children's play area with a miniature railway, a succession of run-down amusement arcades. On the whole Miranda thought Hastings both brash and tawdry, typical of so many of the older seaside resorts, places that had lost their way in the world and had yet to find a new one.

Her mother would hate it, she knew. For some reason this made her smile. She had told her mother she was staying the night with Jenny Lomax. She wasn't sure if Nimmie believed her or not. The idea that she might stay over at Jen's place was preposterous, but her mother didn't know that, she had never met any of the people Miranda worked with.

"Why don't you tell me about the photograph?" she said to Martin. "You said it showed someone you recognised."

"It was so strange," Martin said. "I keep wondering if I imagined it." He squeezed her hand and then let go. She wondered if her question had offended him in some way, but then saw from his face that at least for the moment he was not thinking about her at all. "There was a man who used to walk along the seafront. We didn't see him all that often, but he was around the first summer we came here and Dora never forgot him. She was always on the lookout for him after that. He was a dwarf, and he wore unusual clothes. Straw boaters and striped velvet jackets, rather old-fashioned. Dora used to call him the Circus Man. I don't know if it was the way he dressed that made her call him that, or whether it was because he was a dwarf and she thought dwarfs went with circuses, but whatever it was he fascinated her. Or at least he did when she was a little girl. Later on she became afraid of him. Again, I don't know why. One time when we saw him she said she lost all the sensation in her hands. She thought he was a harbinger of doom."

"You mean a bad omen?"

"Yes. And it wasn't like her at all, to say things like that. Dora was a rationalist. People who believed in the supernatural just made her laugh."

"What was she like, your sister?"

"Oh, Dora was like no one," he said. He stopped walking and gazed out to sea. The waves rasped over the stones. She loved the sea as she knew her father had, though she had no memory of him speaking to her about it. She wondered how different things might have been if he had lived, and supposed not very. People made their own lives, their own choices. It was stupid to blame her father for the way things were, she saw that now. She felt amazed that it had taken her so long.

"She was brilliant at what she did, but she found the world outside her work hard to cope with," Martin said. "She filed the best results in her year at Cambridge, but she ended up earning her living marking exam papers. She fell in love once, but the man broke it off. She needed someone she could depend on, someone she could trust without question. It turned out that person was me." He shook his head. "I've made her sound pathetic, but she was fierce. Fierce in her intellect and fierce in her beliefs. But she was gentle too, and funny. I loved her very much. There are still days when I can't believe she's gone."

Miranda looked down at the ground, at the pink suede sandals she had bought for the trip, thinking that they might be sexy. *They look stupid on me*, she thought. *Only someone like Jen Lomax could wear shoes like these and get away with it*. She knew there were things she should be saying, words that would bring comfort as well as making sense of everything, but she couldn't think of any. Martin's sister was dead. Perhaps some essence of her still existed somewhere but probably not. She wondered what Dora had looked like, whether she had been beautiful.

Even if she had not been, the living could seldom if ever compete with the dead.

"I'm glad you're here," Martin repeated. "It was so nice of you to come."

Nice is nice, Miranda thought. *But it's not enough.*

They ate lunch in a fish and chip shop across from the Stade. The informal atmosphere of the restaurant together with the fact that they had a defined reason for being there seemed to put Martin at ease and Miranda felt herself begin to relax. The talk from the other tables washed over her in a careless cacophony. On the pavement outside three youths stood laughing and joshing. A wide-bottomed girl in velvet track pants pressed her pink-clad buttocks against the glass.

Her hair fell straight to her waist, the colour of brass.

She's like a mermaid, Miranda thought. *A selkie. A fish out of water.* She thought the girl beautiful, but had the feeling Jenny Lomax would not have agreed with her. As Martin rose to pay the bill, Miranda saw someone approach the girl, a child, she thought at first, then realised she was mistaken. It was a man with dwarfism, a man in a pinstripe blazer and a silk cravat. He had a tiny white dog on a leash, a chihuahua, she thought. The sight of the small man with the even smaller dog made Miranda smile.

He patted the girl on the arm, pointing at something beyond Miranda's field of vision. The girl laughed so loudly that Miranda could hear her through the window. She turned to look for Martin, but he had disappeared. Miranda guessed he must be in the toilet.

By the time he returned to the table the man was gone.

"Shall we go?" Martin said. "It's getting on for three now. Are you OK?"

"I'm fine," Miranda said. "I had no idea how late it was, that's all."

She took her bag and got to her feet. As they stepped out on to the pavement she glanced both ways along the street, hoping she would see the man in the blazer again, but there was no sign of him. She wanted to tell Martin what she had seen, but at the same time felt wary of doing so. The description he had given of the man in the photograph, the dwarf who had frightened his sister, seemed to match the man she had seen in the street just five minutes before. It was impossible that they were one and the same; all the laws of logic were against it. The Circus Man was thirty years ago, and this was now.

He was more likely to be a figment of her imagination. She laughed inwardly, thinking that this was what people always said when they saw something they couldn't explain. This was the first time she had put the theory to the test.

I don't know myself at all, she thought. *Or at least not as well as I thought I did.* The idea of herself as an unknown quantity delighted her. She wondered if Dora had been wrong, if the little man in the natty jacket was a good omen, after all.

She reached out and took Martin's hand. It felt right that she should do this, something that only an hour before she would have found impossible. It seemed to her that the whole world had changed. It was just that Martin didn't know that yet.

She felt his fingers tighten around her own.

"Are we ready, then?" he said.

"I think so," she said, and smiled. She thought he was probably talking about their appointment with Juliet Caseby, but from the look on his face he could have meant something else entirely.

The houses north of the Stade were old. Regency, she thought, and some Tudor, a marked contrast with the tottering Victorian terraces that made up the bulk of the town. Narrow cobbled lanes ran off at angles from the main streets, and Miranda caught glimpses of sunny walled gardens filled with lilacs and orange nasturtiums. There was an atmosphere of quiet seclusion, almost of secrecy, as if the beach amusements and the esplanade were just a bright facade for the real town to hide behind.

"I don't remember all this," Miranda said. "I'm not sure my dad even knew it was here."

"I think a lot of people that come here leave without seeing the Old Town," said Martin. "My Aunt Violet used to bring us up here sometimes. There was a second-hand bookshop Dora loved, and a hotel, higher up, where we used to have tea."

"I expect it feels strange, being back here."

"I never thought I would come back," Martin said. "I'm glad I did, though."

He turned towards her, and for a second Miranda thought he was going to kiss her, just as he almost had that time in his office. But at the last moment he seemed to draw back. *He feels guilty*, she thought. *It's because of his sister*. She wondered how it felt, to be so close to someone they had power over what you did even after they were dead.

She did not love her father that way. She had never really felt his presence once he was gone.

Silcox Square was a Georgian terrace, a short run of white-painted houses that could only be reached on foot via one of the twittens. Opposite was a small patch of grass, edged with beach pebbles and seeming to belong to all of the houses simultaneously.

Number 24 had red flowery curtains in the downstairs windows.

"Here we are," said Martin, and pushed the bell. The door opened almost immediately. Suddenly Juliet Caseby was there in front of them.

"Mr Newland?" she said. "How lovely to meet you."

"It's good to meet you, too," Martin said. "This is my friend Miranda. Miranda Coles."

"That's a beautiful name, Miranda," said Juliet. "Were your parents as keen on Shakespeare as mine were?"

"*The Tempest* was my mother's favourite play," Miranda said. "She even directed it once, at university. That's how she met my father. He was doing the lighting."

She could feel herself blushing. She could not remember ever having given so much information about herself to a stranger before. Juliet Caseby's hair was iron grey, clipped close to her head in a style Miranda thought was called an Eton crop. Her back was straight as a metre rule. Her hands, bare of rings and covered with liver spots, were the only sign that age was starting to catch up with her.

She is Shakespeare's Juliet, Miranda thought. *She's how Juliet would be after Romeo has a midlife crisis and runs off to America with a girl of twenty-four on the back of his motorbike.*

Juliet Caseby winked at her and smiled. *It's as if she senses my thoughts*, Miranda wondered. *It's as if we already know each other.*

"Do come in," Juliet said. "I've been looking out some of Gran's things, but I don't know how much use they'll be. I hope you aren't going to feel you've had a wasted journey."

The interior of the house was deep and narrow, a warren of interlinked rooms, reminding Miranda of the alleys and twittens of the Old Town itself. There was a scent of wax polish, a glass bowl of cut chrysanthemums on the hallway table.

"You know, it's funny," Juliet Caseby said. "Ever since Mr Newland wrote to me I've been finding out things about Gran that I never knew."

She led them through to the back, a living room adjoining the kitchen. A tea tray with a cosied teapot stood waiting on a low wicker stool.

"Is this where she lived?" Martin said. "Your grandmother, I mean?"

"It was my great-aunt's house actually, Gran's sister Joanna. Gran moved in here to look after her when she got ill. That was why she had to give up housekeeping for Mr Andrews. She ended up marrying Joanna's doctor. That's often the way though, isn't it?"

There was a photograph on the mantelpiece, a black-and-white snapshot of two teenage girls. One of them was beautiful. Not beautiful in the ordinary way like Jen Lomax. Even with her long nose and crooked mouth this young woman had the kind of looks that inspire poetry or start wars. The other girl wore glasses and a careful smile, and in her straight back and narrow jawline Miranda could easily recognise Juliet Caseby. Her friend, she realised, must be Zoë Clifford.

Between them stood the Circus Man. He was wearing flared trousers with braces, and a pinstriped blazer, and there was a holiday air about him. Perhaps it was the pier in the background, the white horses on the incoming waves. A dog-eared poster advertised boat rides along the coast to Folkestone and Margate.

In the photo the Circus Man looked middle aged, fifty perhaps, fifty-five. It was the same man she had seen outside the restaurant. He appeared not to have aged by a single day.

Owen Andrews was born in a small village a few miles north of Exeter, in Devon. His mother was a teacher, his father a building contractor. From a young age, he showed an aptitude for science and mathematics, and in 1946, at the age of just sixteen, he was awarded a scholarship to study at Oxford. He won several of the major college prizes for mathematics, but left the university before completing his degree. There were rumours that a group of students had mounted a bullying campaign against him, but Angela Norman, Juliet's grandmother, said Andrews had fallen out with one of his tutors.

"What about?" asked Martin. The Caseby woman fascinated him. Partly it was because she had a look of Dora about her, but mostly it was her effect upon Miranda, the way Juliet seemed to have brought her out of her shell. He knew it was not just Juliet. Being away from the office had played its part, as had revisiting a place that resonated with childhood memories. But Juliet Caseby had helped, no doubt about it.

She was dry as a bone, hollowed out, a foreshadowing of what Dora might have become had she lived to grow old. The name Juliet ought not to have suited her, and yet somehow it did. Martin had a sudden and powerful image of her riding pillion on a motorbike, her thin arms hooked possessively about the waist of its rider.

"I'm not sure what it was about," she said. "But from the account Gran wrote in her diary I don't think it was personal. It seems to have been a genuine disagreement about mathematics. I think that's rather wonderful, don't you?"

"I suppose so. How did Owen Andrews end up in Hastings?"

"Once again, I'm not really sure. I think someone left him some property or something. He lived in one of those large houses up on the Ridge and was pretty much alone in the world. I think he hired Gran for company as much as anything. She was devoted to him, I do know that. She won a place at Oxford herself, you know, but all her plans were ruined because of the war. The work she did for Owen Andrews wasn't just housework. You'll think this fanciful, but Mr Andrews was a brilliant scientist. My grandmother helped him with his experiments."

"You said in your letter that Owen Andrews was a watchmaker."

"And so he was, and a very skilled one, but it was really time itself that interested him. Gran never said as much, but I think she had an idea of turning her diary into a book, some sort of official account of the work he was doing. I hadn't looked at it in years, not ever really, not properly. But after you made contact with me I've been reading it again. There's a lot of maths in it, things I can't make head nor tail of, but the descriptions of their day-to-day lives are fascinating. Look," she said. "There's something I want to show you."

She rose from her chair, staggering slightly in a way that suggested she was suffering from arthritis. Martin watched her as she moved towards the sideboard. He found her story captivating, and yet it was difficult to equate the mathematical genius Juliet's grandmother spoke of with the man on the beach he remembered from when he was a child.

It occurred to him that Juliet's grandmother might still have been alive when he and Dora last stayed with Aunty Violet, that she would not have been much older than Juliet was now.

He wondered if Juliet's grandmother and Owen Andrews had ever been lovers.

Juliet was talking to Miranda, something about Louis Breguet and the tourbillon regulator. He had seen a Breguet watch in the small museum attached to the Greenwich Observatory, three rooms packed with watches and chronometers, a mausoleum of time. The Breguet timepiece, he remembered, contained a mechanism that was said to defy gravity.

"Breguet's mind became confused at the end," Juliet was saying. "He left a stack of notebooks, stuffed with calculations that were supposed to overturn all the contemporary theories about how time worked. They were so obscure that not even his son could understand them, and he had worked as his father's amanuensis for most of his life. When the notebooks were finally published they caused a furore. Owen Andrews was trying to make sense of them, and Gran was helping."

Juliet handed something to Miranda, a picture in a cardboard frame. She studied it for a couple of seconds and then passed it to Martin.

It was a photograph of a woman. She looked a little like Juliet Caseby, only not as thin. She was wearing spectacles, and her dark hair had been cut short, framing her face in a mass of curls.

She had Juliet Caseby's firm jaw and dark eyebrows, the same features that had reminded him of Dora. The woman in the photograph did not remind him of Dora, though. It was Dora herself.

He felt his skin turn to ice, a sudden explosion of cold that was like being burned, or having someone douse his chest with a bucket of ice water. His heart jumped in a stuttering dance beneath his ribs. The room and the women receded, spiralling away from him through twisting corridors of corroded time. Perhaps they would be lost forever. He did not care.

"Where did you get this?" he said. His voice emerged as a breathless croak. Juliet Caseby seemed not to notice.

"That's my grandmother, Angela," she said. "It was taken in 1950, just after she came to Hastings to be near Great-Aunt Joanna."

"But it can't be," Martin said, before he could stop himself. Logic told him that it could not in fact be Dora in the photograph, but the likeness was so strong it was uncanny. He had heard it said that everyone had a double, somewhere in the world. He had thought the notion fanciful. Now he knew better.

"Are you all right, Martin?" said Miranda. "You don't look well."

His ears were ringing. He remembered feeling like this before once, when he was a boy, when he tripped over a metal stanchion on the beach and tore his leg open. There was a lot of blood, but Dora said it looked worse than it was.

Get back in the sea, she said. *You need to wash the wound in salt water. It will heal quicker that way.*

He had done as she said. The seawater burned like fire, like he'd been stung by a jellyfish. He hardly dared glance at his leg, though Dora had peered at the cut with interest.

It's wrinkled at the edges, like pink lace.

The wound had healed quickly though, just as Dora had said it would.

"I feel a bit faint," Martin said. "Perhaps it's the fish we had at lunchtime."

"I'll make a fresh pot of tea," said Juliet. "Tea is always the best medicine for indigestion." She stooped to pick up the tray and retired to the kitchen.

"What's wrong?" Miranda whispered. She rested a hand

on his arm. He was glad to feel it there, as he had been glad when she held his hand on the esplanade earlier. Wisps of concern seemed to spiral out from her, like steam.

"The woman in the photo looks just like my sister," he said. "I know that sounds ridiculous, but it's true."

He stared down at his hands, waiting for Miranda to express her disbelief. He found he did not care much what she said. Just saying the words aloud made him feel less insane. At first she said nothing, and Martin wondered if his lunacy had shocked her into silence. For the first time he noticed how many clocks there were in the room, a dozen at least. Their massed ticking sounded like the tapping of many hammers on tiny nails.

It's a time capsule, he thought. *What an eerie place.*

"I think we should go back to the hotel," Miranda said finally. "We can't really talk about this here."

"You don't think I'm mad, then?"

"I don't think you're mad at all. But I know you're upset."

When Juliet Caseby returned with the tea Miranda said they were sorry but they had to be going.

"Martin really isn't feeling well," she said. "But we'll come back and see you again tomorrow if that's OK."

Juliet Caseby nodded, looking anxious. Martin felt bemused by the turn things had taken, the way Miranda seemed to be taking charge. He would never have guessed she had that in her. He realised he had barely known her until now.

* * *

"There's something strange going on here," Miranda said. "I saw that little man. The watchmaker. The man who was in the photograph with Zoë Clifford."

All the time Juliet Caseby was talking Miranda had been feeling increasingly disorientated. Their surroundings were real enough, but there were other things, things that didn't add up. When Martin told her what he had seen in the photograph it was almost a relief. Either both of them were imagining things, or it confirmed her suspicion that they had stumbled into a mystery. This knowledge should have scared her. Instead it seemed to fill her with new insights.

"The Circus Man, you mean?" Martin said. "Are you sure?"

She nodded. "It was while we were in the restaurant. You were paying the bill. I felt sure it was him straight away. Then I saw the picture on Juliet's mantelpiece and I was certain."

"But how can that be? That would make him over eighty years old. More like ninety."

"I know. But he wasn't. He looked the same as he did in the photograph. Should we try to find him, do you think?"

"I honestly don't know. What would we say?" He sat down on the edge of the bed. "I thought this whole thing was just me, you know? That I was seeing what I wanted to see. Do you think the old witch knows what's going on?"

Miranda giggled. "Juliet, you mean? She's not a witch."

"No, but she's strange, and that house is strange. What was she talking to you about?"

"Her grandmother's diary, mostly. Apparently Angela was going to write a book about Owen Andrews, about the time experiments he was doing. Juliet said she was thinking about carrying on the project herself, now that we'd got her interested. I told her she should."

"You liked her, didn't you?"

"Yes, I did. She seemed more real than most people. She wasn't trying to pretend about anything. She said what she thought."

"Does that mean you think I'm pretending?"

"No, of course not." She went to sit beside him on the bed. His face was stricken, clouded with tension. She wanted badly to ease it, if she could. She wanted to tell him that whatever he was feeling it was all right, that it was better to feel even things that seemed crazy than nothing at all. "You miss your sister, that's part of it. That must really hurt."

"You don't understand," said Martin. "What it was like between us. That's something I can never tell you because it was wrong. We led a secret life. Secrets are exciting at first because they make you feel special. But in the end they keep you from knowing what is real. You can't measure your life against other people's, because you can't reveal yourself to anyone. You have each other of course and perhaps while you're both in the world you can make that enough. But if the other person leaves you're left with nothing. You can't even grieve the way you want to. You wouldn't want people to think you were overdoing it."

He pressed a hand to his face, as if he were trying to hold back his emotions with physical force. Miranda remembered the time she had gone out to the garden to call her father inside for supper and found him crying down by the railway line. He was wedged in behind the old wooden summer house that Nimmie had thought would act as a buffer against the sound of the trains. In winter it was damp and full of snails but in summer the boards roasted and cracked and smelled wonderfully of creosote and dry grass. You could take a blanket in there, and a book, and every twenty minutes a train would dash past like a windstorm. The spindly rafters wobbled like strips of Meccano.

Her father's jeans were filthy with mud.

What's wrong, Dad? she said.

Oh God, he said. *Oh God, Miranda, I've made such a mess of my life.* He grabbed her around the waist and pressed his head against her stomach, his tears soaking into her shirt.

Come inside, Dad. Have something to eat. You'll feel better.

Less than three months later he was dead. Miranda felt she should have tried harder to get through to him, though her mother insisted it wouldn't have made any difference.

Do you think I didn't try? Nimmie said to her after the funeral. Her voice rang out like a hammer blow, like a mallet on steel. *I wasted half a lifetime trying. But your father was always so damned selfish.*

"Do you mean that you loved Dora?" Miranda said to Martin.

Martin took his hands away from his face and stared back at her. His eyes were glazed with tears. She could see now he was not just upset; he was also afraid.

"Yes," he said. "Of course I did. We loved each other. Only – far more than we should have done."

Miranda sat very still. She knew what Martin was trying to tell her, that there had been some kind of sexual relationship between himself and his sister. She felt shocked, she realised, but her distress was more for Martin than for herself. Dora was dead now, after all. Whatever had happened between them was at an end.

It was difficult in any case, she realised, to know how much of her shock was real and how much was programmed, an outrage she felt because the world she happened to live in expected it of her. No doubt she would have felt some of the same confusion and disbelief if she had grown up being told it was wrong to kiss another person in public or go outside without your shoes on.

Martin and Dora hadn't hurt anyone. Now Dora was dead and Martin was asking if Miranda would, if she could, accept what had happened. If there was any hope for them beyond this point.

She leaned forward and kissed him on the mouth. For a moment his lips remained taut and unresponsive. Then he was kissing her back. His saliva tasted faintly salty from the fish and chips they had eaten earlier. His face was so close, so present suddenly. She could feel his fingers pressing the back of her head.

The thought of intimate contact with Edmund Wiley had always sickened her. It was not just the fear that he would find her flat chest and bony body unattractive. What she feared was the penetration of her body by another, the idea that she might not be able to stand such dreadful proximity, that she might make some awful faux pas. Now she found that sex was easy. Those parts of male flesh that had aroused such concern in her turned out to be just more body parts, prosaic in their reality as so many human arms and mouths and armpits. She wondered if Martin had been with anyone else since Dora had died. She found the thought exciting, and the flash of guilt she felt on realising that excited her further.

She strained upwards and against him, a stream of bright dots dancing across the backs of her eyelids. She recognised the feeling for what it was, the start of the queasy unspooling of pleasure that for her was like a slow and gliding fall down a long flight of stairs. Martin was already spent, slumped across her like a heap of damp rags. She stroked his hair, marvelling at the way what had just happened had granted her access to him. She could touch him anywhere now, and that would be normal. She adjusted her position so she could breathe more easily.

"Are you all right?" he said at last. "I know you'll think I planned this, but I really didn't."

"I don't think that," she said. "But I'm glad it's happened."

Her own voice sounded strange in her ears, the way it had done when Stephen had once secretly recorded it and played it back to her on their father's ancient reel-to-reel tape machine. She realised she was hungry again, but before she could mention this to Martin she had drifted over the border into sleep. She was woken by him asking her if it was true that she had once been kidnapped.

"It was something Jenny Lomax said, that's all. I'm sure it's nonsense."

She opened her eyes. Bars of shadow and light criss-crossed the room and she realised it was getting on towards evening. It made her uncomfortable to think of Martin discussing her with Jenny Lomax, but she knew what Jen was like, how she had tried to draw her into conversation about Dora. No doubt she had cornered Martin in a similar fashion.

"It's true in a way," she said. "Only it wasn't a real kidnapping. Not like Jen thinks, anyway."

"I didn't ask her about it, in case you're wondering. I would never do that."

"I know you wouldn't. In any case, it doesn't matter now." She turned on her side, facing towards him. "When I was eight years old my mother and father separated for a while. It didn't last long. They were back together within three months. But Dad was very upset. He went a bit mad, I think. One day he drove up to the house while I was playing in the front garden and told me to get in the car. I did as he said, of course – it was just my dad. He drove to the Isle of Sheppey, where a friend of his had a caravan he used for fishing holidays. We had a great time. We collected razor shells and spotted gannets and roasted potatoes over an open fire. Dad kept saying my brother Stephen would be joining us and I thought everything was getting back to normal. I didn't realise Dad had taken me without permission, that my mother had no idea where I was. She was out of her mind with worry and in the end she called the police. I don't suppose she thought she had much choice. She didn't press charges though, not once I was back at home. She told the police it had all been a silly misunderstanding and six weeks later Dad came back to live with us. Perhaps he shouldn't have."

She was crying, she realised, not in the self-conscious, nose-blowing way she occasionally did at films, but in a way that tightened her chest and produced too few tears. Stephen would never talk about their father. Perhaps this was why.

"My father killed himself," she said. "When I was sixteen. I missed a whole term at school because of it, because of Mum, because of everything, really. My teachers said I could start the year again from the beginning, but it didn't seem worth it by then. Too much had gone wrong."

She had never spoken of these things before, not to anyone and certainly not to Edmund Wiley. In telling Martin she had the sense of redressing the balance. He had entrusted her with the secret of himself and Dora. Now she had shared with him the reasons why, until then, her life had been a broken thing, a half-life. It was as if in some curious way they were now even.

She wondered what would happen when they returned to London, whether everything would simply revert to the way it was before. She did not see how it could. She would not let it.

"I'd like to get some fresh air," Martin said. "Before it gets dark, I mean. I thought I'd walk up and have a look at my aunt's old place. Would you like to come with me?"

Miranda shook her head. "You're going to look for him, aren't you? The Circus Man?"

Martin gave no reply and she felt no need of one. She knew she was right, that it was something he had to do. It was the only way he could finally say goodbye to Dora.

"I think I'll stay here," she said. "I've had enough walking. I'll read for a bit instead."

"I'll stay with you if you want me to."

"You go." She smiled. "I'll be fine."

She watched him put on his shirt, his chinos, a v-neck sweater. The casual clothes suited him, she realised, much better than the suits he wore for the office. They gave her a glimpse of Martin as he must have been once, before his life assumed its current pattern.

No pattern is fixed forever, she thought. *There's still time to change.*

She thought that if only he came back, then everything would be all right. *Where else would he go?* she wondered, and began to laugh.

Martin smiled back at her, and she had no doubt that he thought she was laughing from happiness. But in fact she was laughing from terror, the way she used to do at four years old, when her father made her go on the high slide instead of the baby one.

She had done it to please him, of course. On each shiny, swooping descent Ronnie Coles clapped his hands like a mad thing, and she, Miranda, his daughter, had laughed aloud.

Violet's house was at the top of the town. Martin had forgotten how steep Hastings was; also that there were parts of it that stood apart from the rest, lesions of nettle and bramble that overspilled the tightly mapped streets like blots of green ink. The sea lay far below him, colourless, scents of wallflowers and summer bonfires wafted from narrow back gardens. Vast clumps of tangled bindweed garlanded the hedges. As a young child, Dora used to call the convolvulus flowers wedding dresses.

For fairies to wear, she said. *They're so lovely and white.*

Now they shone out of the dusk, pale as ghosts.

He could not get over what had just happened. Miranda's body, light as paper, the flaxen pallor of her underarms and pubis. The way she had strained to meet him at the end, the smell of her transparent as brine.

He felt drained of everything save his awareness of the present moment.

Their mother had not approved of Aunty Violet. She was their father's sister for one thing, her house a muddle of turpentine-soaked rags and dirty dishes. But she took care of Martin and Dora for two weeks each August and Martin supposed that must have balanced the account. The house that had once been Violet's now sported shutters on the downstairs windows and a fresh coat of paint. A ceramic plaque to the right of the door read 'Cressida.' Martin passed in front of the house then turned at the end of the road and began to walk back again. He had no wish to draw attention to himself, and yet he found he could not bear to leave. His memories had been altered just by coming here. He would never again see the place in his mind the way it was before.

It was as if a door to the past had opened and Dora was about to step through it and away from him. It was his last chance to be with her. His eyes filled with tears.

Don't go, he whispered.

I was never here, Martin, she said. *I've been gone for years.*

He started backwards, convinced suddenly that he was being watched, and a second later a light came on in one of his aunt's upstairs windows. It was time to leave. He made his way back down the hill. He went by the quickest route possible, making use of short cuts and twittens he had forgotten existed but that his feet now seemed to find of their own accord. The smoky scent of dusk persisted and deepened, and as he crossed the main road to the Stade and began walking across the shingle between the net shops he had a fleeting image of Dora, jumping from one of the breakwaters and falling headlong on the stones.

Had it been she who cut her leg that time, or he? He found he could not remember any more.

The tide was a long way out, he could tell by the sound. There was someone standing by one of the slip-ramps, a child, he thought at first, or a very old man. As Martin watched the figure turned and began to walk towards him. The shingle scrunched under his feet. A gust of salt-streaked wind blew in off the sea.

It was the Circus Man. He was dressed in a dark-green hooded fleece that reached almost to his knees. He had a little dog with him, a white chihuahua. It galloped across the pebbles like a plump toy pony.

He looks like Father Time, Martin thought. *The only thing that's missing is the scythe in his hand.* He shivered in the breeze, and remembered Dora, grumpy with fright, saying she had lost all the feeling in her feet and hands. *He's just an ordinary person, like you and me*, Martin had insisted. He had taken off her beach shoes and rubbed her feet, and after a couple of minutes she said she could feel the sensation coming back.

"It's a fine evening," the Circus Man said. He had a noble head, Martin saw, handsome features: the dark eyes under heavy brows, the full lips of an aesthete or poet. The dog, mad for the dusk, rolled at his feet.

She did love you, I can see that, Martin thought, thinking of Angela Norman who was also Dora. The idea should have upset him but it did not. He could see now how fitting it was: Juliet Caseby's grandmother with her brilliant mind, this remarkable man who had somehow learned to stop the clock, or turn it back. Martin was not sure which and found he did not care much either way.

Dora and Owen Andrews belonged together.

He felt terrified but also free. He had watched sky divers on television, mad fools who hurled themselves out of aeroplanes. He wondered if this might be how it felt to do a parachute jump, spinning towards Earth at a thousand miles an hour and praying you would remember to pull the ripcord before you hit the ground.

He laughed.

"It is indeed, a fine evening," he said. "I ought to be getting back, though. My wife will be wondering where I've got to."

"It's good to see you, Martin. It's been a long time."

"I don't know you," Martin said. "Everyone I knew here is dead."

"The last time I saw you we were at Paddington Station. You went to buy us both coffee and I almost missed my train."

"I'm sorry," Martin said. "You've mistaken me for someone else."

"Your sister was ill for years before she told you about it. I gave her my watch, though it didn't help, not in the end. She was living on borrowed time."

"I don't know what you're talking about."

"I used to enjoy our talks, Martin. You were always so insistent that time streams could not run parallel to each other without leaking through, that on some level our alternate selves would carry an awareness of each other. *A trace-awareness*, you used to call it. A seepage between universes. I insisted you were wrong, that your theories stemmed from the excess of sentiment typical of the non-scientist. Now I'm beginning to think you might have had something."

Martin was silent. He listened to the sound of the waves, fractionally closer now, and thought about the concourse of Paddington Station. He had been there many times, though not recently. There was a restaurant there he liked, a French bistro that served baked camembert and steak au poivre. He wondered if it was still there.

The white chihuahua came racing out of the darkness and flung itself into his arms. It yelped with excitement and tried to lick his face. Its smooth coat was slightly damp, and smelled of the sea.

"I miss her very much," said Owen Andrews. "Sometimes I find it hard to live without her."

"Dora?" said Martin.

"No," said Owen Andrews. "I mean Angela."

Martin handed over the wriggling dog. It nestled itself in the crook of the little man's arm.

"I really must be going," he said. "It was nice talking to you."

"Take care of yourself," said Owen Andrews. "See you again."

Martin walked back up the beach towards the esplanade,

the shingle shifting heavily beneath his feet. The lights along the promenade shone brightly, and when he looked back once over his shoulder there was nothing but darkness.

They had to check out of the hotel by ten o'clock, but they decided to take one more tour of the Old Town before returning to London. They had coffee in one of the cafés and looked at the sea. Martin said he had forgotten how much he enjoyed the salt air, that they should take another, longer holiday as soon as possible, perhaps in France.

The night before they had made love again, and at some point during the small hours Martin had asked Miranda if she would move in with him.

"Don't you think it's too soon?" she said. "Don't you think we should wait?"

"We've known one another twelve years," Martin said. "I think we've waited long enough already."

She knew what her mother would say, that you should never make important decisions on the spur of the moment, but it occurred to Miranda that all the most important decisions were made on the spur of the moment, that the time apparently spent deciding was simply the time you needed to inform other people of what you intended.

After their coffee they went round the shops. There was a second-hand bookshop that Martin was anxious to find again. He wanted to see if they had any books on antique watches. The interior of the shop was cramped, and Miranda didn't feel like going inside. She browsed the curio shops instead, of which there were many. One had a window display of old pocket watches, and she suddenly thought how nice it would be to buy one, as a surprise for Martin.

The watch she liked best was silver, its dial intricately engraved with a pattern of roses. She examined it for several minutes through the window, then went into the shop and asked if she could have a proper look at it.

"Most certainly you can, my love," said the shop's proprietor. "But just to warn you I don't think that one actually works."

He took a key from beneath the counter and unlocked the casement. The watch felt heavy in her hand, and right, and she knew she must have it. While the shop owner scrabbled around in the back closet looking for a box to put it in, Miranda raised the watch's crown and gave it a twist.

She saw the second hand begin to move. It was a centre seconds, finely honed and tapering, like a needle. Her fingertips, pressed tight to the glass, felt a faint pulse, as if a tiny mechanical heart were beating away.

For a moment time seemed to hesitate, the minutest of gasps, a silently indrawn breath as if at the sight of something wonderful. Then, all by itself, the world started turning again.

timelines: an
afterword

It is five past three in the morning. When Binny opens her eyes the first thing she sees is the black-and-gold Westclox alarm clock that stands on her bedside table. She loves the clock for the sound it makes, its tinny rattling, wheezy as an old man's breathing. She loves its round convex glass with the gilt frame surrounding it, also its face, which lights up in the dark, that samphire-green, marsh-fire glow. She has always seen the clock's ability to illuminate itself as a minor miracle. She cannot understand why it does not arouse a similar excitement in other people.

"How does it do that?" she asks.

"It's luminous," her mother says, in the same tone of voice she might use to say 'its face is black' or 'it is made of metal.' Binny knows the word luminous already. She wants to know how it happens, not what it is called.

She had set the alarm for three-fifteen so she could be sure of waking up in time for the holiday but she never oversleeps, she has woken up anyway. She cancels the alarm, turning the clock with its back to face her and sliding across the small brass lever in its crescent-shaped opening. She pulls herself into her clothes and then puts on her wristwatch. It is a Timex Girl's Wristwatch, with a round white dial and a black leather strap. At night she keeps it on her bedside table, still in its original case, a leatherette box with a hinged lid and a hump of blue velvet inside to keep the watch from sliding around. The watch was given to her as a birthday present by her grandmother, the first grown-up gift she has been given.

She presses the watch against her ear to check that it is still ticking. The watch's mechanism fascinates her. She pictures the cogs and wheels turning inside, like the moving parts inside the Westclox alarm clock only smaller. Sometimes she likes to imagine that the watch has a secret inhabitant, a tiny driver, smoky-voiced and grubby-cheeked, like the engine-stoker she saw once in a television documentary about old steam trains. She thinks of him tapping the pins securing the mainspring with a neat gold hammer, checking the flow of seconds on his time-gauge, shaking his head.

We have an early start this morning. It won't do to take any chances.

She sees no reason why her miniature engineer should not exist. She has been introduced to the world of the microscope through her science lessons. She knows there are plenty of lifeforms that are invisible to the human eye.

She goes out into the hall. The door of her parents' bedroom is open and as she stands there in the orange glow of the overhead ceiling light her mother emerges.

"Have you washed?" Her mother speaks in a whisper because her brother is still asleep, a cramped insistent bundle of bright blond hair and blue pyjamas. Nothing short of a bomb going off would persuade him to wake at this hour. She resents the way her mother never makes Charlie get up until the last minute.

Binny nods. The nod is a lie, but one she knows she will get away with, at least today. From inside her parents' bedroom she can hear the voice of her father talking on the telephone.

"It's up there now, just look out the window. Don't tell me you can't see it?"

There is a short silence then he laughs and says something about a light in the sky. Binny doesn't understand what he's talking about. She asks him about it later, when they're all up and dressed and in the car.

"What was it?" she says.

"A *you-foe*," says her father. "Unidentified Flying Object. A flying saucer." The engine coughs once and then starts.

She doesn't believe him. He has never been very good at telling stories. She wonders who he was calling at three in the morning, too early to be telephoning anyone except in an emergency. Her father made the *you-foe* sound like an emergency, but she senses it was just an excuse to make the call.

She thinks about this for a while then lets it go. It is interesting but not important. The important thing is that they are going to France, that in a little over three hours they will be on the ferry. Outside it is dark and silent, a fugitive world of curtained windows and grey front gardens. The main road is eerily empty, a polished black band of tarmac, and soon they are on the dual carriageway heading for Newhaven. Her eyes catch at the road signs: *Give Way* and

To the Ferry and *Exit Ahead*. In the dawn light they read like messages meant especially for her, some private code for freedom or escape. She has begun to learn that words are magical tools, that she can use them not only to describe the world but also to bring things into it. The little watch engineer is like this – one moment he is just a thought, a squirming at the back of her brain like a maggot inside an apple, but the more she thinks of words to describe him the more he becomes alive. She clothes him with words, laying on his oil-stained boiler suit and scruffy black cap as she used to lay the flat cut-outs of dresses and jackets on the paper dolls in the girls' fashion books she had once enjoyed but was now outgrowing. She knows he will always exist now, whether anyone can see him or not.

Her brother is still mostly asleep. She lays her forehead against the window glass, staring out at the goods lorries, the cat's eyes, the low humped buildings of the ferry terminal. The inside of the car smells of tarmac and new morning and its own worn leather upholstery.

Her grandmother kept the watch in a pillowcase behind the wardrobe as a precaution against burglars. It was a silver half-hunter, and had belonged to her father, Binny's great-grandfather Raymond. It was the only thing of Raymond's Granny had left.

"It doesn't work," said her grandmother. "I took it to the clock man once. He had a shop down by Goring Station. He told me it wasn't valuable enough to be worth mending and that I would be wasting my money. The shop's gone now, it got turned into a butcher's, I think. I haven't been up there for years."

The watch was about two inches across, and contained in a round silver case. The silver tarnished easily. When Binny first saw it, it was the same dull brown as the beach pebbles her grandmother used to decorate her garden.

"Can I clean it?" asked Binny. She was eight years old.

"Are you sure it'll be worth the trouble? You'll get black stuff all over your hands."

When Binny insisted her grandmother gave her an apron to protect her clothing then sat her at the kitchen table with a tin of Silvo metal polish. She showed Binny how to apply the polish by smearing it in a thin layer over the surface of the watch case and then removing it by rubbing with a cotton rag.

"Let it rest for a minute first," she said. "Give it a bit of time to get to work."

Binny read the side of the tin and learned that the Silvo worked by dissolving the metallic salts that formed when the silver came into contact with the air. She was captivated by the process, by the newspaper spread out on the table, by the pungent smell of the Silvo, which Granny said contained a substance called ammonia. Once she acquired the knack of it she found she enjoyed cleaning not only the silver half-hunter but her grandmother's silver butter dish and biscuit barrel, as well as the brass candlesticks and ashtrays that had come from her grandmother's childhood home in Croydon. The brass was an unkind metal, and even the most dedicated scrubbing produced only the faintest of lustres. But Binny found the work soothing in its repetitiveness. She was happy to sit at it for hours, while the kitchen radio played quiz programmes and her grandmother chopped the vegetables for supper.

Granny was still young and cheerful, but her hands were dry and wrinkled from lack of care. In warmer weather her veins stood out like worm casts. She had a gold dress watch, which had come down to her from her mother, Ada. Unlike the silver half-hunter it worked perfectly. It had a delicate soft low tick, so sweet in tone it was almost like music, and a gold bracelet that expanded to fit the wrist.

There were a lot of clocks in her grandmother's house: an electric alarm clock in Granny's bedroom, a battery-powered wall clock in the kitchen, a mahogany bracket clock that was kept on top of the sideboard in the dining room. There was also the cuckoo clock in the living room, brought back by Binny's grandparents from a holiday in the Black Forest. It had heavy brass weights shaped like pine cones, and was wound by pulling down on a chain, rather like the chain of a high-cistern lavatory. The cuckoo clock worked, but as it grew older it became less reliable, and if the weights were tugged in a certain way the plastic cuckoo could be forced to appear. It was forbidden to tamper with the clock, but this only made it more of a temptation. Binny's personal record was fourteen consecutive cuckoos, although Charlie once memorably made it run to twenty-six.

Binny's parents split up when she was fourteen. Two years later they got divorced. The family home was sold, and

Binny's mother used her share of the money to buy a small terraced cottage in a village at the foot of the Sussex Downs. There was a delay in the exchange of contracts, and Binny and her mother and Charlie were temporarily left with nowhere to live. It was decided that the best thing would be for them all to move in with her grandmother.

They stayed there six weeks, a period of time that looked short when it was written down on paper but while it was being lived through seemed to encompass a significant and difficult period of Binny's life. Her brother was bored and sullen away from his friends, and her mother and grandmother squabbled constantly, mostly about Binny's father, whom they both seemed determined to hate but in differing ways.

Her grandmother's house was not used to so much activity and an unreasonable number of things seemed to get broken: a blue-and-white Chinese rice bowl, the back window of her grandmother's Ford Anglia, the television plug socket immediately below the cuckoo clock. There was a splintering crunch as the brass weight plummeted down on to it from above. Binny stared at the splinters of white plastic on the olive-green carpet, barely overcoming the urge to laugh.

"Plug flew up to the cuckoo weight," quipped Charlie, riffing on the title of a film they had seen recently about the inhabitants of a mental asylum.

"It's downright carelessness," Granny said. She was furious. "You can see how he takes after his father."

Binny bit her lip. Before that summer she had never even known her grandmother to raise her voice. The accident with the plug socket had been just as much her fault as her brother's, but it was her brother who got the blame for it, as he seemed to get the blame for all the other petty things that kept going wrong. Binny knew her grandmother favoured her and for this she often felt guilty but secretly glad. It was not that she resented her brother, it was simply that she felt a need for love and sympathy that was sometimes so intense she felt cold to the bone.

She escaped into books. It was the summer of *Wuthering Heights* and *Roadside Picnic* and *Jude the Obscure*.

One afternoon, when her mother had driven her brother into Worthing to buy some new trainers, Binny's grandmother suggested they go for a walk along the beach.

"There's something I want to tell you," she said.

Binny smiled in a way she hoped would inspire confidence. She was tense with excitement inside, wondering what was about to be revealed to her. She considered the possibilities, her imagination fuelled by scenes from her favourite books: her mother was a murderess, her grandfather was not dead but in prison, she had been left a fortune by some almost-forgotten aunt. But for a long time her grandmother walked along without saying anything, her face turned into the wind, her thin grey hair fluttering about her face like streamers of lint. Binny walked silently beside her. She looked out over the shingle, the tamarisk, the ridged pinkish concrete of the promenade, the sea that was never blue but that sometimes at the height of summer was a shimmering translucent green, the colour of jade. She felt an ache inside her, as if something was beginning or ending but she did not know what.

"I was adopted," said her grandmother at last. "I've never told anyone apart from your granddad, not even your mother."

Binny felt disappointed. It didn't seem like much of a secret. She knew other people who had been adopted and none of them made a big thing of it. Her friend Naomi had lived in a council care home until she was three.

"That must have been strange," she said.

"I don't expect you to understand," said her grandmother. "Everything is different now, I know that. But when I was a child people judged these things much more harshly and being born outside of marriage was a reason for shame. Some people were very cruel. It's made me feel like a second-class citizen the whole of my life."

"I think that's terrible," said Binny, and she meant it. She felt an upsurge of righteous indignation on behalf of her grandmother, and a stirring of kinship that had nothing to do with their blood relationship but with the growing sense that in their own way they were both outsiders.

"None of that matters now," Granny said. "I had your granddad, and my two daughters, and then you. That was all the family I needed. But I wanted to tell you because I think it might be important, not for me any more but for you. I never knew my real parents, but when I was the same age you are now Ada and Raymond gave me a photograph of a woman they said was my mother. She had been a domestic servant at one of the London clubs. They said they didn't have any pictures of my father, but that he had been a journalist of some kind and had written for the *Evening Standard* and the *Manchester Guardian*. They told me his name, but I've forgotten it. I think at the time I wanted to forget it, I wanted to forget everything that reminded me of where I had really come from. I know now that I was stupid. Ada and Raymond hoped I would be clever, you see, they hoped I might take after my father. I turned out to be very ordinary, but there must have been something in what they said, because whatever gift my father had has been passed on to you. I feel certain of it every time I look at you. I wanted you to know this. I wanted you to know that you were born to write."

"But you are clever, Gran." It was the first thing Binny could think of to say, and she could see almost at once there was truth in it. Much as she loved her, she had always felt scornful of her grandmother's taste in historical romances, her carefully formed, schoolgirl's handwriting, her hesitations over where to put an apostrophe. But when it came to telling stories Granny had always been a natural. She had an instinct for it, like the grandmothers in the Russian folk tales, like the mediaeval bards. She had always encouraged Binny to make up stories of her own.

Binny remembered the odd little tale she had invented about the people who lived inside watches, the microscopic engineers who kept time flowing smoothly and who were able to decide if it went forward or back. Her grandmother had loved this story. She was always embellishing it, adding new details. It was a game they had continued for years.

"Gran, do you remember Nicky?" Binny asked suddenly.

"Nicky the little watch boy? Of course I do."

Binny had imagined Nicky as a bit of a tearaway. As a teenager he had caused a lot of trouble by letting clocks run down and creating time anomalies, but as he grew older his rebellious instincts began to be channelled elsewhere. He became obsessed with the silver half-hunter, which he was convinced was really a time machine. He had been in the process of trying to mend it but then Binny had stopped playing the game. Now she began to wonder how it would have come out.

She supposed she had been a little in love with Nicky, that a part of her still wanted to believe in him. It excited her now to think that the impulse to create him had not been just chance, but a part of her, something she had inherited, like her small feet and upturned nose and blonde hair.

She wondered what her great-grandfather had looked like, what kind of man he had been. She thought she might give anything to read the articles he had written, to know which books had been his favourites. It struck her that when he had been writing Thomas Hardy would have still been alive.

"Thank you for telling me about my great-granddad," she said to her grandmother. "I think it's an amazing story." She felt proud that her grandmother had trusted her. She wanted to say that she hoped she might one day do something that would make her worthy of the gift she had been given, but she thought it might sound big-headed. She took her grandmother's hand instead, twisting her rings about her bony fingers the way she used to when she was small.

They turned and walked back to the house. Three days later the contracts were exchanged on the cottage. Binny's mother organised the packing, her dark mood transformed overnight into a bright stream of energy. They seemed to have more luggage than they had arrived with and they could barely get it all in the car. Binny sat on the back seat, jammed in between a rolled-up duvet and a box full of wellington boots. She waved through the window to her grandmother, thinking of Jude turning his back on the village of Marygreen and heading for Christminster.

"I found it in one of those junk shops down by the market," Kit said. "It was in a cardboard box with a load of old cutlery. I thought it might be your kind of thing."

The watch was an inch-and-a-half across with a cream-coloured dial. Its maker's name was Smith. It was missing its strap.

"Let's go and get a strap for it now," Kit said. "I'd like to see you wearing it."

"It's gone six already," said Binny. "Most of the shops will be closed."

They hunted around the Lanes for a while, trying to find a jeweller's that was still open but without success.

"It doesn't matter," said Binny. "I'll buy a strap for it tomorrow, in town. I really love old watches. How did you know?"

"I knew you would like it, because I do," said Kit. "We like the same things." He laughed then pulled her towards him and kissed her hair.

"I should go," he said. "But I'll see you soon."

She caught the train with just a minute to spare. She found a window seat and sat down with her legs curled under her and her cheek resting against the glass. She had a book with her, a collection of stories by Carson McCullers, but she felt too tired and too distracted to read. She held the watch tightly in the palm of her hand. Its mechanical pulse was faint yet steady, like an echo of Kit's own heartbeat, and for this reason it comforted her. The watch made her feel safe, somehow. She was afraid to move in case she broke its spell.

, It was almost midnight by the time she got home. As she made her way across the station car park she witnessed an altercation between an elderly man in an ugly red rain slicker and a taxi driver who had just run over his bicycle.

"You can't leave bikes there," the cabbie was saying. "Didn't you see the sign?"

"I leave my bike there every night of the week," the man replied. "You should have been watching where you were going." His voice was high and querulous, the voice of a grumpy granddad in a radio sitcom. Binny hurried away, feeling sick with irritation and pity. The surface of the world felt brittle as ice.

It was October, and in a couple of days the clocks would go back. Binny hated the long dark evenings in the run-up to Christmas. She thought of them as dead days, the old year sloughing its skin. Although it was often colder she found the first weeks of January infinitely preferable.

Her bed sheets were clammy and cold. She turned to face the wall, bunching her limbs together to try and get warm. She was still holding the watch. She had known as soon as Kit gave it to her that she would write about it. The sight of the watch brought back memories, ideas and images that had lain dormant in her since her grandmother had died.

She had missed Granny's funeral because it coincided with a reading she was giving in Kentish Town. The reading had been a big deal at the time, but looking back it seemed like nothing, a dozen or so people gathered in a poky room in the basement of a café to hear a story she now considered derivative and clumsy. She had not looked at the story since for fear that it might be even worse than she remembered. She often wished she had cancelled the reading and gone to the funeral instead. She had tried to get these feelings down on paper but each time she read the work back it seemed shallow and fey.

"You're confusing the facts with the truth," Kit had said to her. "The facts are nothing but a bunch of components, springs and gears and linchpins, stuff like that. The writer's job is to construct something from them, a beautiful machine, a story that is the sum of those facts but also greater than them. When the machine begins to run by itself – that's when you'll know you've managed to tell the truth."

Her mother had told her she should stop seeing Kit because he had been homeless for a while and had three children all by different women. But Binny felt that to see these things as negative was just another way of confusing the facts with the truth. The truth contained these things, as it also contained his greatness as a writer and the soft greyish light in his eyes each time they met.

She missed him when they were apart but she had learned to accept this, to see his physical absence as a flimsy and inconsequential barrier that could easily be traversed by the act of writing.

The story about the watch had begun to take shape in her mind almost at once. Now, as she drifted closer to sleep, she found herself thinking not about Kit, but about Nick, the story's protagonist. She knew already that he was a postgraduate student of Physics at Imperial College, that he had almost drowned as a child, that he had very fair hair and blue eyes. At the start of the story he was walking back to his flat in Clerkenwell with his girlfriend, Sallie. She could hear their voices as they talked together, muffled, like voices heard through a wall.

The watch had belonged to Nick's grandfather. It was a Smith watch, not one of the rarer models, just one of the many thousands that the London firm had manufactured for the army in the years leading up to World War Two. Recently it had begun to lose time. It wasn't much, just half a minute or so each day and nothing that might not be fixed by an experienced repairman but for some reason Nick was reluctant to have the watch interfered with. The watch, like the old man who had owned it, simply wanted to slow down a little.

For some reason this infuriated Sallie.

"It's ridiculous," she said. "A theoretical physicist who doesn't even know what time of day it is."

Nick loved Sallie's rages, and saw them as a subset of her enthusiasms. Everything she expressed she expressed with conviction and forthrightness. Nick envied her a little, although occasionally he wished she would express her opinions a little less loudly.

"Look at this," he said. "This used to be a watchmaker's studio." He pointed to a warped wooden signboard hanging outside what was now an upmarket tapas bar. The shabby industrial sprawl north of Farringdon Station had become a fashionable neighbourhood, glittering with steel and glass and the brash displays of wealth that inevitably characterised the financial districts of the city. But in the narrow closes and disused yards, the cobbled backstreets and converted warehouse buildings, he had never had any difficulty in glimpsing the old Clerkenwell, the watchmakers' quarter as it used to be, where entire streets were once occupied by engine turners and fusée cutters, finishers and escapement makers and pinchbeck welders, the outworkers and parts engineers who had once constituted the lifeblood of the time trade.

The watches these men made were still running. The truth was, thought Nick, that excellence was always an anachronism, yet somehow it always survives.

Sallie glanced at the sign then tugged at his arm.

"Hurry up," she said. "I've got a surprise for you."

They had been out all evening, starting with a glass of champagne at the bar at St Pancras Station and then moving on to a bistro-cum-jazz club that Sallie had recently become keen on, celebrating Nick's appointment as a junior research fellow at Princeton University. Nick had applied for the post on the off chance. Sallie had been ecstatic when he landed it. She had always wanted to live in America.

When they got back to the flat Sallie dashed away into the bedroom and came back holding a small leather-covered box. Inside was a watch, a stainless steel chronograph with numerous complications and his initials and the date engraved on the back.

"Now you can finally get rid of that useless old thing of your granddad's," she said.

Nick felt regret well up inside him, as if something was beginning or ending, only he wasn't sure which. He thought the new watch was quite possibly the most beautiful thing he had ever seen, but the thought of having to part with his grandfather's watch made him feel very sad. He could not think why Sallie felt so hostile towards it, unless it was simply that it had been in his life for longer than she had. He had never heard of anyone being jealous of a watch before, although he supposed it might be possible. He knew Sallie often felt insecure.

They went to bed and made love. The next morning he put his grandfather's watch inside an old spectacles case and slipped it into the drawer of the kitchen table, where it lay hidden beneath a litter of safety pins, old takeaway menus and broken pens. He hoped that Sallie would not notice it there, and as the days went by and he got used to wearing his new watch he gradually forgot about it.

The weeks that followed were mostly taken up with packing and preparing for the move. For practical reasons they had decided to get rid of all the furniture in the flat. Most of it they donated to friends, but none of them had room for the kitchen table. Sallie called a house clearance firm and told them they could have it for free if they would take it away.

It is in Princeton that Nick will make the discovery that will change his life. It is only on the plane over that he realises what has happened to his grandfather's watch. He thinks of it, miles below him somewhere, beginning the next chapter of its story and no longer any part of his. For a moment he feels like crying. Then he takes Sallie's hand and begins stroking her fingers. He knows Sallie is nervous of flying, though she would never admit it, least of all to him.

out-takes

DARKROOM

They crossed at the traffic lights, and on Wimbledon Hill Road there were tall trees and fewer people. After ten minutes' walking they reached the Common. There was a fine drizzle. The ground was soft underfoot and here and there were the muddy runnels left by car tyres. People were walking their dogs or pushing toddlers in buggies. Two pensioners were flying a kite. Lenny stood with Malcolm at the edge of the round pond. The surface was flat as a mirror, its colour the soft grey of clouds. At the margins of the water long grasses with flaxen seed heads quivered lightly in the breeze.

"There's a car in the middle of the round pond," said Malcolm. "Some kids shoved it in there one night about five years ago. It was a green Austin Allegro. The council never got round to fishing it out." He had his hands in his pockets, his shoulders slightly hunched against the breeze. There was a chill in the air and she wondered if he was cold. He was so thin, after all. He was probably more susceptible than most.

"Imagine what that would be like," he said. "If you lived in the pond, I mean."

Lenny laughed.

"It would be like a spaceship falling to Earth. Imagine how it would be written about and spoken of and stripped of its wonders."

"Shall we go and get a coffee?" she said.

Malcolm asked for a latte. When it came he folded his hands around the cup as if to warm them and Lenny wondered about the scabs on his knuckles. He looked bruised all over somehow, as if he'd fallen down in the gutter. Perhaps he had. She knew nothing about Malcolm except what Ted had told her. That he had once been a brilliant student. That somehow he had gone off the rails.

"Why did you drop out of college?" she said suddenly. She wondered if it was all right to ask those sorts of questions or if talking about the past was liable to upset him. Ted had never said.

"I prefer London to Oxford," he said. "You can do what you like here and nobody notices." He took a sip of his coffee and it seemed to put the life back into him. He looked directly at her and drew a deep breath. "I wanted to write a book about Sylvester John," he said. "But my tutor thought I was wasting my time and refused to give me a reference."

She knew there was more to it than that. Ted had told her that Malcolm had gone missing for two days then turned up at the house filthy and incoherent. It turned out he had walked all the way from Oxford to London even though there was plenty of money in his account and he could easily have taken the train. He'd been in bed for six weeks afterwards with pneumonia.

Lenny had never heard of Sylvester John.

"Do you think you'll go back?" she said.

"No," he said. "I ended up hating the place."

They wandered back up the High Street. Malcolm looked about himself constantly, like a tourist in a foreign country. Almost without thinking Lenny put her hand on his arm. She was afraid he might take fright at something and bolt like a startled horse.

Wimbledon Village specialised in the kind of pretty shops you might find in the more affluent market towns of Surrey and Hampshire. She found herself oddly delighted by the items on display, the soft fabrics and polished ornaments, the jade earrings, the hand-blown glass. In one of the windows there was an arrangement of commemorative mugs, not just the gaudy recent issues but hand-painted originals dating from before Queen Victoria. Quite suddenly she found herself wanting to go into the shop and buy something. It seemed to her that the mugs were more than just household utensils, they were coloured fragments of history you could hold in your hand. She knew she wanted to remember this day, standing there with Malcolm in front of that window, yet if someone had asked her why she would have found it hard to put into words. She hesitated then drew back, knowing how much Ted hated mass-produced pottery. It would be difficult to explain why she had bought it.

Her face was reflected next to Malcolm's in the window.

To anyone wandering past they would look like lovers. Malcolm pressed his fingers against the glass. He stared at the objects intently, as if he were trying to memorise them in a specific order.

He looked like he'd been travelling for days.

When they got back to the house she made supper. She served him a half-portion in a small dish, hoping that might make it easier for him to finish it. When he began to eat she felt a rush of pleasure she hadn't anticipated. Later they went upstairs. His body was skinny and pale under his T-shirt. He had long fair eyelashes, the longest she'd ever seen on a man. His eyes were pale turquoise, reminding her of the clear faceted stone in a Victorian tiepin that had once belonged to her grandfather.

He seemed so fragile she felt nervous of touching him. He entered her easily but came too soon.

"Oh God," he said. "I'm so sorry." He buried his face in her shoulder and stroked her cheek. She raised his hand to her lips, mouthing gently at the tender grazed flesh.

"It doesn't matter," she said. "Let's just lie here and talk."

He sighed then kissed her mouth. They lay in silence for a while just holding each other then he opened his eyes and told her what he knew of Sylvester John. He said it had been reading John's stories that had made him want to be a writer himself. Later they made love again and it was successful for both of them. She groaned at the moment of climax and bit his cheek. He gasped heavily and came, digging his fingers deep into the flesh of her shoulders. The bruises were still there after his death, two rows of penny-sized blotches the colour of mould. At around ten o'clock the phone rang. It was Ted. He was calling from the M5 services just south of Bristol.

"I should make it back by midnight," he said. "But don't bother waiting up."

Three weeks after the funeral Lenny landed a new commission. She took a studio at the top of a house in Kensal Rise, a large attic room with a galley kitchen at one end and a shower room and toilet at the other. The day after she moved in Ted phoned and asked her to come back.

He sounded angry but was probably just upset. They'd been together for almost five years. She'd known Malcolm for less than three weeks. She hadn't told Ted what had happened between them. She didn't see what good it would do.

"It wouldn't work," she said. "You'll see that in time."

He swore at her and put the phone down. A minute later he rang back to apologise.

"That's all right," she said. "I understand." They talked about trivial matters, trying to smooth things over. Near the end of their conversation he asked if they could meet for a drink.

"Let's do that," she said. "That would be nice."

Later she put on her jacket and took a bus down to Ladbroke Grove. She browsed the tatty parade of shops just south of the Westway, admiring their eclectic range of imported merchandise. One shop sold fabric by the yard: cheap ginghams, oilcloth, Indian cotton, outlandish fifties florals. She sifted through the remainder bin, selecting a yard of pink silk, some gold netting, a scrap of grey velvet.

The next shop along was a junk shop that specialised in second-hand airport paperbacks and the unwanted leftovers from local house clearances. On the table outside there was a stack of 7" singles and a shoebox full of old photographs. One showed a boy on a beach. Wispy strands of hair clung wetly to the nape of his neck and something in the tilt of his head, the stark angularity of his shoulder blades reminded her immediately of Malcolm. She bought the photograph for fifty pence and then walked home. Buses swept by on the Harrow Road, loading the summer twilight with the reek of diesel. She laid her bag against her chest and held it close.

The couple who had commissioned the doll's house were called Bentall. They were both freelance translators and lived in a narrow mews cottage close to Blackheath Park. Natasha Bentall opened the door. She was slim and quite young, still in her early forties. She had pale skin and smooth dark hair. She took Lenny through into the living room. There were several antique clocks and a large marine aquarium. When Frank Bentall joined them Lenny realised belatedly that the Bentalls were brother and sister. She blushed without knowing why.

They gave her tea in a china mug and showed her a photograph of their godchild.

"We want the doll's house to be something truly special," said Frank Bentall. "Something she can treasure all her life."

They said the design should be left completely up to her. Lenny thanked them and closed her notebook. She wondered what might be the best way to bring up the subject of money but here again the Bentalls made it easy for her. They had a cheque already written out for half the amount. Lenny's pulse quickened when she saw it. It would cover the rent on the flat for the next four months.

Malcolm had first come across Sylvester John's work when he was twelve, in a book of short stories he'd borrowed from the local library. He was drawn to the book because the cover blurb described it as a collection of ghost stories. John's language was descriptive yet uncomplicated, easy for a child to understand. Malcolm liked the stories so much he asked his parents to give him a copy of the book for Christmas. He read it again and again, wondering if he too might be able to write such stories, though it was some years before he dared to try. He wrote his first weird tale when he was sixteen. He decided to set it in Brighton, because he had been there once on holiday and loved it. There had been a puppet show on the pier, a man who walked on stilts, the lilting, grinding lament of the hurdy-gurdy. The memory of the town was simultaneously gratifying and painful. It seemed as good a place to write about as any.

In the hours following Malcolm's death Lenny had gone to his room and removed all his Sylvester John books from beside his bed. She had also taken the file of notes that contained photocopies of the few reviews of John's work Malcolm had managed to unearth as well as colour snapshots of John's birthplace and details of his biography.

Sylvester John had been born in Ludlow, the only son

of an army captain and a Sunday school teacher. He had died at Kensal Green, less than a mile from where Lenny was now living. He had published three novels, as well as the apocryphal diary called *Darkroom Journal* and numerous short stories in magazines she had never heard of, such as *London Gothic* and *Capital Bizarre.*

For the last twenty years of his life he had lived at the house in Kensal Green, a modest Victorian villa in one of the long terraces close to the station. It would have been a poor neighbourhood then, although in recent years the area had undergone radical gentrification. The ground floor of the house was home to a private medical consultancy. The two upper floors, where John had lived, still appeared to be a separate address.

Lenny photographed the house from all angles, then made enlarged drawings from the photographs, accentuating the most prominent architectural details. Finally she transferred the drawings to graph paper, reducing the templates to scale, one foot to the inch.

Ted was a potter. He made tall baluster jugs and loosely thrown wide rimmed bowls. His pieces had clean outlines and no decoration. He had a deep respect for traditional Japanese pottery, a love of the tenmoku and celadon glazes that fired to a liquid shine. For Ted the beauty of a thing was very much tied up with its usefulness.

He had never said as much to Lenny but she had always known he found her work frivolous. He had once asked her why she didn't retrain as an architect.

She had tried to explain to him that she had no wish to design real buildings, that what she wanted was to realise dreams.

For his birthday one year she had organised a trip to Amsterdam. She had taken him to the Rijksmuseum to see the famous doll's house of Petronella Oortman, a seventeenth-century merchant's wife who had spent as much money fulfilling her fantasy as it would have cost her to buy a second home. Ted seemed briefly diverted but quickly bored. He seemed relieved when they were back outside again, and set quickly to planning a walk along the canals.

There were many ways of building a doll's house. As well as the more traditional designs, there were houses with interlocking chambers and secret doors. The furnishings in such houses were kept to a minimum so as not to obstruct the hidden mechanisms that brought them to life. Lenny had once seen a doll's house with no furniture whatsoever, an Oriental piece of unknown provenance that had been part of an exhibition at the V&A. The China House, as it was called, was normally kept locked behind glass, but Lenny had applied for a study permit, allowing her to examine it in the presence of a museum attendant. It was hardly a house at all, more a series of interconnected spaces that might loosely have been described as rooms. The number of chambers that could be accessed seemed to depend on the order in which they were viewed. When she tried to open a 'locked' room the whole mechanism jammed, and she was forced to close all the compartments and start again.

She purchased a folder of slide transparencies of the China House, also the museum's booklet on Chinese puzzle boxes. The booklet stated that boxes by the most renowned makers were highly desirable, and often sold for inflated prices. The specialist collectors displayed their acquisitions proudly, even though there were some boxes that resisted all attempts to open them.

Lenny decided to model the room layout for the Bentalls' doll's house on John's descriptions of Martin Newland's house in *Darkroom Journal*. She began by making a stencil for the living room wallpaper, drawing the pattern freehand and then transferring it to graph paper, exactly as she had done with the plans for the house itself. It was a pattern of fleurs-de-lys, parchment yellow against an off-white background. She traced the finished design onto lining paper and completed it in watercolour.

The next time Ted rang she agreed to meet him for a drink at The Mason's Arms. Ted was already there when she arrived.

He told her he'd started seeing someone.

"Her name's Ruth Dawson," he said. "She works at Lycett's. I thought you should know."

Lycett's was the artists' suppliers where he bought the raw oxides and pigments he used in his glazes. She had a vague memory of Ruth Dawson as tall and rangy, a pleasant open face scattered with freckles.

She felt an upsurge of relief, as if she'd been released from some onerous task.

"I'm pleased for you, Teddy," she said. They talked politely for a while about other things. As soon as she'd finished her drink Lenny got up to leave.

"I've been reading that book Mal was writing about," she said as she was going. "Did you ever have a look at it?"

"Horror stories, weren't they?" Ted said. "Not really my thing."

Lenny walked home, making a detour that took her straight past Sylvester John's house on Ashburnham Road. The ground floor lay in darkness but lights were burning in the upstairs windows. There was a smell of wood smoke and honeysuckle. She imagined John returning home in the evening from one of his walks in Kensal Green Cemetery or from visiting the shabby shops he frequented on the borders of Maida Vale: the stationer's that stocked the notebooks he liked, blue feint with a marbled grey cover, the tiny basement store that sold antique maps and glass paperweights.

She wondered if John had shared the flat with anyone, a friend perhaps, or a lover. Malcolm's notes hadn't said.

The *Evening Standard*'s review of *Darkroom Journal* had described Sylvester John as 'the English Lovecraft'. Lenny had tried reading one of H. P. Lovecraft's stories but could see no connection between his ornate archaic prose and John's language, which tended to be plain and simple, leaving nothing concealed.

She noticed also that whereas Lovecraft's characters were often highly educated eccentrics, John wrote about the kind of people you might easily meet and chat to in the street. The narrator of *Darkroom Journal*, Martin Newland, was a sales rep for a greetings card company. His adversary, Harold Phelps, was a pest-control officer for Westminster City Council.

The novel didn't have chapter headings, just a series of

dated entries such as you might find in an ordinary diary. For the first two-dozen pages or so, the events of *Darkroom Journal* seemed unremarkable. Martin Newland described his home, his neighbours, his various excursions to the firm's clients in Liverpool and Manchester in exhaustive detail. As one of the business's chief representatives, Newland earned good money and had developed a taste for expensive antiques. John revealed only gradually that Newland was able to travel between dimensions, and what he actually dealt in was fiends, or petty devils: semi-aquatic woodlouse-like creatures that swarmed and bred in the cellars of Ladbroke Grove.

Lenny was particularly impressed by John's knowledge and love of beautiful objects. When it came to furnishing the Bentalls' doll's house, his descriptions of Newland's collectables were invaluable.

Her friend Lucy came for supper and Lenny was eager to show her how the project was going. Lucy was most impressed by the doll's house furniture. She particularly admired the long case clock Lenny had made, which looked like an antique timepiece but was actually battery-powered. The case was made from rosewood, which Lenny had waxed and stripped repeatedly until it began to acquire the patina of age. The design of the marquetry had been taken straight from *Darkroom Journal* and featured the rare Sicilian Ladder Orchid, a flower so seldom seen it was thought extinct.

"The detail is incredible," said Lucy. "I don't know how you find the patience."

Lucy designed bathroom tiles. What she really wanted to talk about was Ted. "He seemed such a nice guy," she said. "I thought you were one of the lucky ones."

"I dreamed of owning something like this," said Natasha Bentall. "I think it's every child's dream really." She was looking at the photographs of the work in progress Lenny had brought to show her, and telling her how she had once badgered her parents into taking her to see Queen Mary's doll's house at Windsor Castle.

"It frightened me actually," she said. "It made me feel sick. Everything about it was so perfect it made the world outside seem spoiled."

She showed Lenny some pictures of her godchild.

"Deborah is very precious to me," she said. "She's the closest I'll ever come to a child of my own."

The girl looked about four years old. She had straight mousy hair cut in a pageboy and extraordinary, bright green eyes.

"She's the daughter of Frank's best friend from university," she said. She apologised to Lenny for her brother's absence, and said he was running errands up in town. "To be honest, that's why I asked you to come," she said. "I get so nervous when he's out of the house."

"Nervous of what?" Lenny asked.

"That something might happen to him. I know it's stupid but I can't help it."

Lenny stayed with her until Frank Bentall phoned to say

he was on his way home, and then caught the train back up to town. Instead of going straight home she crossed the Harrow Road and went into Kensal Green Cemetery. The grounds were so extensive that once away from the main gates it was easy to get lost. The central avenues were kept neat and well-weeded but the minor pathways were overgrown, banked heavily on either side with foxgloves and stinging nettles.

Lenny followed one of the paths for almost a mile. The sounds of people and traffic seemed far away. 'If the grey skies and rain-dashed cloisters of Brompton are a foretaste of purgatory, and the ivied avenues of Highgate are where the scholars and poets commune with the spirits of their ancestors, then Kensal Green is the interface between realities,' Sylvester John had written in *Darkroom Journal*. 'It is where the living bid the dead farewell and the dead return to share their news with the living. It is the bus terminal of the dead, a place of common memory and, above all, gossip.'

Malcolm's funeral had been at Lambeth Crematorium. His father, William Foster, had been quick to make it family only and so there had been just the five of them: William and Deirdre Foster, herself and Ted, William's sister Margaret who had driven over from Petworth. The Fosters had compassionate leave but were due to return to Hong Kong the next day.

Lenny didn't know what had happened to Malcolm's ashes. She couldn't bear to think that the Fosters had taken them back to Hong Kong with them, so she didn't think of it. She hoped they had been scattered at Lambeth, just a mile or two away across the river.

Malcolm's notes didn't say how Sylvester John died. He had been sixty-five years old and apparently healthy. Malcolm had told her that John had volunteered for the army in 1939 but had been turned down for active service on account of his short-sightedness. He had worked for the War Office instead, though his service record had subsequently been lost.

After the war John had stayed on in London, working for the MoD and renting rooms from a Major Neville Manley, who owned several substantial houses in Maida Vale. In the January of 1952, Sylvester John had fainted in the street close to St John's Wood Station. He was diagnosed as suffering from strain due to overwork. He was kept under observation for ten days at St Mary's Hospital, Paddington, then spent the following four months in a convalescent home. He resigned from the MoD and soon afterwards the first of his short stories, 'The Mansion House', was published in *Capital Bizarre*.

The police had brought the news at around midday. Ted began to tremble all over. By the time he ushered the two constables inside his teeth were chattering.

"Why didn't he watch where he was going?" he said. "I bet he walked straight out into the road."

Lenny had gone with him to identify the body but waited outside in the car. Her lips felt so numb that every time she spoke she sounded drunk.

Ted lay awake into the small hours, talking. He told Lenny about how he had once come home from a party to find Malcolm in the kitchen covered in blood.

"I thought it was paint at first," he said. "There was glass all over the floor and in the sink but Mal said it was just an accident. I got him down to A&E and he seemed all right after that, although he wouldn't go near the kitchen for several days. When I asked him what had happened he said he thought he'd seen a rat by the waste bin. I poured him a shot of brandy and sent him to bed. It took me ages to clear up the mess. I had a look around for rats but there was nothing, just a couple of dead woodlice." He felt for her hand under the bedclothes. "He was always imagining things, even as a kid," he said. "Always seeing stuff that wasn't there."

She would go to bed around midnight, exhausted, and be wide awake again at two. When this happened five nights in a row she picked up the phone and called Lucy. It was just after three o'clock.

"I'm sorry to wake you," she said. "It's just that I miss him so much."

"What's that?" said Lucy. "Where are you?" She sounded bleary-eyed and confused at first, but soon got back into her stride. She thought Lenny was talking about Ted. She began railing against Ruth Dawson.

"That stupid smile of hers," she said. "As if butter wouldn't melt in her mouth."

"I think she's nice," said Lenny. "I like her."

"You were too good for him, Eleanor," said Lucy. "That's your trouble."

She sounded fully awake now and seemed to be enjoying herself. She told Lenny about her new clients, who were renovating a house in Muswell Hill. "You should see the size of their order," she said. "It'll keep me going till next Christmas, if the cheque doesn't bounce." She chuckled softly and Lenny felt herself begin to relax. After a while Lucy asked if she was all right and Lenny said yes.

"Goodnight then," Lucy said. When Lenny broke the connection, other sounds rushed in but less obtrusively. Traffic passed by on the main road, the engine noise ebbing and flowing with her own breathing.

The four rooms in the central compartment could only be opened in rotation. When one of the rooms was open the others lay flat, folded against one another like theatre scenery. Lenny made the interiors from folded paper, like the pop-up illustrations in the books she had loved as a child. One contained a street market, where barrow boys hawked canaries in bamboo cages. Another was a hothouse garden with carnivorous plants and exotic butterflies. One room was mostly empty, containing nothing but rusty paint tins and old packing cases. This was the room Lenny liked best, and whenever it appeared she would imagine herself sitting on the floor among the tea chests and unpacking them.

The things inside were wrapped in old newspapers: *dustmen's strike, scorching summer, great train robbery.* There was a Doulton tea service, translucent white china scattered with pale pink roses. Ted had always hated factory-made porcelain. He said it was soulless. The window of the room overlooked a beach promenade. There was a white pavilion with gilded turrets and a pier that extended some distance out to sea. When Lenny opened the window she could hear the screams and laughter of children on the carousel, the clamour of the hurdy-gurdy. She longed to go out into the sunshine and look for Malcolm but when she tried the door to the street she found it was locked.

In the end she let herself out by the back door and went straight to Ashburnham Road. The doctor's rooms on the ground floor still lay in darkness but there were lights on upstairs. Lenny rang the bell and waited. After a few moments a light appeared in the hallway and someone opened the door.

The woman was of medium height, with grey hair drawn back from her face in a straggling ponytail. Her slim hand on the latch was covered in age spots. She was wearing a paisley-print housedress that reached to her ankles.

"I'm sorry to bother you," said Lenny. "But did you know a famous writer once lived in your house?"

"It's late," said the woman. Her voice was clear but quiet. Lenny had to strain to catch her words.

"I could come back tomorrow morning if you'd prefer?"

"I don't mean that," said the woman. "I mean it's been more than twenty years since he died and no one's come looking before. I've lived here in this house for forty years."

The hallway was dim and shabby but Sylvester John's rooms upstairs had been kept exactly the way they were when he was alive. Lenny recognised certain things at once from the descriptions of Martin Newland's collectables in *Darkroom Journal*: the antique tea caddy Newland used to store old postcards, the brass prayer bell that had been given to him by a retired army captain who had served in Burma. On a low table close to the door was the Satsuma-ware bowl with the red and gold dragons and next to it the pistol with the engraved barrel and mother-of-pearl handle, the so-called lady's weapon.

Martin Newland had used it to threaten the rat-catcher, Harry Phelps, when Phelps demanded that Newland tell him what was in the cellar.

"I can make tea," said the woman. "Or cocoa if you prefer?"

She disappeared, presumably to the kitchen. As soon as she was out of sight Lenny got up from the sofa and started looking around the room. She hoped she might find a photograph of Sylvester John, something that had thus far eluded her. There were two or three framed snapshots on the mantelpiece. One was of a sandy-haired girl in a blue blouse with the London Eye in the background. Another was of three men in a garden, laughing and drinking champagne, but she couldn't tell if any of them was John.

Beside the photograph stood one of the hand-held projectors that had been popular when she was a child, a white Perspex box that lit up when you pushed a slide in. When she looked through the viewfinder she saw a deserted street flanked by tall terraces. In the foreground a set of steps led to an open front door. The sight of the door filled her with dread. Lenny put the box down quickly, not wanting to see any more of what might be inside.

She crossed to the window and looked out. The room

overlooked the garden. There was a scrubby lawn, a row of dustbins, beyond that the roofs and gardens of Kensal Rise. It was deep dusk and there were lights on in most of the houses. The sky glittered with stars, and the winking lights of jets approaching Heathrow.

The woman served tea in the white porcelain cups with the pink roses. There were biscuits on a plate, yellow langues de chat that were slightly soft in the middle, as if the packet had been left open to the air.

"What was he like?" Lenny asked.

"He was a quiet and gentle man," said the woman. "He always preferred writing to talking. Some people found that difficult to understand."

Lenny finished her tea then asked if she could use the bathroom. The woman directed her into the hallway. The first door she tried opened into a large closet. There was a vacuum cleaner, some coats on hooks, a pile of old newspapers. She was about to shut the door when a faint glimmer of brightness caught her eye. She stepped towards it, pushing aside the coats. At the back of the closet was another door. A pale yellow light was shining from beneath the crack.

A flight of steps led downwards, the bare wood darkened with age and smooth from use. There was a light switch and a single bulb, ancient wallpaper stippled with faded roses.

Lenny leaned over, trying to see what lay at the bottom of the stairs. After about a dozen steps there was a small landing and then a corner turn, making it impossible for her to see all the way down. She moved forward hesitantly, descending as far as the half-landing. From there the steps went down into darkness, but from somewhere far away she could hear the distant sound of children's laughter, the melancholy strain of the hurdy-gurdy.

"Mal?" she called softly, hoping the woman in the next room wouldn't hear.

She stood very still and listened, but the sounds had gone. There was just the faint susurrus of air rising, warm and faintly foetid, from deep underground.

She fought her way free of the coats and closed the door. The one beside it led to the bathroom, a pleasant space with dove-grey tiles and a tall vase of wild flowers on the windowsill. The window, like the one in the living room, overlooked the garden.

The saleswoman wrapped the mug in a double page of the *Evening Standard*. Her hands were large and pink, smooth-skinned and perfectly formed, like the hands of a doll. She asked Lenny if she was old enough to remember Princess Anne's wedding and Lenny said no, but that she'd recognised the picture immediately. It was the same as the one on the first day cover. Her brother was a keen collector of commemorative stamps.

"Her dress was so lovely, I thought," said the saleswoman. "It had a high neck and long sleeves, and those hundreds of tiny pearls. She looked like a real queen in it. Dignified, you know. Not like that other one."

On her way back to Wimbledon tube a storm broke – heavy thunder right overhead and then a cloudburst. Lenny sheltered with five others in the doorway of a newsagent's, watching the rain cut steel diagonals in the steaming air. The downpour ended as suddenly as it had begun. Patches of blue appeared between the clouds. The sun glanced off the wet kerbstones and slid down through the cracks in the pavement.

When she arrived back at the house she went downstairs and continued with her unpacking. She began with the Royal Doulton tea set she and Malcolm had bought in Brighton. They had gone there because Mal had had an idea for a story about a Punch and Judy man. He'd spent a long time in the pier amusement arcade, watching the teenagers playing the fruit machines, the copper cascades of small change. Lenny had sat on a bench in the sun and listened to the laughter and screams of children on the fairground rides, the sweetly lamenting music of the hurdy-gurdy.

Though it was some years ago now, she remembered the day perfectly. The pink-and-white china was grubby with newsprint but it would come up beautifully once it was washed. She usually took Mal his tea at around four o'clock. Sometimes he was so deeply engrossed in his work he didn't even look up when she put the cup down, but when she came back to collect it later it was always empty.

TEN DAYS

Ten days, ten hours, ten minutes. A man is murdered and a woman is charged. The hangman winds his watch and then goes home. I don't suppose you remember that old Cher lyric, the one about turning back time, you're too young. My best friend from law school, Frieda Solomon, used to play that track at the end of every party she ever threw, when we were solidly pissed and everyone was dancing, even those of us who never danced, when discussion had dissolved into barracking and all the ugly home truths began to come out.

The song is about someone who's said something stupid and wishes she hadn't. Hardly a crime, when you think of the appalling things people do to one another every day and can't take back. What are mere words, you might ask, in the face of deeds? I'm not so sure, myself. What if the person Cher is singing to happens to be some hot-shot international trader with revenge on his mind? Or a fighter pilot? Or a president with his finger on the button? Who knows what someone like that might do, if you caught them at the wrong moment?

One thoughtless comment and it's World War Three. Who knows?

If I could turn back time, my dear, I wouldn't change a thing.

It takes about two minutes for a time machine to get going, in my experience. Nothing happens for what seems like forever, then just as you're telling yourself you were an idiot to believe, even for ten seconds, that such a thing would be possible, the edges of things – your fingers, your sightlines, your thoughts – begin to blur, to stumble off-kilter, and then you're gone. Or not gone as such, but *there*. Your surroundings appear oddly familiar, because of course they are. The time you have left seems insubstantial suddenly, a peculiar daydream fantasy. Vivid while you were having it but, like most dreams, irretrievable on waking.

There was a man who lived next door to us when we were children whose house was stuffed to the rafters with old radios. The type he liked best were the wooden console models from before the war, but he kept Bakelite sets too, and those tinny little transistors from the nineteen fifties. His main obsession was a hefty wooden box full of burnt-out circuits and coils he claimed had once belonged to a wireless set used by the French Resistance in World War Two. He was forever trying to restore the thing but I think there were pieces missing and so far as I know he never got it working again.

I used to spend hours round at his house, going through the boxes of junk and watching what he was doing. Our mother couldn't stand Gary Tonkes. She would have stopped me having anything to do with him if she could. Looking back on it now I believe she thought there was something peculiar about his interest in me, but there was never anything like that, nothing you could point a finger at, anyway. When I was thirteen, Gary Tonkes was sectioned under the Mental Health Act. His house was infested with rats, and he kept insisting that one of his radios had started picking up signals from Mars. I remember taking pictures of the house afterwards with the Kodak Instamatic Uncle Henry had given me for my tenth birthday, pretending I was working for MI5. I still feel bad about that. I think now that Gary Tonkes's radio might have been picking up not signals from Mars, but the voices of people who had lived in the house before him, or who would live there in the future, after he'd gone.

Time doesn't give a damn about the laws of physics. It does what it wants.

I think of Helen's basement living room in Camden, the ancient Aubusson carpet faded to a dusty monochrome, the books, the burnt-orange scent of chrysanthemums. I sometimes wish I could go back there, just to see it again, but I know I can't. I've had my turn. And stealing more time could be dangerous, not just for me and for Helen but for you as well.

When I was eighteen, I contracted leukaemia. I was very ill for about ten months and then I recovered. Against the odds, the doctors said, and only after the kind of clichéd regime of brutal chemo you read about in the colour supplements. And yes, there were times I wished they'd give up on me and let me die. I suspect – in fact I know – it was my brother Martin who persuaded me to stick around. His white face at my bedside, I can still see it now. His terror that I wasn't going to pull through. I don't think I've mattered like that to anyone, before or since, and that includes Ray. I hung on and hung on, until suddenly there I was, washed up on the shore of life once more and the tide of those months receding like some lurid sick joke.

But there were side effects. I'd been offered a place at Cambridge to read mathematics. Following my illness I found something was missing: the instinctive affinity for numbers I had taken for granted as an inseparable part of me was, if not vanished, then noticeably blunted. It was like thinking through gauze. My professor seemed confident that I was simply exhausted, that any diminution in my ability would soon be restored. Perhaps she was right. I'll never know now, will I? The university offered me the option to defer my entry for a further year, but I refused.

I turned down my place, partly from the terror of failure and partly to match the drama that was playing out inside my head with something concrete that could be measured in the world outside. I was having a breakdown, in other words, and in the aftermath of that I switched to Law. I know it doesn't sound like much, when you put it like that, but the decision hurt a lot at the time. It felt like the worst kind of defeat. I won't say I ever got over the loss, but I learned to live with it, the same as you do with any bereavement. And in time I even came to enjoy my legal studies. There is a beauty in the law, in which the abstraction of numbers is countered by the wily and intricate compromises of philosophy. Call it compensation, if you like. An out-of-court settlement that if not generous has at least proved adequate.

I'm good at my job, I think, and it has provided me with a decent living in return. And whenever I find myself growing maudlin for what might have been, I remind myself that the law has also provided me with what Martin jokingly refers to as Dora's file on the doomed: an interest that began as a tree branch of curiosity and grew into a passion.

If I am known to the public at all, it is for my articles and radio broadcasts on the subject of capital punishment, and the fatal miscarriages of justice that have been associated with this barbaric practice. For many years, the essays I wrote for various history and politics journals formed the limit of my ambition for my researches. It was Martin – of course it was! – who first suggested I should write a book, and the more I thought about the idea the more I liked it.

My first thought was to write a monograph on capital

punishment in general: a philosophical treatise, to be accompanied by a thorough debunking. A literary bollocking, if you like. I soon came to realise how dull such a volume would be, unless you had an interest in the subject to begin with, which would make the whole thing pointless, a sermon to the converted. I came to the conclusion that a more personal approach would work better, an in-depth study of specific cases, of one specific case even. What better way to demonstrate the brutality of state-sanctioned murder than to tell the story of one of its victims? To show that murder is always murder, even when enshrined in law, with the same practical margin for error and moral depravity that murder entails?

My decision to write about Helen Bostall was made quickly and easily. As a story, her case had everything you might look for in a decent thriller. The condemned criminal was also a woman, which made the case a cause célèbre, even at the time. People are fascinated by women who kill in much the same way as they are fascinated by genetic freaks, and with the same mixture of self-righteous indignation and covert repulsion.

For my own part, I became interested in Helen because I admired her writing, and also because from the moment I first encountered what passed for the facts of her case, I found myself convinced she was not guilty. Not that I would have ceased to admire her, necessarily, if she had been a murderer – Edwin Dillon was an arrogant prick, if you ask me – but her innocence made her the perfect candidate for my thesis. I would do her justice, I decided, if not in deed then in word, at the very least.

I've read interviews with biographers in which they wax on about having a special kinship with their subjects, a personal relationship across time that could never have existed in reality. I would once have dismissed such speculation as sentimental codswallop.

Not any more, though.

Helen Bostall was born in 1895, in Addiscombe, Croydon. Her father, Winston Bostall, was a doctor and lay preacher. Her mother, Edith, had worked as a teacher, though she gave up her career entirely after she was married. The two were well-matched, forward-thinking people who gave their only daughter Helen every opportunity to develop her intellectual awareness of the world and her place within it.

I might have been content, Helen wrote in her 1923 pamphlet essay 'On War, on Murder', *content to take up my place among the teachers, preachers, poets and painters I had learned to admire as a very young woman, to speak my protest, but timidly, from inside the very system I was protesting. It was the spectacle of war that made me a radical, that fired in me the conviction that the system I was protesting had to be broken.*

The war, and more specifically the death on the Somme of her cousin, Peter Arnold Bostall, the son of her father's brother Charles. Peter and Helen, both only children and of a similar age, had been close throughout their childhoods. At the outbreak of war in 1914, Peter had just graduated from Oxford and was considering whether to take up a junior fellowship offered to him by his college, or to embark on a research trip to Madagascar with his other uncle, his mother's brother, the entomologist Rupert Paxton.

It is not known whether Peter and Helen had plans to marry, although judging by the letters the two exchanged while Peter was at Oxford it is certainly a possibility. There is no doubt that Helen was devastated by her cousin's death, locking herself away in her room for several weeks afterwards and ultimately falling ill with pneumonia. She emerged from her illness a different person, determined to play her part in creating a more just society, a society in which a death such as her cousin's would not be possible. When the war ended she took up lodgings in Hampstead, close to the house where John Keats once lived, and began taking in private pupils. During the hours she was not teaching, she was studying and writing. She also joined a suffragist group. Her parents, though initially upset by her abrupt departure from the family home and concerned for her health, were tentatively supportive of her aims.

Until she met Edwin Dillon. Then everything changed.

Edwin Dillon was thirty years old, a journalist on the *Manchester Guardian* who had written a number of inflammatory articles on the employment conditions of factory workers in the north of England. He had lost three fingers of his left hand in an unspecified industrial accident, although there was some talk that he had inflicted the injury himself, to avoid conscription.

He came south to London in 1919, quickly establishing links with the community of Russian anarchists and dissident Marxists living there in exile from the Bolshevik revolution. It was likely to have been Dillon's views on free love that set Helen's parents so thoroughly against him, although it could simply have been that they didn't much like him.

Hector Dubois, the proprietor of the Liberty Bookshop in Camden and a former associate of Dillon's, testified in support of Helen Bostall at her trial. He described Edwin Dillon as 'a man you needed to be careful around, a man who held a grudge'. There were also rumours that Dillon's original motive for coming to London had to do with a woman he had made pregnant in Manchester and later abandoned. Attempts to trace this woman ended in failure and so the rumours remained unsubstantiated.

Whatever the reason, Winston and Edith Bostall were determined that their daughter should have nothing more to do with Edwin Dillon. When Helen announced that she was intending to move into Dillon's rooms in Camden, her parents threatened to cut all ties with her. Perhaps they hoped to call her bluff. If so, it was a gamble that backfired. In the February of 1927, Helen gave up her Hampstead lodgings and moved into the basement flat at 112 Milliver Road.

I soon found myself accruing vast amounts of information, not just on Helen Bostall but on her whole family. I can imagine many editors dismissing most of it as irrelevant – who cared about Winston Bostall's run-in with a colleague in 1907 (over the involuntary committal of an unmarried mother to a mental asylum, if you're interested) when the incident had zero connection to the case in hand? But the more I dug into the private lives of the Bostalls and their circle, the more I became convinced they were important. Crime does not arise in a vacuum. A murder is simply the flash point in a gradual accretion of narrative. The various strands that make up that narrative – Winston Bostall's mortal hatred of violence, Edith Bostall's inability to conceive another child, Peter Bostall's ambiguous relationship with his uncle, Rupert Paxton – may all be contributing factors in its final outcome.

And besides that, I was interested. The Bostalls were an unremarkable family, on the face of it, and yet their lives provided a snapshot of an entire era. In the conflicts and setbacks they encountered, it was possible to discern the birth of the modern age and the decline of empire, the fireworks and anxieties that occurred when the two collided. Was it any wonder that a woman like Helen Bostall – educated, resourceful and unwilling to settle for the life that society had preordained for her –ended up finding herself directly in the firing line?

The shadow side of my researches was the strange vacuity surrounding the person of Edwin Dillon. Information about the Bostalls was plentiful, and easy to come by. This was partly because of the crime, of course – call someone a murderer, and suddenly every detail of their life becomes interesting, becomes *evidence* – but that was not the only reason. The Bostalls – Helen herself, but also Winston, Edith, Peter, Rupert, and especially Rupert's wife Marina, who was Russian and embraced the literary arts as her birthright – were all copious, inveterate letter writers and journal keepers. Their histories remained bright, remained present.

Searching for information about Edwin Dillon came to seem like staring into a black hole. I became convinced that if Dillon hadn't been murdered, he would have disappeared from history altogether. I turned up odd pieces of his journalism here and there, but finding images of the man himself was another matter. Aside from the blurry photograph that was so often in the newspapers at the time of Helen's trial, Edwin Dillon might as well have been invisible.

In the end I decided it would be better to set all the background material aside for the moment and concentrate on the timeline of the case itself. It was like working on a proof, in a way – carry one distinct line of enquiry through to its logical conclusion and the rest will follow.

The actual order of events was easy enough to assemble from the trial records. A little before eight o'clock on the evening of the 20th of January 1928, a Mrs Irene Wilbur, a widow who lived in the ground floor apartment of 112 Milliver Road, was disturbed by what she called a 'furious altercation' in the flat below. Concerned by what she heard – "It sounded like they were bashing each others' brains out," was what she said on the witness stand – she left her flat and hurried to the Red Lion public house, approximately a minute's walk away, hoping to enlist the aid of the publican in locating a police constable. When asked why she did not call at Dillon's apartment herself, she insisted she was afraid to. "The noise they were making," she said. "It was as if the devil had got into them."

The publican of the Red Lion, Gerald Honeyshot, confirmed that Irene Wilbur came into the pub soon after eight o'clock. He left with her more or less immediately and they walked together to Camden Town Underground Station, where they were able to secure the services of PC Robert Greystowe, who passed by the station regularly on his beat.

The three then returned to 112 Milliver Road, where on entry into the hallway they found the house silent, and the door leading to Dillon's apartment standing ajar.

I knew straight away there'd been a murder done, Irene Wilbur claimed in her statement. *You could feel it in the air. Something about the silence. It wasn't right.*

At this point, Greystowe gave instructions for Wilbur and Honeyshot to remain upstairs in the hallway while he entered the basement apartment alone. He called out to 'Mr and Mrs Dillon' as he entered, but there was no reply. A short time later he re-emerged, and informed Wilbur and Honeyshot that they would need to report to the police station on Highgate Road immediately, in order to give their witness statements. He did not offer them any further information at this point, but by the end of the evening both Wilbur and Honeyshot knew that Edwin Dillon had been murdered. According to PC Greystowe, he had discovered Dillon within moments of entering the flat. He was in the kitchen. His clothes were soaked with blood, and more blood was spreading in a large puddle across the kitchen tiles.

Edwin Dillon was pronounced dead where he lay. He had been stabbed five times. Two of the wounds were serious enough to have killed him.

* * *

There was no sign, anywhere, of Helen Bostall. An officer was left on duty outside the house, and when Helen eventually returned home at around eleven o'clock, she was taken immediately into police custody. On being asked where she had spent the evening, she said she had been at the house of a friend, Daphne Evans, who lived in Highgate. Daphne quickly confirmed Helen's alibi, but when officers asked if they might search her flat, according to PC Greystowe she seemed to become agitated.

"I suppose you have to come in," she said in the end. She had been about to go to bed. When asked why she was reluctant to let police officers enter her apartment, she said it was because she was in her dressing gown.

The apartment was tidy, with no signs of disturbance, let alone the murder weapon. Two porcelain teacups – according to Daphne Evans they were the same teacups she and Helen had been drinking from earlier that evening – stood drying in the drainer beside the sink. It was only after half an hour's searching that officers discovered the small valise on top of the wardrobe in Evans's bedroom. The valise contained clothes that were later positively identified as belonging to Helen Bostall, together with a forward-dated ticket for the boat train from Victoria and a number of notebooks and letters, either addressed to Helen Bostall or filled with her handwriting.

It was clear that Helen Bostall had been planning her getaway, that she had been keeping her plans hidden from Dillon, that she had not intended for him to accompany her on her journey. When asked why this was, she stated that she had decided to break with Dillon permanently and was determined not to get into an argument with him. "Edwin's temper had become unreliable. I didn't want him to cause a scene."

When the prosecuting counsel pressed her on whether she was, in fact, afraid of Dillon, she hesitated and then said no. "Edwin was domineering, but I was used to that," she said. "He would never have done me physical harm."

When questioned about the row she'd had with Dillon on the evening of his death, Helen Bostall seemed completely bemused. "I barely saw Edwin all day," she said. "I was working in the library for most of the morning, then in the afternoon I saw three of my private pupils, at Milliver Road. I have no idea where Edwin was at that time. He came back to the flat at around six o'clock. He seemed tired and irritable, but no more so than usual. I told him I was going to Daphne's, that I would be back around eleven. Those were the last words I spoke to him. I left the flat soon afterwards." She hesitated. "We really didn't have much to say to each other any more."

The police seemed determined right from the start that Helen was the killer. She had a motive – Dillon's coercive behaviour – and she had her escape already planned. A further breakthrough came the following day, when the murder weapon – a serrated steel kitchen knife with a scratched wooden handle – was discovered jammed into a crack in the wall separating the back garden of 112 Milliver Road from the garden of 114. The blade was caked in dried blood, later proved to be of the same blood type as Edwin Dillon's. Three clear fingerprints were found on the handle – all Helen's.

Helen freely admitted that the knife was hers, that it had come from her kitchen. She strongly denied that she had used it to murder Dillon. When asked who she thought had killed her lover, she said she didn't know. "Edwin was always falling in and out of love with people. He thrived on dissent. He didn't have friends so much as sparring partners, political cronies most of them, people he knew from before we met. I gave up having anything to do with them a long time ago."

When asked why that was, Helen Bostall stated that she no longer cared for their company. "They were all men, obsessed with themselves and their own self-importance. They barely knew I existed. I'm sure some of them hated Edwin – he could be obnoxious. Whether any of them hated him enough to want to kill him I have no idea."

For two or three days, attention veered away from Helen as the police went in search of Dillon's political associates, many of whom, as Helen had suggested, turned out to have grievances against him. Then on February 5th, just as things were starting to get interesting, officers received an anonymous tip-off concerning a Louise Tichener of Highgate Village. This person – or persons – insisted that Miss Tichener had been conducting an affair with Edwin Dillon, and that Helen Bostall had known about it. When found and questioned, Tichener, who belonged to one of the suffragist groups also attended by Bostall, readily confessed to the affair, with the additional information that Dillon had been planning to leave Bostall, and marry her.

"We were going to leave London," Tichener said. "We were happy."

Helen confirmed that she knew Tichener by sight from the women's group, but denied she knew anything about an affair between her and Dillon. She reaffirmed that her own relationship with Dillon was as good as over, and the idea that she might have murdered him out of jealousy was ridiculous. "What Edwin did with his time or his affections was none of my business," she said. "If it is true that this young woman put her trust in Edwin, I would have been afraid for her, not jealous."

But the tide had turned. Louise Tichener's evidence, together with Irene Wilbur's statement, the clothes and travel tickets hidden at Daphne Evans's flat – the evidence seemed damning. Paradoxically, Helen's fortitude under questioning – her refusal to break down on the witness stand – may actually have helped in securing a conviction.

Helen Bostall was found guilty of murder and sentenced to death. She was hanged at Holloway Prison on the morning of August 14th, 1928. Three weeks after her execution the hangman, Arthur Rawlin, resigned from the prison service and took up a position as a warehouseman for a minor shipping company part-owned by friends of his brother, a decision that meant a considerable drop in his standard of living. More than one enterprising journalist clamoured for Rawlin's story, but he refused to comment, saying merely that he was done with the hanging game and that was that.

* * *

I thought that was interesting. Rawlin wasn't the first hangman to lose his stomach for the profession, either. John Ellis, who executed Edith Thompson in 1923, ended up committing suicide. Although some said it was his alcoholism that did for him, most people agreed that Ellis never got over the appalling brutality of Edith's execution. There have been others, too – look them up if you don't believe me. It was thinking about Arthur Rawlin that prompted me to call on Lewis Usher. Lewis was an old client of mine – I'd helped him fight off the property acquisitions company that wanted to tear down the historic Methodist chapel that backed on to his home in Greenwich and turn it into a Tesco Metro – and it was during our war with Sequest Holdings that I happened to find out that he was an expert on British murder trials as well as an enthusiastic collector of murder memorabilia. I always enjoy going to see Lewis – he tells the most amusing anecdotes, and his house on Crooms Hill contains more weird and wonderful collectables than you'd hope to see in most provincial museums. When I visited Lewis on that particular afternoon in late November, I was hoping he might have something enlightening to tell me about the Bostall execution and I was not disappointed.

"Do you think Arthur Rawlin resigned his job as a hangman because he came to believe that Helen Bostall was innocent?" I asked him.

"It's a strong possibility," Lewis said. "There was more to it than that, though. People gossiped that Arthur Rawlin was in love with Bostall, that he believed he was, anyway. The prison governor reported that he used to visit Helen

Bostall in her cell, during the run-up to her execution. There was a strange little article about it in the *Evening Standard* afterwards. You'd probably put it down to Stockholm Syndrome now, but it really was quite odd." He spooned more sugar into his tea. "You do know I have his watch?"

I felt my heartbeat quicken. "Arthur Rawlin's watch? The one he used to time his executions?"

"I think you'll find it was Albert Pierrepoint who used to do that. Rawlin might have copied him, I suppose. There was certainly a cult of personality around Pierrepoint at the time. It's Rawlin's watch though, definitely, whatever he used it for. I have the full provenance."

"Could I see it?" I found myself becoming excited in a way that seemed completely out of proportion with what Lewis had told me. It was just a watch, after all. But it was as if I knew, even then, that I was about to make a significant discovery, not just about Arthur Rawlin but about Helen Bostall.

"Of course. Won't be a tick." He eased himself out of his chair and shuffled off towards the side room where he kept most of his collection. I couldn't help noticing he seemed to be relying on his cane more than he had on my last visit. Still, he seemed in good spirits. I gazed around the living room – the ancient red plush sofas, the fake stuffed dodo in its glass case, the walls and mantel shelf crowded with photographs of his wife, the stage actress Zoë Clifford, dead from a freak bout of pneumonia some ten years before. The place had become something of a haven for me during the Sequest case, which had happened to coincide with the first stage of my breakup with Ray. How glad I had been to come here, to escape from my own thoughts and misgivings into this cosy little corner of theatreland, where the fire was always lit and the stories were always taller and more preposterous than my own.

A place suspended in time, a lacuna in the fraying fabric of the everyday world.

"Here it is," Lewis said. I jumped, startled. I'd been so absorbed in my thoughts I hadn't noticed him come back into the room. He was carrying a small bag, made from yellow silk with a drawstring opening. "I can show you the papers too if you'd like to see them, but this is the watch."

He passed me the bag. I reached cautiously inside. Things inside bags make me nervous. You don't know what you're getting into until it's too late. In this case, Rawlin's watch, which was a full-case silver pocket watch about two inches in diameter. The front of the case was engraved with a lighted candle. On the back was a skull, the eye sockets and nasal cavities etched out in darker relief. The classic vanitas, life and death, light and darkness, the universal allegory for time's passing.

Perfect for a hangman, I thought.

"He may have commissioned the engraving personally," Lewis said, as if reading my thoughts. "Although the design isn't unusual for the time. The Victorians were heavily into mourning jewellery, as you probably know."

"Yes," I said. "It's more my brother's area, to be honest." I flipped open the front of the case. The watch's white enamelled face was simple and plain, as if in deliberate contrast to the gothic extravagance of the case. There was a date stamped on the dial, 1879, and the name of the maker – Owen Andrews. The name meant nothing to me but I made a mental note to ask Martin about it later.

"It's a tourbillon watch," Lewis added. "Very expensive, even at the time. An ordinary working man like Rawlin would have had to save several months' salary to purchase this."

"What's a tourbillon?"

"A means for stabilising the watch's mechanism, so it doesn't lose time. Here." He opened the back of the watch, revealing its workings, which resembled a complicated mechanical diagram, all gears and levers. "And have a look at this."

He angled his hand, showing me the inside back of the watch's case, and the photograph that had been secreted there. The image showed a young woman, with short dark hair and light eyes, a narrow, straight nose and a high lace collar: Helen Bostall.

"There is a possibility that the photograph was placed inside the watch later – after Rawlin's death, I mean," said Lewis. "It's unlikely though. You won't read much about this in the newspapers, but if you delve a little deeper you'll find there are several contemporary accounts, from colleagues and family and so on. All of them agree that Rawlin was living in a fantasy world."

"About him and Helen being in love, you mean?"

"Yes, that, but it went even further." He chuckled. "I read one letter from Rawlin to his younger brother where he was going on about travelling back in time to prevent the execution he himself had carried out."

"That's ridiculous. Poor man."

"Plenty would say he got what he deserved. Not everyone would feel sorry for a hangman."

I did, though. We can't all choose our jobs, and was Rawlin so different from the soldiers sent out to kill other soldiers on the battlefields of World War One? I tried to imagine how he must have felt, becoming properly aware for the first time of what his job meant, what it was he actually did, and the imagining was not pleasant.

"Too bad we can't bring him back to talk to the Americans," I said. I smiled to myself, thinking how Martin would disapprove of my poor taste in jokes. He would love to see this watch though, I thought, which gave me an idea. "Please say no if you want to," I said to Lewis, "but could I possibly borrow this? Just for a day or two? I'd like to show it to my brother."

"The watch?" He fell silent, and I was fully expecting him to demur, to begin explaining how he didn't like to let items from his collection leave the house, especially an item like this, which must be valuable even aside from who had once owned it. "I'd like you to have it," was what he actually said. I felt so surprised and so shocked that for a moment I couldn't answer him.

"Lewis, don't be silly. I couldn't possibly. I'm sorry I asked," I said, when I had regained the use of my tongue.

"I mean it," he insisted. "I've been wanting to leave you something – in my will, I mean. To say thank you for being such a good friend to me. But it's difficult to know what someone might like. If I know you like this, then you've made my task easier. You'll be doing me a favour."

"You're not ill?"

"Dying, you mean? No, no more so than usual. But I am eighty-six."

"Lewis," I said. "Thank you."

"It's my great pleasure. So long as you don't use it to go running off after repentant hangmen."

We both laughed at that. Both of us, at the same time. But I've sometimes had the feeling – call it hindsight, if you want – that neither of us really thought it was funny.

Helen's defence rested on the fact that the evidence against her was circumstantial. No one – not even Irene Wilbur – claimed to have seen her in the vicinity of Milliver Road at the time of Dillon's death, and no matter how many times the prosecution cross-examined Daphne Evans over Helen's alibi, she never deviated from her original statement: Helen had arrived at her apartment just before seven, they ate some sandwiches Daphne had prepared and talked about Edwin. Helen still felt guilty for what she was planning – to walk out on him without a word of warning – but Daphne remained adamant she was doing the right thing.

"I never liked Edwin," she said. "He wasn't trustworthy. I was glad when Helen decided she was leaving him. I knew she wasn't happy."

When asked whether she considered Dillon to be a violent man, Daphne hesitated before replying and then said yes. "I would have said he could be capable of violence," she added. "I was afraid for Helen, just sometimes, but she always told me I was being foolish so I had to believe her."

* * *

The prosecution's most important witness was Irene Wilbur. Her insistence that there had been a 'furious altercation' at 112 Milliver Road just before eight o'clock was more instrumental in securing a guilty verdict than Helen Bostall's fingerprints on the murder weapon. You didn't have to be a lawyer to understand that anyone could have used that knife, that the killer would have been likely to grab the first weapon that came to hand, especially if the murder had been opportunistic rather than planned. That Helen Bostall kept a carving knife in her kitchen drawer was hardly damning evidence.

On the other hand, Irene Wilbur was adamant that she had heard two people yelling at each other, that one of them had been a woman. And she had Gerald Honeyshot of the Red Lion to back her up regarding the time.

Why would Irene Wilbur lie? When asked by the prosecution if she had any reason to dislike or resent Helen Bostall, if there was any previous bad feeling between them, Wilbur was equally adamant that there was none. "I barely knew her," she stated. "I'd not been living at Milliver Road for more than a fortnight. I'd seen Miss Bostall a few times to say hello to but that was all. She seemed friendly enough. A bit aloof perhaps but not what you'd call unpleasant."

In fact, Irene Wilbur had been resident at 112 Milliver Road for just ten days. The defence did not appear to find anything suspicious in that, and why would they? People move house all the time. Wilbur's assertion – that she had moved to Camden from Putney because she had numerous friends in the area – seemed entirely reasonable.

I don't know what kept me picking away at Irene Wilbur,

but I did. I didn't like the way she had been so relentless in the way she'd given her evidence, so determined, almost, that Helen was guilty. Wilbur had persisted, even while knowing that Helen might face a death sentence if convicted. Why such animosity towards a woman she claimed not to have known? I didn't get it. Those who did think to criticise Wilbur at the time did so on the grounds that she was a natural attention-seeker, altogether too enamoured of seeing herself in the newspapers. An interesting hypothesis, but I wasn't so certain.

Was it possible, I wondered, that Irene Wilbur had been a stooge? Most newspaper accounts of the trial made mention of Wilbur's 'smart' attire, and several made particular mention of a jade and diamond brooch she wore. Everyone seemed to agree she was 'a handsome woman'.

After pursuing the matter a little further, I discovered that Irene Wilbur had moved away from Milliver Road less than a week after Helen's execution, that she had returned to her old stamping ground of Putney, and to considerably smarter lodgings than she had occupied previously.

If Irene Wilbur had been paid to provide false evidence, it suggested not only that Dillon's murder had been carefully planned, but that Helen had been intended to take the blame for it all along.

If this was so – and once I stumbled upon the idea I found it difficult to give up the conviction that it was – then Irene Wilbur would have to be connected with Edwin Dillon in some way, or rather with his enemies, who would scarcely have risked employing a stranger to do their dirty work.

On top of my research into the lives of Helen Bostall and Edwin Dillon, I now found myself grubbing around for any information I could find about Irene Wilbur. I soon discovered she had been married at the age of twenty-one to a Major Douglas Wilbur, who had been killed at the Battle of Amiens in World War One. They had one child, a daughter named Laura, born in the February of 1919, a full six months after her father's death.

Those dates seemed odd to me. Of course it was entirely possible that Major Wilbur had been afforded leave prior to the Amiens campaign, that Laura could have been conceived then, but it didn't fit somehow, not to my mind, anyway. Douglas Wilbur had been an experienced, valuable and loyal officer. It was inconceivable that he would have left his post immediately before such a crucial offensive.

There was also the fact that Irene Wilbur was thirty-eight years old at the time of Laura's birth, that during the whole of her twenty-year marriage there had been no other children.

What had changed?

If Douglas Wilbur was not in fact Laura's father, who was?

I looked back once again over the trial records, focussing on any mention of Irene Wilbur's home life, no matter how minor. Which is how I came to notice something that had not registered before, namely that Laura Wilbur had not been resident at Milliver Road, that at the time of the murder she was staying instead with a person Irene Wilbur described as a 'near relative', a Mrs Jocelyn Bell, close to the Wilburs' old address in Putney. When questioned about why her daughter was not in fact living with her, Irene Wilbur said it was a matter of Laura's schooling.

Once again, it was possible. But by now I was coming to believe it was more likely a matter of Irene not wanting her daughter anywhere near a house where she knew there was going to be a murder. Wilbur would not be staying long at Milliver Road, in any case. Far better to keep Laura at a distance.

I was filled with a sense of foreboding, the feeling that always comes over me when I understand I have made a discovery about a case that has hitherto kept itself obstinately hidden. I knew that I was close to something, that the pieces of the truth were more than likely already assembled, that it was simply a matter of arranging them in the correct order.

The first step, I decided, was to try and find out a little more about Jocelyn Bell. And in the meantime I still had to talk to Martin about the hangman's watch.

People say we're alike, Martin and I, but I'm not so sure. We look alike, and I think what our mutual friends might be picking up on is our shared tendency towards poking around in subjects no one else gives a damn about. We both like finding things out. Of the two of us though, I believe it is Martin who is the better human being. Martin cares about people, which is why he is so good at his job. When I tell him this, he always insists that I must care about people too, or I wouldn't put such time and effort into fighting their corners.

Perhaps he's right. But I still think what I enjoy most

about my work is the thrill of argument, the abstract battle of opposing forces. If 'doing good' happens to be a side effect of that I'm not going to knock it, but it isn't the driving force behind what I do.

I don't think so, anyway. You'd better ask Martin.

I hope he meets someone else. He's borne up remarkably well since Miranda died, but that's Martin all over, never one to make a fuss.

I was always the one who made a fuss. Getting cancer then going crazy then marrying Ray. Martin was there for me through all of it, no matter how much I managed to screw up.

He can cook a mean curry, too.

"Have you ever heard of a watchmaker called Owen Andrews?" I asked him once we'd finished eating. I poured us both another glass of wine. It was odd, the way his face changed. A lot of people might not even have noticed, but I'm used to watching other people's body language and I know Martin back to front anyway. The moment I said the name Owen Andrews, it was as if someone had suddenly switched a light on inside him, then just as rapidly flicked it off again. Something he didn't want to talk about? Or felt uncertain of? Could have been either. I'd been telling him about my research, my various theories about Irene Wilbur. I'd deliberately held off mentioning Arthur Rawlin because once you get Martin on to the subject of watches it's difficult to get him off it again.

I knew he'd be interested, but the extremity of his reaction surprised me, all the same.

"I've heard of him, yes," Martin said finally. "But what does he have to do with Irene Wilbur?"

This is going to sound strange, but I decided more or less in that moment that I wasn't going to tell Martin I had Rawlin's watch in my possession. Not yet, anyway.

It wasn't that I didn't trust him. I would trust Martin with my life, and perhaps that was the problem.

It was as if – and I know how bizarre this sounds, especially coming from an unreconstructed rationalist like me – I sensed already that something was going to happen, something involving the watch. I think I was afraid that if Martin got wind of what I meant to do, he would say it was dangerous and try to stop me.

I'm not good at taking advice – once I have a mind to do something, you might as well try *advising* a stampeding mare with a swarm of bees on her tail. No one knows this better than Martin and normally he'd stay out of it, but in this case?

Let's just say I wanted to keep my intentions under wraps.

"Nothing," I said. "At least nothing directly." I told him about Arthur Rawlin and Arthur Rawlin's posthumous obsession with Helen Bostall, and then added that my old client Lewis Usher knew someone who knew someone who'd purchased Arthur Rawlin's watch in a private auction.

"It's by a London maker, apparently, this Owen Andrews," I said. "Lewis seems to think that Rawlin attached mystical properties to the watch, that he believed it could reverse time, or something. He's going to try and dig out the documents for me – Lewis, I mean. I wondered if you knew anything about this Andrews guy, that's all."

"Only that he trained in Southwark, and that his watches are vanishingly rare," Martin said. He sighed. "There are entire internet forums devoted to Owen Andrews. He's one of those people other people are always talking about, probably because we know so little about him. There are still ongoing arguments over exactly when he was born. There's speculation that he had access to Breguet's late notebooks. I don't believe it myself. I don't see how he could have done. The notebooks weren't in the public domain for at least a century after Breguet's death."

"Who's Breguet?"

"Abram Louis Breguet, a Swiss watchmaker. He's best known for making a watch for Marie Antoinette and almost losing his head for his trouble. But for horologists, Breguet is most famous for inventing the tourbillon."

Martin went off into a long-winded explanation of what a tourbillon was and how it worked, how before Breguet, no pocket watch could keep accurate time over a long period because of gravity, which acted as a drag weight on the mechanism, speeding it up or slowing it down by as much as sixty seconds in every hour. Breguet placed the whole mechanism inside a revolving metal cage he called a tourbillon, or whirlwind. The tourbillon kept the mechanism in stasis, twirling it around its own axis like a sidecar on a fairground ride.

The tourbillon watch was like a planet, spinning in space. In every sense that mattered, it was weightless.

"Think of a tornado," Martin said. "A wind itself has no substance, but it has incredible power. It renders everything weightless before it, even massive objects like houses and cars."

I zoned out a bit towards the end, not because what Martin was telling me wasn't interesting, but because I couldn't see how any of it related to Arthur Rawlin and a possible time machine. Then Martin said something else, something jaw-dropping. I was dragged back into the conversation with a physical jolt.

"What was that about the notebooks?"

"Breguet's notebooks," Martin repeated. "His doctors always insisted he was senile by then, but according to his son, Breguet was lucid and rational right up until he died. His late writings suggest he had been trying to create a kind of super-tourbillon, a mechanism he believed would eventually enable human beings to travel through time. He called it the Time Stasis. I can't believe anyone would take it literally, quite honestly, but some of the people on the forums believe Owen Andrews made it his mission to put Breguet's theory into practice."

"To make a watch that could turn back time?"

Martin shrugged. "If you like."

"That's incredible."

"If it were true, maybe. But I've seen some of Andrews's pieces and they're just watches. Andrews was gifted but he wasn't a magician. All that time travel stuff – it's just the horological equivalent of urban myth."

I thought there was something heroic about it, nonetheless – the lone mechanic, pitting himself against logic like a gladiator fighting a tiger. I reminded myself that all the most radical advances in science seemed like lunacy before they were proven.

"It's a beautiful word," I said to Martin. "Horological."

"Are you still convinced Helen Bostall was innocent?" he asked.

"More than ever. And I believe Arthur Rawlin thought so, too – that's why he felt so guilty over her death."

"You're determined to prove it, aren't you? Through your book?"

I laughed. "I suppose I am."

I didn't just want to prove it, though – I can admit that now. I wanted to change it. But I wasn't about to blow my cover to Martin.

Three days later I performed an experiment. Just one little trip back, five minutes or so. *Brain of Britain* was on the radio, which made it easy to tell if anything had actually happened. I had a second go at some of the questions, which would have upped my score if I'd been keeping tally, which I wasn't. It would have been cheating, anyway.

Jocelyn Bell turned out to be Jocelyn Leslie, an artist. She won a scholarship to study at the Slade, and when her father – a successful Yorkshire businessman of a conservative cast of mind – refused to let her go, she continued to paint in secret, making her own way to London two years later. She enjoyed a moderate popularity for a time. Although there were those who dismissed her efforts as 'primitive' or 'naive', Lavinia Sable, who wrote art criticism for several London papers under the pseudonym Marcus Fell, insisted that in spite of having almost no formal training, Bell's work showed a keener understanding of European modernism than many of her better-known contemporaries.

I liked the sound of Lavinia, who apparently attended private views and press gatherings for years as Marcus, with no one being any the wiser. Lavinia was easily interesting enough to fill a book in her own right, but Lavinia was not my mission and after spending a day or two reading up on her I laid the material reluctantly aside and went back to the matter in hand, namely Jocelyn Bell.

On arrival in London, Jocelyn found work first as an assistant housekeeper at a private boarding school for girls, then as a secretary and assistant to the curator of one of the more progressive galleries on Cork Street. It was here, I'm certain, that she first encountered Leonard Bell, who was friendly with several of the artists represented there.

Leonard Bell was actually Leonid Belayev, a Russian émigré and a member of the radical socialist group based in Camden called the Four Brothers. The group was founded in the 1890s, and unlike many similar loose associations that fractured and splintered at the outbreak of war, the Four Brothers remained intact as a group well into the 1920s.

At some point during 1924, Edwin Dillon began attending their meetings.

Here at last was the breakthrough I'd been searching for. Jocelyn Leslie married Leonard Bell in 1902. They had one son, Malcolm, in 1903, although letters sent by Jocelyn to a friend in Manchester reveal that differences were already making themselves felt between the couple and by 1905 their marriage was over in all but name. Leonard Bell kept in close touch with his family, though – I think he was probably still living under the same roof for some years after he and Jocelyn separated, a fact that would almost certainly have led to gossip amongst the neighbours. Not that Jocelyn or Leonard gave much of a damn for bourgeois convention. They remained friends, and when Leonard eventually began a long-term affair with another woman, the woman quickly became Jocelyn's friend, also.

That woman – and you can imagine my satisfaction when I was able to prove this for sure – was Irene Wilbur. There were in fact several dozen letters from Leonard to his lover, preserved amongst Jocelyn Bell's papers at the Women Artists Forum in Hammersmith.

As a bonus, the letters also revealed to me the identity of Malcolm Bell's soon-to-be fiancée: Louise Tichener.

Frustratingly, I was never able to find out much about Irene Wilbur herself, and I can only assume her willingness to go along with the murder plot had more to do with her wanting to protect Leonard Bell than with any active animosity towards Helen Bostall. The true identity of Dillon's murderer also remained hidden from me, although I'm more or less positive it wasn't Bell himself. Leonard was a hardened activist – he would have known better than to put himself directly at risk.

After weeks of rooting around in various archives of obscure research papers I came to the conclusion that the most likely suspect was a much younger man, Michael Woolcot, who seems to have known Dillon when he was living in Manchester. The two had some sort of falling out – either in Manchester or soon after Woolcot's own arrival in the capital. So far as I know they were never reconciled, although mysteriously there was one final meeting between them, in a Camden public house, just ten days before Dillon's murder. The meeting was remarked upon by a moderate socialist named West, a journalist who wrote a satirical column for an independent newspaper called *The Masthead*, lampooning many of the personalities associated with the more extreme wing of the movement.

They say that if you sup with the devil you should use a long spoon, West wrote in his January 20th column, just one week before the murder. *Judging by the outbreak of cosy camaraderie at The Horse's Head last Thursday evening, it would seem there are those who set little store by such sage advice, even those we might consider our elders and betters.* West goes on to reveal the identities of both Dillon and Woolcot, referring to the latter as 'an upwardly mobile cur of the Belayev persuasion' and to the meeting itself as 'a council of war'.

Which can only beg the question, West writes, *of who exactly is at war here, and with whom?*

Whether the police were ever made aware of West's column, or possessed enough insider knowledge to make sense of the connection, I have no idea. Leonard Bell was questioned briefly, along with two dozen or so other regular and irregular members of the Four Brothers group, though the comrades' universal disdain for the official forces of law and order would have meant the chances of anyone letting anything slip were practically nil.

Helen Bostall's ticket for the boat train was forward-dated to February 3rd, a date that turned out to be less than a

week after Dillon's murder. It seems likely that someone –
someone friendly with Leonard Bell or one of his cronies
– knew about Helen's travel plans. For Bell's plan to succeed,
it was crucial that Dillon be killed well in advance of
Helen's departure for the continent. I believe it was Dillon's
meeting with Woolcot, staged by Bell as an opportunity for
reconciliation, that set the stage for the murder. No doubt
Woolcot had been instructed to arrange a second, more
informal meeting, to take place at Dillon's flat.

Putting all the evidence together, it finally became clear
to me that it was those ten days that formed the crucial time
period, the ten days between Dillon first meeting Woolcot at
The Horse's Head, and his eventual death.

If Helen Bostall could have been persuaded to bring her
journey forward – to leave London soon after New Year, say
– then Bell would either have had to shelve his plans, or risk
being exposed as complicit in Dillon's killing.

Regardless of Dillon's fate, Helen Bostall herself would
have been saved.

If only someone could have told her, I thought, and
almost immediately afterwards I thought of Arthur Rawlin.
Had he tried to use the watch? I wondered. If so, he had
obviously failed.

As to why Bell wanted Dillon dead in the first place, the
reasons remained obscure to me. All I could think was that it
must have been down to some intricate power struggle within
the Four Brothers. Truth be told, I didn't care much. Not then.

* * *

I knew from the start that the best place to approach Helen would be at one of her suffragist meetings. The very nature of such gatherings would mean there would always be new faces in evidence, strangers who might turn up for a couple of meetings and then disappear again. It would be relatively easy to mingle with the women without drawing undue attention to myself. The main thing was not to go overboard in trying to fit in. I chose clothes that were unobtrusive rather than authentic: the three-quarter-length coat I normally wore to court hearings in winter, a dark, paisley-patterned skirt I hardly ever wore but couldn't bear to throw out because I liked the material so much, a pair of black lace-up shoes. In every sense of the word, plain clothes.

By now you're either wondering what on earth I'm talking about, or if I can possibly be serious, which is absolutely fine.

I kept putting off the actual – journey? I told myself I needed to do more research, which was at least partly true. In order to keep myself safe, I had to know that particular bit of Camden well enough to be able to walk around it blindfolded, if need be. But mostly I was just scared. Scared in case the watch didn't work and scared in case it did.

What if it worked in one direction but not in the other?

I wanted to know though, I wanted to *see*. The closer it came to the date I'd set myself, the more impatient I felt. Impatient with my fear. Impatient with my delaying tactics.

When Ray phoned the night before to ask me if I was going to some private view or other his agent was organising, I almost bit his head off.

"Are you OK, Dottie?" he said. He hadn't called me Dottie for years, not since we separated.

"I'll be there, don't worry," I said, not answering his question and not knowing if I would be there, either. "I've got a lot on at work, that's all. Say hi to Clio for me."

Clio is Ray's daughter, the child he has with Maya. I should make more of an effort with Maya, I suppose, but it's difficult. We're such different people, and although chumming up with her ex-husband's new wife seemed to work for Jocelyn Bell, I'm not sure it's for me.

Clio, though. She's eight years old and a miracle. I could never tell this to anyone, not even Martin, but occasionally it breaks my heart that she isn't mine.

There is a lever inside the watch, a silver pin that slides from side to side inside a moulded slit – imagine the back of an old wind-up alarm clock, the little lever you use to engage the alarm function, or to turn it off. There is no clear indication of what the purpose of this lever might be, and when you first engage it, nothing seems to happen. Say 'nothing happens, full stop', if you like. I won't mind.

I once had a conversation with Martin, years ago when we were kids, about whether ghosts existed. When I asked Martin if he believed, he said it didn't matter. "If ghosts exist, they'll go on existing whether we believe in them or not."

It's the same with this. And if I tell you that what time travel reminds me of most of all is the time before my illness, I wonder will you believe that either? The time when I was so in love with numbers – when I could listen to numbers conversing the same way you might listen to music, when I felt the thrum of numbers in my blood, intricate as a crystal lattice, sound and rhythmic and basic as the beat of a drum.

I turned the lever, and the rush of numbers filled my head, blazing in my veins like alcohol, like burning petrol. The music of the primes, du Sautoy called it, and I could hear it again. I closed my eyes and counted backwards. I could feel the boundaries of reality expanding, unfurling. Bobbing deftly out of reach of my hands, like a toy balloon.

I ducked under the boundary wire and followed. Time filled me up, chilly and intoxicating.

Yes, but what's it *like*? I can hear you asking.

Like a triple slug of Russian vodka that's been kept in the icebox, that's what it's like.

I started going on practice runs. Just silly things: walking past my front door in the middle of last week, going to a concert at the Barbican I'd wanted to attend when it was actually on but happened to miss. I thought it would be difficult to get the timing right, but in fact the mechanism was extremely accurate, once you got the hang of it. I found it mostly came down to imagining: knowing where you wanted to be and forming an image of the place and time inside your mind. This sounds irrational I know, but that's how it was.

I spent a lot of time in Camden, just walking around. You'd be surprised how little it's changed. Even when houses, whole streets have been torn down and built over, the old shadows remain.

The city has a shape. You can sense it, if you feel for it, even if you're sleepwalking and perhaps especially then, London's presence wrapped closely around you like a horsehair blanket.

The suffragist meetings took place in rooms about the Quaker Meeting House, on Bentley Street. During the day it was mostly quiet, but in the evenings it livened up considerably, mainly because of The Charlady, a public house and pie shop on the corner of the street opposite. I went in daylight the first time, just to be safe. Muggings were common then in this part of London and I didn't feel like exposing myself to unnecessary risk.

You think of the past as cleaner, but it really isn't. Horse shit, engine oil, smoke, blood, piss, beer, the rotting detritus from the market, piled at the kerb. Not London as it might be in a theme park, but a London you'd recognise instantly, just from the stench. Cars are creeping in already: hackney cabs and omnibuses, gentlemen's conveyances. And the bikes – the thrilling thring of bicycle bells, boy couriers speeding along. *Oi, miss, get on the pavement, why dontchyer? Bleedin' 'eck.* A flower and matchbox seller, a puckered scar across one cheek and her left hand missing. I reach into my pocket to find the right coins, then remember I don't have the right coins, not at all. Exactly the kind of stupid blunder I'm supposed to be on guard against. The peddler gazes at me with tired eyes and I look away in shame. The next time I come I bring her a paper packet of corned beef sandwiches but she is no longer there. Not in the same place, anyway. I remind myself of what I'm here for, and move swiftly along.

Another time, I stand in a shop doorway opposite and watch the women arrive for their meeting. I'm amazed to find that I recognise some of them, from the letters I've read, from the blurred photographs in the Women's Studies archive in the British Library. One of them, a young poet named Kathleen Thwaite, is accompanied to the door of the meeting house by her husband, Austin Gears. I know that Kathleen is to die in 1937, on a protest march against Franco's fascists in Madrid. It makes my heart ache to see her, and the urge to do something, to warn her in some way, is all but overwhelming. I turn quickly away, hoping to catch a glimpse of Helen Bostall instead. On this occasion at least she appears to be absent.

Has my being here, even to stand motionless in the street, altered things somehow, and for the worse? I push the thought away. It is coincidence, that's all. She will be here next week, and if not then, the week after. It need not matter.

The next time, I file inside the hall with the other women. No one talks to me or takes particular notice but many smile. I feel accepted as one of them. More than that, I can *imagine* myself as one of them. It is almost as if I have experienced this life, this version of my life anyway, this Dora Newland who attended suffragist rallies in Hyde Park, who conducted furious arguments with her uncle about being allowed to travel down through Italy with another woman friend. Casting Henry – dear Henry, who indulged our every whim when we were children – in the role of authoritarian guardian makes me smile.

We sit on hard wooden chairs in the draughty space – three small attic rooms that have been converted into one larger one – and listen to a Mrs Marjorie Hennessey tell us about her experience of studying politics at the Sorbonne. She is an impressive woman, commanding and authoritative, and I cannot help wondering what happened to her, how come she failed.

So many women, I think. It is depressing to consider how many of us have been discouraged, disparaged, forced to reconsider, turned aside from our dreams.

I want to rush up to Marjorie Hennessey and tell her not to give up, not to drop by the wayside, not to fall silent.

"She's wonderful, isn't she?" It is the interval and we are queuing up for tea. The woman who speaks to me seems shy and rather young, and I have the feeling this is her first time here also. Her cheeks are flushed pink.

"Admirable," I say, and for a second I experience a sensation close to vertigo. *I am here, and I am speaking to someone*, I think. I hug my bag as if seeking support from it. Inside the bag are the keys to my flat, my purse, my Kindle ereader, my mobile phone, all those other insignificant trifles that don't exist yet. *I come from the future*, I think, in what Martin always calls the MGM voice. I want to laugh out loud. I glance over at the chalk board, where Marjorie Hennessey has been drawing diagrams illustrating the economic implications of women withdrawing their labour from the home.

I wonder how my new friend in the tea queue would react if I were to tell her that almost a century later we're still fighting the same battles. Again, I want to laugh. Not that it's funny.

"We need more like her," I say instead, because that also is still true. Now more than ever, we need more anger, more knowledge. "Shall we sit down?"

We take our tea and sit at one of the wooden trestles at the side of the hall. The woman tells me her name is Barbara Winton and she's a socialist.

"They say there's going to be another war," she says. "We have to join with our sisters in Europe – we must prevent war, at all costs."

She is learning German, and corresponding with the daughter of a friend of her father's, who lives in Frankfurt. "Her name is Gisela. She's a sculptor. Don't you think that's marvellous? She's asked me to go out and visit her and Daddy says I can. It feels – I'm not sure how to explain – as if a whole new life is beginning."

"I hope you're right," I say. I tell her that I'm studying Law, that I am hoping to practise at the bar. I see confusion on her face – my age, probably – which is swiftly succeeded by a kind of wonder, mixed with mischievous delight. Women have been allowed access to the legal profession for less than a decade, after all.

"Well done, you," she says. "I think that's marvellous."

Her excitement is contagious. It is only as we are about to resume our seats for the second half of the programme that I finally catch sight of Helen Bostall. She is near the back of the room, talking to a woman with an upright posture and hawkish nose whom I recognise at once as Daphne Evans.

I gaze at them, dumbstruck. I feel like a spy. As I move towards my seat I see Helen turn, just for a moment, and look directly at me.

Instead of the blank, flat gaze of a woman casually scanning the crowd, what I see in her eyes – indisputably – is recognition: *you're here*. I feel cold right through. My hands begin to shake. I'm going to drop my cup, I think, then realise it's all right, I no longer have it. Barbara Winton has taken it from me and returned it to the tea bench at the back.

That was when I lost my nerve. Instead of sitting down again I pushed through the crowd to the door and then rushed down the stairs, almost tripping over my paisley skirt in the process. Once outside I felt better. There was the usual rowdy hubbub coming from The Charlady, the same stink of greasy Irish stew and overloaded dustbins. I made my way to an access lane between two rows of terraces and took out the watch. I engaged the lever without looking at it – not looking had become a kind of superstition with me – and stood there in the dark, counting primes and feeling that odd, trembling dream state take hold until I became aware of the sound of traffic – motor traffic, I mean, buses and police sirens – on Camden High Street.

I was back. I breathed in through my mouth, tasting exhaust fumes and the tarry scent of someone's spent cigarette. I stood still for some moments, letting the world come back into focus around me and feeling the relief I felt each time: that I had conducted an extremely risky experiment – heating flash powder in a petri dish, say – and managed to get away without blowing my hands off.

I never experimented with going forward, not even by one day. I had a terror of it, a paralysing phobia. It was a deal I made, I think – with God, the devil, myself, Owen Andrews? *Bring me safely home, and I'll keep our bargain.* Well, I guess it worked.

The next time I went back, I was prepared. So, it seems, was Helen. She was waiting for me this time, at the bottom of the stairs outside the meeting house. She told me later that she'd waited there at the start of every meeting since she'd first seen me, knowing I would be returning but not knowing when.

"Dora," she said quietly. "You're here at last." She caught my hands in both of hers. Her fingers were cold. It was December, and she was smiling in a way that suggested she was greeting an old friend, someone she knew well but hadn't seen in a while. Pleasure, and sadness, as if she knew our time together would be short.

"I don't understand," I said, and sighed. Who was I to talk? "How did you – how do you know me?"

"Knowing everything you know – do you need to ask?" she said. "The order in which things happen doesn't matter, surely? Just that they happen. I'm so pleased to see you."

She leaned forward to embrace me, and I found myself almost believing – there was such joy in seeing her, such emotion – that this was indeed a reunion and not, as I knew it to be, our first meeting.

"Come," she said. "We can go back to the flat. Edwin's away – in Manchester. That's what he says, anyway."

"You don't think he really is?"

She shrugged. "Edwin tells me what it pleases him to tell me. Sometimes it's the truth and sometimes it isn't. I had to give up caring which a long time ago."

We came to Milliver Road. I'd been to the house of course – what I mean is I'd stood outside it many times. I knew 112 as a spruce, bay-fronted terrace with replacement windows. The house in Helen's time seemed smaller, meaner, the exterior paintwork chipped and blistering. A flight of steps led steeply down to a basement forecourt.

"We've had problems with damp," Helen said. "The woman who lives upstairs says there are rats, too, but I've never seen them."

"Mrs Wilbur?"

She gave me a puzzled look. "Mrs Wilbur? Mrs Herschel lives on the ground floor. There's no Mrs Wilbur."

"It doesn't matter," I said. So my researches had proved

correct – Irene Wilbur hadn't moved in yet. There was still time.

"Let's go in and get warm," Helen said. "I'll light the stove."

"We were happy here once, Edwin and I," Helen said. The stove was well alight. Soft lamplight threw shadows on the whitewashed walls of the cosy front sitting room. Framed prints, showing images from a Greek bestiary. An orange-and-green Aubusson rug. Books, books everywhere, overflowing the alcove shelving and piled on the floor. A stack of handwritten pages lay fanned across a low wooden table. It was a good room. A room I felt at home in.

I also knew I'd been there before.

"Have you eaten?" Helen asked.

I laughed. "It's been a hundred years at least," I said.

"I can warm up some soup. I made it yesterday."

"That would be lovely." I wasn't hungry – quite the opposite – but I was curious to see how food might taste here. In fact, it tasted like potato soup, thick and nutritious and well seasoned. We ate, dipping bread into our bowls, and I asked Helen what she was working on.

"I've been helping to edit a collection of essays by women on the subject of war," she said. "I want to include writing by German women as well – letters, memoir, whatever I can get hold of. The publisher was against this at first but I managed to persuade them how important it is, essential, even. You don't think it's too soon?"

I shook my head.

"I'm glad. We have to use every weapon we have."

"Weapon?"

"To make people understand what war really is. The madness of it." She fell silent, head bent. "Dora, I know I shouldn't really ask you this, but do we succeed? Do we succeed at all?"

I know I shouldn't answer, and I don't, not then, but the following week, when I know that Helen will be at her meeting, I return to Milliver Road for one final visit. I have an envelope with me, addressed to Helen. I post it through the front door of the house, hear it fall on to the scuffed brown linoleum of the communal hallway. Inside is a second-hand copy of John Hersey's memoir, *Hiroshima* in the original Pelican edition, its pages faded and brittle but clearly readable, the most concise response to her question that I can think of. What good will it do? None at all. But Helen asked me a question and she deserves an answer.

"That doesn't matter now," I said in 1927. "What I mean is – it matters, but there are more urgent things to think about. Urgent for you, anyway."

"You're frightening me."

"In a month's time, Edwin is going to be murdered. If you stay here you are going to be blamed for it. There will be a trial and—"

"You're telling me I'm going to be hanged. For a crime I had nothing to do with."

I stared at her, horrified.

"I thought it was a dream," she said, more quietly. "That man. He sat on the edge of my bed and told me about it. He was crying. He seemed quite mad. When I told him to go away he did. I wish I'd been kinder."

Arthur Rawlin. So he had used the watch to try and save her, after all.

"None of that is going to happen," I said quickly. "But you must leave London, and Edwin. You need to pack your things and get as far away from here as you can."

She nodded slowly. "I've been planning to go, anyway. To leave Edwin, I mean. Whatever we had – it's over. I could say he's changed but really I think it's me. I see him differently now." She paused. "I see everything differently."

"Can you think of any reason why anyone would want to kill Edwin?"

She was silent for a long time, lacing and unlacing her fingers. Finally she sighed. "I really don't involve myself with Edwin's business any more, but I do know there are people in the Four Brothers he's fallen out with. Badly. Edwin believes, I don't know, that we should do something to signal the start of the revolution. Something dramatic, something violent even. He says he has people standing by – bomb makers." She shook her head. "I don't know how much of this is true, and how much is just talk. The more he drinks the more he talks, Edwin. That's something I've noticed. Not that half the brethren would see much wrong if Edwin really is planning to blow people up. I think mainly it's about power within the group – who has it and who doesn't. There are some who see Edwin as a threat, who think he's getting above himself. I'm sure they'd be more than happy if he were out of the way. Can you believe that?"

"I can more than believe that."

"They don't like him because he's clever, because he doesn't give two hoots about their old hierarchies. Because he's from Manchester, even." She turned to look at me. "I keep asking myself if it's partly my fault that things have gone this far. If I could have talked to him more, maybe? But I've come to understand that Edwin never cared about what I thought, not even at the beginning. He wanted an audience, that's all. Now that I no longer listen, he cares even less."

I was tempted to tell her about Ray and me, but decided that would be unfair. Ray's no bomb maker, just another man with an ego who needs it stroking. Now that I no longer have to live with him, I can even enjoy his company from time to time. "Where will you go?" I said instead.

"I have a friend, Elsa Ehrling, in Berlin. She says I can stay with her as long as I need. I can teach English. And there are other things I can do to make myself useful. Elsa says workers for peace need to make their voices heard in Germany, now more than ever."

You'd be right there, I thought, but did not say. I'd interfered enough already. Besides, she would be safe in Berlin, at least for a time.

"I would wait until the new year – but not much longer," I said. "And tell no one what you are planning – not even Daphne. You can write to her from Berlin. She will understand."

"I know she will. And, Dora – thank you."

We talked of other things then: the book she dreamed

of writing on poetry and war, my love of numbers and the loneliness I'd always felt in having to abandon them.

"But you never did abandon them – your being here is proof of it. You can see that, surely?"

She was right in a way, I suppose. But I'm no Sophie Germain.

The stove gave out its warmth, and we sat beside it. I understood that this was the moment of change, that if I had indeed met with Helen before, I would not do so again. That I had done what I had come to do, and that this was goodbye.

I felt time tremble in the balance, then come to a standstill. There are moments when time lies in stasis, and this was one of them. But time always moves on in the end.

"I'm pregnant, by the way," Helen said as I was leaving. "Edwin doesn't know, don't worry."

My heart leapt up at her words. I think I knew this was your story, even then.

Edwin Dillon lived. With Helen gone and their plans in ruins, Leonard Bell must have decided that murdering him was too much of a risk. Or perhaps he waited, hoping for a better opportunity and never finding it. A year later, the Four Brothers disbanded. Leonard Bell went to Germany, where he became part of the communist movement dedicated to getting rid of Adolf Hitler. He was arrested and deported back to London in 1934. Edwin Dillon headed a splinter group, also calling itself the Four Brothers, and believed to be one of the main instigators of the notorious plot to assassinate Oswald Mosley in 1936. He served four years for his involvement, and although it is not known whether it was prison that made him lose his appetite for radical politics, he cut loose from all his Four Brothers contacts and after the war returned to working as a freelance journalist. You can find feature articles by Edwin Dillon in the archives of *The Times*, *The Guardian* and *The Glasgow Herald*, among other places. He died in 1971.

He was briefly involved with the Irish writer Eimear Mowbray, with whom he had one son. Douglas Mowbray also worked as a journalist, and was known to be a fervent supporter of the IRA. Douglas died aged thirty-one, when he killed himself and his young daughter Gemma by driving off a bridge on the outskirts of Belfast. His son Padraic, who was also in the car at the time, survived. I have been unable to trace his whereabouts. There is every possibility that he is still alive.

Real history is a mass of conflicting stories. According to the official records, Helen Mildred Bostall was tried and found guilty of the murder of Edwin Patrick Dillon and sentenced to death. The execution was carried out on August 14th, 1928. History seems content with this judgement, though there are many, including myself, who would argue that capital punishment is never justified.

There are also anomalies, if you care to look for them. The Library of the Sorbonne records the publication, in 1941, of a pamphlet by Ellen Tuglas with the title *On War: the imaginary reminiscences of hell's survivor*. The work was originally written in English, although a French translation was provided by Ivan Tuglas, a Russian exile resident in Paris since the 1920s and Ellen's common-law husband until his death in 1952.

On War is a peculiar work. Lodged halfway between fact and fiction, it has aroused some interest among scholars of World War Two literature because it appears to predict the nuclear destruction of Hiroshima. *I remember where I was when they told me*, states the unnamed narrator. *I have never before felt able to speak my feelings aloud, but what I wanted, when I heard, was simply to be there. To be not guilty of this thing, to help one person up from the rubble, even if such an action brought about my own destruction. I yearned to haul myself across bleeding Europe with my coat in tatters and no money in my purse. You will say that these feelings were selfish and I would not blame you for saying so. Some crimes are so huge there can be no recompense.*

On War is dedicated to Ellen's daughter, Isobel Elsa, who was eleven years old at the time of its publication.

I knew Ray's mother was called Isobel, but she was old, and living in Paris, and I never met her. She died three years ago. I know that Ray sent her photos of you when you were born. I imagine they were there beside her bed on the day she died.

Ray was always meaning to take you over there, so she could get to know you. It's too late now, but that's Ray all over. He loses track of time.

Dearest Clio. We can only cheat time for so long, and I

knew when I went back to Milliver Street that final time it should be the last.

Your great-grandmother, though: Ellen Tuglas, whose name was once Helen Bostall. I should have guessed she would find a means of letting me know our escape plan succeeded, and that her name would be Clio. Clio, the daughter of memory, the muse of history. I should have known that – through you, Clio – Helen and I would one day meet again.

I carried on writing the book, of course I did, my account of Helen Bostall and how she was hanged for a crime she didn't commit. I'd come so far with my research I didn't feel like giving up – and as a story, as I say, it had everything: bomb plots, political feuding, affairs of the heart, as many double crosses as you might find in *Tinker, Tailor, Soldier, Spy*. My editor at *History Recollected* even thinks she's found a publisher for it. I doubt it'll make me rich but it should do all right.

You can read the book when you're older. Make of it what you will. Godmothers can be boring, can't they, especially godmothers who also happen to be lawyers? At least you can tell yourself that your boring lawyer godmother once changed the world. A little bit, anyway. I don't imagine you'll be telling anyone else.

acknowledgements

My original research for *The Silver Wind* included a great deal of reading on the subject of clocks and watches, and particular mention should be made of M. Cutmore's *Watches 1850 – 1980* (David & Charles 1989) and David Thompson's *Watches in the Ashmolean Museum* (Ashmolean Museum 2007) and *Watches* (British Museum Press 2008). The story 'Darkroom' was originally published in 2008 in the anthology *Subtle Edens*, edited by Allen Ashley for Elastic Press. The story 'Ten Days' first appeared in 2016 in *Now We Are Ten*, edited by Ian Whates for NewCon Press. My thanks to those editors and publishers, and also of course to David Rix of Eibonvale Press, who first gave a home to the earlier version of *The Silver Wind* in 2011. My heartfelt gratitude to Gary Budden, Cath Trechman and the whole inspiring crew at Titan Books for offering me the opportunity to substantially revise the text, and to bring these characters and their stories to a wider readership. Thanks as always to my remarkable agent, Anna Webber, of United Agents.

about the author

Nina Allan is the recipient of the British Science Fiction Award, the Novella Award and the Kitschies Red Tentacle. Her story 'The Art of Space Travel' was a Hugo finalist in 2017 and the original version of *The Silver Wind* was awarded the Grand Prix de L'imaginaire in 2014. Her most recent novel is *The Dollmaker*. Nina lives and works in Scotland, on the Isle of Bute.